TROY

FALL OF KINGS

DAVID & STELLA GEMMELL

TROY

FALL OF KINGS

BANTAM PRESS

LONDON · TORONTO · SYDNEY · AUCKLAND · JOHANNESBURG

TRANSWORLD PUBLISHERS 61–63
Uxbridge Road, London W5 5SA
A Random House Group Company
www.booksattransworld.co.uk

First published in Great Britain
in 2007 by Bantam Press
an imprint of Transworld Publishers

A CIP catalogue record for this book
is available from the British Library.

ISBNS 9780593052259 (cased)
9780593052266 (tpb)

Addresses for Random House Group Ltd companies outside the UK
can be found at: www.randomhouse.co.uk
The Random House Group Ltd Reg. No. 954009

The Random House Group Ltd makes every effort to ensure that the papers used in its
books are made from trees that have been legally sourced from well-managed and credibly
certified forests. Our paper procurement policy can be found at:
www.randomhouse.co.uk/paper.htm

Typeset in 11/14pt Sabon by
Falcon Oast Graphic Art Ltd.

Printed in the UK by
CPI Mackays, Chatham, ME5 8TD

6 8 10 9 7 5

Mixed Sources
Product group from well-managed
forests and other controlled sources
www.fsc.org Cert no. TT-COC-2139
© 1996 Forest Stewardship Council
FSC

Fall of Kings is dedicated to the memory of Olive and Bill Woodford, and to Don and Edith Graham, without whom the book would have been neither started nor completed.

ACKNOWLEDGEMENTS

With grateful thanks to James Barclay, Sally and Lawrence Berman, Tony Evans, Oswald Hotz de Bar, Steve Hutt, Howard Morhaim, and Selina Walker.

RHODOPE MOUNTAINS

R. Nestos
• Kalliros

• Xantheia   THRAKI

• Ismaros

SAMOTHRAKI

Carpea

IMBROS

Mt Olympos ▲   Dardanos   • Zeleia

Troy ◉

LEMNOS   Mt Ida ▲   • Thebe Under
                                   Plakos

THESSALY

LESBOS

EUBOEA

KIOS

Thebes • Aulis

Athens   KARIA

ITHAKA

KEPHALLENIA   Mykene ◉   • Miletos
                     Argos •

Pylos •   Sparta •   KOS

THERA   RHODOS

KYTHERA

KRETOS   Knossos

Phaistos •

THE
GREEN
GREEN

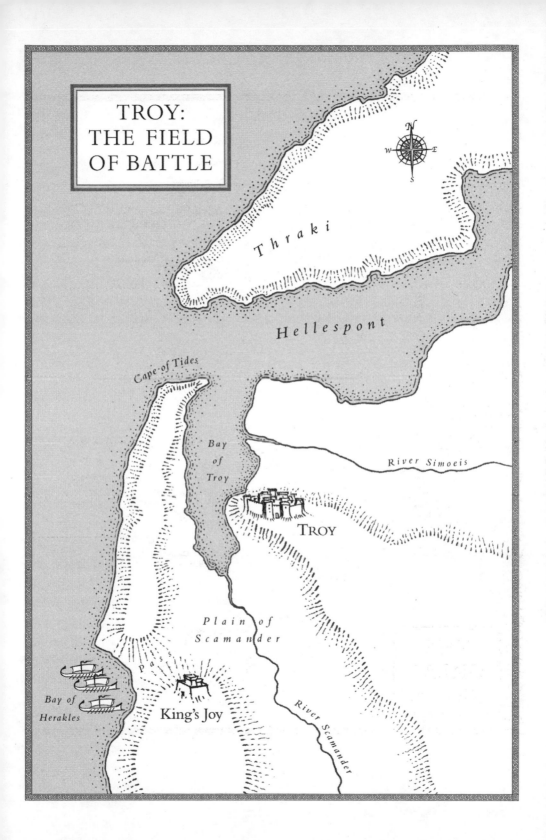

TROY:
THE FIELD
OF BATTLE

Thraki

Hellespont

Cape of Tides

Bay
of
Troy

River Simoeis

TROY

Plain of
Scamander

Pass

Bay of
Herakles

King's Joy

River Scamander

'Beware the wooden horse, Agamemnon King, Battle King, Conqueror, for it will roar to the skies on wings of thunder, and herald the death of nations.'

'A pox on riddles, priest!' replied the king. 'Tell me of Troy and of victory.'

'The last king of the golden city will be Mykene. The gods have spoken.'

The oracle of the Cave of Wings

PROLOGUE

A BRIGHT MOON SHONE LOW IN THE SKY ABOVE THE ISLE OF IMBROS, its silver light bathing the rocky shoreline and the Mykene war fleet beached there. The curve of the bay was filled with ships, some fifty war galleys and more than a hundred barges drawn up so tightly there was not a hand's-breadth between them. On the beach the Mykene army sat round scores of cookfires, eight thousand soldiers, some preparing their weapons, sharpening swords, or burnishing shields, others playing knucklebones or dozing by the flickering fires. The beach was so crowded many of the sailors had remained on their ships rather than jostle for a strip of rocky ground on which to lay their blankets.

Agamemnon, king of the Mykene, and warlord of the western armies, stood outside his canopied tent, his gaunt frame wrapped in a long black cloak, his cold eyes staring out to sea towards the east, where the sky glowed red.

The fortress of Dardanos was burning.

With luck, and the blessing of the war god Ares, the mission had been totally successful. Helikaon's wife and son would be lying dead in the blazing fortress, and Helikaon himself would know the full horror of despair.

A cold wind blew across the beach. Agamemnon drew his cloak

round his angular shoulders and turned his gaze to the men labouring to build an altar some distance away. They had been gathering large stones for most of the day. The round-shouldered priest, Atheos, was directing them, his thin, reedy voice sounding shrill as a petulant seagull. 'No, no, that stone is too small for the outside. Wedge it closer to the centre!'

Agamemnon stared at the priest. The man had no talent for prophecy, which suited the king. He could be relied upon to say whatever Agamemnon wished him to say. The problem with most seers, Agamemnon knew, was that their prophecies became self-fulfilling. Tell an army that the portents were dark and gloomy and men would go into battle ready to break and run at the first reverse. Tell them victory was assured and that Zeus himself had blessed them and they would fight like lions.

On occasions, of course, a battle would be lost. It was unavoidable. All that was then needed was someone to blame. Which was where idiots like Atheos were so useful. Talentless and flawed, Atheos had secrets. At least, he thought he had. He liked to torment and kill children. Should any of his 'prophecies' fail Agamemnon would expose him to the army, and have him put to death, saying the gods had cursed the battle because of the man's evil.

Agamemnon shivered. If only all seers were as talentless and malleable as Atheos. Kings should not be subject to the whims of prophecy. Their destinies should be chained entirely to their will and their abilities. What glory was there in a victory preordained by capricious gods? Agamemnon's mood darkened as he recalled his last visit to the Cave of Wings.

Damn those priests and their noxious narcotics! Damn them and their riddles! One day he would have them all killed, and replaced with men he could trust. Fools like Atheos. But not yet. The priests of the cave were highly regarded by the Mykene nobility and by the people and, in the midst of a great war, it would be foolish to risk wiping them out. And he only had to endure the Time of Prophecy once every four years.

The last time had been just before sailing to Imbros. Agamemnon and his chosen Followers had gathered at the Cave of

Wings, on the hills outside the Lion City. Then, as two centuries of ritual demanded, the king of the Mykene had entered the torchlit cave. The air was thick with smoke from the opiate fire, and Agamemnon had kept his breathing shallow. Even so bright colours had swirled before his eyes, and he had grown dizzy.

The dying priest had drifted in and out of consciousness, and when he spoke the sentences had been broken and confused. Then his eyes had opened, his bony fingers circling the king's wrist. 'Beware the wooden horse, Agamemnon King, Battle King, Conqueror, for it will roar to the skies on wings of thunder, and herald the death of nations.'

'A pox on riddles, priest!' replied the king. 'Tell me of Troy and of victory.'

'The last king of the golden city will be Mykene. The gods have spoken.'

And there it was. The fulfilment of dreams, the promise of destiny. Though the priest had yet to succumb to the hemlock, and was struggling to say more, Agamemnon pulled back from him and fled the cave. He had heard all he wanted.

Troy would fall to him, and with it all the riches of Priam's treasury. The relief had been colossal. Though few were aware of it, the Mykene empire was bleeding to death, its wealth leached away to finance armies of conquest. Each successful invasion had only exacerbated the problem, for with greater lands to occupy and hold, greater amounts of gold were needed to train fresh soldiers. The Mykene gold mines, for so long the bedrock of military expansion, had failed. Agamemnon had been left with only two options: to reduce the size of the army, which would inevitably lead to insurrections, revolts and civil war, or to expand Mykene influence into the rich lands of the east.

For such a campaign to succeed Troy had to fall. With its limitless treasury under his control Mykene domination could be guaranteed for generations.

It was rare for Agamemnon to feel content, but at this moment, under the bright stars of Imbros, he luxuriated in the feeling. Gold looted from Thraki had paid for the invasion fleets, the fortress of Dardanos had been taken, and Troy would follow.

Even the defeat at Carpea could be used to advantage. Hektor and his Trojan Horse had killed his ally, the idiot Peleus, and left the young warrior Achilles king of Thessaly. Inexperienced and impressionable, he would be easy to manipulate.

A brief moment of irritation cut through Agamemnon's thoughts. Achilles was with Odysseus, somewhere to the southwest. Had he heard yet of his father's death? I should have kept him with me, thought Agamemnon. But no matter. When he does hear his heart will burn with the need for vengeance, and he will return.

Hearing movement to his right, Agamemnon turned. Three soldiers in black cloaks and breastplates of burnished bronze discs approached him. One was dragging a skinny, black-haired child of around ten years old. The group halted before the king.

'As you ordered, Agamemnon King,' said the first, hurling the child to the stones.

'As I ordered?' responded Agamemnon, his voice low, his tone icy.

'You . . . you said bring a virgin for the sacrifice, lord.'

'To sacrifice to the god Poseidon, for safe crossing and our victory,' said Agamemnon. 'To send him an unsoiled young woman, to please his nights. Would this little wretch please your nights?'

The soldier, a tall wide-shouldered man with a thick black beard, scratched at his chin. 'No, lord, but the villagers had mostly taken to the hills. There were only old women and children. This one was the oldest child.'

Agamemnon called out to the priest. Atheos hitched up his long white robes and scurried across the sand. Pausing before Agamemnon, he held both hands over his heart, then bowed his head.

'Will this scrawny creature suffice?' asked the king. He knew the answer before he asked the question. The priest tried to hide his delight as he looked upon the frightened girl, but Agamemnon saw the lust shining in his eyes.

'She will, great lord. Yes, indeed.' Atheos licked his thin lips.

'Take her then and prepare her.'

The child began to cry once more, but Atheos slapped her soundly across the face.

*

The distant glow to the east was fading, hidden by a sea mist that had sprung up along the shoreline. The bright moon vanished behind a screen of clouds. The now naked girl was hauled across the sacrificial altar. Agamemnon walked down to watch the ceremony. If it were done expertly, the child would be split open and her heart ripped from her body while she still lived. Then the priest would read her entrails for portents of victory.

The soldiers began to gather, standing silently, waiting for the blood to spurt. While two of them held the girl, Atheos took out a long curved knife, and began to chant the name of Poseidon. The cry was taken up by the army, thousands of men, their voices rumbling like thunder.

Atheos turned towards the altar, knife raised.

Then came a moment so unexpected and risible that laughter broke out. A clay pot flew over the crowd, cracked against the head of a soldier, then went on to shatter against the priest, drenching him in a foul-smelling liquid. Shocked into immobility, Atheos stood very still, his knife arm still raised. Then he gazed down at his dripping robes.

Agamemnon was furious. He scanned the crowd, seeking the culprit, determined to have him flayed alive. Then a second clay pot shattered among the spectators. Movement in the air caught Agamemnon's eye, and he saw several small dark objects falling from the sky. They were being hurled from the mist, beyond the beached ships. One of the missiles struck a cookfire. What followed was horrifying.

The clay ball exploded, spraying flames into the crowd, setting light to clothing and skin. The massed men panicked and fled towards the high hills. One, his tunic burning, blundered into the priest Atheos. There was a great whoosh, and the priest's robes ignited in blue and yellow flame.

Atheos dropped his knife and began to beat at the flames with his hands, but then his fingers caught fire, and he screamed and began to run towards the shoreline, seeking the sanctuary of the cold sea. Flames danced over his body, setting light to his hair.

17

Agamemnon saw the priest stagger and fall. His robes were burned away now, his skin blackened. Yet still the flames clung to him, devouring his flesh.

Another campfire exploded close by. Agamemnon ran to higher ground, clambering up over jagged rocks. He turned and gazed back. Only then, as the wind picked up, dispersing the mist, did he see the huge ship out in the bay, with its twin banks of oars, and a billowing white sail, emblazoned with a rearing black horse. Rage and frustration ripped through the Mykene king. Though he had never seen the vessel he knew its name. All who sailed the Great Green knew the name of *that* ship. It was the *Xanthos*, the flagship of Helikaon the Burner.

Down at the shore sailors had scrambled from the decks of their ships and were trying to launch them. It was no easy task, for they were so closely packed. One galley almost made it. But as the crew climbed back aboard two missiles struck it. Fire arrows lit the sky, curving up from the *Xanthos* and then down on to decks slick with *nephthar*. The galley began to burn. Crewmen, their clothes ablaze, leapt into the sea.

Agamemnon watched in impotent fury as more fireballs rained down upon his fleet, fierce flames flowing over dry timbers, and seeping down into the holds. The easterly wind fanned the fires, which leapt from ship to ship. Terrified of the inferno, the Mykene sailors fled back towards the hills.

The *Xanthos* moved slowly across the bay, clay balls of *nephthar* striking vessel after vessel, fire arrows slicing through the air behind them. A score of Mykene ships and some forty of the barges were on fire now, the flames rising high into the air.

Out on the bay the moon emerged from behind the clouds, shining upon the Death Ship. A warrior in armour of bronze climbed to the prow and stood gazing at the devastation he had caused. Then he raised his arm. Banks of oars dipped into the water, and the *Xanthos* swung away towards the open sea.

A white figure scurried past Agamemnon. The skinny girl had crawled from the altar and was running away into the hills. No one tried to stop her.

Book One
DARKNESS FALLS

I

Farewell to the queen

HELIKAON STOOD AT THE STERN OF THE *XANTHOS*, STARING BACK AT the burning fleet. He felt no satisfaction as the flames lit the night sky. Removing his helm of bronze he leaned against the stern rail and turned his gaze towards the east. Fires were also burning in the distant fortress of Dardanos, and the *Xanthos* was heading slowly back towards them.

The breeze was cool upon his face as he stood alone. No one approached him. Even the sailor at the great steering oar kept his gaze firmly fixed to the east. The eighty oars of the great vessel slid rhythmically into the night-dark water, the sound as regular as heartbeat.

Halysia was dead. The queen of Dardania was dead. His wife was dead.

And his heart was a ruin.

He and Gershom had climbed the steep cliff to where her body lay, little Dex snuggled up beside her, the black stallion waiting close by. Helikaon had run to her, kneeling and lifting her into his arms. There was a savage wound in her side, and the ground around her was slick with blood. Her head had flopped back, her golden hair hanging loose.

Dex had cried out, 'Papa!' and he had hugged the three-year-old

21

to him. 'We must be very quiet,' whispered Dex. 'Sun Woman is sleeping.' Gershom had lifted the boy into his arms. 'We jumped over it,' said Dex excitedly, pointing to the chasm and the burned bridge. 'We ran away from the bad men.'

Helikaon had cradled Halysia to him. Her eyes opened then, and she smiled up at him. 'I knew . . . you would come,' she said.

'I am here. Rest. We will get you back to the palace and staunch your wounds.'

Her face was pale. 'I am so tired,' she told him, and his vision misted as tears formed.

'I love you,' he whispered.

She sighed then. 'Such a . . . sweet lie,' she said.

She spoke no more, nor ever would, and he knelt there, holding her close.

Across the chasm the sounds of battle grew closer. He did not look up. Hektor and the Trojan Horse had driven the Mykene along the defile towards Parnio's Folly, and there the enemy made their last stand.

But Helikaon did not care. He stroked his fingers through Halysia's golden hair, and looked down into her dead gaze. Other men came climbing the cliff. They stood round him silently. At last he closed Halysia's eyes. He gave orders for her body to be carried back to the fortress, then slowly made his way to meet Hektor.

'There is still some fighting to the northeast,' Hektor told him. 'The enemy general tried to battle his way to the coast. We have them penned.'

Helikaon nodded.

'We took a few prisoners,' said Hektor. 'One told us Agamemnon and a war fleet are on Imbros. I don't think we can hold here if they come. The Seagate is ruined, and my men are weary.'

'I will deal with them,' said Helikaon coldly. 'You finish the resistance here.'

Calling his men he had returned to the *Xanthos* and set sail into the night. He had expected to face battle with a screen of war galleys protecting the main fleet. But the Mykene, with the arrogance of conquerors, believing themselves safe from attack, had beached their entire fleet on Imbros for the night.

A mistake Agamemnon would now be rueing.

The *Xanthos* sailed serenely on, the burning fleet lighting the sky behind the great ship, the screams of the dying like the cries of distant gulls. The weight of guilt settled on Helikaon as he stood alone, and he remembered his last conversation with Halysia the previous spring. He had been preparing to raid along the Mykene coastline, and she had walked with him down to the beach.

'Be safe, and come home to me,' she said, as they stood together in the shadow of the *Xanthos*.

'I will.'

'And know as you journey that I love you,' she told him.

The words had surprised him, for she had never said them before. He had stood there in the dawn light like a fool, not knowing how to respond. Their marriage had been, as all royal weddings were, a union of necessity. She had laughed at his confusion. 'Is the Golden One speechless?' she asked.

'I am,' he admitted. Then he had kissed her hand. 'It is an honour to be loved by you, Halysia. I mean that with all my heart.'

She had nodded. 'I know that we do not choose whom to love,' she said. 'And I know – I have always known – that you yearn for someone else. I am sorry for that. I am sorry for you. But I have tried, and I will continue to try, to bring you happiness. If it is just a portion of the happiness you have brought me, then you will be content. I know this.'

'I am already content. No man could have a finer wife.'

With that he had kissed her, then climbed aboard the warship.

Such a . . . sweet lie.

Memories cut into him like talons of fire.

He saw black-bearded Gershom walking down the central deck. The big Egyptian climbed the steps to the stern. 'She was a great woman. Fine and brave. That was a mighty leap across that chasm. She saved her son.'

The two men stood in silence, each lost in his own thoughts.

Helikaon stared ahead, at the flames in the sky over the fortress. Warehouses had been set ablaze, and many of the wooden buildings beyond the palace. Women and children had been killed, as well as many of the defenders, and the fortress city would be shrouded in grief tonight, and for many nights to come.

It was close to midnight when the *Xanthos* finally beached again on the rocky shore directly below the ruined Seagate. Helikaon and Gershom walked slowly up the steep path. At the gate they met soldiers of the Trojan Horse, who told them Hektor had captured the Mykene leader and several of his officers. They were being held outside the city.

'Their deaths should be long, and their screams loud,' said Gershom.

Fewer than twenty Mykene had been taken alive, but these included their admiral Menados. He was brought before Hektor on the open ground before the great Landgate. The few captured warriors, their hands bound, sat huddled close by.

Hektor removed his bronze helm, then ran his fingers through his sweat-streaked golden hair. He was tired to the bone, his eyes gritty, his throat dry. Passing the helm to his shield-bearer Mestares, he unbuckled his breastplate, lifting it clear then dropping it to the grass. The Mykene admiral stepped forward, touching his fist to his own breastplate in salute.

'Ha!' he said with a grim smile. 'The Prince of War himself.' He shrugged, and scratched at his black and silver chin beard. 'Ah well, it is no dishonour to lose to you, Hektor. Can we discuss the terms of my ransom?'

'You are not my prisoner, Menados,' Hektor told him wearily. 'You attacked Helikaon's fortress. You killed his wife. When he returns he will decide your fate. I doubt ransom will be in his thoughts.'

Menados swore softly, then spread his hands. He stared hard at Hektor. 'It is said you don't approve of torture. Is that true?'

'It is.'

'You had better make yourself scarce then, Trojan, for when

Helikaon returns he'll want more than our deaths. Doubtless he will burn us all.'

'And you will deserve it,' Hektor replied. Then he stepped in close, keeping his voice low. 'I have heard of you, and of your many deeds of courage. Tell me, Menados, how does a hero find himself on a mission to murder a woman and a child?'

The admiral gave Hektor a quizzical glance, then shook his head. 'How many dead women and children have you seen in your young life, Hektor? Scores? Hundreds? Well, I have seen thousands. Lying twisted in death on the streets of every captured city or town. And, yes, at first it turns the stomach. At first I pondered the waste of life, the savagery and the cruelty.' He shrugged. 'After a while, and more mountains of corpses, I no longer pondered on it. How does a hero find himself on a mission like this? You know the answer. The first duty of a soldier is loyalty. When the king orders, we obey.'

'You will pay a heavy price for that loyalty,' Hektor told him.

'Most soldiers pay a heavy price in the end,' replied Menados. 'Why not just kill us now, cleanly? I ask this as one warrior to another. I do not want to give the evil bastard the pleasure of my screams.'

Before Hektor could answer he saw Helikaon walking towards them past the captured men, the big Egypteian Gershom with him. Behind them came a score of angry Dardanians, knives and cudgels in their hands. Menados drew himself up to his full height, and placed his hands behind his back, his expression stern, his face unreadable. Helikaon halted before him.

'You came to my lands with fire and terror,' he said, his voice cold as winter. 'You murdered my wife, and the wives and children of my people. Is murder the only skill you Mykene ever seek to master?'

'Ah,' said Menados, 'we are to have a debate about murder? Had I won here I would have been declared a hero of the Mykene, having defeated a king of evil. But I lost. Do not seek to lecture me, Helikaon the Burner. How many helpless men have you killed? How many women and children died in your raids on Mykene villages?'

Beyond them the mob of Dardanians was moving in on the bound Mykene prisoners.

'Back!' yelled Helikaon, turning towards them. 'There are buildings burning in our city, and many there need help. Go! Leave these men to me.'

He stood in silence for a while, then glanced at Hektor. 'What do you say, my friend?' he asked. 'You captured him.'

Hektor looked at his comrade, seeing his anger and his need for vengeance. 'The road a soldier walks is narrower than a sword blade,' he said. 'A step one way and he weakens, becoming less of a fighter; the other and he becomes a monster. Tonight Menados strayed from this path and is cursed for it. His tragedy is that he serves Agamemnon, a man without pity, a man devoid of humanity. In any other army Menados would have remained true to his heart, and been remembered as a hero. Before you make a judgement on the matter of his death, I will tell you one story, if I may.'

'Make it brief.'

'When I was a boy,' Hektor went on, 'I heard the tale of a Mykene galley beached on the isle of Kythera, close to a fishing village. A fleet of pirate vessels came into sight, ready to raid the village, kill the men and the children, and enslave the women. The captain of the galley, though he had no links to the village, nor any friends there, led his forty men into battle against great odds. Twenty-two of his men died, and he was severely wounded. But the village was saved. The people there still celebrate their day of deliverance.'

'And that was you, Menados?' Helikaon asked.

'I was younger then and knew no better,' the admiral answered.

'Back in the summer,' said Helikaon softly, 'I saw a soldier weep, because in the midst of battle he accidentally killed a child. I led that soldier into the fight. I took him to that village, and I made him a murderer. You are correct, Menados. I have no right to lecture you, or any man, on the vileness of war.'

He fell silent and turned away. Hektor watched him, but his expression was unreadable. Finally he swung back to Menados.

'For the sake of that child, and the villagers of Kythera, I give you your life.' He turned to Hektor. 'Have your men escort the prisoners to the shore. There is a damaged Mykene galley there. It is barely seaworthy. But let them take it and try to reach Imbros.'

Menados stepped forward, as if he would speak, but Helikaon raised his hand, and his voice was cold. 'Do not misjudge me, Mykene. If ever I see you again I will cut out your heart and feed it to the crows.'

The men of the Trojan Horse rode southwest from Dardanos, until the city of Troy came into sight. Only then did Hektor order them to make camp in a wood just outside the city. Here they sat, the night cold, a bitter wind leaching the heat from their campfires, their thoughts grim. Just beyond the hill their families waited, loved ones they had not seen for more than two years.

On the brow of the wooded hill Hektor stood silently, a deep sadness clinging to his spirit. Tomorrow there would be a parade for these survivors, their entry to the city met with cheers. But the men who had given most to this ghastly war would not ride through the flower-strewn streets, nor have garlands placed over their shoulders by adoring young women. The lifeblood of those heroes had already soaked into the soil of distant Thraki, their ashes scattered by the winds of a foreign land. Or they had drowned in the Hellespont, or fallen before the walls of Dardanos.

Even among the survivors there were those who would not enjoy the acclaim they deserved. A victory parade, according to Priam the king, was no place for cripples and amputees. 'By the gods, boy, no one wants to see the truth of war. They want to see heroes, tall and strong, striking and handsome.' The comment had angered Hektor, not because it was harsh and ungrateful, but because it was true. And so he had ordered the wounded and the maimed to be taken to the healing houses after dark, ferried into the city in secret, as if covered in shame.

Hektor glanced towards the wagons recently arrived from the city. Only one had brought food for his men. The other two were filled with two thousand new white cloaks, so the crowds would not see weary men, exhausted by years of battle, coming home bloodstained and filthy. Instead they would gaze in wonder at shining heroes.

His brother Dios climbed the hill to stand alongside him. 'A cold night,' he said, drawing his cloak more tightly around him.

'I do not feel it,' answered Hektor, who was dressed in a simple, knee-length tunic of faded yellow.

'That is because you are Hektor,' said Dios amiably.

'No, it is because I have spent two long years in Thraki, trudging through snow and ice in the mountains. You do not have to stay with us, brother. Go back to the warmth of your house.'

'You are gloomy tonight. Are you not glad to be home?'

Hektor stared down at Troy, and thought of his wife and son, and of his farms and the horse herds on the northern plain. He sighed. 'I am not yet home,' he said. 'How is Andromache?'

'She is well. Angry, though. She railed at Father for keeping the army out here tonight. They deserve better, she told him.'

'They are both right,' said Hektor. 'The men do deserve better, but tomorrow they will revel in the adulation. The parade is important. It will help disguise our failure.'

'How can you speak of failure?' asked Dios, surprised. 'You did not lose a single battle – and you killed an enemy king. I call that a victory. So do the people. So should you.'

Unaccustomed anger touched Hektor then, but he kept it from his voice. 'We crossed the straits to defend the land of Thraki, and to protect King Rhesos, our ally. Rhesos is dead. Thraki is lost. Our enemies gather across the Hellespont, ready to invade. All the northern trade routes are lost to us. Does this sound like victory to you?'

'I hear you, brother,' said Dios softly. 'However, you and your men went to Thraki to *assist* in the defence. The defeats were suffered by Rhesos, not by the warriors of Troy. Your legend is unblemished.'

'A pox on legends,' snapped Hektor. 'And a double pox on the twisted realities of politics, where defeats can be melted down and recast as golden victories. The truth is that the enemy has gained control of the north. Now Agamemnon will come against us in our own lands. And he will come with a great army.'

'And you will destroy him,' said Dios. 'You are the Lord of Battles. Every man round the Great Green knows this. You never lose.'

Hektor glanced at his younger brother, seeing the admiration in his eyes. Fear touched him, cramping his belly. During the battle at Carpea he had been no more than a single sword-thrust from death. A well-aimed arrow, or a cast spear, could have pierced his throat. A slinger's stone could have cracked his skull. Indeed, had Banokles not led a near-suicidal charge at the enemy rear his spirit would now be walking the Dark Road. He thought of telling his brother of the fears, of the trembling hands and the sleepless nights. And, worse, of the growing pain in his left shoulder, and the ache in his right knee. He wanted to say, 'I am a man, just like you, Dios. Just like every man sitting back there at the campfires. I bruise, I bleed, I age. And, if I go on fighting battle after battle, then one day my luck will run out, and my lifeblood with it.'

But he did not say any of it. To Dios, to the army, to the people of Troy, he had long since ceased to be Hektor the man. Now he was like tomorrow's parade, a false, yet glittering, symbol of Trojan invincibility. And with every day of war that passed he became more firmly chained to that lie.

Dios spoke again. 'Wait until you see Astyanax. The boy has grown, Hektor. Nearly three years old now. And what a fine, bold child he is.'

Hektor relaxed then, and smiled. 'I long to see him. I shall take him on a ride through the hills. He will enjoy that.'

'I took him myself, not more than a week ago. Sat him before me and let him hold the reins. He loved it. Especially the gallop.'

Hektor's heart sank. Through the long, grim and bloody months of warfare he had dreamed of taking the boy on his first ride, of holding the child close to him, listening to his laughter. Amidst the terror and brutality of war this one small ambition had nurtured him. 'Was he frightened?' he asked.

'No! Far from it. He kept shouting for me to go faster. He is

29

fearless, Hektor. No more, of course, than one would expect from a child of yours.'

A child of yours.

Save that he is not mine, thought Hektor. Masking his sadness, he looked across at the city. 'And Father is well?'

Dios said nothing for a moment. Then he shrugged. 'He is getting older,' he replied, dropping his eyes.

'And drinking more?'

Dios hesitated. 'You will see him tomorrow,' he said at last. 'Best you form your own judgement.'

'That I will.'

'And what of Helikaon? Word reached us that he sank Agamemnon's fleet. Burned them all. That lifted the spirits, I can tell you.'

The bitter wind picked up again, hissing through the branches overhead. This time Hektor shivered, though not from the cold. He saw again the pale, dead face of Helikaon's wife, the beautiful Halysia, as her body was carried into the fortress. Hektor had heard the story of her last ride. Taking her son with her she had mounted a huge black horse, and ridden through the enemy, down the defile towards the bridge known as Parnio's Folly. They had pursued her, knowing they had her, for the bridge had been destroyed by fire. Caught between murderous soldiers and a deep chasm Halysia had heeled the stallion forward and leapt it across the wide gap. Not one rider had dared to follow her. She had saved her son, but not herself. During the ride she had suffered a deep spear wound, and had bled to death as Helikaon reached her.

The voice of Dios brought Hektor back to the present. 'We need to discuss the route for the victory parade. You will ride Father's ceremonial war chariot. It is being burnished now, and layered with new gold leaf. It will be brought out to you before dawn. Father has two pure white horses to draw it.' Dios smiled. 'You will look like a young god!'

Hektor took a deep breath, and transferred his gaze to the city. 'And the route?' he asked.

'The entire regiment will ride up through the lower town, then through the Scaean Gate and up the avenue to the palace, where Priam will greet them, and give awards to the heroes you have named. This will be followed later by a feast of thanksgiving in the Square of Hermes. Here Father hopes you will make a speech. He suggests you tell the gathering about the victory at Carpea, as it is the most recent.'

'Dardanos is the most recent,' Hektor pointed out.

'Yes it is, but the death of Halysia makes it too sad a tale.'

'Of course,' said Hektor. 'We cannot have tales of blood and death spoil a story about war.'

Khalkeus the bronzesmith sat in the torchlit *megaron* of Dardanos, rubbing at the numbed fingers of his left hand. After a while sensation returned, the tips beginning to tingle. Then the trembling started. He stared down at the palsied limb, willing the movement to stop. Instead it intensified. It was as if invisible fingers had grasped his wrist and were shaking it. Irritated now, he made a fist, then crossed his arms so no one would see the tremors.

Not that there was anyone to see. The Gyppto, Gershom, had told him to wait in this cold, empty place for Helikaon. Khalkeus stared around the *megaron*. Blood had stained the mosaic floor. The splashes and spatters had dried, but elsewhere, on the rugs and in the deeper grooves of the mosaic, it remained sticky and uncongealed. A broken sword lay by a wall.

Khalkeus strolled across and picked up the weapon. It had snapped halfway down the blade. Khalkeus ran his thick fingers over the metal. Poorly cast, with too much tin, he decided. Copper was a soft metal, and the addition of tin created the harder, more useful bronze. But this blade had been hardened too much, becoming brittle, and had snapped on impact.

Returning to his couch Khalkeus sat once more. His hand had stopped trembling, which was a blessing. But the palsy would return. It was the curse of bronzesmiths. No one knew what caused it, but it always began in the fingertips, then the toes. Soon he would be limping along with the aid of a staff. Even the god of smiths, Hephaistos, was said to be lame. Old Karpithos, back in

Miletos, had gone blind in the end. He had sworn it was the melting copper putting poison in the air. Khalkeus had no way of testing this theory, but he favoured it enough to have his forges built outside now, so any poisons would be dissipated by fresh air.

You cannot complain, he told himself. Fifty years old, and only now does the trembling start. Karpithos had endured the tremors for close to twenty years before his sight failed.

Time drifted by and Khalkeus, never a patient man, began to grow more irritated. Rising from his couch he walked out into the night air.

Black smoke was drifting up from the centre of the fortress, where the kitchens still smouldered. Despite their obvious enthusiasm for destruction, thought Khalkeus, the enemy had been largely incompetent. Many of the burned buildings had suffered superficial damage only. And the support struts of the bridge at Parnio's Folly had been ignored by the Mykene. They had hacked at the bridge planks with axe and sword to weaken them, then poured oil on the flat timbers, before setting them ablaze. The idiots did not realize it was the support struts, set deeply into the cliffs on both sides, that gave the structure its strength. Whoever had designed them had been a master at his craft. With them still in place, undamaged by fire, the bridge could be rebuilt within days.

Khalkeus glanced to his right. In the moonlight he saw three men hauling a wide handcart on which the bodies of several women and children had been laid. A wheel struck an uneven patch on the road, making the vehicle judder. One of the dead women slid side-ways. The movement caused her torn tunic to ride up, exposing her buttocks. Instantly the three men stopped pulling the cart, and one of them hurried back to cover her nakedness.

How strange, thought Khalkeus. As if she would care.

He wandered back into the *megaron*. Several servants were placing fresh torches in the brackets on the wall. Khalkeus called out to one of them. 'You there! Bring me some bread and wine.'

'And you are?' the man asked, his tone surly.

'Hungry and thirsty,' replied Khalkeus.

'Are you a guest of the king?'

'Yes. I am Khalkeus.'

The servant grinned. 'Truly? The Madman from Miletos?'

Khalkeus sighed. 'I am not from Miletos but, yes, that is what some idiots call me.'

The man brought him a platter of black bread, some cheese, and a jug of watered wine. The bread was not fresh but, smeared with the cheese, it was palatable enough. Khalkeus sipped his wine and glanced towards the great doors, and the moon shadows beyond them. He wished Helikaon would come, so that he could conclude his business here and head back to Troy and his new forges.

His first attempts at smelting metal from the red rocks had proved disappointing. Even the hottest furnace produced a useless spongy grey mass. The fires, he decided, needed to be even hotter, and to this end Khalkeus had ordered the construction of a new furnace on the north plateau of Troy where the wind was keen.

But he needed more time, and more gold.

He was convinced Helikaon would understand. If Khalkeus succeeded the rewards would be colossal. Swords, spears, arrowheads and armour could be fashioned from the red rocks, which were plentiful all across the east. No need for expensive tin to be shipped from far islands beyond the Great Green, or soft copper from Kypros and other Mykene-held lands. Metal implements – ploughs, nails, barrel ties – could be produced at a fraction of the price of bronze.

The blazing torches were replaced twice before Helikaon returned. Flanked by five young men he strode into the building, shouting for a servant to bring some water. His handsome face was smeared with grime, his long dark hair tied back in a ponytail that reached his shoulders. Moving to the carved throne the young king slumped down, leaned back, and closed his eyes. Several of the men with him began speaking. Khalkeus listened as they complained of the insurmountable difficulties facing them. *This* could not be done because of *that*, and *that* was impossible because of *this*. Khalkeus felt his irritation flare. Stupid men with lazy minds. Instead of solving problems they wasted time seeking reasons why no solutions were available. Why Helikaon should allow such fools around him was a mystery.

A servant brought a silver wine cup and a jug brimming with cool water. Helikaon filled the cup, and drained it.

A young man with a wispy red beard spoke up. 'Rebuilding the bridge alone will take months, and there is not enough timber to reconstruct the warehouses and other buildings destroyed by the Mykene.'

'Nor enough carpenters and woodworkers,' added another man.

'And certainly not enough brains,' stormed Khalkeus, heaving his bulk upright. The men about the king stopped speaking, and swung towards Khalkeus. He marched forward, staring them down. 'I saw the remains of the bridge. It can be repaired in a matter of days. By the gods, Helikaon, I hope these morons are better fighters than they are thinkers.'

'My friends,' said Helikaon, to the angry men around him, 'this is Khalkeus. Now, before you decide to hate him you should understand that he will not care. Everyone hates Khalkeus. So put aside your anger, and leave us to talk.'

Khalkeus waited until the men had walked away, ignoring the cold glances they gave him as they passed. Then he approached Helikaon. 'I am close to the answer,' he said, 'but I need more gold.'

Helikaon took a deep, slow breath, his face hardening. Khalkeus, suddenly nervous, looked into the king's eyes, and saw no friendliness there. On the contrary, the sapphire gaze was hostile. 'Have I . . . done something to offend?' asked Khalkeus.

'To offend? What a paradox you are, Khalkeus. Genius and idiot in one fat package. You called my men morons. You walk into my hall with no greeting, no consoling words for the agonies that have been experienced here, merely a brazen demand for more of my gold.'

'Ah!' said Khalkeus. 'Now I understand. Yes, of course. The absence of feigned sympathy was offensive. My apologies. However, I do need more gold. I think I am close, Helikaon. The furnaces need to be hotter to burn out more of the impurities. Then I think—'

34

'Enough!' roared Helikaon, surging to his feet, and drawing his bronze knife. Shocked and frightened, Khalkeus took a backward step. His mouth was dry, and both his hands were trembling now. Helikaon moved in, grabbing Khalkeus' tunic with his left hand, the right bringing up the dagger, until the gleaming blade hovered above Khalkeus' left eye. For a moment neither man moved, then Helikaon swore softly, and let out a long breath. Sheathing the knife, he returned to his seat and filled the silver cup with more water. He drank deeply, and when he looked again at Khalkeus his eyes were no longer full of rage.

'The men you insulted,' said Helikaon, 'came home to find their wives and children murdered. And, yes, they are not skilled crafts-men or artisans. They are sailors. I kept them with me today to give them something to do, something to think about, other than the terrible losses they have suffered. You do not understand that, though, do you? No man who talks of *feigned* sympathy could understand.'

Khalkeus was about to speak, but Helikaon raised his hand. 'No, let us not discuss this further. I am sailing for Troy tomorrow. You will remain here. I want the bridge repaired and a new Seagate constructed. Then you can organize workmen to rebuild the warehouses.'

'I have much work to do back in Troy,' responded Khalkeus. Then he saw the cold glint reappear in Helikaon's eyes. 'But, of course, I would be happy to help here.'

'That is wise of you.'

Khalkeus sighed. 'Then they must be the first wise words I have said today. You were correct, Helikaon. I am an idiot. You are the last man I would wish to offend – and not because I need your gold, but because you have stood by me, and supported me when others called me a madman. So I hope you will forgive me, and that we can put these moments of anger behind us.'

Helikaon's face relaxed, but he did not smile, nor was there any warmth in those bleak, violent blue eyes. 'We are what we are,' he said. 'Both of us. You are oblivious of the sufferings of others, but you have never burned men alive and revelled in their screams.'

He fell silent for a moment, then spoke again. 'You say the bridge can be rebuilt swiftly?'

Khalkeus nodded. 'It could be functional within twenty days. I doubt you will want it more than that, at this time.'

'Why so?'

'You are a rich man, Helikaon, but your continuing riches depend on trade. Every gold ingot you use to rebuild Dardanos could prove to be a reckless waste should the Mykene invade again. And you may need all your gold if this war drags on.'

'So you would advise . . . ?'

'Make temporary repairs, at little cost. And move your treasury from Dardanos.'

Helikaon shook his head. 'The first I cannot do. There is no nation here, Khalkeus, merely a mix of races who have come to Dardania in search of wealth: Hittites, Phrygians, Thessalians, Thrakians. And many more. They obey my laws, and pay my taxes because I shield them from their enemies, and crush any who oppose me. If they come to believe that I have lost faith in my ability to defend my own land, then they will lose faith in me. Then I will be facing not only invasion from the north, but insurrection from within. No, the repairs must be solid and built to last.'

'Then they will be,' agreed Khalkeus. 'And, at the risk of offending you once more, what of my earlier request? With this war showing no sign of ending my work is even more vital.'

'I know. Help my people here and I shall ensure you have gold waiting for you in Troy.' Helikaon pushed himself wearily to his feet. 'You have great faith in these red rocks, Khalkeus. I hope it is not misplaced.'

'It is not. I am convinced of it. By next summer's end, Helikaon, I will bring you the greatest sword in all the world.'

II

The masks of Priam

THE DREAM WAS TERRIFYING. XANDER WAS HANGING ABOVE A BLACK pit. When he looked down he saw scores of blood-red eyes staring up at him, and bright fangs waiting to rip at his flesh. Xander glanced up, seeking reassurance from the man whose strong grip held firmly to Xander's wrist.

Then he screamed – for the man holding him was a corpse, grey, rotting flesh peeling back from his bones. The decaying sinews at the wrist and the elbow began to stretch. The bones of the fingers broke away and Xander fell into the pit.

He awoke with a start, his legs drawing up in a spasm of movement. Eyes wide, he stared around the small, familiar resting room in the House of Serpents. Slowly his heartbeat returned to normal, the panic fading. He heard again the words of Odysseus. 'My Penelope tells me there are two kinds of dreams. Some come through a Gate of Ivory, and their meanings are deceitful. Others come through a Gate of Horn, and these are heavy with fate.'

Xander sat up. Sunlight was bright outside the shuttered window, but the young healer was reluctant to open it. Once he did so his time of rest would be over, and he would once again walk among the dying and the maimed.

'The dream is a deceit,' he whispered. 'It is merely a mixture of memories and fears.' In that moment he pictured again the fury of the storm four years before, crashing down upon the *Xanthos*. Then only twelve, Xander had been on his first sea journey. Swept over the side by a colossal wave he should have drowned, but a powerful hand had grasped his wrist. The warrior Argurios had hurled himself across the rainswept deck to grab Xander before the sea could swallow him.

'Memories and fears,' whispered Xander, breathing slowly and deeply, now recalling the dissection of the beggar's corpse a few days before.

The surgeon Zeotos had opened the flesh of the dead man's arm, peeling it back from the elbow. 'See,' said the old man, 'how the muscles attach, and the tendons. Remarkable!' Four healers and five students had attended this grisly display of the surgeon's skill. One of the youngsters had fainted, striking his head on the wall as he fell. Xander and the other three students had briefly enjoyed a feeling of superiority over their hapless colleague, until Zeotos had sawn through the chest bone and slit open the cadaver's belly. Once the intestines were exposed the stench that filled the room was beyond bearing, and the young men had fled to the corridor beyond, the sound of the surgeon's laughter following them.

These two memories – the cadaver and the ship in the storm – had blended to form the awful dream.

Feeling calmer Xander rose from the bed and moved to a stone basin set on a table beneath the window. Splashing water to his face he pushed his wet fingers through his curly hair. Refreshed, he opened the shutters, allowing sunlight in. There was little warmth in it, and the cold breeze heralded the onset of winter.

'Xander!' came the voice of Zeotos. The young student turned to see the white-bearded surgeon at the door of the resting room. 'You have to return to work now,' he said, his face a mask of exhaustion. Xander felt a rush of guilt. The old man had worked throughout the night without rest.

'You shouldn't have let me sleep so long, sir,' he said.

'The young seem to need their sleep more than the old,' answered Zeotos. 'That said, I am now going to steal that bed of yours. There are two men out there with deep stomach wounds. Keep an eye on them both, boy. If their bellies begin to distend come and get me as fast as you can. Understand?'

'Yes, sir.'

The previous night almost two hundred cavalrymen had been brought to the House of Serpents under cover of darkness. They were all grievously wounded and had suffered greatly in the embattled crossing of the Hellespont and the long journey to the city from Dardanos. Carried on jolting, overloaded carts and horse-drawn litters, many had died along the way.

Zeotos lay down on the bed, and gave a low groan of pleasure. Xander left the old man and made his way to the courtyard, where most of the injured were lying under canopies on cushioned pallets. There was little noise, despite the numbers crowded there, just the occasional groan of a soldier having a wound tended, or the mumbled delirium of a dying man. The smoke from fragrant herbs burning on the altar of Asklepios helped keep insects away. Xander saw the head of the house, Machaon, and the three other healers moving among the wounded. Elsewhere trained servants busied themselves, bringing fresh water, removing soiled linen and applying clean bandages.

Xander knew where he was most needed. Those with a chance of life and recovery were receiving the best care from both healers and servants. The dying lay alone. Xander moved swiftly to the row of beds nearest the altar. The first man he came to had been wounded in the chest and lower back. His face was haggard and grey, and death was not far off.

'Are you in pain?' whispered Xander, leaning over the man.

The dying soldier looked into Xander's eyes. 'I've suffered worse. You see the parade?' he asked. 'Heard them ride by, crowds cheering.'

'I caught a glimpse,' Xander told him. 'Hektor rode in a golden chariot, and the riders followed him in ranks of four. People threw flowers on to the street.'

The soldier's smile faded. 'You can go now, healer. There's others with greater need than me.'

'Can I get you anything? Water?'

The soldier winced. 'Another year of life would be good.'

Xander moved on. Three other warriors had quietly died, and he called servants to remove the bodies. The dying watched the departure of the dead, their faces grim.

Late in the afternoon old Zeotos appeared again, hurrying across the courtyard. 'The king is coming,' the surgeon grunted. 'Machaon wants you to meet him and Prince Hektor at the gates. He himself must perform an immediate amputation. And I cannot be seen here.'

Xander nodded his understanding. Zeotos had been banished from Troy after the Mykene attack in which the king's daughter Laodike had died. Priam had blamed the old surgeon for her death. Zeotos had travelled the countryside plying his craft, never straying far from Troy, but had fallen on hard times. Machaon had heard of his plight and covertly returned him to the House of Serpents, fearful the impending war would stretch their resources beyond their limit.

As Xander hurried nervously to the gates to greet the king he could hear the sound of marching feet. Out in the sunlit square a troop of Royal Eagles was heading towards the temple, escorting a covered litter. Beside them walked Hektor, still in the ceremonial armour and flowing white cloak he had worn in the parade. The litter stopped and Priam the king climbed out. Dressed in long blue robes, he lifted his arms high and stretched his back.

'A pox on this . . . moving hammock!' he spat. 'I should have ridden my chariot. A king shouldn't be carried around like a heap of laundry.' Looking round, he glared at Xander. 'Who are you, boy?' he rasped.

Xander was speechless. He had seen the king before, but only from a distance, at games and ceremonial events. He was struck now by the resemblance between Priam and his son, both tall, broad and exuding power. The older man was slightly stooped, and it was clear he had celebrated his son's return with plenty of wine, yet his personality dominated the sunlit square and even the heavily armoured Eagles seemed diminished in his presence.

Hektor stepped forward. 'You are Xander,' he said, smiling.

'Yes. Yes, lord,' the young healer replied, throwing himself belatedly to his knees.

'Stand up, Xander. You are a friend of my wife, and no friend kneels in my presence. Now, bring us to our wounded comrades.'

As they passed through the dark gates into the temple, Xander heard Priam grumble, 'Cripples depress me, and there is always a stink around the dying. It sticks in the nostrils for days.' Hektor appeared not to hear him.

They stepped into the courtyard and there was silence for a moment, then ragged cheering arose from the sick and broken men. Even those on the threshold of the Dark Road raised their voices for their king and commander.

Priam raised his arms and the cheers redoubled. Then he spoke and the irritable rasp Xander had heard moments before was replaced by a deep, warm, booming voice which easily reached the injured men at the far wall.

'Trojans!' he cried, and all other sound ceased. 'I am proud of you all. This victory you have won for Troy will be spoken of for a thousand years. Your names will be as familiar to Father Zeus as those of Herakles and Ilos.' He beamed and raised his arms again to acknowledge the cheers, then he and Hektor walked among the beds.

Xander was baffled. Moments before he had heard the king complaining of this visit as a tiresome duty. Perhaps he had misheard, or misunderstood the words. Now he watched Priam speaking softly to the dying, listening kindly to babbled tales of saintly mothers and wives, even joking with amputees, and saying to each one, 'Your king is proud of you, soldier.'

Xander stayed at his side, sometimes translating the mumbled words of a soldier in his last moments, sometimes lifting a man's hand so he could touch the king's robes. He stole an occasional look into Priam's face, but could see nothing there but kind concern and compassion.

Hektor was always a step behind his father, and greeted each man by name. As they slowly made their way round, not missing one bed, the sun moved down in the sky and Xander saw the lines on Hektor's face deepen and his shoulders sag. In contrast, his father seemed to gain energy from the visit.

As the sun disappeared over the houses of healing, and torches were lit around the courtyard, they returned to the gates again, where an ornate chariot, encrusted with gold and gems, had been drawn up. Priam turned to his son. 'Now let us return to the living, and enjoy this day of triumph.'

'It was good for the men to see us together,' Hektor replied mildly.

Priam looked at him with anger in his eyes. His voice again was cold and rasping. 'Never ask me to do that again, boy. A king is not a nursemaid. And the smell in there was nauseating.'

Xander saw Hektor's jaw set, but he stepped lightly into the chariot and took up the reins. Priam climbed in beside him. 'You should have left them all on the beach at Carpea. They would have welcomed an honourable death for their king and their city,' he said.

Hektor flicked at the reins and the two white geldings leaned in to the traces, the chariot pulling smoothly away, the Royal Eagles loping alongside.

Back in the courtyard the men were talking excitedly about the visit of the king, and how he had spoken of his pride in them. Xander, saddened by Priam's deceit, spoke of it to Zeotos later that night. 'He seemed so . . . so genuinely interested in them, so warm, so compassionate. In truth, though, he cared nothing for them.'

The surgeon chuckled. 'You heard him tell the men he was proud of them, and tell Hektor he was a king not a nursemaid?'

'Yes.'

'And you assume he was lying to the men, and telling the truth to Hektor?'

Xander nodded. 'Am I wrong, sir?'

'Perhaps, Xander. Priam is a complex man. It is possible that his words to the injured and the dying were heartfelt, and that his callous comments to Hektor were made to disguise his emotions.'

'You think so?' Xander's heart lifted.

'No. Priam is a cold and wretched creature. Although,' Zeotos added with a wink, 'now it might be me who is lying. The point is, Xander, that it is unwise to form judgements on such little evidence.'

'Now I am completely confused.'

'Which was my intention. You are a fine lad, Xander, honest, direct, and without guile. Priam is a man so drenched in deceit even he would no longer know which – if any – of his statements was genuine. In the end it doesn't matter. The men who heard him praise them had their spirits lifted. Indeed, some of them may even recover now, and it would then be fair to say that Priam healed them. So do not be downcast by a few callous words from a drunken king.'

Andromache climbed the long hill towards the palace, moonlight glinting on the golden, gem-encrusted gown she wore. Her long, flame-red hair was decorated with emeralds in a braid of gold. She was weary as she walked. Not physically tired, for she was young and strong, but drained by a day of jostling crowds and cloying conversations, rich with insincerity. Andromache could still hear music and laughter from the square. There was no joy in the sound. The atmosphere at the feast had been tense, the laughter forced and strident.

The men had talked of victory, but Andromache had heard the fear in their voices, seen it shining in their eyes. Priam lifted the crowd with a powerful speech, in which he extolled the heroic virtues of Hektor and the Trojan Horse. But the effect was ephemeral. All at the feast knew the reality.

Many merchant families had already left the city, and most of the warehouses stood empty. The wealth that had flowed like a golden river into the city was slowing. Soon it would be merely a trickle. How long then before the enemy were camped outside the walls, readying their ladders and their battering rams, sharpening their swords and preparing for slaughter and plunder?

Which was why, Andromache knew, everyone wanted to be close to her husband Hektor, talking to him, clapping him on the back, telling him how they had prayed for his safe homecoming. This last was probably true. More than the huge walls, more than the power of its soldiers, and the wealth of its king, Hektor represented Troy's greatest hope for staving off defeat. Everywhere else the news was grim: trade routes cut off, allies overcome or suborned, enemy armies rampaging beyond the Ida mountains, and across the straits in Thraki.

Andromache walked on, two soldiers alongside her holding burning brands to light the way. Two others, of Priam's elite Eagles, followed, hands on sword hilts. Ever since the attack on her by Mykene assassins, Andromache had been shadowed by armed men. It was galling, and she had never become used to it.

She thought back to the night long ago on Blue Owl Bay when, disguised, she had walked among the sailors and the whores, and had listened to Odysseus telling tall tales. That was the night she had met Helikaon – a night of violence and death, a night of prophecy.

There could be no such anonymous nights now. Her face was too well known in Troy. Otherwise she might have returned to the palace, slipped into a servant's tunic, and made her way down to the lower town, where she could dance and sing among honest people.

As they climbed towards the palace she saw several drunken men asleep on the street. The soldiers with her eyed them warily. One of the drunks awoke as they passed. He stared at her, then rubbed his eyes. His expression was one of wonder. He struggled to his feet and staggered towards her. Instantly the swords of the Eagles rasped from their scabbards.

'It is all right,' Andromache called out. 'Do not harm him.'

The drunk halted before her, staring at the golden gown she wore, the torchlight glittering on the gems woven into its strands. 'I thought . . . I thought you were a goddess from Olympos,' he said.

'I am Andromache. You should go home.'

'Andromache,' he repeated.

'Be off with you,' ordered one of the soldiers.

The drunk tried to stand tall, but then staggered. He glared at the soldier. 'I was at Kadesh,' he said, raising his right hand. In the flickering light Andromache saw it was maimed, the first three fingers cut away. 'Trojan Horse,' he went on. 'No parades for me, boy. Now I piss in a pot for the dye makers, and I sleep on the street. But I could still piss on you, you arrogant turd!'

Andromache swiftly stepped between the man and the angry soldier. Unpinning a golden brooch encrusted with gems from the shoulder of her gown, she pressed it into the man's ruined hand. 'Accept this gift, soldier, from Hektor's wife,' she said, 'in tribute to your courage.'

He stared down at the glowing gold, and she saw there were tears in his eyes. 'I am Pardones,' he said. 'Remember me to your husband.'

Then he turned away, and stumbled into the darkness.

The sun was blazing low on the horizon as the *Xanthos* sailed into the great Bay of Troy. Not a breath of wind blew across the water, and only the sound of the oars dipping and rising broke the sunset silence.

In the distance the city gleamed as if cast from burning gold. The last of the sunlight shone upon its gilded rooftops and bannered towers, casting glittering reflected shards of light from the spear-points and helms of the sentries upon the battlements.

Gershom the Egypteian smiled as he gazed again upon the city. It was indeed impressive, but as he looked at the awestruck expressions of the crew nearest to him he wondered how they would react should they ever see the wonders of Thebes, the city of a hundred gates, or the towering white pyramids, or the Great Lion. Troy was breathtaking, but it mirrored the people who had built it. The city had not been constructed with thought to beauty, nor aligned with the stars to please the gods who dwelt there. It was, first and foremost, a fortress, solid and strong, with high walls and gates of oak and bronze. The majesty of Troy was almost accidental, Gershom thought, a blending of impressive masonry and brilliant sunsets.

There were few other ships in the bay. Four fishing boats had spread their nets, and three new war galleys were being put through manoeuvres close to the southern shore. Gershom watched them for a while. The rowers were inexperienced, oars clashing at times as the galleys were halted, or spun, or urged to ramming speed. So many ships had been sunk these last few seasons, and hundreds of experienced sailors drowned or killed in sea battles. Now novices would take to the sea and die in their hundreds.

The *Xanthos* sailed on, reaching the King's Beach just as the sun dipped below the horizon. Oniacus called out orders to the rowers. Immediately the two banks of oars on the port side lifted clear of the water, while those on the starboard side dipped and pulled. The stern of the *Xanthos* swung smoothly towards the beach. 'And . . . NOW!' yelled Oniacus. All the oars struck the water simultaneously. The hull of the *Xanthos* ground into the sand, then came to rest. Oars were swiftly shipped.

Then the deck hatches were opened. Gershom walked over and helped the crew unload the cargo. More than a thousand cuirasses were passed up and dropped over the side to the sand. The armour worn by the Trojan Horse was well crafted, discs of bronze overlaid like fish scales on breastplates of leather, and – unlike the bodies of the proud men who had worn it – far too valuable to be left behind on the battlefields of Thraki.

The armour was loaded on to carts, then carried back up through the lower town and into the city. Finally the deck hatches were closed. Oniacus moved past Gershom, heading to the prow. The men of the skeleton crew settled down on the raised aft deck, blankets over their shoulders against the chill of the evening, while their comrades made their way up to the town, beneath the walls of the golden city.

Gershom saw Helikaon, cradling in his arms his sleeping son Dex, greeted by the huge Trojan prince Antiphones. Gershom turned away and strolled to the prow. Oniacus was leaning against the rail and staring out across the bay at the new war galleys. His handsome young face was set and angry, and there was violence in his eyes.

'Is there anything I can have sent down to you?' asked Gershom. 'Wine, perhaps?'

Oniacus shook his head. 'Wine helps you to forget, they say. I don't want to forget. And I don't want to talk, either.'

'Then don't talk,' said Gershom softly. 'Two friends should be able to stand together in silence without awkwardness.'

The silence did not last long, nor did Gershom expect it to. It was not that Oniacus was a gregarious man, but the grief welling up in him could not be restrained. He began by talking of his two sons, what fine boys they had been. Gershom said nothing; it was not necessary. Oniacus was not really talking to him, but instead speaking to the night, to the shades of his boys, to the gods who were not there to protect them and their mother when the Mykene fell upon Dardanos with bright swords. Sadness was followed by rage, and rage by tears. Finally there was silence again. Gershom put his arm round Oniacus' shoulder.

Oniacus sighed. 'I am not ashamed of tears,' he said.

'Nor should you be, my friend. It is said that the gates of paradise can only be opened by the tears of those left behind. I do not know whether that be true. It should be, I think.'

Oniacus looked at him closely. 'You do believe we live on, and that there . . . there will be some reward for those innocents whose lives were . . . were stolen from them?'

'Of course,' Gershom lied. 'How could it be other?'

Oniacus nodded. 'I believe that. A place of happiness. No terrors or fears, no cowards or killers. I believe that,' he said again.

They stood together for a while watching the galleys upon the still waters. 'The balance is wrong,' said Gershom, pointing to the nearest vessel. 'See it veer?'

'Too much strength on the port side oars. They need to switch some of the rowers,' Oniacus told him. The anguish could still be seen in his eyes, but now he was focused on the galley. 'Pushing the oarsmen too hard,' he said. 'All they'll get is sprained shoulders and shattered confidence.' He looked at Gershom, and forced a smile. 'Time for you to get ashore. The many delights of Troy are waiting, and you do not want to be standing here discussing the training of sailors. Do not concern yourself about me. I shall not slash open my throat, I promise you.'

'I know that,' replied Gershom. 'I will see you tomorrow.' With that he swung away. Oniacus called out to him, and he turned.

'Thank you, my friend,' said Oniacus.

Gershom walked to the aft deck, gathered his cloak and swung it to his shoulders. Then he climbed over the deck rail and lowered himself to the sand.

He strolled across the beach towards the path to the lower town. At the wide wooden bridge spanning the fortification ditch he saw two sentries in armour of burnished bronze, long spears in their hands. Across the bridge a crowd had gathered round some of the sailors from the *Xanthos*. One of the sentries smiled at Gershom. He was a young man, but his face and arms bore the scars of combat.

'News of your victories reached us two days ago,' he said. 'It was welcome as sunshine after snow.' People clustered round the crew, patting them on the back and calling out praises and blessings. Gershom eased himself round the edge of the crowd.

A man suddenly clapped his hand on the Egypteian's shoulder. 'Here is another of them!' he shouted happily.

As more men turned towards Gershom he shook his head. 'No, no,' he told them, raising his hands. 'I am merely a traveller.'

Losing interest immediately, they turned their attention once more to the other sailors. Gershom pressed on. A dark-haired girl stepped from the shadows into the moonlight and linked her arm in his. Gershom glanced down into her face. She was pretty, with pale eyes, either blue or grey. It was too dark to tell. He could see the girl was young, though. Her white ankle-length tunic was close-fitting, her small breasts barely stretching the fabric.

Taking her hand, he lifted it from his arm. 'I am in no mood for sport,' he told her gruffly. 'And if I were it would be with a woman, not a child.'

The girl laughed. 'If you *were* in the mood you could not afford me – not even as a prince of Egypt.'

Gershom paused then, his eyes raking her slim form, seeking any sign of a hidden weapon. His identity had been kept secret – or so he had thought. If this young whore knew of him, how many more had heard? Men who would seek the reward still on his head? He glanced around nervously, half expecting to see Egypteian assassins dart from the shadows.

'Do I frighten you?' the girl asked him.

'Go and find someone else to annoy,' he told her, walking on. The girl ran after him. Gershom felt his irritation rise.

'I saw you in the sea,' she said. 'Great waves crashing over you. You were very strong.'

Gershom paused again, his curiosity aroused. 'All right, you know who I am. Who sent you, child, and for what purpose?'

'Xidoros sent me . . .' Suddenly she cocked her head. 'Yes, yes,' she said, talking to the darkness, 'but that is just pedantic.' She frowned and seemed to be listening. Then she threw up her arm. 'Oh, go away!' she snapped. Turning back to Gershom she said: 'He says he didn't send me, that he merely said we should speak.'

Gershom swore softly. Back in Thebes there was a house with high walls where the moon-touched were kept for four years. In that time diviners and healers, astrologers and magicians would be called upon to heal them, or drive out the demons that robbed them of sanity. Surgeons would drill holes into their skulls; healers would feed them strange herbs and potions. If at the end of four years they were still not cured, it was taken as a sign that the gods were calling for them. They were then strangled. Gershom had heard of no such houses of caring in barbarous Troy. Which was why sad lunatics like this child were allowed to wander the streets.

'Where do you live?' he asked the girl. 'I will see you safely home.'

She looked up at him, and her face was suddenly sad. 'There is a mist inside your head,' she told him. 'It is swirling and thick, and it stops you from seeing. You stumble around like a blind man.' She shrugged. 'But then there are times when I long to be blind myself. Just to listen to people and hear only the words they speak, and not the sly whisperings inside their heads.' She smiled again. 'Come, I will walk *you* home.'

'You know where I am going?'

'Yes, I know. You are going to the Beautiful Isle with me, and then you will be called to the desert, and there will be voices in the fire, and fire in the heavens, and the fire will melt away the mist in your head, and you will know all that I know, and see more than I will ever see.'

'Very intriguing,' said Gershom, 'but I meant do you know where I am going *now*?'

'Oh! Yes, I do. The House of Stone Horses.'

'Well, that is true enough. Now, where do *you* live?'

She gave a soft laugh. 'My guards are looking for me, so I must go. But I will see you tomorrow at Hektor's palace.' With that she hitched up her white tunic and darted away.

Gershom thought of chasing her, and handing her over to the city watch. Some of the areas of the lower town were known to be dangerous, and a moon-struck child like this one could find herself in peril. But even as the thought occurred he saw her vanish into a dark alley, and out of his sight.

With a shake of his head the big Egypteian walked on towards the palace of Helikaon.

III

The amber goddess

EARLY MORNING SUNSHINE BATHED THE STREETS OF TROY AS HELIKAON left the House of Stone Horses and strolled through the town. The business of the day was beginning: merchants were setting up their stalls in the marketplaces; servants and slaves were carrying bundles of cloth, or produce wrapped in dry reeds. The varied sounds of the city washed over Helikaon as he walked: hammers beating upon metal from the Street of Armourers, the braying of donkeys, the clucking of hens, the yelping of dogs, and the cries of the gather-men, competing to draw crowds to their stalls.

It felt strange to be back in Troy. The war seemed far away now, the death of Halysia a dark nightmare, unreal and bizarre.

He had awoken this morning to a soft, warm body beside him. In the instant before full consciousness asserted itself he had thought to open his eyes and gaze down at Halysia. Instead it was Dex, his thumb in his mouth, his head resting on his father's shoulder. Helikaon had stroked the fair hair back from the boy's brow. Dex's eyes had opened, then the child had fallen asleep again.

Easing himself from the bed Helikaon had risen and dressed. He chose a white tunic, embroidered with gold thread, and a wide belt embossed with gold leaf. He felt uncomfortable in such finery, but it was fitting for his meeting with Priam. Lastly he took a scabbarded dagger, and tucked it into his belt. It was unlikely that assassins would be abroad on the streets of Troy, but not impossible.

In happier days Helikaon had walked these streets in the company of Hektor or his brothers Antiphones or Agathon. Those had been the days of innocence, when the future had promised wonders. It was here on these streets, ten years ago, that he and Hektor had argued about the merits and drawbacks of marrying for love alone.

'Why would you want to?' Hektor had asked. 'All actions of a prince must strengthen the realm. Therefore a wife should bring a handsome dowry, land, or promises of alliance with her father's kingdom. A prince can find love wherever he wishes thereafter.'

'I do not agree,' Helikaon had replied on that far-off day. 'Odysseus loves his wife, and is happy. You should see them together, Hektor. You would change your views in a heartbeat. Odysseus says that life without Penelope would be like a land without sunshine. I want a wife who brings me happiness like that.'

'I hope you find her, my friend,' Hektor had said.

And he had. He had found the woman of his dreams. How ironic then, he thought, that it should have been Hektor who had married her.

He paused to examine some Egypteian jewellery on display, and was immediately accosted by an elderly merchant, a slender, dark-skinned man with henna-dyed hair and beard.

'You won't find better, sir. Not anywhere in the city.' The man lifted a heavy brooch of amber, decorated with gold wire. 'Sixteen silver rings, sir. A real bargain.'

'In Egypte last season,' Helikaon commented, 'sixteen silver rings would buy a sack of these baubles.'

'Perhaps, sir,' replied the man, his dark eyes narrowing. 'But, since there is now no trade with Egypte, who knows what price amber is fetching today?'

'Wise words,' Helikaon agreed, casting his gaze round the marketplace. 'There are fewer stalls than I recall from my last visit.'

'A few have left,' said the merchant. 'More will follow, I think. My brother packed up his wares as soon as the fortification ditch was dug. Too early, I said. But he always was timid. Now they say there's going to be a wall to protect the lower town. If that's true I'll follow my brother.'

'An interesting point,' observed Helikaon, with a smile. 'You will stay only as long as the lower town is *badly* defended?'

The merchant chuckled. 'Priam is a good king. Has to be said, though, that he's careful with his wealth. If he has now approved the expense of a wall round the lower town it will only be because he cannot stop the Mykene coming to this land. Well, I have walked through the ruins of towns plundered by the Mykene. I'll not wait to see such sights again.'

Helikaon nodded. 'I see the logic in your words, but surely still more merchants will quit the city if Priam builds *no* wall to defend them?'

'Yes. Who'd be a king, eh?'

On the stall Helikaon's eye was taken by an amber pendant, upon which an artist had incised the figure of the goddess Artemis, her bow extended, the string drawn back. It reminded him of Andromache, and of how she had stood on the balcony of Priam's *megaron*, calmly shooting arrows down into the Mykene attackers. Lifting the pendant he examined it more closely. It was finely carved.

'You are a wonderful judge of jewellery, sir,' said the merchant, immediately slipping back into his sales patter, 'for you have chosen the pride of my collection.' He was about to go on when Helikaon interrupted him.

'Before you speak let me say I am in no mood to haggle today. So, this is what we will do. You will name one price. If I like the price I will pay it instantly. If not I will drop this bauble back to the stall and walk on. Now . . . name the price.'

The old merchant licked his lips, then rubbed at his chin. As he did so he stepped out from behind the stall, appearing deep in thought. Helikaon stood quietly as the merchant observed him. 'Twenty silver rings,' said the man, at last.

'I agree,' Helikaon told him, with a smile. 'You are a clever man. What is your name?'

'Tobios.'

'A Hittite?'

The merchant shrugged. 'I suppose that would depend upon who asked. The land in which I was born is fiercely contested. The pharaohs would say I am a foul-hearted *Hittite* desert-dweller, but the land is currently ruled by Emperor Hattusilis of the Hittites. Therefore, I am now considered to be a foul-hearted *Egypteian* desert-dweller. Life for my people is always complicated.'

Helikaon smiled. 'Such complications help to sharpen the wits,' he said. As he spoke he counted out the twenty silver rings, and laid them on the stall. 'If you choose to remain in the city, Tobios, come and see me at the House of Stone Horses. I am Helikaon of Dardania and I always have need for men of good judgement.'

Tobios bowed his head and touched his heart in the Hittite manner.

Helikaon walked on, the amber pendant in his hand. The price had been high. The merchant had looked at his clothing, appraising, through its quality, the wealth of the wearer. The white tunic was of Egypteian design, woven from the finest thread. The engravings on his belt were filled with gold leaf. Even his sandals were fashioned from crocodile skin, brushed with gold. Had he not been dressed for a meeting with King Priam he would have worn old, comfortable clothes and bought the pendant for two-thirds of the price.

Moving on through narrow streets and open squares he reached the mighty Scaean Gate, with its six guardians of stone, and passed through to the upper city, its palaces and gardens and avenues. Indications of wealth lay everywhere. Women wore heavy necklaces, bracelets and earrings, and even the men sported expensive torques or wristbands.

At the palace Helikaon was ushered through to the gardens, where nobles hoping to see the king were allowed to wait in comfort, rather than in the crowded *megaron*. There was a chill in the air, and several braziers filled with burning charcoal had been set up.

Helikaon looked about him, nodding greetings to those he knew. Then he turned – and his stomach tightened. Just paces away, a rust-coloured cloak round her shoulders, stood Andromache, sunlight glinting upon the red-gold of her hair. She was wearing a long yellow gown that sparkled like summer sunshine. Helikaon's mouth was dry, and he felt nervous and awkward. Andromache stepped towards him.

'I was so sorry to hear of Halysia's death,' she told him. 'Though my heart was lifted by the manner of it. The gods will cherish her, I think.'

'Perhaps. But in life she deserved better,' he replied. 'From life, from me. The people loved her greatly, though, and they will not forget her, I think.'

'And how is the boy?'

'Dex is brave, but scarred now. Last night he had nightmares and ran to my room. I slept with him curled up against me. A child should not have to see his mother die.'

'But when he grows,' she told him softly, 'he will know she loved him – so much that she was willing to give her life for him. It will sustain him.'

Andromache had seen his handsome face soften, and the sad smile he gave. She wanted to reach out and hug him in that moment, remembering that he too had watched his mother die. Instead she had forced herself to stand still, and say politely: 'I hope you will bring your son to visit us while you are in Troy.'

'I would like that, Andromache.'

She had felt herself redden as he spoke her name. 'I am here to see the king,' she told him suddenly, the comment both redundant and ridiculous, since the only reason anyone was in the garden was to see the king. Angry with herself, she went on, 'I meant to say I have been *called* here to see the king. A ship arrived yesterday from Thera with a message from the High Priestess. It probably concerns Kassandra. As you know, she is to become a priestess at the Temple of the Horse. You did know that?'

Sweet Artemis! Help me to stop babbling!

'Yes, I did. I am to take her on the *Xanthos* next spring. Are you well?' he had asked suddenly, concern in his eyes. 'You seem flushed.'

'I am well. Just a little warm.'

'I shall fetch you some water,' he had said, and moved away.

There were many people in the garden waiting to see the king. As Helikaon walked away the crowd parted for him. Andromache could see he was oblivious of the effect he had on the people around him. He did not seem to notice the envious glances from the men, nor the openly admiring stares from the women.

A shadow fell across her. She looked up to see her husband Hektor. He too was looking across at Helikaon, his face expressionless. Andromache thought she saw sadness in his eyes.

'What is wrong, husband?' she asked, taking his arm.

He shrugged and drew her close. 'What could be wrong when I have you beside me? Did I miss any interesting conversation with Helikaon?'

'No, not really. I asked him to bring his son to see us.'

Hektor's brow furrowed, and she felt him tense. 'Why did you do that?' he asked.

'Why would I not?' she responded, suddenly uncertain. When he answered her the anguish in his voice was so great that the words slid through her defences like daggers.

'How many of his sons do I need in my house, Andromache?'

The shock was so great she felt sick. Hektor had promised to raise the boy Astyanax and love him as he would his own child. He had been true to his word, and Andromache had never before heard him express such feelings as these. Rarely at a loss for words, she had no response. She merely stood and looked at her husband, seeing yet again the resemblance to his father. Until this moment he had reflected everything that could have been great in Priam – courage, compassion, kindness – but now she wondered just how many of his father's weaknesses he had also inherited.

Turning away from him without a word she walked to a brazier, reaching out her hands and rubbing them over the fire as if seeking warmth. There was anger in her, but not with Hektor. She was angry with herself. Of course her husband would be hurt by her invitation! He knew she loved Helikaon. She had confessed to Hektor on their first evening alone that she had shared a bed with Helikaon. Having survived an assassin's blade Helikaon had fallen into a fever, poison in his blood. A healer from the desert told Andromache that Helikaon appeared to have lost the will to live. He suggested a naked woman be brought to his bed to remind him of the joys of life. A few nights later, fearing Helikaon was dying, Andromache had let fall her dress and slid into the bed alongside him. The following morning, when Andromache returned to his room, Helikaon had told her he had dreamed of her. She had realized then that he had no memory of their lovemaking. Not only had she allowed him to believe the dream, she had later kept from him the knowledge that he had a son.

Standing by the brazier she found her mood sliding downward, bleak thoughts filling her mind. She had arrived in this city as a young priestess, proud and honest, determined that the deceptions and deceits of Troy would not sully her. She would not be drawn into a world of lies and intrigue. Stupid, arrogant girl, she chided herself. Since her arrival she had become pregnant by one man while betrothed to another, had seduced the old king to make him believe her son was his, and had poisoned Hekabe, the dying queen of Troy.

But Hekabe had been a queen of malice, she told herself, who murdered my sister and would have murdered my friends. And as for seducing Priam, what other course had there been? Had he discovered the truth Astyanax would have been taken from her, perhaps killed, and she would have been executed, and Helikaon too.

Evil will always seek to justify its actions, she reproached herself.

Her thoughts bleak, she turned towards Hektor. Before she could speak to him she heard a young soldier call out to him. It was Polydorus, the king's bodyguard. He crossed to where Hektor stood.

'The king is asking for you both,' he said, glancing at her, 'in the Amber Room.'

Propelled by the wind the Trojans called the Scythe, the great flock of golden birds flew south, leaving behind them the icy peaks of the Rhodope mountains and the fierce winters of Thraki. Driven by migratory instinct the birds dipped and swooped, skimming over the waves and isles of the Great Green. Early morning sunshine gleamed upon feathers of yellow and black as the golden cloud flew above the city of Troy.

Upon a high balcony, and dressed in an old robe of faded gold, Priam gazed up at the migrating flock of orioles. They swooped above him, twisting and turning in the sky, as if drawn to the king's golden robe. Priam raised his arms and called out to them. 'I am your king too, little birds.'

For a few moments the arrival of the flock made the old king forget his troubles. He recalled that his beloved Hekabe had studied the migratory habits of scores of birds: white-tailed eagles, pygmy owls, pelicans, lapwings, and many more whose names he had now forgotten.

The golden orioles, though, were special to Troy, Hekabe had insisted. If their migration to the coasts of Egypt began before the feast of Ares then the winter would be harsh and cold, and full of storms and great winds.

And the feast of Ares was still eighteen days away.

Suddenly the golden birds scattered, and were gone. A cold breeze whispered across the palace, making the king shiver.

'Fetch me a cloak!' he called out to his aide Polydorus. The soldier emerged on the balcony bearing a new cloak of green wool, edged with gold thread. 'Not that useless rag,' snapped Priam. 'My own cloak, if you please.' Polydorus returned with an old brown garment, frayed at the edges. Swirling it round his shoulders, Priam walked to the edge of the balcony.

In the early morning he could hear movement all over his city: donkeys braying and roosters crowing, the sounds of carts and horses' hooves on the stone roads, the shouting as soldiers changed shifts and seamen made their way down to the beach for dawn sailings. He imagined bleary-eyed bakers kneading dough, and tired whores making for their beds. Atop the Great Tower of Ilion the four night torches still flickered.

Priam's eye was constantly drawn to the dark shape of the tower. He used to climb its steep steps every morning to watch the sun rise and look over the city, but he had neglected the practice in recent days.

'How long since I last went to the tower, Polydorus?'

'In the high summer, lord.'

'So long? Time flies swifter than the orioles. I will go tomorrow. The people should see their king keeping watch over them.'

'Yes, lord,' said Polydorus. 'Shall I bring your wine?'

Priam licked his lips. The thought of wine was tempting. Indeed he ached for the taste. 'No,' he said at last, the effort of will bringing with it a surge of anger. 'No wine today, Polydorus.' There was a time when he had enjoyed his wine as a man should, as an enhancer to the joys of dancing, singing and sex. Now he thought of it constantly, organizing his day around bouts of heavy drinking. Not today, though. Today he would need his wits about him. No wine will pass my lips until tomorrow, he promised himself.

'Are my visitors here yet?'

'I'll see, lord.' The young soldier slipped away.

Alone now, Priam thought of Andromache, visions of her bringing a tightness to his chest and a warmth in his belly. It was too long since he had seen her. His gaze was caught again by the Great Tower. He could not see it without thinking of her. He first met her on its heights, when she had refused to kneel to him, as had his own Hekabe so many years before. Andromache! He allowed himself to remember her as he saw her that day, in a yellow gown, her flame hair tied back roughly, her eyes bold, gazing at him in a way no young woman should look at a king. He had tried to frighten her, but even as they stood on the parapet together and she knew he could send her smashing to the stones below with a single push, he saw in her eyes that she was ready to reach out and take him with her on the Dark Road to Hades.

And later, when she had finally surrendered to him, as he had known she would, he had glanced out into the darkness and seen the torches on the Great Tower ablaze. He knew then that his entire life had been destined for that one act. All the battles he had fought, all the sons he had sired – mostly a waste of energy and seed – even the years with his beloved Hekabe had faded into grey futility. His night with Andromache had fulfilled the prophecy. The Shield of Thunder had brought forth the Eagle Child, and Troy would last a thousand years. He was a king complete, yet his loins still ached for her. Not a day went by when he did not regret the promise he had made her. She had agreed to share his bed – but only until she fell pregnant. She had demanded his word that he would honour that agreement. And he had given it. Fool!

Even so, he had been convinced she would return to him. Trapped in a loveless marriage with an impotent husband. Of course she would.

Yet she had not, and it still mystified him.

'Hektor and Andromache await you in the Amber Room, lord,' Polydorus said, emerging from the doorway. 'I have sent a soldier to find Helikaon.'

'He is Prince *Aeneas*,' snapped Priam. 'A noble name, long held in high esteem by my family.'

'Yes, my lord king. I am sorry. I forgot for an instant.'

Priam strolled from his chambers and along the wide corridor, Polydorus following him. The room where his guests waited was on the south side of the palace, away from the cold winter winds. Even so, there was a chill in the air.

Waiting for him were Andromache, Hektor and the young Dardanian king. Leaving Polydorus outside to guard the door Priam stepped inside to greet them. As he did so he could not stop his eyes lingering on Andromache, the curve of her breasts beneath the yellow gown, the bright green of her eyes, the lusciousness of her lips.

Tearing his gaze away he said, 'Aeneas, my boy, I grieve for you. When my own dear Hekabe died it was as if my heart had been pierced by a flaming arrow.'

Priam gazed round the room. There was tension here. Andromache was sitting stiffly, her hands folded on her lap. Hektor was standing behind her, his expression stern, his eyes cold. And Aeneas seemed oddly ill at ease. Did they know what he was about to ask them? The priestess had only arrived late yesterday, but since then might have spoken of the matter to a servant. Instantly he dismissed the thought. The priestess was a tight-lipped old witch, and hardly likely to gossip to palace servants. No, there was something else here. Pushing this minor problem from his mind he focused on the matter at hand.

Looking at Aeneas, he asked: 'Is it still your intention to risk the winter seas and voyage west?'

His kinsman nodded. 'We need the tin,' he said simply. 'With all the sources through Kypros drying up, and the Hittites using all the tin they can get, we must seek it from farther afield. If I leave directly, I can get to the Seven Hills well ahead of Odysseus, who will probably winter on Ithaka as he always has.'

Though perilous, it was a good plan, Priam knew. Without tin there could be no bronze for the smiths to work, without bronze no swords, no spears, no shields, no helms. Without bronze there could be no victory over the Mykene.

'And you will take the *Xanthos*? You will not pass unnoticed in that fire-hurling monstrosity.'

'No, I will not,' agreed Aeneas. 'But with a full complement of eighty she is faster than any galley, and will withstand the stormy seas. Added to which she will carry more tin than any three galleys could. As to monstrosity, well . . . I do not doubt Agamemnon would agree with you.'

Then Hektor spoke. 'If any ship can make it to the Seven Hills in winter, and return safely, it is the *Xanthos*. We must assume Agamemnon will attack again in spring, be it Dardanos, or Thebe Under Plakos, or Troy itself, and we must have the armour for our troops. I agree: Helikaon should leave as soon as possible.'

'As soon as possible, yes,' said Priam, walking to a small carved table and pouring himself a goblet of water. He glanced again at Andromache. She was wearing a necklace of sea horses carved

61

from ivory. Sea horse clasps held back her thick red hair. She sat with her hands in her lap and watched him gravely. If she wondered why she had been asked there she gave no indication.

'There is something else we must discuss,' he told them. 'Yesterday a representative of the High Priestess arrived from Thera. It seems, Andromache, a decision has been made about your young friend, the renegade priestess.'

'Kalliope. Her name was Kalliope.' Andromache's voice was low, but the king could hear the tension in it.

'Yes, Kalliope. As we all know, the punishment for a runaway is to be buried alive on the isle to serve the Sleeping God. This punishment still stands. They require the girl's bones to be returned to Thera in the spring for burial there, where her soul will be chained to serve the Minotaur for all eternity.'

Andromache opened her mouth to speak, but Priam held up his hand. 'Let me finish. Those who aid a runaway must also suffer. Burning is the usual punishment. But the two Mykene soldiers who helped her are now valued members of the Trojan Horse. As patron of the Blessed Isle I have decided that they were unknowing dupes. The High Priestess can make her own representations to Odysseus, who also helped the girl. However, this leaves you, Andromache.'

Hektor's response – as Priam had expected – was swift.

'Andromache was not responsible for Kalliope's actions,' he said, an edge of anger in his voice. 'She had no idea the girl had left Thera until she turned up at my farm. I will not allow anyone to punish my wife for something she did not do.'

'Yes, very well,' said Priam impatiently. 'The High Priestess does not seek to punish her. She asks that Andromache bring the renegade's bones to Thera. Andromache is, after all, the reason the girl fled the isle. I have agreed that Andromache should travel to Thera with the bones of Kalliope to make this act of contrition. Kassandra was due to go to Thera in the spring anyway. Now my two daughters will go together.'

Hektor's anger flared. 'This is insane! Andromache cannot go. This is just a ploy of Agamemnon's. He has tried to have

Andromache killed before. We all know the High Priestess is his blood kin. Now, with her help, he seeks to lure Andromache on to the Great Green. By the spring Agamemnon's fleets will once more control the sea routes. It is a trap.'

Priam stared at his son coldly. 'Of course it could be a trap!' he snapped. 'But I cannot refuse. If I do I risk Troy's being cursed by Thera. Such a curse will strengthen our enemies, and cause our allies to think twice about coming to our aid. But, as ever, we will out-think them. We will not wait for spring. Andromache and Kassandra will sail for Thera on the *Xanthos*. Tomorrow.'

For a moment there was silence. Priam looked at his son, and saw all colour had drained from his face.

'No,' said Hektor. 'This I will not allow.'

The reaction surprised Priam. Hektor was a fine strategist, and a man who understood that risks were necessary in war. Priam switched his gaze to Andromache, expecting her to speak up. She always had an opinion. Instead she sat very quietly, eyes downcast. Then Aeneas spoke.

'It is a clever plan,' he said, 'but I must agree with Hektor. The risks are very great. Sailing to Thera in winter, when the days are short, will mean sailing in darkness in treacherous weather. It will also bring us close to the pirate havens.'

'The risks are high,' agreed Priam. 'But look at what we face. Our enemies outnumber us, our trade routes have been blocked. In the spring the Mykene may come to our shores in their thousands. Then we will need the *Xanthos*, and all the allies we can muster. With the blessing of Thera we can hold those allies steady. You think I want to risk Andromache and Kassandra to the perils of the winter sea? I do not. But I see no other choice.'

'Then I will go too,' said Hektor.

'What?' Priam was stunned. 'Now *that* would be a nonsense and you know it. If word got out that *you* were on the Great Green, in a single ship, every Mykene war fleet would be mobilized. No. I have already promised King Ektion that you and the Trojan Horse will ride south to little Thebe. Enemy armies are ravaging his lands. They need to be crushed, or at the least forced back.' Stepping in, he patted Hektor's shoulder. 'Have faith, my son,' he said. 'Aeneas is a fine sailor and I trust him to master the perils of the sea.'

'It is not the sea . . .' Hektor began. His words tailed away and, with a shake of his head, he walked out on to the balcony.

Thirsty now, Priam called out to Polydorus. The door opened and the young soldier entered. 'Fetch wine!' ordered the king.

'Yes, lord, but you said—'

'Never mind what I said!'

Hektor stood out on the balcony for some time, taking deep draughts of air into his chest. Finally he returned to the Amber Room. Facing Priam, he said, 'As the king orders, so shall it be.'

With that he turned towards Helikaon, who rose from his seat. Hektor gazed upon his old friend, and felt a deep sadness sweep over him. This was the man his wife loved, whose son she had borne. Forcing a smile he said, 'Take care, Helikaon. And bring Andromache safely home.'

Helikaon said nothing, and Hektor understood. No promises could be made, for the Great Green in winter was hazardous enough, without the added perils of pirates and enemy ships.

Stepping forward, Helikaon embraced him. Hektor kissed his cheek then pulled away, turning back to his father. But Priam was not looking in his direction. Instead he was gazing hungrily at Andromache. Without a farewell to his wife or his father Hektor left the room.

He paused outside and leaned against the wall, feeling the cool of the stone against his brow. The turmoil in his mind was like a fever, and his heart was sick.

During the campaign in Thraki, all he could think of was returning home, to Troy, and to the woman he adored. He knew Andromache loved another, and that Astyanax was Helikaon's son. Yet when he was with his wife and the boy he could put those hurtful facts out of his mind. He had never considered what it would be like when Helikaon was in Troy as well, knowing Andromache's heart belonged to the Golden One and not to him, knowing the child who called him Papa was really another man's son.

Hektor had spent all his young life trying not to be like his father, treating other men with honour and respect, and women with gentleness and courtesy. When Andromache told him she was pregnant with Helikaon's child he had accepted it, knowing he could not give her sons himself. But then he had not known her; they had scarcely met. Over the years he had grown to love her deeply, while she still thought of him as a brother, a good friend. He had never shown her how much this had hurt him, until today when she had spoken so blithely of bringing Helikaon's boy Dex to the palace. And now she was to set sail with her lover on a long journey by sea, where they would be together all the time.

Never in his life had he so much wanted to throw himself back into the war, to fight and, yes, to kill. At that moment war, and perhaps death, seemed wonderfully simple. It was life that was so complex.

He looked up. Coming towards him along the corridor he saw his brothers Dios and Paris. They were speaking together in hushed tones. Dios saw him, and his expression brightened. Then Paris saw him too. Despite the sadness in his heart Hektor could not help but smile as he saw Paris was wearing a breastplate and carrying a bronze helm under his arm. No one, he thought, could look more ludicrous in armour. Paris had always been lacking in co-ordination, his movements clumsy. To see him masquerading as a warrior was almost comical. Dios was wearing no armour, merely a white tunic and a leaf-green cloak.

'Well, what did you decide without us, brother?' asked Dios, his smile fading.

'Nothing that need concern you, Dios. We talked only of Helikaon's planned voyage to the west.'

Paris pushed forward and stared up into his brother's eyes, his expression angry. 'You will not send Helen back to Sparta,' he said.

'Why would we?' responded Hektor, surprised.

'You think me an idiot? That is what Agamemnon demanded. That is what caused this stupid war.'

Hektor sighed. 'I do not think you an idiot, Paris. But you are not using your mind now. The demand for Helen was merely an excuse. Agamemnon does not want her, and knew when he made the demand that Father would have to refuse.'

'I know that!' snapped Paris. 'It does not alter the fact that Agamemnon has used the refusal to gather allies. Therefore to accede to his demand would weaken the Mykene alliance. Not so?'

Hektor shook his head. 'Not any more, Paris,' he said. 'Had we agreed at the start, then, yes, perhaps our enemies would not have been so numerous. No longer, brother. A king is already dead, and a queen has been murdered. This war will be to the death. No drawing back. Either Mykene will fall, or the Golden City.'

'They will come here, then?' asked Dios. 'We cannot stop them?'

'They will come, from the north, from the south, from the sea. Agamemnon, Menelaus, Achilles, Odysseus . . .' His voice tailed away. 'And all the lesser kings, bandit chiefs, and mercenary bands seeking plunder.'

'But you will be here to defeat them,' said Dios.

'If the gods will it, Dios, then, yes, I will be here. As will you, my brothers.'

Dios laughed aloud, and clapped Paris on the back. 'You hear that, Paris? You are going to be a hero.' Taking the helm from Paris' hands Dios placed it on his brother's head. It was too large and slid down over his eyes. 'It is as if great Herakles himself has returned from Elysium!'

Paris dragged the helm clear and threw it at Dios, who ducked. The helm struck the wall and clanged to the floor. Paris lunged at Dios, grabbing his tunic. Dios staggered and they both fell. Dios scrambled up, but Paris grabbed his ankle, and tried to drag him back. Hektor smiled and his thoughts went back to the days of childhood. Dios and Paris had always been close. Dios unruly and disobedient, Paris quiet and scholarly, they were an odd pair.

Priam's voice suddenly thundered out. 'What in the name of Hades is going on here?'

The two brothers ceased their wrestling and climbed to their feet. Priam advanced down the corridor, his face flushed, his eyes angry. 'By the balls of Ares, are you morons?' he shouted. 'Sons of Priam do not squabble like children.'

'Sorry, Father,' said Paris. 'It was my fault.'

'You think I care whose fault it was? Get out of my sight, the pair of you!' He pointed to the dented bronze helm. 'Whose is this?'

'Mine, Father,' Paris told him. Priam hooked his foot under the brow of the helm and skilfully flicked it up in the air towards Paris. The young man reached out hesitantly, and the helm struck his fingers. With a cry of pain he leapt back, and the helm once more bounced to the floor.

'I must have been sick with fever the day I sired you,' Priam sneered, turning on his heel and striding back to the Amber Room. As the insult echoed in the air Paris looked crestfallen.

Hektor picked up the fallen helm and handed it to him. 'He has much on his mind, brother,' he said.

'Perhaps,' answered Paris bleakly, 'but what difference does that make? When has he ever missed an opportunity to humble his sons?'

Dios stepped in and curled his arm over his younger brother's shoulder. 'Do not take it so seriously, Paris,' he advised. 'Priam is old, and increasingly frail. With luck we will both live long enough to piss on his funeral pyre.'

Paris grinned. 'That is a happy thought,' he said.

The three brothers walked out of the palace into the mid-morning sunlight. Dios and Paris set off for the lower town, while Hektor made his way back to his own palace. There he found little Astyanax, with his nurse, playing in the gardens. The child, dressed in a small leather breastplate and helm, was bashing a toy sword against a shield held by the nurse. Then the boy saw him and cried out, 'Papa!' Dropping his wooden blade he ran at Hektor, who fell to one knee and caught him, flinging him high in the air, then catching him. Astyanax squealed with delight. Hektor hugged him close.

'Will you be the monster now, Papa?' asked Astyanax.

He gazed into the child's sapphire-blue eyes. 'What does the monster do?'

'He kills people,' Astyanax told him.

Hektor lifted the small helm from the boy's head, and ruffled his red hair. 'Can I not just be Papa for a while, and give you a big hug?'

'No!' cried Astyanax. 'I want to kill the monster.'

Hektor put the boy down, then dropped to his knees. 'You can try,' he growled, baring his teeth in a snarl, and giving a great roar like a lion. Astyanax squealed and ran back several paces to hide behind the nurse. Then, picking up his wooden sword and waving it, the little boy rushed at Hektor.

IV

Blood in the market

PLOUTEUS THE MERCHANT HAD FALLEN IN LOVE WITH TROY DURING his six years in the city. Despite being a foreigner he had been warmly accepted by his neighbours and treated with courtesy by his fellow merchants, and had come to regard the golden city as the home of his heart, if not his blood. He was also considered a lucky man, for his ships always seemed to find a way through the blockades, bringing silks and spices up from Miletos, and even smuggled copper from Kypros.

Life was good for Plouteus, and he gave thanks every day at the temple of Hermes, offering white doves to the winged-heeled god of merchants. Ten times a season he also made sacrifices to Athene, guardian goddess of Troy, and once a year he made a donation of ten gold ingots to the temple of Zeus the All-Father. Plouteus was above all else a man of religion and piety.

He was also known in his homeland as a man of steadfast loyalty – a reputation he had been proud of all his life. Until today.

Plouteus sat quietly with his guest in a secluded corner of his garden, a brazier burning close by. The visitor was younger and slimmer than the portly Plouteus, and where the merchant was ruddy-faced and friendly, the newcomer was hollow of cheek and cold of eye. A chill breeze blew across the garden. Dancing embers whirled up from the brazier. The newcomer swore softly. Plouteus saw his hands brushing at his blue cloak and guessed some hot ash had settled on the garment. Plouteus rubbed at his eyes. Bright sunlight made them water, and caused his head to ache. 'It would be warmer inside,' said his guest.

'Yes, it would,' agreed Plouteus. 'But out here, in the cold, Actonion, no one will hear us.'

'You already know what is required,' said Actonion, tugging at his thin black chin beard. 'We need to speak no more of it.'

'You do not understand the nature of the task you are suggesting,' argued Plouteus.

Actonion raised his hand, wagging his finger. 'I am *suggesting* nothing, Plouteus. I have brought you instructions from your lord. Your king desires the death of an enemy. You and your sons will kill this man of evil.'

'Just like that?' snapped Plouteus, reddening. 'My boys are brave enough, but they are untrained. And I – as you can see – have fully enjoyed the fine foods of Troy. Why is it that we are asked to do this? Why not men of blood like yourself? Why not soldiers or assassins?'

The newcomer's cold eyes hardened still further. 'So,' he said, 'now you seek to question our master's wisdom. You worm! Everything you have here Agamemnon King has given you. You swore to serve him in any way he desired. Now you baulk at the first danger.'

'It is not the first,' said Plouteus, defiance in his voice. 'My sons and I have gathered information, sent reports. We have risked our lives many times. But once we have accomplished this task today – if indeed we can – our usefulness will be at an end. Can you not see that? When our troops come in the spring would it not be valuable to have loyal men *inside* the city?'

'Of course. And we will have,' replied Actonion. 'You think you are the only spies in Troy?' He rose from his seat. 'As I have told you, Helikaon is at the palace, meeting with Priam. When he leaves he will walk back down through the lower town. You and your sons will waylay him, and strike together.'

'He has been kind to us,' observed Plouteus sadly.

'So I am told,' Actonion sneered. 'You have dined at his house, and made trade deals with him. He gave your youngest son a pony, on the day of his manhood. That is why you have been chosen for this task. We have tried sending soldiers. We have tried sending assassins. Always he has eluded death. He is cunning, and crafty, and he has strength and speed. But few men seek to protect themselves from their friends.' He drew his cloak around him and stepped away from the brazier. Glancing back he said, 'Once it is done get down to the beach as fast as you can. Take any wealth you can carry.'

'Will you be on the ship waiting for us?' asked Plouteus.

'No. I shall remain in Troy for a while, but you will not see me again, Plouteus. Well . . . unless you fail. Agamemnon King has little time for those who break faith with him. Now best prepare yourself. You have a friend to kill.'

Tobios the jewel merchant hitched his heavy wool cloak up round his neck, and stamped his feet against the cold. The early morning crowd had thinned now, as people headed off to the eating houses and their midday meals. It had been a good day so far, he thought. The pendant Helikaon had purchased had ensured that, but Tobios had also sold three brooches and an amber bracelet. He was tempted to summon his servants, pack away his stall, and head for home and a warm fire. However, thoughts of the many years he had spent on the borders of ruin and starvation prevented such extravagant behaviour. Chilled to the bone, Tobios remained where he was, huddled against the canvas windbreak behind his stall.

There would be time enough for such idle behaviour, he told himself, when the winter had fully set in. Then he could spend more time in the workshops, supervising the crafting of brooches and bangles, rings and ornaments. Amber had been popular now for several seasons. It would not last. Trojans were fickle when it came to fashion. Five years ago it had been rubies, coral, and cloaks and tunics of crimson. Red had been the colour. Then, for a short while, black had gained the ascendancy. An Egypteian merchant named Cthosis had perfected a dye that allowed black garments to be washed without the colour leaching out. Ebony and obsidian bangles and earrings had been the fashion then among the women of Troy.

Now it was amber. What next, wondered Tobios? Blue was a strong possibility. Lapis lazuli never entirely went out of fashion, and it could be very pricey. The bluer the lapis the more expensive the stone. Many women – and men, for that matter – had been seduced by being told their eyes were the colour of lapis lazuli.

He caught sight of the Mykene merchant Plouteus and his sons entering the square. He waved a greeting but, immersed in a deep, and obviously serious, conversation, they did not see him. Perhaps even the notoriously lucky Plouteus was feeling the pressures of this senseless war. So far his ships had escaped either seizure or sinking. Which was galling. Not that Tobios wanted to see honest sailors killed upon the Great Green, but Plouteus' luck meant his trade goods could be sold more cheaply, which kept prices down, cutting margins and lowering profits. Others of the merchant group were growing envious of the man, but Tobios had no time to waste on such destructive emotions. Plouteus was, it was said, a religious man, paying homage to many gods. In return, perhaps, they were favouring him. Tobios would have dearly liked to bribe the gods of this land, but if he did there was no doubt the Prophet would get to hear of it. If that happened then death would surely follow. Or worse. Some years back it was said the Prophet had cursed a man and given him leprosy. And one of Tobios' servants told a story of a man who annoyed the Prophet and woke up the following morning blind in both eyes.

Better to risk the wrath of anonymous gods, who might or might not exist, than to anger the Prophet, who certainly did.

The Scythe was blowing hard now, hissing round and beneath the windbreak. Tobios retrieved his old woollen cap from the shelf below his stall and tugged it over his dyed red hair.

As he straightened he saw the king's son Paris heading towards him. The boy was wearing armour, and carrying a dented helm.

Tobios cast his gaze round the marketplace, seeking the plump Helen, who usually walked with him. They were a sweet couple and Tobios liked them. Helen was a plain, matronly woman, with mousy hair and a sweet smile. Her husband obviously adored her. Whenever he shopped alone he would buy the most extravagant pieces for her – jewels that only a beautiful woman would dare to wear. The following day she would quietly return and exchange them. Helen's taste was for the simple. She chose brooches for the shape of the stone, or the beauty of the grain, preferring works in silver to those of gold.

Tobios smiled at the young man as he approached the stall. 'A chill morning, lord, to be sure,' he said.

'I envy you your cloak, Tobios,' responded Paris. 'Armour does not keep out the cold.'

'So I have been told, lord. Are you expecting a battle today?'

Paris gave a boyish grin. 'If there were one, Tobios, I would be as much use as feathers on a fish.'

'Skill at fighting is much overrated,' confided Tobios. 'In my long life I have discovered that to be fleet of foot is infinitely superior to having skill with weapons. Though better than both is to be quick-witted.'

'Have you been in many wars?' asked Paris, as he examined a bangle of cunning design.

'Too many, sir.' Tobios shivered as dark memories assailed him. Changing the subject, he said: 'That piece you hold was crafted by my grandson. It is the first competent example of the skills to come.'

Out of the corner of his eye Tobios saw Helikaon moving through the crowds. He frowned. He hoped he had not come to return the pendant he had bought. Returning his attention to Paris, he waited patiently as the young man examined the bracelet more closely. It was fashioned of braided silver wire, wrapped round, and through, seven small fire opals. Young Aaron was becoming a fine craftsman.

'If I may make so bold, lord, the lovely Helen would find this piece especially appealing.'

Before Paris could answer the air was rent with a piercing shout. 'Father! No! It is not him!'

Tobios peered round and saw the portly Plouteus fighting with Helikaon. For a heartbeat it looked comical, a fat, middle-aged merchant in a crimson, ankle-length tunic, grappling next to a pie stall with a slender, white-garbed warrior.

As Tobios looked more closely he saw the warrior was not Helikaon. It was Prince Deiphobos, one of Priam's bastard sons, known as Dios. Tobios wondered why a placid man like Plouteus would risk insulting a king's son – but then a spray of red spattered across Dios' tunic. Sunlight glittered on the bright blade in Plouteus' hand. Dios reached out to grab Plouteus' wrist, but the merchant wrenched his hand loose of the grip and plunged the blade again into Dios' chest. The victim's clothes were blood-drenched now, and rivulets of red streamed down his legs. Yet still he fought on. Plouteus' sons rushed in. Tobios thought they had come to pull their father clear. Instead they too drew knives and began to hack at the injured prince.

'Paris! Paris!' shouted Dios, and Tobios saw him reach out to his brother. Then another blade slammed into his body and he doubled over, blood spewing from his mouth.

Tobios glanced at Paris. The young prince was standing statue-still, frozen in shock and fear. Tobios snatched Paris' sword from its scabbard and ran at the killers, shouting at the top of his voice, 'Murderers! Assassins!'

Plouteus' younger son swung towards Tobios. There were blood splashes across his face, and the skinning knife he held dripped gore. He looked at the jewel merchant, then dropped his blade and ran. The elder son grabbed his father and was pulling him away when the red-headed merchant arrived. Tobios lashed out with the sword blade. It caught the young man high on the temple, slashing the skin, and sending blood spraying. He fell sideways, then staggered several steps.

'Assassins!' shouted Tobios again. 'Hold them!' Another stall-holder ran up behind the injured assailant and hit him with a club. He pitched forward unconscious.

Standing alongside the body of Dios, his face stricken, the merchant Plouteus looked into the eyes of Tobios. He was shaking his head.

'I never wanted this,' he cried. 'I swear by all the gods, Tobios, I had no choice . . .'

'You worm!' shouted an angry man in the crowd. Tobios recognized him as the trader Actonion. Running forward, he plunged his dagger into Plouteus' neck, forcing it deep. Blood spouted from the wound and Plouteus pitched to his face on the stones.

Tobios knelt beside Dios. The prince's eyes were open, but they could see nothing. The stab wounds to his face and neck were no longer bleeding. The man who had killed Plouteus also knelt beside the body. Tobios looked up into the dark eyes of Actonion.

'I would have thought such a famed fighter would be bigger,' Actonion commented, staring down at the corpse.

'Famed fighter?'

'Did someone not say this was the dread Helikaon?'

'They were wrong. This is Deiphobos, son of Priam.'

Pushing himself to his feet, Tobios turned back towards his stall. Paris was still standing there, slack-jawed, his eyes full of tears. 'He's dead, isn't he?' he whispered.

'A man stabbed that many times usually is.'

Paris groaned. 'He called out for me and I didn't go to him. I couldn't move, Tobios.'

'Then go to him now,' said Tobios softly. 'It is not right for the son of a king to lie alone in the dust of a marketplace.'

But Paris seemed rooted to the spot. 'Oh, Tobios, I failed him. My greatest friend and when he needed me I did nothing.'

Tobios held his tongue, and sought to hide his contempt. Paris was spineless, but he was a good customer. Merchants did not stay in business long if they drove such away. Then he saw the young man was staring at him, his expression imploring. Tobios sighed. He knew what the prince needed. What all cowards needed.

'You could have done nothing, lord,' he said, putting as much sincerity into the lie as he could muster. 'The first blows would have been fatal. By rushing in you would have risked being killed yourself, for nothing. You acted wisely.'

Paris shook his head, but said nothing.

A troop of soldiers arrived too late in the marketplace. They lifted the body of Dios, and carried him back towards the Scaean Gate. Tobios looked around for Actonion, but the man had gone.

How odd, he thought. Priam would surely reward the man who had killed the assassin of one of his sons.

Leaving Priam and Helikaon deep in conversation in the Amber Room, Andromache made her way down to the *megaron*, where she spotted Antiphones among the crowd. He was hard to miss, for he was still the largest man in Troy, though much of his weight was now muscle. Where once he had enjoyed bouts of almost Heraklean eating, he was now famed for his ferocious training regimes. Andromache liked him greatly but was in no mood for idle conversation.

'Have you seen Hektor?' she asked him swiftly.

'A few moments ago. He left the palace.' He leaned towards her and whispered, 'You seem troubled, dear one.'

'This has been a difficult day,' she told him.

'There are many difficult days now. Hektor also seemed downcast. Is all well between you?'

Andromache paused before answering, and when she did the words sounded hollow in her ears. 'There is love between us, Antiphones. Ultimately, therefore, all will be well. I have to believe that.'

'He adores you. So I hope you are right,' said Antiphones. Andromache looked into the big man's eyes and knew he wanted to say more, but the conversation was interrupted by the arrival of the king's son and chancellor, Polites. Stooped and balding, Polites seemed to age a year for every season that passed. His face was pale, his eyes dark-ringed, his mouth permanently downturned.

'We need to speak, Antiphones,' he said.

'You forget your manners, brother,' Antiphones admonished

him. Only then did Polites notice Andromache. His tired face reddened with embarrassment.

'I am sorry, sister,' he said. 'Please forgive me.'

'No need to apologize, Polites. You are obviously more in need of Antiphones' company than I. Therefore I will leave you both to talk.'

Andromache left the *megaron* and, trailed by two bodyguards, made her way back towards the palace of Hektor. Once outside her problems returned to haunt her. She understood Hektor's fears. There had been honesty between them from the first, so he knew she loved Helikaon. Now the thought of his wife sailing across the Great Green with his friend must be burrowing into his mind like a maggot in an apple.

Her heart in turmoil, Andromache paused by a well. One of her guards, thinking she was thirsty, drew up a bucket. Andromache thanked him, and sipped a little water from a wooden ladle. Thoughts of Kalliope suddenly filled her mind. Sweet, damaged, brave Kalliope. And she remembered the vile killers, the blazing farm, and Kalliope, standing tall on the hillside shooting arrows down at the assassins. Tears formed as she struggled to hold to that heroic image. But she could not, and cold reality made her see again the black shaft ripping into Kalliope. Now all that remained of her lover were the few bones Andromache had gathered from the ashes of the funeral pyre. They were contained in an ebony and silver chest beneath a window in her bedchamber.

Andromache had dreamed of returning the bones to the Blessed Isle and burying them in the tamarisk grove beside the temple of Artemis. Now the High Priestess planned to hurl Kalliope's bones into the pit, and chain her spirit to serve the Minotaur for ever.

'Are you well, lady?' asked Ethenos, the younger of her guards. 'You are looking very pale.' He was a serious young man, and cousin to the murdered Cheon, who had died along with Kalliope on the day of the assassins.

'I am fine,' she told the fair-haired soldier. It was a lie.

Kalliope had adored the goddess Artemis, had prayed to her many times a day. Had her adoration been repaid in any way?

Raped as a child, betrayed by her family, and then murdered by assassins. Not twenty years old when she died. Now, even after death, she was to be brutalized.

For a moment only Andromache thought of praying to the goddess, but the voice of her anguish screamed out then. *You think Artemis, or any of the gods, cares a whit about your life, or Kalliope's? Think on it! Have any of your prayers ever been answered?*

Suddenly Andromache smiled, but her thoughts were bitter. When she first left Thera she had wanted nothing more than to return to the Blessed Isle, to her simple life with Kalliope. She had prayed for that, and the freedom she had never known before or since. And in her first unhappy days in Troy she had daydreamed about Helikaon taking her away on the *Xanthos*, and had prayed for that also. Now, as if twisting a knife in her gut, the gods had decided she would have both prayers twistedly fulfilled.

Cold anger coursed through her. The demi-god would not have Kalliope – not even if the fate of worlds hung on it. Yes, she would take bones to Thera, but not those of her lover.

The decision made, she dropped the ladle into the bucket and walked on. At the palace she dismissed her guard, nodded to the soldiers at the side gates, then stepped through into the courtyard gardens. She saw Astyanax playing in the dirt, Hektor kneeling beside him.

Her love for Astyanax was like nothing she had ever experienced. It was as if he was tied to her with tender ropes. Each time she left him, even for a day, there was a dull ache in her heart. An entire winter without him would be close to unbearable. Her heart began to pound with increasing panic. She feared for his life. She feared traitors, and spies and poison, and the dagger in the night.

Then the sun moved beyond the clouds, and shone down on her child, and the powerful man beside him. The two were dishevelled and covered with dust, as if they had been rolling on the ground. They were kneeling, facing each other, engrossed in something in the dirt between them. The boy pointed, to an insect or a leaf perhaps, and raised his small face in enquiry to his father. The expression of love and tenderness on Hektor's face made a lump form in Andromache's throat.

The panic passed. He loves Astyanax, she thought, and he will never stop. He will guard the boy with his life.

Quietly, unnoticed, she went into the palace.

V

Men of copper and bronze

ENTERING HER HIGH, AIRY APARTMENTS ANDROMACHE GREETED THE two young handmaids who sat in an outer room embroidering heavy cloth. Both were Women of the Horse, and wore hip belts crafted from bronze discs, threaded with gold wire.

Andromache recalled the first day she had seen such a belt. Heavily pregnant, she had been walking with Hektor along the Street of Goldsmiths. A young woman with braided blond hair was standing by a stall. Her tunic was long and white, and around her hips hung a disc belt. 'I would like one of those,' Andromache had said.

Hektor had stared at her curiously. 'I think you do not know what the belt signifies,' he said softly.

'No, I do not.'

'If ever you get one it will mean I am dead.'

Andromache had learned then of the Women of the Horse, wives and daughters of soldiers killed serving with the Trojan Horse. The belts were crafted from the breastplate discs of the fallen.

Andromache's handmaids were sisters, raven-haired daughters of a warrior named Ursos who had died in the battle for Dardanos. They would work in the palace until suitable husbands were found from among the ranks of the Horse. The elder, Penthesileia, was tall, with deep-set eyes and a strong chin. Her sister Anio, younger and more nervous, was slight of build and pretty.

'Is there anything we can do for you, lady?' asked Penthesileia.

'No. Have you eaten?'

'Yes, lady,' said Anio. 'There is fresh bread in the kitchen. Shall I fetch some?'

Andromache smiled at her. The girl was fifteen years old, and desperately eager to please. 'I need nothing at the moment,' she told her. 'Why don't you and your sister go for a walk? Familiarize yourself with the palace.'

'We are your handmaids,' said stern Penthesileia. 'We must serve you.'

Andromache sighed. 'Yes, you are my handmaids, and you will also be my friends. You are not slaves. You are daughters of a hero. If I need you I will call for you.'

'Yes, lady,' answered Anio. 'You have a guest waiting in your chambers. The Princess Kassandra.' She suddenly looked nervous. 'She is . . .' she dropped her voice, 'talking to herself.'

'She does that,' Andromache told her. 'Do not let it concern you.'

Walking through to her inner rooms Andromache heard Kassandra speaking. 'I did not see it, Dios. I don't see everything.' She sounded distraught. When Andromache entered the room she saw Kassandra sitting staring at a wall. Dressed in her usual black, her wild hair pulled roughly back with combs, she was alone.

Andromache took a deep breath and approached the girl. 'I'm so glad to see you, Kassandra,' she said, sitting beside her on the couch. 'I've missed you these past few months.'

Kassandra's head drooped forward, and she sighed. 'Did you know Vora died?' she asked.

'Who is Vora?'

Kassandra's eyes had a faraway look. 'Vora was a dolphin. She was very old. Cavala, her mate, sings of her. He will spend a year travelling the Great Green singing her song in every place she loved, then he will follow her to the ocean of the South Wind, and they will be together again.'

Andromache smiled. 'Perhaps he will swim to Thera with us.'

'No. He is frightened of Thera. He won't go there. I am frightened of it too. I never expected to be.' Kassandra sighed and leaned forward, her hands on her lap. She looked then just like a child again.

Andromache put her arm round Kassandra's shoulder. 'There is no need for fear. Thera is a place of beauty and serenity. You will like it there.'

'Thera is where the world will end,' whispered Kassandra. 'I will rise into the sky like an eagle, and three kings will die with me . . .' Her voice tailed away.

Andromache kissed her cheek. 'Why not come into the gardens with me? We can shoot our bows. You used to enjoy that. It will lift your spirits.'

Kassandra straightened, and suddenly smiled. 'Of course!' she said. 'We must prepare them. It can begin now. I would like that. It's very important!'

She ran to the far wall and took two bows and two quivers of arrows down from the rack. Then she rushed into the outer room. Andromache followed. Kassandra ran to the sisters.

'Put down that embroidery,' she ordered them, and pushed the bows into their hands. 'You must learn to shoot! The Women of the Horse with shaft and bow!' She swung back to Andromache. 'You see? You see, Andromache?' Her head jerked, and she turned away. 'What? Yes . . .' she said to the wall. Then she nodded, and sighed. Looking into Andromache's eyes she smiled sadly. 'Too soon,' she said. 'But you will remember, Andromache? The Women of the Horse? You will teach them the bow?'

'Be calm, little sister,' said Andromache softly. The girls were standing very still, their eyes watchful. Andromache put her arms round Kassandra's slender shoulders. 'Come, let us take our bows and go to the garden,' she said, retrieving the weapons from the sisters.

'You will remember?' cried Kassandra.

'I will. I promise. I will teach them to shoot.' Turning to the sisters she asked, 'Would you like to learn the bow?'

'I can shoot a little,' Penthesileia said. 'Father taught me. And, yes, I would enjoy taking up a bow again.'

Andromache felt the tension fade from Kassandra. The young princess looked at Penthesileia and smiled. 'You will be a warrior woman of Troy, and great songs will be sung of your bravery.' Pulling away from Andromache, she said: 'We will not need the bows now.'

Andromache returned the weapons to the inner chamber and led Kassandra through the palace and into the gardens where the shadows were lengthening. Hektor saw them and walked over, Astyanax sleeping in his arms. Andromache smiled at her husband, who leaned in and kissed her. 'I am sorry for your hurt today,' she told him.

Hektor nodded. 'It is already forgotten.' She knew it was a lie, but it was well meant.

Kassandra stepped up to him. She took his free hand and kissed it and held it against her cheek. 'I will not see you after tomorrow. You will remember me kindly, won't you? Not as a little mad-woman.' Tears suddenly fell to her cheeks.

Instantly Hektor passed the sleeping boy to Andromache, and took Kassandra into his arms.

'I will miss you,' he said, kissing her brow. 'I love you and I always have. You are my little sister, and I treasure you.'

'I am not mad, Hektor. I do see things.'

'I know.'

In the silence that followed a soldier burst through the courtyard gates and ran across the garden towards them. 'Hektor! Lord Hektor!' He stopped and hesitated as if suddenly aware of the impact of his news.

'Well?' said Hektor, releasing Kassandra, and facing the soldier. 'Speak, Mestares, my friend. No one is going to slice out your tongue.'

'It is Dios, lord . . . he has been killed. Murdered in the lower town.'

For a moment there was silence. Then Andromache realized she could hear the sound of her heart beating. Her friend Dios dead? It seemed impossible.

'It was the Mykene merchant, Plouteus,' explained Mestares.

'He and his sons. They attacked him in the marketplace. Plouteus was killed by someone in the crowd. One of his sons fled. The other was captured. Paris was there. He will know more than I.'

'Paris? Was he hurt?'

'No, lord.'

A female servant came into the garden and hurried up to them. 'Lord Hektor,' she cried. 'The king has sent for you.'

Hektor's face was ashen, and he left the garden without a word of farewell to Andromache or Kassandra. The servant girl approached Andromache. 'Shall I take the boy, lady?' she asked softly.

Andromache nodded and passed the child to her. Astyanax moaned a little then settled his head on the girl's shoulder. As the servant moved away a cool breeze whispered across the garden, rustling the dried leaves on the pathway. Andromache saw Kassandra standing there, her large blue-grey eyes full of tears.

'You knew he was dead, didn't you?' said Andromache. 'You were speaking to his spirit.'

Kassandra nodded. 'The fat merchant had weak eyes. He thought Dios was Helikaon.'

Andromache recalled seeing Dios earlier that day. He had been wearing a white tunic, similar to Helikaon's. Odysseus had once remarked upon the resemblance between the two men. 'They look alike,' he had said, 'but they are very different. They are copper and bronze. Both have value.' His eyes had twinkled mischievously. 'In a whorehouse a man needs copper rings to buy his pleasure. In battle, though, a man needs sharp bronze in his hand. Helikaon is bronze. Dios is copper.'

Kassandra's voice cut through her thoughts. 'Dios will be honoured in death. His bones will lie in the city he loved. That is important, you know.'

'Yes,' said Andromache. 'I am sure that it is.'

Kassandra leaned in close. 'Kalliope wants you to take her home. You can carry her back to the tamarisk grove, where she was most happy. Where she sat with you on that midsummer's night. You remember?'

Andromache could not answer, but she nodded, tears coursing down her face.

'You can speak to her there,' said Kassandra. 'You will feel her in your heart.'

Andromache shook her head. 'No,' she said, 'I cannot take her home. I will not allow her spirit to be chained.'

Pale pre-dawn light shone through high windows as Andromache kissed her sleeping son, and allowed herself a few heartbeats to enjoy the warmth of his cheek against her face. Then she stood and strode from her apartments.

Dressed in an ankle-length tunic of yellow wool, and wrapped in a heavy, grey-green cloak, she made her way through the quiet palace and out into the night. Kassandra was already waiting at the portico, her slight figure also enveloped in a dark cloak. Close by, servants held torches, illuminating a four-seat chariot. Horses shifted nervously and whinnied softly in the flickering light.

Suddenly Hektor appeared out of the gloom. In full armour, and ready for travel, he picked up Kassandra and swung her high like a child before placing her gently in the chariot. She looked flustered and pleased. Then he kissed Andromache and handed her into the vehicle too. She smiled down at him and touched his cheek. They had talked long into the night. Today he would ride south to protect her father's lands, while she sailed enemy seas to Thera.

'May the gods keep you from harm,' he said, 'and bring you back to me.'

The charioteer touched the reins lightly to the horses' backs, and, surrounded by a troop of cavalry, the chariot set off down the stone road towards the bay. The two women held on tightly as the vehicle bumped through the wakening streets. At the Scaean Gate they paused as the great gate was opened, and the noise of the wooden wheels, creaking harness and snorting horses died away.

Sadness settled on Andromache as she thought again of Dios. She regretted missing the ritual farewell tomorrow, but promised herself that wherever the *Xanthos* beached that night she would speak her own words of goodbye to his shade. The chariot lurched forward, and she grabbed the rail as the vehicle thundered towards the beach.

And there, in the distance, she saw the mighty *Xanthos*. Twice the size of any ship on the King's Beach, the *Xanthos* lay half in, half out of the water, listing slightly to one side. Despite her great bulk, the warship had grace and beauty. As the chariot clattered down to the beach, drawing up close to the *Xanthos*, the first rays of the rising sun speared over the horizon, turning the polished oak timbers to gold.

The *Xanthos*, still and serene, was surrounded by people: crewmen shinning up ropes to the top deck, beachmasters and their workers loading cargo, early-rising fishermen and home-going whores lingering to watch the launch. As she climbed down from the chariot Andromache wondered for a moment how they were going to get on board, but as they neared the ship a sturdy wooden ladder was passed down to the sand at the stern. At the top she could see the reassuring figure of Gershom leaning down over the rail. He waved and called out a greeting.

Then curly-haired Oniacus trudged across the sand. 'Can you manage, lady? You can sit in a sling if you prefer.'

'To be hauled up like livestock, Oniacus? My sister and I can manage a ladder.' She softened the sharp words with a smile, remembering the man had only recently lost his family at Dardanos.

'The rest of your belongings are already aboard,' he said. 'They are stored at the rear of the lower deck.'

'And the ebony box?' she asked.

Oniacus nodded. 'Safe, lady, alongside your luggage. Your bow is there also, and two fine quivers. Let us hope you do not find use for them – beyond practice, I mean.'

Andromache saw Kassandra was about to speak, and cut across her. 'Thank you, Oniacus,' she said. 'We also took your advice and brought extra warm clothing. Oiled woollen cloaks and leggings.'

'That is good. The weather may be savage cold and wet.'

Andromache took Kassandra by the arm and led her to the ladder. 'You go up first,' she told her. 'I will follow and steady your foot if you slip.'

Kassandra laughed. 'You think I am some drooling defective who has never climbed a ladder?' Lifting the hem of her dark, ankle-length tunic, she almost ran up, taking Gershom's hand and leaping over the rail. Andromache followed her.

Safely on the aft deck, by the carved steering oar, Andromache glanced round for sight of Helikaon. He was not yet aboard, and she felt a pang of disappointment. The crewmen amidships were hauling aboard cargo – bales of embroidered cloth, sturdy wooden chests, nets full of bread and fruit, and hundreds of small amphorae strung together with twine and padded with straw. Other crewmen then lowered the goods to the hold.

Oniacus vaulted over the deck rail, then opened a hatch in the deck by Andromache's feet. Climbing down to the second oar deck he called out greetings to the men below. The buzz of conversation continued as the oarsmen began to swap stories and catch up on news of their comrades. All of them seemed cheerful at the prospect of getting under way.

Andromache felt it too, the exhilaration running through the golden ship. She glanced at Kassandra. The girl's eyes were bright, her cheeks flushed, and she gazed round her with wonder. Because of her strangeness it was easy to forget that Kassandra was little more than a child – and a child about to embark on a great adventure.

'Let us get you both settled,' said Gershom. 'We are sailing soon.' He stared hard at Kassandra, as if he knew her. 'Come,' he said, then led the two women along the central aisle.

Andromache could see some of the *Xanthos'* battle scars. There were fire-blackened rows of decking that needed renewal, and part of the starboard rail had been roughly repaired with planks. Three carpenters were busy replacing a section of rail on the port side. They were hammering feverishly.

As she reached the tabernacle, the box at the centre of the ship into which the mast sank securely, Andromache saw a circular wooden seat had been built round the thick oak mast. Plaited ropes had been fixed as handholds. There were half-finished carvings round the edges of the seat.

'We are expecting some rough weather,' explained Gershom. 'Even the most experienced of sailors can feel nausea in winter storms. The centre of the ship heaves about least in rough seas. Come here if you feel unwell, or if a storm is looming.'

Andromache nodded and glanced at Kassandra. The girl looked a little frightened now, and her face had turned pale. Gershom continued on towards the foredeck. Glancing down through open hatches, Andromache could see the oarsmen taking their places in the rowing seats on the lower deck. They were laughing and shouting and passing water skins back and forth. They kept their eyes averted, but she knew they were all aware of the two princesses walking above their heads.

On the foredeck a yellow canopy had been set up to make a private space for the women. Gershom explained this was where the pair could sleep and spend their days during the voyage. Andromache was used to such arrangements on her trips to and from Thera, but Kassandra looked aghast.

'It's so small,' she whispered to Andromache.

Andromache was about to point out that the *Xanthos*' foredeck was roomier than any other on the Great Green when silence fell over the ship. She looked back to see Helikaon climbing on to the aft deck. His long dark hair had been tied back in a ponytail, and he was wearing a simple tunic of faded blue. A change came over the crew, a quiet that spoke more of respect than fear, she believed. She sensed the power in him. It called out directly to her blood, and she tore her gaze away, her face reddening.

Eight burly crewmen ran to the foredeck and, splitting into two teams of four, untied two long ropes fastened to a thick support. Andromache was intrigued. 'What are they doing?' she asked Gershom.

'Getting ready to haul up the anchors. The *Xanthos* is a heavy beast, and hard to launch. We drop anchors a little way from our mooring place; then, when the men heave upon the ropes, it helps pull the hull into the water.'

From all over the King's Beach Andromache watched men come running. Crewmen from other ships, fishermen, beachmasters, even foreign traders all worked together, putting their shoulders to the golden hull of the *Xanthos* to push her out into the bay.

For a moment it seemed the ship would not move. Then a voice shouted, 'Again!' There was a pause, the timbers creaked, there was a deep groaning sound, the ship moved forward a pace, then another, then suddenly she slid into the water and they were free and afloat. The men on the foredeck tied off their ropes, leaving the stone anchors sluicing water on specially strengthened sections of planking.

The people on the beach cheered as the eighty oars were run out. Then came the deep voice of Oniacus from below decks, supplying a rhythmic beat for the rowers.

> 'One *was an oarsman,*
> *They say he was a bad man,*
> One *was a slinger,*
> *And certainly a sad man.*

> 'One *was a whoreson,*
> *They say he was a madman,*
> One *was a singer*
> *Who never was a glad man.*'

The *Xanthos* moved smoothly away from the beach. The wind was from the north, from Thraki, and the galley made slow progress for a while as the oarsmen battled the strong headwind to get out of the shallow bay of Troy. The ship moved as if through glue.

'Let's pick it up, you lazy cowsons!' yelled Oniacus. 'Mark of Four!'

> 'One *had a sword trick,*
> One *had a treasure,*
> One *had a big prick,*
> One *had the pleasure.*'

The oars sliced into the churning water and the ship picked up speed, but it was heavy going, the tide and the wind seeking to drive the great vessel back towards Troy. The two women stood hand in hand watching the golden city recede slowly behind them.

'I will never see Troy again,' Kassandra said. Andromache had heard her speak these words before, and she had no argument, so she said nothing but put her arm round her and gently turned her so they faced the way they were travelling.

'We must look forward,' she said, 'not dwell on our sadness.' The image of her son's sleeping face invaded her mind and tore at her heart.

'The ship is very slow,' said Kassandra, staring at the muddy water creeping by below them. She seemed disappointed.

'We will soon be reaching the cape. After that you will see your dolphin bay and King's Joy.'

The Cape of Tides was the farthest point north they had to travel. After that the ship would turn south for the long voyage down the coast. As the *Xanthos* cleared the Bay of Troy the fierce current in the straits snatched at her. The vessel lurched, then picked up speed. The prow began to swing. The skill of the oarsmen came into play, those on the port side, closest to the land, dipping their blades and pulling hard, those on the starboard lifting their oars clear. The *Xanthos* straightened. Gershom shouted an order and six crewmen sprang to haul up the yard. The great sail was unfurled, flapping ferociously against its stays, and as the black horse came into view the men all shouted. The rowers drew in their oars. The strong north wind filled the sail.

And the *Xanthos* leapt forward on its journey south.

VI

The Great Circle

CLOUDS HAD BEGUN TO GATHER AS THE *XANTHOS* SAILED SOUTH DOWN
the coast, heading towards the distant chain of islands known as
the Great Circle. Standing at the prow Gershom stared at the sky,
his mood brittle. Though he did not speak of it he still had nightmares of shipwrecks and drowning, where he clung again to the
driftwood with bleeding fingers as the storm raged around him.
The big man shivered at the memory, and focused on the dark,
lowering clouds.

He had been an oarsman on a cargo ship, overloaded with
copper ingots. It had broken up in what sailors called 'a blow'.
Gershom had been the only survivor. He did not often allow himself to dwell on those dreadful days after the wreck, but he was
feeling ill at ease on this voyage.

The Egypteian glanced back to where the passengers were standing on the rear deck. Andromache was gazing out at the barren
islands, but the dark-haired, moon-touched girl was staring at him
again. He found her gaze unsettling.

Helikaon joined him at the prow. 'We'll find a secluded bay,' he
said, 'and put out scouts.'

'You think we could be attacked this close to Trojan
waters?'

'Probably not, but then I expect Dios felt safe in a Trojan marketplace.'

Gershom fell silent for a moment. The assassination two days ago had shocked them all – especially when, under torture, the killer's son had admitted they were seeking to kill Helikaon. His father's poor eyesight had led him to attack Dios. Gershom looked at his friend, seeing the hurt in his eyes. 'In Egypte,' he said, 'the priests say a man's life is calculated in a celestial sand measure. When the sand runs out his life ends.'

'We do not hold to that belief,' replied Helikaon. 'I wish it had been me in that marketplace.'

'You would prefer to be dead?'

Helikaon shook his head. 'I wouldn't *be* dead. I would never have walked among the crowds unarmed, and I do not believe a fat merchant would have been fast enough to surprise me.'

Gershom smiled then. 'Karpophorus surprised you, my friend. But, yes, you are a tougher man than Dios ever was. Even so, you are not invulnerable. Do not let arrogance blind you to that fact.'

Helikaon took a deep breath, and let it out in a sigh. 'I know what you say is true, Gershom. And I liked that fat merchant, so, perhaps, he would have got close to me. We will never know.'

'Was the son executed?'

'Not yet. The other boy was discovered hiding in a warehouse. They are both to die tomorrow. Priam has decided they will burn alive on Dios' funeral pyre, and serve him on the Dark Road.'

'They deserve no less,' commented Gershom. He flicked a glance to the rear deck and cursed softly. 'Why does she keep staring at me?'

Helikaon laughed. 'She is barely more than a child. Why does she bother you so?'

'I have never been comfortable around the insane. They are so . . . unpredictable. I saw her in Troy, after we docked. She told me my head was full of mist, and that one day I would see clearly. Her words have been going round and round inside my head. What do they mean?'

Helikaon put his hand on Gershom's shoulder and leaned in

close. 'One moment you say she is insane, the next you look for meaning in her words. Is that not itself a sign of madness?'

Gershom grunted. 'And that is why I am uncomfortable around them. I fear their afflictions can be transmitted, like the plague. If I stand too close I will begin howling at the moon.'

'She is not insane, my friend. Cursed would be more accurate. As a babe she was struck down with the brain fire. Most infants die when afflicted with it, but she recovered. From that moment she was fey.'

'Could she be a true seer?'

Helikaon shrugged. 'Kassandra once told me that she and Hektor, and I, would live for ever. Later she said she would die high in the sky, sitting upon a rock, and that three kings would take to the clouds with her. Does either sound like genuine prophecy to you?'

As Helikaon spoke the clouds suddenly cleared and brilliant sunlight sparkled upon the sea. Islands of dull grey and brown rock were instantly transformed into shining silver and red gold. Light from the setting sun shone brightly on the undersides of the rain clouds, turning them to glistening coral. Gershom gazed in awestruck wonder at the glory of the sunset.

'Have you ever seen such beauty?' whispered Helikaon.

Gershom was about to agree when he saw that Helikaon was staring towards the rear of the ship. Gershom turned and saw Andromache, framed in golden light, her yellow dress shimmering, as if formed from molten gold. She was smiling and pointing out to sea. Gershom swung his gaze to starboard and saw a dolphin rise from the water, then dive deep.

'It is Cavala,' he heard Kassandra cry happily. The girl ran to the starboard rail and called out. The dolphin gave a high-pitched squeal, as if answering her, then leapt high into the air, spinning as it rose. Drops of water sprayed from its body, the bright sunlight turning them to diamonds.

It swam alongside for a while, occasionally leaping and diving, but when the *Xanthos* swung towards a protected bay he gave a last cry then disappeared towards the west.

Gershom saw the dark-haired girl was once more looking at him. She looked sad, and he was suddenly sorry for her. He lifted his hand and waved.

She answered him with a smile, then turned away.

The moon was high, the night cold, as Helikaon, wrapped in a heavy cloak of dark wool, climbed to the top of the cliffs overlooking the southern sea. Most of the crew were sleeping on the beach below, huddled together for warmth. Others – much to the annoyance of the cooks – were crouched close round the early breakfast fires burning on the sand.

It would get much colder yet, Helikaon knew. There would be ice and snow in the Seven Hills, and sleet storms along the way. Squatting down away from the wind he stared out to sea, picturing the route along the coast and then through the Great Circle to Thera. With luck they should encounter no war fleets this late in the year, and few pirate captains would have the nerve to attack the *Xanthos*.

No, the dangers would come further west, and on the journey home. He sighed, and corrected himself. Dangers from the sea, anyway. His thoughts darkened as he recalled the merchant Plouteus. A good, honest man, and a shrewd trader. Helikaon would never have considered him a threat, and Gershom was right: the fat merchant *would* have got close enough to make a mortal strike. How many others had been approached, hired, threatened or suborned? Were there men on this ship waiting for the opportunity to kill him?

He thought again of the merchant's son Perdiccas. He had been babbling and begging by the time Helikaon arrived in the cells. One of his eyes had been burned out, and he was bleeding from a score of shallow wounds. The torturers were weary, and disgusted with the lack of information. At first they thought the lad was showing great bravery, but then decided he actually knew nothing and they had been wasting their time and their skills. Helikaon had knelt beside the weeping Perdiccas.

'Do you remember me?' he asked softly.

'I do . . . I am so sorry, lord. So sorry.'

'Why was the attack so hurried? You could have come to my home, or waited for nightfall. Why in broad daylight?'

'Father was told you were sailing south either that day or the next. There was no time for planning.' He burst into tears again. 'Please forgive me, Helikaon.'

'I forgive you. You stood by your father. What else could you do?'

'Will the torture end now?'

'I think that it will.'

'Thank the gods.'

Helikaon had left him then, climbing away from the stench of the dungeons, and out into bright sunlight. Perdiccas would not be thanking the gods when they dragged him out and threw him, bound and gagged, on to the funeral pyre of the man he had murdered.

He thought over what the doomed young man had told him. The Mykene had known he was sailing south. Did this mean there was a traitor on board the *Xanthos*, or within Priam's inner circle? Or could it simply be a sailor bragging to a whore about his coming travels, and the whore passing on the information to a Mykene spy?

If the latter then there was no harm done. No one on the crew knew their destination, only that they were heading south. If, however, there was a traitor within the palace, then the enemy would know he was heading for Thera.

The wind dropped. The eastern sky was growing paler now, the dawn approaching. In that moment Helikaon heard the sound of furtive movement. Stepping swiftly to his left he drew his sword and spun.

A few paces away a shaggy goat rose on its hind legs and leapt for the shelter of the rocks. Helikaon smiled, sheathed his sword, and made his way back along the cliff top. He paused to gaze down on the *Xanthos*, his thoughts a mixture of joy and regret. She was the ship of his dreams, and he still remembered everything about the first day of her maiden voyage, from the clumsy crewmen who dropped an amphora of wine to the sudden wind which blew Khalkeus' hat over the side. What a day that had been! The crew were terrified of sailing the Death Ship – even Zidantas, who always claimed to fear nothing, was ashen when the storm struck.

Zidantas!

Murdered and beheaded by the Mykene. As Dios had been murdered, and Pausanius, and Argurios and Laodike. And little Dio, and his mother Halysia.

The memories were painful, but there was no anger in him as he stood in the pale light of the pre-dawn. It was as if the ghosts of the past were floating around him, offering silent comfort and continued friendship. You are growing maudlin, he warned himself. The dead are gone, and you are alone here.

Even so he felt calmer than he had for a long, long time.

On the beach men were stirring now, heaping wood upon the fires, seeking to banish the cold of the night. Helikaon saw Andromache rise from her blankets. His heartbeat quickened as he remembered the kiss they had shared on the night of battle in the *megaron*. Angrily he tore his gaze from her. Do not think of that night, he warned himself.

Movement out to sea caught his eye. The crews of two small fishing boats were casting weighted nets in the waters beyond the bay. Helikaon watched them for a while. The boats were old, probably built in the days when the grandfathers of the fishermen were young men, full of hopes and dreams.

Wars will come and go, he thought, but there will always be fishermen.

He strolled down the cliff path and leapt to the sand, making his way to a cookfire. A sailor ladled broth into a wooden bowl and passed it to him. Helikaon thanked him, took a hunk of bread, and walked on, further along the beach. Sitting on a rock he ate his breakfast. Kassandra came towards him, her cloak trailing in the sand. 'I am looking for your friend,' she said. 'Where is he?'

After a moment Helikaon realized she meant the goat. 'Perhaps he is hiding.'

'Why would he hide?' she asked, cocking her head to one side.

'I think you frighten him,' he joked.

'Yes, I do,' she answered seriously. 'I can't help that. Can I finish your bread?'

'Of course you can. But there is more bread and good broth at the cookfire.'

'Yours will taste better,' she told him. 'Other people's food always does.'

Removing her cloak she laid it on the sand like a blanket and sat down. As Helikaon watched her eat he was touched by sadness. For all her father's wealth, and her own intelligence and beauty, Kassandra was forever lonely, locked in a world of imagined ghosts and demons. Will they truly care for her on Thera, he wondered? Will she find happiness there?

The dark-haired princess finished the bread in silence, shook the sand from her cloak and swirled it round her shoulders. Stepping in, she kissed Helikaon on the cheek. 'Thank you for the bread,' she said, then spun and ran away down the beach towards the ship.

For three days the *Xanthos* sailed on, untroubled by bad weather or enemy ships. On the fourth day three Kretan galleys gave chase, but with the wind at her back the *Xanthos* raced clear of them. It was some days before the first heavy rain of the voyage arrived. The sea began to surge, the wind picked up and storm clouds gathered overhead. Then, with a clap of thunder, the heavens opened.

Andromache and Kassandra took refuge in the tent prepared for them on the forward deck, but a fierce gust of wind tore through the canvas. With the ship tossing and sliding Andromache hooked her arm through a safety rope and drew Kassandra to her. She heard Helikaon shouting out orders to the oarsmen, his voice firm. Crewmen ran to furl the black horse sail, straining at the ropes. Twisting round, Andromache glanced back, seeking Helikaon. He was standing on the rear deck, gripping the rail, his long dark hair streaming out in the storm wind like a banner.

Lightning flashed overhead, and the rain lashed down.

Kassandra cried out, though not in fear. Andromache saw her eyes were shining with excitement. A huge wave burst over the prow, a wall of water striking the two women. Kassandra was torn free of Andromache's grip. Landing on her back, she struggled to rise. The prow of the *Xanthos* was lifted by another wave. Kassandra fell heavily again, her body spinning down the rainswept deck.

From his position on the circular seat constructed round the mast Gershom saw the girl fall. There was little danger of her being swept overboard but, helpless as she was, he feared she would crack her skull against a rowing bench. A child as frail as Kassandra could easily break her neck in such an accident.

With the ship being tossed like driftwood Gershom knew there was no way to reach her on foot. So, releasing his hold on the safety rope, he flung himself to the deck, and dived towards the girl. Kassandra cannoned into him. Gershom threw his arm round her waist, drawing her to him. The *Xanthos* pitched again, hurling them both against the mast. Gershom managed to twist his body to take the impact on his shoulder. Grunting with pain, he threw out an arm. His hand struck something hard, and his fingers closed round it. It was the base of the seat by the mast. Rolling to his knees, he lifted Kassandra on to it. 'Take hold of a rope,' he ordered her. Kassandra did so, and Gershom hauled himself up alongside her.

The weather worsened, the rain becoming torrential. Gershom could see the rowers straining at their oars, and heard Helikaon shouting more orders to them. Glancing to port the Egyptian saw the outline of a rocky outcrop. Slowly, battling now against the wind, the *Xanthos* moved behind the shelter of the headland.

Protected from the worst of the wind by high cliffs, the *Xanthos* steadied. Helikaon ordered the oars shipped and the anchors lowered. The rowers stood up from their benches, stretching their muscles and walking the deck.

After a while the rain eased, and patches of blue could be seen in the sky. Gershom glanced down at the dark-haired girl snuggled against him. 'You are safe now,' he told her, hoping she would move away.

'I was always safe,' she replied, resting her head on his shoulder.

'Foolish girl! Your neck could have been snapped like a twig.'

She laughed then. 'I am not intended to die on this boat.'

'That's right. Helikaon tells me you are going to live for ever.'

She nodded, and smiled. 'So will you.'

'That is a thought to cherish. I have never liked the idea of dying.'

'Oh, you will die,' she said. 'Everyone dies.'

Gershom felt his irritation rise, and tried to quell it. The girl was, after all, moon-touched. Yet the question had to be asked. 'How can I both live for ever and die?'

'Our *names* will live for ever.' She frowned and cocked her head to one side. 'Yes,' she said. 'For ever is inaccurate. There will come a day when there is no one left to remember. But that is so, so far away it might as well be for ever.'

Gershom asked, 'If I am dead why would I care that my name is known by strangers?'

'I did not say you would care,' she pointed out. 'Do you know where we are?'

'Inside the Great Circle. Helikaon says we will soon reach Thera.'

Kassandra pointed to the headland. 'That is the isle of Delos, the centre of the Circle. It is a holy site. Many believe Apollo and Artemis were born there.'

'But not you?'

She shook her head. 'The sun and the moon did not grow like flowers upon the sea. But Delos is a holy site. There is strong power there. I can feel it.'

'What kind of power?'

'The kind that speaks to the heart,' she told him. 'You have experienced it, Gershom. I know that you have.' She smiled. 'Tonight I shall build a prayer fire, and you will sit with me under starlight. Then you will begin to know.'

Gershom pushed himself to his feet. 'You can build your fire where you like, princess, but I will not be sitting there. I have no wish to see what you see. I just want to live, to draw in breath and to drink sweet wine. I want to take a wife and raise sons and daughters. I do not care about my name living for ever.'

With that he walked away from her, striding towards the rear deck.

It was late in the afternoon before the storm completely cleared. Helikaon glanced at the red-streaked sky. The winter sun was falling rapidly, and soon it would be dark. 'Rowers, to your positions,' he called. The men hurried to their benches, unlashed the oars and ran them out. Oniacus sent teams fore and aft to raise the anchors. Then he climbed to the rear deck and took up his position at the steering oar.

'South,' Helikaon told him.

'At the call of three,' Oniacus sang out to the rowers. 'One – ready! Two – brace! Three – PULL!' Eighty oars sliced into the water, and the *Xanthos* surged away from the small island and out towards the open sea. 'And . . . pull! And . . . pull! And . . . pull!'

Oniacus continued to sound the rhythm for a while. Then, with the oarsmen rowing in perfect unison, he let his voice fade away.

As they cleared the headland Helikaon saw several fishing boats in the distance, but no sign of enemy warships. The wind was favourable and six sailors were standing alongside the mast, ready to raise the yard and unfurl the sail. The men looked to Helikaon, but he shook his head. 'Not yet. Stand easy,' he called. Walking to the port side he stared down at the two banks of oars. They were rising and falling in perfect rhythm. Then he moved to starboard, and studied the movement.

'Oar six, lower starboard,' said Oniacus.

'Yes,' Helikaon replied. 'What's wrong with him?'

'Hatch cover slammed on his finger. Nothing serious. Probably lose the nail.'

Gershom, who had joined them, stared over the side. 'I can see nothing wrong with oar six,' he commented.

'Look harder,' Helikaon told him.

The Egypteian narrowed his eyes. 'I cannot see what you see,' he admitted at last.

'The rhythm is fine, but the oar is not biting as deeply as it should. There is a slight imbalance in our forward motion. If you close your eyes you will feel it.' Helikaon saw Gershom staring at him disbelievingly. 'It is not a jest, my friend.'

Gershom swung to Oniacus. 'You could feel this . . . this imbalance from one oar in eighty? Speak truly now!'

Oniacus nodded. 'The pain in his hand is causing him to jerk slightly as he dips his oar. I told him to rest it today, but he is a proud man.'

Several black-headed gulls appeared overhead, swooping and diving. 'Did you feel that?' said Gershom suddenly.

'What?' asked Oniacus.

'One of the gulls shat on the deck. Wait while I adjust my stance to take in the new weight distribution.'

Oniacus laughed. 'We are not mocking you, Gershom. If you had spent as many years as we have aboard ship you too would feel every small change in the performance of the *Xanthos*. As our supplies dwindle and we ride higher in the water, or if the sail is wet, or the oarsmen are weary.'

Gershom seemed unconvinced, but he shrugged. 'I will take you at your word. So, where are we heading tonight?'

'Perhaps Naxos, perhaps Minoa. I have not yet decided,' said Helikaon.

'A good trading settlement on Kronos Beach,' put in Oniacus.

'And a Kretan garrison,' replied Helikaon.

'True, but local militia. I'll wager they wouldn't object to a little profit. And I am tired of dried meat and thin broth. You will recall there is a fine baker there.'

'Oniacus has convinced me,' said Gershom. 'Where is Kronos Beach?'

'On the island of Naxos,' Helikaon told him.

'The largest island of the Great Circle,' added Oniacus. 'A place of great beauty. It is where I met my wife.'

An uncomfortable silence followed. Then Helikaon spoke. 'Oniacus is right,' he told Gershom. 'It is a beautiful island, but Minoa may be the safer alternative. The king there has not yet declared himself in the war. He is a canny man, and will wait until he is sure which side will be victorious. More important, he has only five war galleys, and will be in no hurry to attack the *Xanthos*.'

Moving away from Gershom Helikaon signalled the men standing by the mast to raise the yard, and unfurl the sail. Once the black horse fluttered into view Oniacus called out the order to ship oars.

The rain began again, lightly spattering the deck. Helikaon stared down towards the prow. The small tent had been repaired and he could see Andromache and Kassandra standing by the rail.

'Has Andromache done something to offend you?' asked Gershom.

'Of course not. Why would you think that?'

'You have hardly spoken to her on the voyage.'

It was true, but he did not wish to discuss it with Gershom. Instead he strolled down the central aisle towards the two women. As he came closer he saw they were watching a dolphin. Andromache looked up as he approached, and he felt the power of her green eyes. But it was Kassandra who spoke. 'Cavala is still with us,' she said, pointing to the dolphin.

'Did you hurt yourself when you fell?' he asked her.

'No. Gershom caught me. He is very strong.' She shivered. 'I wish we had a fire. It is very cold.'

Helikaon saw her lips were blue. Shrugging off his heavy cloak he draped it over her shoulders. She drew it tightly around her.

'Sit in the tent for a while, away from the wind,' he advised.

She smiled up at him. 'Are you worried about me? Or do you want to speak privately to Andromache?'

'I am worried about you, little cousin.'

'Then I will,' she said. 'For you.'

Ducking her head she disappeared into the small tent. Helikaon was suddenly nervous. He met Andromache's gaze. 'I have rarely felt so awkward,' he said.

'Is that why you have avoided me since the voyage began?' Her gaze was cool, and there was suppressed anger in her voice.

'Yes. I do not know how to . . .' His voice tailed away. What could he say? That all his life he had dreamed of finding love, and that she was the embodiment of that dream? That every day since he had met her she had been in his heart? That when he fell asleep at night her face shimmered in his mind, and upon waking his first thoughts were of her?

He sighed. 'I cannot say what is in my heart,' he said at last. 'Not to the wife of a dear friend, and the mother of his son.'

'Yes,' she said, 'the son of the man I love – and love with all my heart.'

The words, spoken with such intensity and passion, tore into him. He stepped back from her. 'I am glad for you,' he managed to say. He saw there were tears in her eyes. Swinging away from her, he returned to the rear deck. Gershom looked at him closely.

'Are you all right? You are ashen.'

Helikaon ignored him and turned to Oniacus. 'Southwest to Minoa,' he ordered.

VII

The truth of prophecy

ALKAIOS THE KING WAS NOT AN AMBITIOUS MAN. THE ISLAND OF Minoa, with its rich fertile soil, supplied enough wealth to keep him and his three wives happy. Regular income from trading cattle and grain enabled him to maintain a small fighting force – five war galleys to patrol the coast, and some five hundred soldiers to defend the land. Neither the galleys nor the small army were strong enough to make the kings of neighbouring islands fear invasion, or so weak that they encouraged those same kings to consider attacking Minoa. At twenty-eight years of age Alkaios was content with his life.

Success, as the king had discovered many years before, lay in harmony and balance. That path had not been easy for Alkaios. As a child he had been passionate and outspoken, much to the chagrin of his father, who had impressed upon him the need to control his emotions. All decisions, his father had maintained, had to be based upon rational thought and careful consideration. He had continually mocked his son for his inability to think clearly. At the age of twenty Alkaios had finally realized his father was right. The understanding that followed freed him, and he went to his sire, thanked him, plunged a dagger into his heart, and became king.

After that no one mocked him and harmony and balance

abounded. On the rare occasions when someone put that harmony under threat Alkaios found the dagger to be a source of instant relief.

Not today, though, he thought irritably. Today there was little balance to be found.

Yesterday he had been preparing to move to his palace on the west coast, away from the harsh northern winds of winter. Two of his wives were pregnant, the third delightfully barren. The trading season had been – despite the war – more profitable than last summer. The gods had, it seemed, smiled upon Alkaios. Then the Mykene galley had returned, and now – his journey southwest delayed – he was forced to play the genial host with two of Agamemnon's creatures, one a snake, one a lion. Both were dangerous.

The pale-eyed Mykene ambassador Kleitos was pointing out how greatly Agamemnon King would appreciate it if next summer's Minoan grain could be used to feed the armies of the west, once the invasion of Troy began.

The voice of Kleitos droned on. Alkaios was barely listening. He had heard it before. Minoan grain was shipped all over the Great Green and the profits were high. Supplying Agamemnon would be – as Kleitos so disingenuously put it – an 'act of faith'. The profits for Alkaios, he maintained, would be handsome, and paid from the sacked treasury of Troy. Alkaios had suppressed a smile at this. As his father had once said, 'You don't pull a lion's teeth until you see the flies on its tongue.' At the thought of lions Alkaios flicked a glance at the second Mykene, the warrior Persion.

Powerfully built, with a black, forked beard, Persion stood silently by, one hand on his sword. Alkaios knew his type. The arrogance in his dark eyes spoke of victories. This was a warrior, a killer, and probably at times an assassin. Persion stood unblinking and statue-still, his presence a mute warning. Those who went against Agamemnon's wishes did not survive very long.

Alkaios leaned back in his chair and called for more wine. A servant crossed the floor of the *megaron* and filled his cup. A cold breeze was blowing through the old building, and Alkaios, getting to his feet, strolled to a burning brazier set near the north wall. Kleitos followed him.

'This war will be won in the summer,' he said. 'The greatest fleet ever seen will bring seventy thousand men to the walls of Troy. The city cannot withstand our might.'

'Interesting,' mused Alkaios. 'Do I not recall a similar comment from you last year?'

'There have been unexpected setbacks,' answered Kleitos, his lips thinning. 'There will be no more, I can assure you.'

Alkaios smiled inwardly. 'Forgive me,' he said mildly, 'but are you assuring me you are *expecting* no further unexpected setbacks? If you had expected them in the first place they would not have been unexpected. That is the very nature of surprise, Kleitos. That it is *always* unexpected. So, essentially, you are maintaining that Prince Hektor and his Trojan Horse, and wily Priam, and deadly Aeneas, have no capacity left to surprise you. Bold assertions, if I may say so.'

Kleitos blinked, then his eyes narrowed. 'I am a soldier. Word games do not interest me. What I am saying, Alkaios King, is that Troy is doomed.'

'I expect you are correct,' responded the king amicably. 'However, only last year I was speaking to King Peleus of Thessaly. He told me how much he was looking forward to destroying the Trojan Horse, and forcing the braggart Hektor to kiss the dirt at his feet. I learned only yesterday that they met at Carpea, but I do not recall hearing of any dirt-kissing.'

He could see Kleitos was growing angry, and knew it would not be long before soft words gave way to hard threats. It annoyed him that he would have to find a way now to placate the creature. To irritate Agamemnon's ambassador was enjoyable, but not wise.

The conversation was interrupted by a pounding on the wide door of the *megaron*. A servant swiftly pulled it open, just long enough to allow a stocky soldier to enter. Alkaios saw it was his captain of cavalry, Malkon. A strong breeze blew through the building. Cinders danced up from the brazier, causing Kleitos to step back. Malkon advanced towards the king. He was a short, wide-shouldered man wearing a breastplate of bronze. Thumping his fist against the armour he bowed his head to Alkaios.

'What is it, Malkon?'

'A large . . . galley, lord, has beached at Thetis Rock.' Alkaios noted the hesitation and looked closely at his captain. 'They are travelling to Thera,' the soldier went on, 'bringing a new priestess to serve the Minotaur. They request permission to spend the night on the beach, and to purchase supplies.'

'I see,' replied the king, his mind racing. Malkon had full power to grant such permission, and would not have interrupted him had this been the only concern. He was a sharp, intelligent man, and therefore the interruption meant the new arrival posed some threat, or a complication beyond the capacity of a captain to resolve. A king of a neighbouring island, perhaps? He dismissed the thought at once. Malkon would have granted permission instantly. No, the captain's decision to refer the matter to him had to be connected with the presence of the Mykene.

Which meant it was a Trojan vessel, or some ally of Priam's. But why the emphasis on its being a *large* galley?

Realization struck home like a lance, though the king's expression did not change. He looked into Malkon's blue eyes. 'A ship bound for Thera,' he said slowly. 'So late in the year. Ah well, the gods demand we must offer them our hospitality. Not so, Kleitos?' he asked suddenly, looking at the Mykene.

'We must always offer respect to the lords of the earth,' answered Kleitos. 'Otherwise they will withdraw from us their favour, or curse our endeavours.'

'Quite so, and admirably put.' Swinging back to the soldier, he said, 'Go and tell the newcomers they are welcome to stay the night.'

Malkon nodded and strode back towards the door. As he reached it Alkaios called out to him. 'Are there any among them known to us?'

Malkon cleared his throat. 'Aeneas of Dardania, my lord. He is taking a daughter of Priam to be a priestess.'

'The Burner is *here*!' roared Kleitos. 'This is insufferable! He must be held by your forces. Agamemnon King will reward you handsomely.'

'I cannot hold him, Kleitos,' said Alkaios. 'The ship is bound for the temple at Thera, and, as you said yourself only moments ago, we must give respect to the gods.' Turning back to Malkon, he called, 'Invite King Aeneas and his passengers to the palace this evening.'

The soldier walked swiftly from the *megaron*. Alkaios turned to Kleitos. 'Do not be so glum, my friend,' he said, laying his arm over the Mykene's shoulder. 'That man of yours, Persion, looks like a fighter.'

'He is. What of it?'

'Did you not say, when introducing him, that he was kin to a great Mykene hero?'

'Yes. His uncle was Alektruon, a hero foully murdered by the man you are inviting to your table.'

'As a king, and a man who worships the gods, I cannot, for profit or malice, interfere with those engaged in serving them. However, Kleitos, the gods value honour and bravery above all other virtues. Not so?'

'Of course. All men know this.'

'Persion has suffered a great loss. Alektruon the Hero was of his blood, and blood cries out for vengeance. The gods would surely understand – even applaud – were he to honour his uncle by challenging to single combat the man who killed him?'

The light of understanding shone in the other man's pale eyes. 'By Ares, yes! My apologies, Alkaios King. I misjudged you. It is a fine plan.'

The moon was bright above the cliffs, its silver light reflecting from the timbers of the *Xanthos*, giving the ship a spectral glow. Fires had been set upon the beach, but the men of the crew were not relaxing round them. Many wore light leather breastplates and short swords. Others had strung their bows. Only the cooks went unarmed as they prepared the night's meal.

Helikaon called the first sentries to him, and the eight men gathered close. Helikaon's voice was low, but there was an under-lying urgency that was not lost on them.

'You must consider this a hostile harbour,' he warned them. 'There are two Mykene vessels in the next bay, and by now they will know we are here. Find yourselves positions high on the cliffs, and stay alert.'

Nearby, dressed in an ankle-length gown of unembroidered green wool, Andromache sat by a fire watching him. What a contradiction you are, she thought. One moment volatile and unpredictable, the next as cool and rational as a grey-bearded veteran. She stared at his profile in the moonlight. As if he felt her gaze he turned suddenly and looked at her, his sapphire eyes emotionless and cold.

Andromache turned away. Rising from beside the fire she brushed sand from her gown and walked to the shoreline. She was angry with herself. When Helikaon had come to the prow, in the golden glow of the sunset, she had wanted to tell him the truth: that she loved him as she would never – could never – love another. Instead, with one careless phrase, she had left him believing Hektor was the man she adored. There was nothing she could do now to draw back those words, nor could she explain them.

Oniacus and Gershom came walking across the sand. Both men waved a greeting to Andromache, then joined Helikaon. The sentries loped off to their positions on the cliffs, and Andromache heard Gershom voice his concerns about the coming feast. 'Why risk this?' he asked. 'You know there could be Mykene there.'

'You think I should find a cave and hide in it?'

'That is not what I meant. You are in a strange mood tonight, Golden One. You carefully pick the best sentries. You set up defensive positions and prepare us for an attack. Then you blithely decide to wander out where your enemies can strike you down.'

'There is no ambush planned, Gershom,' Helikaon told him. 'They have a champion who means to challenge me after the feast.'

'Is this a jest?'

'Not at all. Alkaios had a servant come and warn me.'

'You know this champion?'

109

Helikaon shook his head. 'His name is Persion. He is kin to a man I killed some years back. Alkaios says he has the look of a fighter.'

Gershom swore softly. 'A pox on it! A fighter? You've no choice then.' He glared at Helikaon. 'You should have listened to Oniacus, and travelled to the island that has the talented baker.'

Helikaon shrugged. 'There would have been Mykene there too, my friend.'

'Well . . . kill him quickly and take no chances.'

Helikaon gave a tight smile. 'That is my plan.'

They talked on for a while, but Andromache moved away from them, her stomach tight with fear. Helikaon was going to fight a duel tonight. Her mouth was dry. If he died, a part of her would die with him. Do not even think it, she warned herself. He is Helikaon, the Golden One. He stood with Argurios on the stairs, and fought the best the Mykene could send against him. He defeated them all.

She heard his footsteps on the gritty sand, but did not look at him, instead focusing her gaze on the moonlit waves.

'It is best if Kassandra does not attend the feast,' she heard him say.

'She told me earlier that she would not go,' Andromache told him. 'She is frightened. She says there will be a red demon there. She does not want to see it.'

'A red demon? By the gods, her condition worsens every season,' he said, sadness in his voice.

Now Andromache looked at him, her green eyes radiating her anger. 'Her *condition*? You all think her insane. She is not. She truly *sees*, Helikaon. And, yes, the power of her visions comes close to driving her mad. She is little more than a child, and yet she has already witnessed the day of her death.'

'I do not believe that,' he said. 'I have heard seers make predictions. I have listened to oracles. Sometimes what they predict comes to pass, but then often I could have predicted the same outcome, and I am not a seer. The gods – if they exist – are capricious and wilful, but they are always fascinating. You think they would devise a world entirely lacking in surprise for them, where everything was preordained?'

Andromache shook her head. 'Why do men always leap from one extreme to the other? Just because one event is predestined does not mean that an entire life is mapped out, heartbeat by heartbeat. I have seen the truth of prophecy, Helikaon. On Thera, on the beach at Blue Owl Bay, and in Troy, with Kassandra.'

Helikaon shrugged. 'Then you had better dress yourself for the feast,' he said, 'lest you be late and miss the entrance of the red demon.'

'Dress myself?' she countered, nonplussed.

'The gown you are wearing is . . . functional, but hardly fitting for a royal feast.'

'How foolish of me!' she snapped. 'I must have gone to the wrong chest. I opened mine, the one that holds clothes for a sea journey. I shall return immediately to the *Xanthos* and borrow some royal robes from the crew.'

Helikaon flushed, then smiled. 'I am an idiot,' he said gently. 'Please forgive me. Did you bring no jewellery either?'

She glared at him. 'No.'

He stepped forward, opening the leather pouch at his side. From it he took a heavy pendant of gold and amber, which he passed to her. Upon it was a beautifully carved image of Artemis holding her bow. The amber was warm in her hands. Idly she stroked her fingers across the flawless surface, feeling the grooves of the carving.

Looking into his eyes she asked, 'Why were you carrying it?'

'It caught my eye in a market,' he said, with a shrug that was too casual. She knew then he had bought it for her. 'It would honour me if you would wear it tonight,' he said.

'Then I shall,' she told him, lifting it to her neck. Stepping behind her he fastened it. 'Your hands are remarkably steady for a man who is going to fight tonight. Are you so unconcerned?'

'Yes,' he answered. 'You think me arrogant?'

'Of course you are arrogant, Helikaon. You have much to be arrogant about. However, you do realize that everyone can be beaten? No one is invincible.'

Helikaon grinned. 'And that is the thought you would like me to carry into battle, that I might be maimed? Or killed?'

'No!' exclaimed Andromache. 'Not at all. I didn't want you to go into the fight over-confident, that is all.'

'Little danger of that now,' he said. 'Come, we should go. It is ill-mannered to keep either kings or killers waiting.'

Gershom belted his heavy woollen cloak against the strong breeze from the north and thought fleetingly of fine food and a warm bed. Ten nights of cold fitful sleep on winter beaches had left him nostalgic for the luxurious palaces of Egypt, the splendour of white-walled Memphis, the awesome majesty of Luxor. Places of soft sheets and softer women. But, more than anything else, places of warmth!

He sighed. As Prince Ahmose, those palaces had been his, but as Gershom the outlaw his home was wherever his blanket lay. Now is not the time to meditate on all that is lost, he told himself. There were Mykene on the island, and the *Xanthos* needed to be guarded against attack. Helikaon had sent scouts up into the cliffs to the south, and across the shingle headland to the east. To the west thin woodland grew almost down to the beach. More scouts lay hidden in the perimeter of the wood, overlooking the cliff path to the king's citadel.

Crewmen free of guard duty settled by the cookfires. All the men remained alert, keeping their weapons close by. Yet despite the awareness of peril there was laughter and some singing in the gathering darkness, for these were men used to war and its dangers.

Gershom glanced at the star-filled sky, then sought out Oniacus. 'We will rotate the guards when the moon reaches its height,' he told the crewman. 'No one will get a full night's sleep tonight. See the wine is given out sparingly.'

'Much as I love the *Xanthos* I would sooner be guarding Helikaon,' replied the younger man. 'What if there is treachery there tonight?'

Gershom had similar thoughts, but he did not voice them.

Instead he said, 'Helikaon knows this king and trusts him. You think he would take the wife of Hektor and the daughter of Priam into danger?'

Oniacus' face darkened. 'Kassandra did not go with them,' he said, looking round in sudden alarm. 'She said she would be with you.'

Gershom cursed. The wretched girl was nothing but trouble. He and Oniacus strode among the crew, asking if any had seen the girl. It was surprising how few had noticed her. A dark-haired princess in the midst of young, strong men ought to have drawn their eyes. But it seemed she walked among them like a wraith. One of the cooks, however, recalled seeing her beside a narrow cliff path, which he pointed out. Then Gershom remembered the prayer fire she had spoken of.

'Stay alert, Oniacus,' he said. 'I will find her.' Snatching up his sword, he strode into the night.

As he climbed the path he could see the king's citadel awash with light far to his right. To the left the land was in darkness, but bright moonlight showed a narrow trail up towards a rocky outcrop shrouded in trees. The trail was narrow, perhaps made by animals, but he followed it confidently. The sounds of night, the shrill creak of tree beetles and the croaking of frogs, pressed in on him as he left the sea behind. Small creatures rustled in the undergrowth and close by he heard the bleating of unseen goats. He started to sweat under his wool cloak and paused for a moment. A faint smell of burning herbs drifted past his nostrils, and he turned his head slowly, seeking its source. His eye caught the faintest glow of fire-light reflected on the rock above him.

Climbing carefully in the moonlight he found a deep cave in the cliff side, facing south and protected from the northerly winds. Here a fire had been set against the far wall, and smoke swirled up to the low ceiling.

'Kassandra?' he called, but there was no reply. Ducking his head he moved deeper into the cave. The smell from the fire was acrid, and faintly perfumed. The smoke stung his eyes, and he crouched down, low to the rocky ground, seeking fresher air. 'Kassandra!' he called again. His voice sounded strange to his ears. 'Kass-an-dra!' he said, then chuckled at the weirdness of the sound. He slumped down, resting his head on his arm, and stared into the fire.

It was a poor effort, scarcely more than a small dry bush blazing. Except that the leaves did not seem to be burning. Flames danced around them, bright as captured sunlight, leaving the foliage unmarked. Small though the fire was, it gave off a great deal of heat. Gershom clumsily undid his bronze cloak brooch, then let slip the garment. The effort drained him, causing him to breathe heavily, drawing in more of the sickly sweet smoke. He found himself growing drowsy, yet his eyes remained open, staring into the fire. The sounds of the night drifted away. The blaze seemed to be drawing him in, and his mind swirled with bright colours. And then the fire was gone, and he was dreaming.

He found himself floating in the moonlight above the palace garden in Thebes and laughed. How curious, he thought. I am dreaming, and I *know* I am dreaming. Below him he saw a female servant moving furtively, a newborn babe in her arms, wrapped in a blanket embroidered with gold. The woman was crying as she ran through the night-dark garden and out into the street beyond. Gershom recognized her, though she was far younger than he remembered. The last time he had seen Merysit she was frail and silver-haired, crippled with arthritis. A sweet-natured woman, she had been his nursemaid for seven years. Intrigued, he watched as the weeping woman ran down the shadowed street to a broad river bank, where she crouched low in the bullrushes. She hugged the babe to her, but its head flopped sideways, the eyes open and unseeing. In the bright moonlight Gershom saw the infant was dead. A bearded old man wearing the ragged clothes of a brickmaker moved out of the shadows. Then another woman appeared, dressed in the flowing robes of the desert people. She too had a babe, but this one was alive. Merysit tenderly wrapped the living child in the golden blanket and ran back to the palace.

Gershom followed her up to the royal apartments, where his mother was sleeping. There was blood upon the sheets. The queen opened her eyes. Merysit sat upon the bed, and passed the babe to her. It had begun to cry.

'Hush, little Ahmose, you are safe now,' whispered the queen.

It is just a dream, thought Gershom, fear flowing through him. Just a dream.

The image shifted, and he was soaring like a hawk above a burning desert. A multitude was crossing the sands: hard-faced men with worried eyes, women dressed in bright robes, small children darting among flocks of sheep and goats. And he saw himself, his beard streaked with silver, a gnarled staff in his hands. A young boy ran up to him, crying out a name.

Gershom blinked and the vision faded, becoming once again a fire within a cave. Desperate to be away from the fire he struggled to rise, but then slumped down. The blazing twigs shifted and turned red. He saw shining rivers of blood flowing through a land of darkness and despair. He saw the face of his brother Rameses, grey with grief.

Then the fire grew again, filling his vision. Flames blazed high into the sky, and he heard the roar of a thousand thunders. Darkness blotted out the sun. Gershom watched in horror as the sea rose up to meet roiling black clouds. The fury of the vision caused him to cry out, and cover his face with his hands. Yet still he saw . . .

Finally the fire burned out, and cool, fresh air blew into the cave. Tears streaming from his eyes, he crawled out into the night, and collapsed on the wet earth of the entrance. Kassandra was sitting there, slim and straight, a crown of olive leaves round her head. 'And now you begin to see,' she said softly. It was not a question.

Gershom rolled on to his back and stared up at the stars. His head began to clear. 'You put opiates in the flames.'

'Yes. To help open your eyes.' His head was aching now and he sat up and groaned. 'Drink this,' she said, passing him a water skin. 'It will clear your head.'

Pulling the stopper free he lifted the skin and drank greedily. His mouth felt as dry as the desert he had observed. 'What was it I saw?' he asked her.

She shrugged. 'They are your visions. I do not know what you saw.'

'At the last I saw a mountain explode and destroy the sun.'

'Ah,' she said, 'then I am wrong, for I *do* know that vision. It will not destroy the sun, merely block out its light. It is a true vision, Gershom.'

Gershom drank more water. 'My head is still full of mist,' he said. 'Upon the fire mountain there was a great temple in the shape of a horse.'

'Yes, it is the temple on Thera,' she answered.

Gershom leaned forward. 'Then you must not go there. Nothing living could survive what I saw.'

'I know,' she said, pulling the crown of leaves from her head, and shaking twigs from her long dark hair. 'I will die on Thera. I have known this since I was old enough to know anything.'

He looked at her then, and his heart was full of grief. She looked so fragile and alone, her eyes haunted, her expression sad. Gershom reached out to draw her into a hug, but she moved back from him. 'I am not frightened by death, Gershom. And all my fears will end on the Beautiful Isle.'

'It did not look beautiful to me,' he said.

'It has had many shapes, and many names, through the ages of man. It will have more yet. All of them beautiful.' She sighed. 'But this night is not about my life and death. It is about you, Man of Stone. Your days upon the sea are almost done. You made a vow, and soon you will be required to honour it.'

Gershom's thoughts flew back to the time Helikaon had been close to death. With the surgeons and healers of Troy powerless to save him Gershom had sought out a mysterious holy man, a desert-dweller known as the Prophet. Even now he recalled with absolute clarity the first meeting, and the words spoken there. The white-bearded Prophet had agreed to heal Helikaon, but for a price. And not one to be paid with gold or silver. 'I will one day call for you,' he told Gershom that night, 'and you will come to me, wherever I am. You will then do as I bid for one year.'

'I will become your slave?'

The Prophet's answer was softly spoken, and Gershom remembered the subtle note of contempt in it. 'Is the price too high, Prince Ahmose?'

Gershom had wanted to refuse. Pride had demanded it. He had wanted to shout that, yes, this price was too high. He was a prince of Egypt and no man's slave. Yet he did not speak. He sat quietly, scarcely able to breathe through his tension. Helikaon was his friend, and had saved his life. No matter the cost, he had to repay that debt.

'I agree,' he had said, at last.

Now, in the moonlight, he looked at Kassandra. 'He will call for me soon?'

'Yes. You will not see Troy again, Gershom.'

VIII

The crimson demon

KLEITOS, THE MYKENE AMBASSADOR, SAT QUIETLY NURSING A CUP OF
wine. The atmosphere in Alkaios' *megaron* was subdued, the fifty
or more guests eating and drinking in near-silence. There was
tension in the room and Kleitos watched as people furtively
glanced at Persion and Helikaon, sitting at opposite ends of the
king's table.

For Kleitos tonight was an answer to prayer, a gift from the gods
to a man who obediently served them. His life had been singularly
blessed. Above all he had been born into a land and a people loved
by the gods. The Mykene were the greatest race of the Great Green,
more noble, more heroic than any other. Agamemnon King
epitomized this greatness. He had seen before all others the danger
Troy represented to all the nations. He had recognized in Priam a
despot, determined to subdue all free peoples to his will. While others
had been bribed or seduced by the wily Trojan king, Agamemnon had
not been fooled. Because of his wisdom the vileness of Troy would be
cut away, its walls torn down, its people enslaved.

Tonight, as a foreshadowing of that great day, one of the worst
enemies of the Mykene, a man of true evil, was to be struck down
by the righteous strength of a Mykene warrior. It would be a night
of justice, a night for the gods to rejoice.

The heavily pregnant woman on his left leaned across him, trying to reach a platter of fruit. Her arm brushed his, spilling a little of his wine.

'My apologies, Lord Kleitos,' she said. Kleitos wanted to slap her. Instead he smiled, reached for the platter and placed it before her.

'None are needed, Arianna Queen,' he told her, instantly turning his head away, in the hope the fat sow would understand he had no wish to converse with her. But the woman, like most of her sex, was uncomprehending, and could not take a simple hint. She insisted on talking to him, continuing the conversation they had started earlier.

'But I do not understand, ambassador,' she said. 'You say Priam was planning to plunge the world into war.'

'Yes. To make himself master of the world.'

'Why?'

He stared at her. 'Why? Because . . . he is evil, and a tyrant.'

'I meant what would he gain from sending armies to attack his neighbours? He is already the richest king. Armies are costly. Each area, once subdued, would need to be patrolled and forts built. Endless armies roaming the vassal lands would drain even Troy's great wealth.'

'What would he gain?' he repeated, trying to give himself time to think. 'He would be seen as a conqueror, and a great warrior king. He would have fame and glory.'

'And this would be important to him?'

'Of course it would be important. All true men desire fame and glory.'

'Ah,' she said. 'I am confused again now. Is he a true man then or an evil tyrant? Or somehow both?'

'He is evil, as I have said.'

'So the evil also desire fame and glory. How then do we tell them apart?'

'It is not always easy,' he replied, 'especially for women. One must rely on the wisdom of great kings like Agamemnon.'

'I have heard of his greatness,' said the queen. 'My husband talks of his conquests, of the numbers of cities he has overcome, the slaves and the plunder he has gathered. From Sparta in the south all the way north to Thraki. I am not good with numbers. Is it fourteen kings and princes he has slain, or sixteen?'

'I have not kept count,' Kleitos told her. 'It is true, though, that Agamemnon King is a warrior without peer.'

'A man of fame and glory,' she said.

'Indeed so.'

She leaned in then. 'Ah, yes, I think I have a grasp on it now. Priam fooled us all, disguising his plans for domination with forty years of peace. Such cunning approaches genius, don't you think?'

Arianna smiled sweetly, then turned away to speak to other guests. Kleitos stared malevolently at her. One day, he promised himself, she will pay for such disrespect. Just as her husband would suffer for his sly, mocking tone.

He glanced along the table at Helikaon. The villain seemed relaxed. He was smiling and chatting to some merchant. Kleitos noticed, though, that he hardly touched his wine cup. Alkaios was engaged in conversation with the wife of Hektor. Kleitos was impressed with her. She had not arrived at the feast, as had other women, bedecked in jewellery, but wearing a simple green gown and a single pendant. Such behaviour entirely befitted a woman travelling without her husband. Torchlight shone on her red-gold hair, and Kleitos found himself staring at the curve of her neck, his gaze flowing down to her breasts. Hektor was a lucky man to have found such a wife. Tall, graceful, demure in her dress and her manner, she was a beauty. Kleitos wondered if Agamemnon King would grant him Andromache as a prize when the city fell. Probably not, he decided ruefully. Her son would have to be executed, and women rarely forgave such necessities. No, he realized, she would have to be killed too.

Towards the end of the feast a storyteller was called out, a young man with tightly curled blond hair and the face of a girl. Kleitos disliked him the instant he walked before the assembly. He was obviously the soft-bellied son of a rich man, who never had to fight for what he wanted, or struggle to stay alive in a harsh world.

His voice, though, had range, and his story was well told. The tale itself was exceptional, but then it was devised by Odysseus, and Kleitos had already heard it from the master himself. Now *there* was a man who could tell stories.

The girl-faced bard entertained the crowd with the exploits of the sea king and the sorceress, and told of the battle with the dread one-eyed giant, Cyclops. At the conclusion the bard opened his arms and bowed deeply to Alkaios. Applause thundered out, and the king tossed the man a pouch of copper rings.

In the silence that followed the performance Kleitos flicked a glance at Persion. The warrior nodded, then pushed himself to his feet.

'I have a grievance,' he said, his voice ringing out. 'A blood grievance with a murderer seated at this table.'

Even though Andromache had been waiting for this moment its arrival was still shocking. She looked down the table at the young Mykene warrior. His dark eyes were shining, his expression one of exultation. He looked a man of great determination, powerful and unbeatable. Andromache felt fear begin to swell. Fear cannot be trusted, she warned herself. It exaggerates everything. It is both treacherous and dishonest.

Despite these rational thoughts, when Andromache looked again at Persion she still saw a warrior of almost elemental power. When she turned her gaze to Helikaon he seemed altogether more human, and therefore vulnerable. Closing her eyes she summoned again the image of him fighting on the stairs, invincible and unconquerable. A sense of calm returned to her.

Alkaios called out: 'A feast is a time of comradeship, Persion. Can this matter not wait until the morning?'

'In respect to you, Alkaios King, I have waited until the feast was concluded. However, the gods and Mykene honour demand I seek retribution for the atrocities committed against my family, my land, and my king.'

Alkaios climbed to his feet. 'And whom do you seek retribution against?' he asked.

121

Persion drew himself up and stabbed out a hand, his finger pointing down the table. 'I speak of Helikaon the Vile and Accursed,' he said.

Alkaios turned to Helikaon. 'You are my guest,' he said, 'and should you request it the laws of hospitality demand that I refuse this man's challenge to you.'

'I make no such request,' answered Helikaon, rising to his feet. 'Might I enquire of my challenger which of his family have suffered at my hands?'

'The mighty Alektruon,' shouted Persion, 'overcome by your warriors and beheaded by you – though first you put out his eyes to make him blind in Hades.'

Andromache heard murmurs from the crowd at this, and saw some men staring coldly at Helikaon.

'The *mighty* Alektruon,' Helikaon told the company, 'was, like all Mykene, merely a blood-hungry savage preying on those too weak to resist him. I killed him in single combat, then cut off his head. And yes, I pricked out his dead eyes before throwing the head overboard to be devoured by fishes. Perhaps one day I will regret that action. As it is I regret not cutting out his tongue and ripping off his ears.'

Helikaon fell silent for a moment, then looked around the *megaron*, scanning the crowd. 'You all know the reality of the Mykene honour this wretch speaks of. It lies in the ruins of your cities and towns, the rape and plunder of your women and lands. The arrogance of the Mykene is colossal. My accuser talks of the gods and Mykene honour as if the two are somehow linked. They are not. I believe with all my heart that the gods loathe and despise Agamemnon and his people. If I am mistaken then let me die here, at the hand of this . . . this miserable creature.'

Persion shouted out an oath, drew his sword and stepped away from the table.

'Put up your sword!' demanded Alkaios. 'You invoked the gods, Persion, and now you will wait while all the rituals are observed. This duel will follow Olympian rules. Both fighters will be naked, and armed with stabbing sword and dagger. Let the priest of Ares be summoned, and the women allowed to withdraw.'

Andromache sat very still as the other women rose and left the room. Alkaios looked at her. 'You cannot stay, lady.'

'Nor will I go,' she told him.

Alkaios moved in close to her, his voice barely audible. 'In this I must insist, Andromache. No woman must be present at a blood duel.'

'Helikaon is my friend, King Alkaios, and I will bear witness to these proceedings. Unless of course you wish to order the wife of Hektor dragged from your *megaron*?'

He gave a wan smile. 'Sadly, sweet Andromache, the mention of your husband's name no longer carries the weight it once did. Despite that, I will grant your request. Not through fear, nor thoughts of future gain. Simply because you are the wife of a great man, and one I admire.'

Looking up, he summoned a soldier to him, a short, stocky man with a strong face and bright blue eyes. 'Malkon,' he murmured, 'the lady Andromache wishes to see the duel. Take her to the Whisper Room, and ensure no one disturbs her.'

Andromache rose to her feet, and smoothed the folds of her green gown. There was much she wanted to say to Helikaon, but her mouth was dry, her heart beating fast. His sapphire gaze turned to her, and he smiled. 'I will see you soon, lady,' he told her.

'See you keep that promise,' she told him, then turned and followed the stocky soldier out of the *megaron* and along a corridor.

They came to a set of stone steps leading up, through a narrow doorway, to a rooftop overlooking the town and the sea. The wind was blowing fiercely. Andromache shivered. Malkon crossed the rooftop to a second doorway, and Andromache followed him. The soldier entered the room. Andromache paused in the doorway, suddenly concerned. The room was dark and windowless. In the moonlight she could see the dark shape of Malkon by the far wall. He seemed to be kneeling. Then came another light, thin as a sword blade, from low in the wall, and Andromache saw the soldier had removed a slim section of panelling. He rose and crept quietly back to the door.

'If you stretch out upon the rug, lady,' he said, his voice a whisper, 'you will be able to see the centre of the *megaron*. I will wait outside.'

Andromache glanced into the darkened room, with its sliver of light, and hesitated.

'You wish to change your mind, and return to your ship?'

'No.' Stepping into the room, she crouched down on the floor and edged in close to the sliver of light.

It was coming from torches flickering in the *megaron* below. The field of vision was narrow, and she could just see the edge of the feast table, and the central flagstones of the *megaron*. There were servants moving about, scattering dry sand on the floor. The sound of the grains striking the flagstones seemed loud in the room. One of the servants leaned in to another and whispered, 'I'll wager two copper rings on the Mykene.' The words echoed unnaturally in Andromache's ears. So this was how the Whisper Room gained its name, she thought. Spies would lie here listening to conversation in the *megaron* beneath them.

The servants departed and an elderly priest arrived. His robes were black, and upon his spindly shoulders he wore the twin red sashes that denoted a follower of Ares.

'You have called upon the god of war to witness this duel,' he said. 'Let it be understood then that Ares has no wish to see anything but a fight to the death. There will be no calls for mercy, no surrender, no flight. Only one combatant will walk away. The other will shed his lifeblood upon these stones. Let the duellists step forward.'

The first man Andromache saw was Persion. In the torchlight the pale skin of his torso seemed white as marble against his dark, suntanned arms and legs. As he walked forward he was stretching the muscles of his arms and shoulders, loosening them for combat. Then she saw Helikaon. Persion seemed taller, and wider in the shoulder than Helikaon, and once again Andromache felt her fear grow. Both men were armed with sword and dagger, the bronze glinting like red gold in the torchlight.

'I call upon the gods to bear witness to the justness of my cause,' said Persion. Then he stepped in close and whispered something no one in the hall heard. But the sound carried to Andromache.

'I was there when we killed your brother. I set the flames to his tunic. Oh, how he screamed! As you will scream, Helikaon, when I cut the flesh from your bones.'

Helikaon did not reply, or even seem to hear.

'Let the duel begin!' called out the priest, stepping back from the two fighters.

Instantly Persion leapt to the attack, his sword lancing towards Helikaon's head. The Dardanian danced to his left, avoiding the blow. The crowd gasped. A long red line had appeared across Persion's belly, a shallow cut that began to leak blood. It streamed down over his genitals and thighs. Persion shouted an oath and attacked again, slashing out with his sword. Helikaon blocked the blow. Persion stabbed out with his dagger. This too was parried. Helikaon hurled himself forward, hammering a head-butt into the Mykene's face, smashing his nose. Persion fell back with a cry. Helikaon stepped in, his sword slashing left and right with dazzling speed. Then he withdrew. The cut to the flesh of Persion's belly was now joined by three other long wounds. Once again Persion rushed at Helikaon. This time the Dardanian stepped in to meet him, easily blocking and parrying the Mykene's lunges. Helikaon's dagger flashed out, slicing the skin of Persion's cheek, which flapped down from his face like a torn sail.

Persion screamed in rage and frustration, hurling his knife at his · tormentor. Helikaon swayed to his right and the weapon sailed harmlessly past, clattering against the far wall. Persion charged. Helikaon sidestepped. A crimson spray erupted from Persion's arm, and Andromache saw the limb had been deeply slashed. Blood was spurting now from ruptured vessels.

'Call upon the gods again, wretch,' taunted Helikaon. 'Perhaps they did not hear you.'

Persion advanced again. Blood was pouring from him, and Helikaon too was spattered with gore. The Mykene darted forward. His foot slipped. Helikaon leapt, slashing his sword across Persion's mouth, splitting the skin and smashing the man's front teeth. Persion fell to his knees, spitting blood. Then he struggled to his feet and swung back to face his enemy.

Helikaon showed no mercy to the wounded man. Again and again his sword and dagger cut and sliced the Mykene. One vicious slash ripped away an ear, another tore into his face, cutting away his nose. Not a sound came from the crowd, but Andromache could see the looks of horror on their faces. This was not a fight, not even an execution. It was cold-blooded annihilation. With every fresh and painful cut a cry of pain was torn from the mutilated Mykene. At the last, his body drenched in blood, which had begun to pool at his feet, he dropped his sword, and just stood there, blood streaming from him.

In that moment Helikaon tossed aside his sword, stepped in swiftly and rammed his dagger into Persion's heart. The Mykene sagged against him, and let out a long, broken sigh.

Helikaon pushed the dying man from him. Persion's legs gave way and he tumbled to the floor.

Andromache had seen enough. Rising to her feet, she waited as Malkon replaced the panel of wood. Then the two of them returned to the rooftop. The wind had died down but it was still cold.

The soldier led Andromache down the steps and out to the road leading to the beach. He walked with her in the moonlight until they were within sight of the *Xanthos* and the cookfires of the crew. Then, without a word, he turned back to the palace.

Andromache was met by Oniacus and other crewmen. She told them Helikaon had conquered. None was surprised. Paradoxically, though, they were all relieved.

Desiring no company, she moved away from the campsite to a small section of beach close to a wood. Sitting alone by the water's edge, a thick cloak wrapped around her, she could not push the images of the combat from her mind. Helikaon, in a cold fury, cutting and slashing an increasingly helpless opponent. Andromache saw again the spraying blood. By the end of the duel

Helikaon's naked body had been almost as crimson as that of his opponent.

Towards midnight she saw Helikaon walking along the beach towards her. His hair was still wet from the bath he must have taken to remove the blood.

'You should be beside a fire,' he told her. 'It is bitterly cold here.'

'Yes, it is,' she replied.

'What is wrong?' he asked her, sensing her mood. 'One of our enemies has been defeated, we are provisioned for the journey to Thera, and all is well. You should be happy.'

'I am glad you survived, Helikaon. Truly I am. But I saw Kassandra's red demon tonight, and he filled me with sadness.'

He looked confused. 'There was no demon,' he said. 'What are you talking about?'

Reaching up she pressed her finger against the skin of his neck. As her hand came away there was blood upon it. 'You missed a spot,' she said coldly.

Then he understood, and his voice deepened with anger. 'I am no demon! The Mykene brought this upon himself. He was the one who set fire to my brother.'

'No, he was not,' Andromache told him. 'King Alkaios talked to me of him during the feast. He said Persion had fought many duels in the lands of the west. But he had not been to sea before. How then could he have taken part in the first attack on Dardanos?'

'Then why would he say what he did?'

'You do not need to ask that.'

She was right. Even as he had spoken the words Helikaon had known the answer. Persion had tried to make him angry and unsettle him for the fight. Angry men are mostly reckless, and reckless men do not last long in duels. He sat back and stared at Andromache. 'He was a fool then,' he said, at last.

'Yes, he was,' she agreed, with a sigh.

'You sound as if you regret his death.'

She swung to face him, and he saw that she too was angry. 'Yes, I regret it. But more than that, I regret watching you torment and destroy a brave opponent.'

'He was evil.'

Her hand snaked out, cracking against his face. 'You hypocrite! *You* were the evil one tonight. And the foulness of what you did will be spoken of all across the Great Green. How you tortured a proud man, turning him into a mewling wreck. It will be added to your heroic list of accomplishments: gouging the eyes from Alektruon, setting fire to bound men at Blue Owl Bay, raiding unarmed villages in the west. How dare you speak of the savagery of the Mykene when you are cast from the same bronze? There is no difference between you.'

With that she pushed herself to her feet to move away, but he surged up and grabbed her arm. 'Easy for you, woman, to criticize me! You do not have to walk into ruined towns and see the dead. Nor bury your comrades, or see your loved ones raped and tortured.'

'No, I don't,' she snapped, her green eyes flashing. 'But those Mykene who returned to settlements you destroyed will have seen it. They will have buried loved ones you killed or tortured. I thought you a hero, brave and noble. I thought you intelligent and wise, then I hear you talk of all Mykene as evil. Argurios, who fought and died beside you, was a hero. And he was Mykene. The two men with Kalliope who saved me from assassins, they were Mykene!'

'Three men!' he stormed. 'What of the thousands who swarm like locusts through the lands they conquer? What of the hordes waiting to descend on Troy?'

'What do you want me to tell you, Helikaon? That I hate them? I do not. Hate is the father of all evil. Hate is what creates men like Agamemnon, and men like you, vying with each other to see who can commit the most ghastly atrocity. Now let go of my arm!'

But he did not release her. She dragged back on his grip, then angrily lashed out with her other hand. Instinctively he pulled her closer, his arm circling her waist. This close he could smell the perfume of her hair, and feel the warmth of her body against his. Her forehead cracked against his cheek, and he grabbed her hair, to prevent her butting him again.

And then, before he knew what he was doing, he was kissing her. The taste of wine was on her lips, and his mind swam. For a moment only she struggled, then her body relaxed against him and she responded to the kiss, just as she had on the stairs four years before. He drew her closer, his hands sliding down over her hips, drawing up her dress until he felt the warmth of her skin beneath his fingers.

Then they were lying down, still entwined, her arms round his neck. He felt the hunger in her kisses, matching his own. She was beneath him now, and her legs opened, her thighs sliding over his hips. With a groan of pleasure he entered her.

Their lovemaking was fierce. No words were spoken. In all his life he had never known such intensity of passion, such completeness of being. Nothing existed in all the world, save this woman beneath him. He had no sense of place or time, nor even identity. There was no war, no mission, no life beyond. There was no guilt, only a joy he had experienced only once before, in a delirium dream on the point of death.

Andromache cried out then, the sound feral. Her body arched against his. Then he too groaned and relaxed against her, holding her close.

Only then did he become aware of the lapping of the waves on the shoreline, the whispering of the breeze through the treetops. He looked down into her face, into her green eyes. He was about to speak when she curled her arm round his neck, and drew him into a soft embrace. 'No more words tonight,' she whispered.

IX

Voyage of the Bloodhawk

A HALF-DAY'S SAIL TO THE EAST, IN A PROTECTED BAY ON THE ISLE OF
Naxos, the sailors of the *Bloodhawk* and the crews of four other
galleys sat in a circle round the legendary storyteller Odysseus. His
voice thundered out a tale of gods and men, and a ship caught up
in a great storm which flew high into the sky and anchored on the
silver disc of the moon. The audience cheered wildly as the stocky
king embellished his tale with stories of nymphs and dryads.

Sitting quietly a little distance from the circle, the warrior
Achilles listened intently. He enjoyed the tales of Odysseus,
especially those where mortal men defied the gods and won the
day. But mostly he loved the images they contained, comrades
standing together like brothers, caring for one another, dying for
one another.

'How did you get down from the sky?' yelled a man in the
crowd.

Odysseus laughed. 'We took down the sail, cut it in half, and
strapped the pieces to the oars. Then, using the sail as wings, we
flew down. Tiring work, I can tell you, flapping those oars.'

'The last time you told that tale,' shouted another man, 'you said
you called on Father Zeus, who sent fifty eagles to bring you
down.'

'That was a different tale,' thundered Odysseus, 'and I didn't want to waste a sail. Now if any other cowson interrupts me I'll soak him in oil and swallow him whole.'

Achilles smiled. There was no one like Odysseus. He gazed fondly at the old king. He was dressed in a tunic of faded red, his ornate belt of gold straining round his large belly. His beard was more silver than red now, and his hair was thinning. And yet he radiated a power that was ageless.

They had first met many years ago when Achilles was still a child in his father's palace at Thessaly. He had crept from his bed-chamber and hidden with his sister Kalliope on the wide gallery above Peleus' *megaron* to listen to the tales of his father's guest. He had been thrilled then with the stories of heroes, and both the children had sat wide-eyed.

Thoughts of his sister brought with them a sense of sadness and loss, and he remembered his first real conversation with Odysseus, after the fall of the Thrakian city of Kalliros. The Ugly King had brought a fleet of supply ships up the river, and had then enter-tained the troops. Achilles had invited him to dine with him in the captured palace.

Odysseus had been tired after his performance and the meeting had been stilted. Somewhere during the evening Kalliope had been mentioned. Odysseus' eyes had hardened. 'A fine, brave girl,' he said. 'I liked her enormously.'

'She betrayed the house of Peleus,' Achilles had replied.

For a moment Odysseus said nothing. He swirled the wine in his cup, then drained it. 'Let us talk of other matters, Achilles, for I am not one to insult a man at his own feast.'

The response had surprised the young warrior. 'I was not aware that I said anything that could give birth to an insult. I was merely stating a fact.'

'No, lad, you were *merely* repeating a great lie. I do not believe Kalliope was capable of betrayal, any more than you are. She left Thera because a seer told her a friend would be in grave danger. She made her way through great perils to save that friend. And she died doing so.'

'That is not what I meant,' said Achilles. 'She betrayed my father.'

'And now we really must stop talking about her,' said Odysseus, rising from the table, 'otherwise we will come to blows. And I am too old and fat to trade punches with a young warrior like you. Thank you for the meal.'

Achilles had risen to clasp hands with the older man. 'Let us not part with ill-feeling,' he said. 'As a child I loved your stories. They inspired me. They made me determined to be a hero. All my life I have struggled to live up to that dream.'

Odysseus' expression had softened. 'There is more to life than heroism, Achilles. There is love and friendship, and laughter. It seems to me you know too little of those.'

Achilles had been embarrassed then. 'I know of them,' he said defensively. 'When we were young Kalliope and I were very close. And a man could have no greater friend than my shield-bearer Patroklos. I have known him since we were children.'

'Let us have some wine,' said Odysseus, reseating himself, 'and we'll talk of the woes of the world and how, through the brilliance of our minds, we can set them to rights.'

And they had talked long into the night. As they were draining their fifth flagon of wine, while the pearly light of dawn appeared in the east, Achilles had confessed he had never enjoyed a conversation so much.

Odysseus had laughed. 'We are not rivals, you see, lad,' he had explained. 'I am too old to be competition for you. And, you know, that is why you lack friends. You are Achilles, and you compete for everything. Most young men are in awe of you, or frightened of you. Only Patroklos feels no awe in your presence, for he was brought up with you and knows all your weaknesses as well as your strengths.'

He thought for a moment, then went on. 'I've heard your father speak of your childhood. It was the same then. He talked of your winning all the foot races, the wrestling matches, the spear-throwing, as well as the swordplay. You crushed all those other youngsters, never losing. You can admire a man who constantly defeats you. Rare to like him, though.'

'Hektor is liked,' Achilles had argued.

'Ah, you have me there. When I arrived tonight two soldiers escorted me to your presence. Who were they?'

'I did not notice.'

'Hektor would have done. He would also have told me, if asked, the names of their wives and children.'

'That is clever of him.'

'True, but he doesn't do it because it's clever. He does it because he cares. And that is why his men love him.'

'I hear in your voice that you are fond of him too.'

'Yes, I am. It is a tragedy to be his enemy. But I didn't choose to be.'

'It seems to me that you are a good judge of men, Odysseus.'

'And of women, which – if we are not careful – will bring us back to talking of your sister. So now, since the dawn is rising, I am going to seek my bed.'

'Will you answer one question before you go?'

'It depends on the question.'

'Why do you dislike my father?'

'I will avoid that path, Achilles. No man should seek to come between father and son. You are a fine young man, and you have a good mind. So I will offer you some advice. Trust your instincts, and make judgements on what your heart tells you. The heart will not betray you, Achilles.'

As the months of war ground on Achilles had thought of this advice many times, especially when dealing with his father. As a child he had seen Peleus as a great king, powerful and brave. It was not an image he wanted to lose. Yet time and again he found him-self making excuses for the man, for his pettiness, his cruelty and, worse, his tendency to blame others for his mistakes. Then the jealousy began. Where Peleus had been proud of his son's achievements he now began to berate him for 'stealing his glory'. Every success Achilles achieved in battle was belittled.

In the end, with Thraki taken and Hektor and his surviving men fleeing towards the eastern coasts, Peleus had relieved Achilles of command of the army, and sent him with Odysseus to Naxos to bargain with King Gadelos for supplies of grain and meat.

'You want me to be a merchant?' he had asked his father, unbelieving.

'You will do as I command. Agamemnon needs food for the army. It will flatter Gadelos to have a great hero as part of the delegation.'

'And who will lead the attack on Hektor? He is no ordinary general. His mere presence is worth a hundred men.'

Peleus had reddened. 'I will lead the attack. Peleus, king of Thessaly, will destroy this Trojan.'

Angry then, Achilles had spoken without thinking. 'You have shown precious little appetite for battle so far, Father.'

Peleus had struck him, open-handed. 'Are both my children destined to betray me?' he had shouted.

Shocked by the blow, Achilles had finally voiced the thoughts of his heart. 'I loved Kalliope, and I do not believe she ever betrayed anyone.'

'You dog!' Peleus' hand lashed out again, but this time Achilles had caught his fat wrist.

'Do not ever attempt to strike me again,' he said, his voice cold.

He had seen the fear then in his father's eyes, and the last vestiges of childhood admiration had vanished like mist in the sunshine. Peleus had licked his lips nervously and forced a smile.

'I am sorry, my son. The pressures of war . . . You know I value you above all men. My pride in you is colossal. But allow me a little pride too,' he pleaded. 'I will hunt down Hektor, and bring us a victory. But I need you to go to Naxos. Otherwise men will say that the defeat of Hektor was won by you. Do this for me!'

Saddened and sickened by the wheedling tone, Achilles had stepped back. 'I will do as you bid, Father. It will be good to get away from here for a while, and I enjoy the tales of Odysseus.'

'The man is a fat braggart, worthless and vain. Do not listen too closely to his lies, boy.'

Achilles ignored the comment. 'Remember, Father, that Hektor is a warrior without peer. When you corner him it will be a fight to the death. There can be no withdrawal, no pulling back. The man is a lion. Once you grab his tail only one of you will walk away alive.'

Achilles had left the following day, travelling on the *Bloodhawk*, the sleek war galley manned by Ithakan sailors, veterans who had served Odysseus for many years. Achilles had tried to be friendly with the men but, as always, they were in awe of him, treating him respectfully but keeping their distance.

The days at sea, and the enforced idleness, had at first found him tense and bored, but gradually he had relaxed, and had begun to see why the Great Green held such fascination for sailors. The vast, eternal sea freed the mind from petty thoughts and vain ambitions.

Now, as he sat on the beach at Naxos, listening to Odysseus, he realized he had no great desire to return to Thraki, or even to fight in the war against Troy. A part of him wished merely to be a sailor, an oarsman, travelling the sea.

Odysseus concluded his tale to thunderous applause, and the listeners cried out for more.

'Too old and tired to go on,' Odysseus told them, and strode away to a cookfire.

Achilles saw several soldiers approach him. In the conversation that followed Achilles saw Odysseus turn as still as a statue, and he wondered what was being said. Others of the crew gathered round. Achilles saw Odysseus glance across at him. Obviously some important news was being imparted. Achilles thought of walking across to join the men, but at that moment Odysseus stepped away from them, moving towards him. Achilles rose to greet him.

Odysseus looked shocked. His face was grey and there was sweat upon his face. He looked into Achilles' eyes and sighed. 'There is word of your father's battle with Hektor,' he said.

Achilles could tell from his expression that the news was not good. 'Is he dead?'

'Yes. I am sorry, lad. Hektor destroyed him and his army at a place called Carpea.'

Odysseus fell silent. Achilles looked away, staring out over the night sea.

'I feared this,' he said softly. 'I tried to warn him. But he was hungry for glory. Did he die well?'

Odysseus shrugged. 'I did not hear all the details. But you must get back. King Gadelos is still neutral. Tomorrow we will see if he can spare a galley to take you north.'

'You will not be returning with me?'

Odysseus shook his head. 'There was other news, Achilles. I must return to Ithaka immediately.'

Achilles looked into the ashen face of the old king, and knew then that it was not the death of Peleus that had stunned him. Odysseus seemed to have aged ten years.

'What has happened, my friend?'

'A pirate fleet, with several hundred warriors, has invaded Ithaka. They have taken my Penelope.'

Achilles said nothing for a moment. His warrior's mind focused on the problem.

'You have only forty men,' he said. 'We must request aid from the Kretan galleys, or find willing warriors on the mainland.'

Odysseus shook his head. 'The Kretans have orders to patrol the seas around Naxos. Only a direct order from King Idomeneos could change that. And he is far away, fighting near little Thebe.'

'So you will go against them with but a single ship?'

Odysseus' eyes blazed. 'Penelope is the love of my heart and the light of my life. I will sail at dawn.'

'Then I shall come with you, my friend.'

The older man was touched. Reaching up, he clasped Achilles' shoulder. 'I thank you for that, lad. I truly do. But you are a king now, and your place is at home, not fighting another man's battles.'

'No, Odysseus, you are wrong. I was a man before I was a king, and no true man walks away when a friend needs him. So, no more arguments. I am coming with you.'

Odysseus sighed. 'I cannot say that I am not relieved. Very well then. We sail tomorrow. There is a man I must find who might help us.'

'Is he a warrior with a great army?'

'No,' answered Odysseus. 'He is an old pirate named Sekundos.'

X

The Blessed Isle

AS SHE HAD EVERY EVENING FOR FORTY YEARS THE HIGH PRIESTESS OF
Thera walked out on to the cliff top, in the giant shadow of the
Temple of the Horse, and watched the sun descend into the sea. In
high summer she would view the sunset from directly beneath the
great head, but as winter deepened, and Apollo's Arc became more
shallow, she would observe it from a sheltered bench, facing
southwest.

She smiled as she thought of Apollo's Arc. Not that she did not
believe in the sun god. Far from it. Iphigenia believed in all the
gods, most especially the demi-god beneath the island, whose fury
the temple had been founded to appease and gentle. What made
her smile was the myth that golden Apollo climbed into his fiery
chariot every day and flew it across the sky, pursuing his errant
sister, the virgin Artemis, whose white chariot was the moon. What
nonsense. As if two gods would waste their immortality in so fruitless a pastime.

Pain lanced through Iphigenia's chest and she cried out and
staggered. Her left arm spasmed in an agonizing cramp. She
staggered to the bench and collapsed on to it. Reaching into the
pouch at her waist she took a pinch of the powder there, placing it
on her tongue. The taste was sharp and bitter, but she swallowed

it down and sat quietly, taking deep, calming breaths. After a while the pain faded, though her arm ached for some time.

In the far distance she saw the tiny dot of a ship moving through the necklace of islands surrounding Thera. During winter ships rarely ventured far on the Great Green, fearing the sudden squalls when Poseidon swam. They certainly did not travel to Thera without invitation. Yet now two were here, the Egypteian ship and this newcomer.

The Gypptos had arrived yesterday, but had offered no reason for their visit. The leader, a lean, hard-faced young man named Yeshua, had sent two barrels of dried fruits as a gift offering, and requested permission to remain on the beach for a few days. Iphigenia had granted his wish, presuming they had repairs to make to their vessel. A strange craft it was, with its high curved prow and crescent sail. It seemed flimsy against the solidly crafted galleys of Mykene or Kretos.

The after-effects of pain left Iphigenia feeling cold and nauseous. Wrapping her cloak more tightly round her thin shoulders she leaned back against the bench. Craning her neck, she looked up at the horse. Even now she could vividly recall her feelings when she had first seen the isle and its monstrous temple. She had been barely fourteen, tall and thin and without the curves which caught men's eyes. Her failure to attract suitors had left her shy and ashamed, but when Iphigenia had gazed upon the giant horse she had been filled with a sense of purpose, of destiny.

'Lady!' Her reverie was interrupted by a young priestess with dishevelled yellow hair who ran up to her, breathless. 'It is the *Xanthos*! The *Xanthos*!' The girl was terrified, as well she might be.

Iphigenia looked sternly at her. 'Are you sure, Melissa?'

'Yes, lady. Kolea told me, and she has seen it many times. Kolea is from Lesbos. Her father is an ally of Troy.'

'I know who her father is, foolish girl!'

'I'm sorry, lady. Kolea told me it is Helikaon's ship. No other ship on the Great Green is that big. Should we hide?'

'Hide?' Iphigenia surged to her feet. 'From a murderous

brigand? I am Iphigenia, daughter of Atreus the Battle King, sister to Agamemnon. You think that I will hide?'

Melissa flung herself to her knees, her forehead to the floor. 'Forgive me, lady!'

Pain seared again through Iphigenia's chest. Biting back a cry, she sat back down and took a second pinch of powder. It was too much, she knew, and the colours of the sunset sky began to dance and swirl. But the pain died down.

'Send Kolea down to greet the *Xanthos*,' she told Melissa. 'Tell her to bring any messages to me immediately.'

She looked out to sea again. The *Xanthos* was beating its way across the great harbour, passing the black isle in the centre. The young priestess hitched her skirt to her knees and ran off towards the jumble of stables and living quarters behind the temple.

'Melissa!' the older woman barked. The girl stopped in her tracks and swung round, dust swirling about her bare feet. 'Behave with dignity. A priestess of Thera does not run like a frightened peasant. She does not panic.'

The girl flushed. 'Yes, lady.' She turned and walked quickly towards the stables.

Iphigenia smiled grimly. She knew how they all saw her – tall and forbidding, her iron-grey hair pulled back fiercely, emphasizing her hawk nose and fierce brows. They could not see beneath the wrinkled, sagging skin the remains of the young priestess who had also run like a colt, intoxicated by this life of freedom and unexpected pleasures. They saw only a woman grown old in the service of the Blessed Isle.

She looked up at the horse. 'Well, great stallion, what does this mean? Helikaon the Burner here at Thera. The enemy of my blood and of my house.'

The thought that the *Xanthos* was on a raid flashed into her mind and was as quickly dismissed. Priam the king was patron of the island and, much as she abhorred the man's excesses, she had to admit he performed the duties of a patron with efficiency, delivering both gold and the power of his protection to the Blessed Isle. If the sanctuary of Thera were lost both Trojans and Mykene would rue it. All sides knew that. No, Helikaon must be acting as messenger. She had not expected so early a reply to her embassy. Her heart beat faster. Perhaps she had been successful, and Andromache would be lured back to Thera in the spring.

Her hand to her chest, she relaxed against the bench. Eager though she was to find out why the *Xanthos* had arrived, she no longer had the strength to walk down to the harbour. This was a problem, since men who landed on the Blessed Isle were permitted no further than the wooden receiving hall on the black sandy beach. Therefore she would have to either allow the Burner to walk up to the temple, or use intermediaries to ascertain his purpose. To admit a man into the temple – especially one as vile as the Burner – would be sacrilege, yet to depend on others, with less guile than she, would be to risk misunderstanding the true purpose of his visit.

Conceding that a man might walk the island was not without precedent. Priam had entered the temple forty years before. Iphigenia had been fourteen then, newly arrived on the isle, and she had looked with curiosity on the virile king and his young queen, a woman of dark beauty and darker ambition.

The priestess placed her hand against the horse's massive hoof. 'You were more impressive back then, my friend,' she said, marvelling anew at the skill of the builders. Craftsmen from Troy and Hattusas had built the main block of the temple from limestone, a huge rectangular building with a tower at one end. Then skilled carpenters from Kypros and Athens had shaped oak timbers around it, creating the illusion from a distance of legs, neck and a great head. Egypteian artists had travelled to the Blessed Isle to coat the wooden horse with whitewashed plaster, and then added paints and dyes to give it life. Much of the paint was chipped now, and bare timber showed through, cracked and pock-marked. From the sea, though, the white wooden horse still looked magnificent, a massive sentry standing guard over the island.

Rising again and moving to the edge of the cliff, Iphigenia could see the great galley with its black horse sail beached below. Men were milling about. Soon she would know.

She had been angry when Queen Hekabe had ordered Andromache be sent to Troy. There was a strength and energy in the girl which should never have been wasted on furthering men's ambitions. Andromache herself had been furious. She had stormed into the gathering chamber and confronted Iphigenia.

The priestess smiled fondly at the memory. Green-eyed Andromache feared her, just like all the other women here. But such was the strength of her spirit that she could, and often did, conquer that fear and fight for causes she believed in. Iphigenia had admired Andromache for her stand on that day. Closing her eyes she pictured the angry young priestess. Her lover Kalliope had been standing anxiously close by, her eyes downcast.

Andromache had refused to leave Thera, and Iphigenia had tried to explain how the circumstances were special.

'Special?' stormed Andromache. 'You are selling me for Priam's gold! What is *special* about that? Women have been sold since the gods were young. Always by men, though. It is what we have come to expect from them. But from *you*!'

And *that* had hurt, like a dagger deep in her belly. Iphigenia had fought for decades to keep Thera safe and independent from the powers of kings. Sometimes it required steadfast courage, but often it needed compromise.

Instead of seeking to dominate Andromache, and cow her into submission, Iphigenia had spoken softly, her words full of regret.

'It is not just for Priam's gold, Andromache, but for all that gold represents. Without it there would be no temple on Thera, no princesses to placate the beast below. Yes, it would be wonderful if we could ignore the wishes of powerful men like Priam, and do our duty here unmolested. Such freedom, however, is a dream. You are a priestess of Thera no longer. You will leave tomorrow.'

Andromache had not argued further, which showed that she had grown in wisdom in her two years on the Blessed Isle, and was beginning, at last, to grasp the need for such compromises.

Andromache would probably not show such understanding when she returned to Thera in the spring, Iphigenia knew. She would be furious when she discovered the betrayal. But her fury was as nothing when set against the needs of Thera. The security of the temple was vital; more important than any single life.

At last she heard the snorting of donkeys and the clink of bridles. Iphigenia eased herself up and moved to the cliff edge. Below she could see three figures on donkeys slowly climbing up the winding path from the harbour. The priestess Kolea led the way. She had turned in her seat and was chattering to the others, a dark-haired girl Iphigenia did not know, and . . . Andromache.

The old priestess raised her hand to her heart. Andromache here already? Across the winter seas all the way from Troy!

'No!' she whispered. 'It is too soon. Far too soon.'

Andromache sat upon the little donkey's back as it slowly plodded up the steep, narrow trail. Far below, the *Xanthos* had been half drawn up on the black beach. Men, seeming no larger than insects from this height, scurried around it.

She glanced back at Kassandra. Mostly when visitors were carried up this treacherous path they sat their mounts nervously, aware that the slightest slip of a hoof would send them plummeting to their deaths. Not Kassandra. She seemed in a dream, a faraway look in her eyes.

Back on the beach, when Andromache had ordered Oniacus to fetch the ornate box from its place in the hold, Kassandra had gone with him, returning with an old canvas sack, which she carried on her shoulder.

'What do you have there?' Andromache had asked.

'A gift for a friend,' answered Kassandra, giving a shy smile.

'Could you not have brought it in a . . . more suitable container? The High Priestess is a formidable and angry woman. She will be looking for any action that might be regarded as an insult to her, or to the order.'

'You do not like her,' said Kassandra.

Andromache had laughed, but there was little humour in the sound. 'No one *likes* Iphigenia, little sister. Like her brother Agamemnon, she is cold, hard, and unfeeling.'

'You are just angry because she let your father send you to Troy.'

'She *sold* me for gold.'

Kassandra had carried her sack away and walked towards the two priestesses sent to greet them. Andromache knew one of them, Kolea, the youngest daughter of the king of Lesbos. She had arrived in the same season as Andromache. Kolea, with her long dark hair drawn back from her face in a tight ponytail, was taller and slimmer than Andromache remembered. The priestess smiled a greeting. The other girl was around Kassandra's age, fair-haired and freckled. She seemed frightened.

Helikaon had moved across the sand to stand alongside Andromache. She was very conscious of his warm body, not quite touching hers. Each time they had spoken since that night on Minoa she had trembled a little at the sound of his voice. She feared she was blushing, and lowered her head.

'Hektor and Priam both believe this invitation reeks of treachery,' he said softly, concern deepening his voice. 'They fear you are being lured to Thera on Agamemnon's orders. But there are no other ships here, or close by, only a small Egyptian trader. I do not know the High Priestess, so I cannot judge her motives. But you do.'

Andromache looked into his sapphire eyes, and saw they were clouded with anxiety. 'She dislikes me,' she replied, making herself speak firmly and clearly, 'and will have reasons of her own for wanting me here. But we have discussed this already, at length. It could be a trap. But she is the First Priestess of Thera before she is Mykene. I do not believe she would do her brother's bidding if it would harm the reputation of the Blessed Isle. More likely, she wants to punish me rather than betray me.'

'Through Kalliope, you mean?' he said, indicating the ornate box she carried. She nodded. 'When will you return, my love?' he asked quietly.

'In the morning.'

'I will watch for you at first light.'

'I will be here.'

'If you are not, I will come for you with my men. Make sure the old witch understands that.'

'She is a daughter of Atreus, and a Mykene princess. She would understand that without being told. Do nothing rash!'

He leaned in close, touching her hair, and lightly tapped the box she carried. 'Rash actions may be necessary if the witch discovers you are lying to her.'

Andromache's mouth was dry. 'What are you saying?'

'I know you, Andromache,' he whispered. 'You would never surrender the soul of your friend to serve a monster. It is not in you. Where did you find those bones?'

'Xander brought them for me. They are the skull and thigh bone of a murderer.'

Helikaon had grinned then. 'Well, he and the Minotaur should suit each other.'

Iphigenia sat alone in the coolness of the temple's great gathering room. The carved, high-backed chair was uncomfortable, but the High Priestess no longer had the strength to stand for long.

When the two visitors finally arrived they stepped out of bright sunlight into the temple, and stood blinking as their eyes adjusted to the gloom. Andromache, her hair shining red in the light from the doorway, was dressed in green and carried only an ebony box. Kassandra's dark hair was also unbound. Her face was pale and gaunt and her eyes were feverish as she squinted round in the near darkness. On the floor she dropped an old canvas sack.

Kolea stepped forward. 'My lady, these are—'

'I know who they are,' Iphigenia said forbiddingly. 'You may go now.' The girl bobbed her head and fled back to the sunlight.

Pushing herself to her feet Iphigenia stepped towards Andromache. 'I am glad your sense of duty has not deserted you,' she said. Then she paused, for Andromache was staring at her intently, her expression one of sadness. For a moment this confused the old priestess, then realization dawned.

'Do I look so shocking?' she asked coldly.

'I am sorry to find you unwell,' Andromache told her. The sincerity in her words touched Iphigenia.

'I have been ill, but let us not dwell on the matter. Your arrival is a surprise. We expected you in the spring.'

'A ritual to appease the Minotaur should not be so long delayed,' responded Andromache, and Iphigenia saw her expression change. Gone was the concern for her health, replaced by a look of defiance Iphigenia remembered well.

'You brought Kalliope's remains?'

'I have.' Andromache put the ornate box on the ground and was about to open it when Kassandra stepped forward, and laid her sack down at Iphigenia's feet.

'*These* are Kalliope's bones.' Kassandra bent down to the sack and drew forth a dull grey cloth. Unwrapping it she revealed a shining white thigh bone and a skull.

Iphigenia looked from one woman to the other.

Andromache was ashen. 'How could you do this, Kassandra?' she whispered.

'Because Kalliope asked me to. She wanted to come home, to the Beautiful Isle where she was happy. She wants to be laid in the earth of the tamarisk grove, close to the shrine to Artemis.'

'You don't realize what you have done.' Andromache stepped forward, fists clenched. For a moment Iphigenia thought she would strike the girl. Instead she reached out and took the bones from Kassandra's hands, clutching them to her. She glared defiantly at Iphigenia. 'You will not have her. Not her bones, not her spirit.'

Iphigenia ignored her and called to Kassandra. 'Come here, child, and let me look at you.' Kassandra stepped forward and Iphigenia took her hands. She spoke softly. 'The tamarisk grove, you say?'

'Yes.'

'And you knew I had no intention of chaining her spirit?'

'I knew. This was not about bones, but about luring Andromache to Thera.'

'Yes, it was. And I have both succeeded and failed,' said Iphigenia, reaching up and stroking a dark lock of hair back from Kassandra's brow. 'So much has been spoken about you, child, and I see now that most of it was nonsense. You may be moon-touched, but Artemis has gifted you with the sight. So tell Andromache why I wanted her here.'

Kassandra turned to her sister. 'She wanted to save you from Agamemnon, not deliver you to him. But she thought you would arrive here in the spring when the sailing season starts again, just before the siege begins. Then there would be no way for you to return, and you would be forced to remain here.'

'For what purpose?' demanded Andromache. 'Do you care so much for me, lady?' she asked sarcastically.

Iphigenia released Kassandra's hands. 'The Blessed Isle only remains free because its leaders have always been strong, fearless and unafraid of the world of men. I am dying, Andromache. You can see that. Thera will need a new leader soon. I had hoped it would be you.'

Andromache fell silent, and stood staring into Iphigenia's face. Finally she spoke gently. 'But I am married now, and I have a son.'

'And neither of them will survive the onslaught on Troy,' Iphigenia replied gravely. 'You will die too, or face slavery, if you remain there.'

Anger rose again in Andromache's eyes. 'That may be the Mykene view,' she replied, 'but it is not mine. First there is Hektor and his Trojan Horse. Then there are our allies of courage, like Helikaon and my father Ektion. But even aside from the men of war, there must be some among the enemy who will draw back, even now, from the folly of pride and envy that is Agamemnon.'

Iphigenia's shoulders sagged and she returned to her chair with relief. 'Pride?' she asked quietly. 'You think it is pride that drives Agamemnon? It is not, and that is why this war cannot be brought to a peaceful conclusion.'

Kassandra sat down at Iphigenia's feet, resting her dark head on the old woman's thigh.

'Why then?' asked Andromache. 'And do not tell me about poor Helen and the great love Menelaus has apparently developed for her.'

Iphigenia gave a cold smile. 'No, Helen has no real part to play here – though if Priam *had* returned her then Agamemnon's armies would not have been so mighty. But that is of no matter now.' She looked into Andromache's green eyes. 'Do you know what my father had painted upon his shield?'

Andromache frowned. 'It was a snake, I am told.'

'A snake eating its own tail,' said Iphigenia. 'Atreus had a dry sense of humour. His generals were constantly urging him to attack and conquer other lands. My father fought many battles, but only against those who were threatening us. An army is like a great snake. It must be fed and motivated. The more lands a king controls, the greater his army needs to be. The greater the army, the greater the amount of gold needed to maintain it. You see? As the conqueror strides into each captured city his treasury grows, but so must his army, in order to hold this conquered land. Atreus understood this, hence the snake. For when an army is not fed, or paid, or motivated, it will turn upon itself. Therefore the conqueror is forced to take his wars further and further from his homeland.'

Iphigenia lifted a hand, and called out. Instantly a priestess emerged from behind a column and ran forward. 'Water,' Iphigenia demanded. The priestess ran the length of the hall, returning swiftly with a pitcher and a silver cup. Iphigenia took the cup from her and drank deeply, then returned her attention to Andromache. 'Agamemnon no longer has a choice. He must build an empire – or fall to a usurper from within his own army.'

'But there are gold mines in Mykene land,' argued Andromache. 'Everyone knows Agamemnon is rich, even without conquest.'

'Yes, three mines,' said Iphigenia. 'Only one of them now produces enough colour to maintain even the miners. The largest, and once the richest, collapsed upon itself two seasons ago.'

Andromache was shocked. 'You are saying Agamemnon has no gold?'

'He has *plundered* gold, but not enough. He has *borrowed* gold, but not enough. He has *promised* gold, and far too much. His only hope is for Troy to be defeated, and the wealth of the city to fall into his hands. And it will, Andromache. The armies he brings will be as many as the stars in the sky. With them will be Achilles – like Hektor, unbeaten in battle. And wily Odysseus, fox-cunning, and deadly in war. Old Sharptooth will also be there. Greedy he may be, but Idomeneos is a battle king to be feared. Troy cannot withstand them all.'

'All that you say may be true,' said Andromache. 'But you know I would not – could not – desert my son.'

'Of course I know,' Iphigenia told her sadly. 'In the spring you would have had no choice, and by summer's end nothing to return to. But now I cannot save you. I am tired now, Andromache. But you are young and strong. So take Kalliope's bones to the tamarisk grove, and pour wine in remembrance of her. I liked her, you know. She suffered much before she came here.'

She held out her arm to Kassandra. 'Support me, child, and help me to my bedchamber. I fear the strength is almost gone from these old bones.'

Kassandra put her arm around her. 'One day we will have no bones,' the girl said happily, 'and our dust will swirl among the stars.'

XI

The call of destiny

HELIKAON SLEPT FITFULLY THAT NIGHT, CONCERN FOR ANDROMACHE disturbing his rest and colouring his dreams. He found himself in darkness, as if at the bottom of a deep well, and he could see Andromache high above him, framed by light, her hair wild around her head, her hands reaching out to him. Then she was in his arms and he could feel the curves of her body, and smell salt in her hair, but she was cold as stone and he realized she was soaking wet, her face pale and lifeless. He cried out but his voice was thin, like a distant gull, and he could not help her.

He awoke with a groan and threw back his blankets. The fire had burned low, and it was cold on the beach. All about him were sleeping men, huddled close together for extra warmth. Helikaon glanced up at the great horse on the cliff above. It was a clear night, the stars bright round a crescent moon, and the face of the horse shone balefully in the moonlight.

He shivered and stood, rubbing warmth into his bare arms. He would not sleep again. He would watch for Andromache and be ready to climb the cliff path to find her. He had told himself he would wait until the first light of dawn but he was impatient to see her again, and anxious for her safety.

He looked around. To his left, down by the shoreline, he saw a powerful figure standing staring out to sea. Gershom had seemed withdrawn these last days, spending much time on his own. Anxious for conversation to divert his thoughts from Andromache, Helikaon picked his way carefully between the sleeping men and walked across the black sand of the beach. Gershom heard his approach and turned to meet him.

'You were wrong about her, Golden One,' he said. 'She has the sight.'

Helikaon raised his eyebrows and smiled. 'She read your palm?'

'No. She opened my mind.' Gershom shook his head and gave a harsh laugh. 'Nothing I say could convince you.'

'You are probably right. But you are troubled and we are friends. So speak anyway.'

'In a cave on Minoa I learned who I am.'

'What was to learn? You are a runaway Gyppto prince.'

'No, Helikaon, I am a changeling. The child my mother bore was stillborn. A servant carried the babe's body down to the river bank. There she was met by two desert people . . . slaves. They gave her a baby to replace the dead boy. They gave her . . . me.'

'Kassandra told you this?'

'No, she showed me. She made a fire and burned opiates upon it. When I breathed the smoke it filled my mind with visions.'

'How can you know they were true?'

'Believe me, Golden One, I know. I saw so much.' He sighed heavily. 'Destruction and despair. I saw Troy and I saw you . . .'

'Do not speak of Troy, my friend,' said Helikaon quickly. 'I know in my heart what will befall the city. I need no prophecies, whether true or false.'

'Then I will offer none. But I understand now why you have sent so many of your people across the sea to the Seven Hills. A new land, and a new nation, far from the wars and the treacheries of the old empires.'

'It is just a settlement, Gershom, and the people there are from many nations and races. They bicker constantly. Only luck and the blessings of the gods have stopped them ripping each other to pieces. The settlement will probably not survive more than a few seasons.'

'No, Helikaon, you are wrong. The hardships they face will bind the people together. They will endure, I promise. You will see.' Gershom smiled. 'Well,' he went on, '*you* may not see, I do not know that, but your sons will, and their descendants.'

Helikaon looked at his friend. 'You are beginning to make me uncomfortable. Have you become a seer now?'

'Yes, I have, and I know I must travel to the desert, and then return to Egypt.'

'The pharaoh will kill you if you go back!' said Helikaon. Concern for his friend welled up to vanquish his own anxieties. 'I think Kassandra has poisoned your mind.'

'No, do not think that. She is a sweet, sad, broken child. But her visions are true. I believe what I saw was also true. We will know before the dawn.'

'What will we know?'

Gershom pointed to the Egypteian ship drawn up further along the beach. 'If what I saw was real then I will be summoned to sail upon that vessel tomorrow.'

Helikaon suddenly shivered, the cold night seeping into his bones like freezing water.

'Let us stop this now!' he cried. 'You are talking madness, Gershom. Tomorrow we will all sail for the Seven Hills and you can put all thoughts of Kassandra and visions from your mind.'

Gershom looked into Helikaon's eyes. 'What is it that frightens you about prophecy, my friend?' he asked softly.

'I am not frightened by it. I just do not believe it. I too have consumed opiates and seen the whirling colours. I have seen people's faces suddenly blossom like flowers, and heard dogs yapping in strange tongues I could almost understand. I saw a man once who dropped down to the floor and turned into a score of frogs. Do you think he really turned into frogs? Or did the opiates confuse my mind?'

'They confused your mind,' agreed Gershom. 'As indeed they might have confused mine. I will not argue that. If no one comes for me from that ship, Golden One, then I will board the *Xanthos* and rejoice.'

'Good,' said Helikaon, clapping his friend on the shoulder. 'And after dawn, when we sail, I will mock you for this conversation. Now let us get back to a fire. This sea breeze is chilling my blood.'

Despite his lightness of tone Helikaon felt tense and anxious as they walked back to the campfires. He stared at the Egypteian ship. No one was moving around it, the crew all asleep on the beach. Gershom added dry sticks to the glowing coals of a fading fire. Flames sprang up. He stretched himself out on the sand and fell asleep almost instantly.

Helikaon swirled a thick blanket round his shoulders and seated himself close to the small blaze. Clouds started forming in the eastern sky, and the sky grew darker as the moon was obscured. Before long a light rain started to fall. Helikaon sat alone, heavy of heart.

Like Zidantas before him, the big Egypteian had excavated a deep place in Helikaon's heart, and the Dardanian king found himself grieving for the loss of his friend, suddenly sure that the desert folk would come for him in the morning. Since the *Xanthos* had rescued him from the sea, Gershom had become an invaluable crewman on the galley, and Helikaon's right-hand man and friend, one to whom he entrusted not only his life, but his feelings, fears and hopes. He had saved Helikaon on several occasions, not only in battle but also when he brought the Prophet with healing maggots to cure him after the assassination bid.

Remembering that time, when he lay helpless in Hektor's palace and Andromache had nursed him, brought back thoughts of his lover, and he turned and looked up again at the cliff path, in hope of seeing her walking down. But it was too dark and wet to see well, and he shrugged his blanket closer round him, and waited patiently for first light.

It was nearly dawn, and campfires were glittering like stars upon the beach far below, guiding the way as Andromache trod down the cliff path. The ground was uneven, the trail in places narrow and broken. Lowering clouds had covered the moon and the journey back to the ship was growing perilous. It began to rain, lightly at first, but soon the path became slick and treacherous. The wind picked up, tugging at her green dress and the borrowed cloak she wore.

Now the rain came pelting down, sharp and cold, stinging the skin of her face and hands. She moved on even more slowly, one hand tracing along the crumbly cliff wall. Her sandalled feet slipped and slid on the wet ground. Anxious though she was to return to Helikaon and the *Xanthos*, she was finally forced to stop. Crouching against the cliff side, she drew her cloak around her.

Alone on the path, she found herself thinking back over the events of the previous day. She had dreaded seeing Iphigenia again, remembering her dislike of the cold, hard-faced Mykene woman. Now she saw her differently. Was it just that she was dying? Did that knowledge allow her to see the old woman with clearer eyes? Or was it merely pity that changed her perception of the priestess?

Most of the women sent to Thera had no wish to serve the demigod, and many of them wept at being removed from the world they knew, a world of dreams, of hopes of love and family. Perhaps Iphigenia had been such a woman once. Andromache saw again the moment Kassandra had knelt beside the priestess and rested her head on Iphigenia's lap. Iphigenia had reached out and stroked the girl's hair. Andromache had looked into her face then, and thought she saw regret there. Did Iphigenia, with that one caress, think on an empty life, robbed of the chance to have her own children?

The rain began to die down, and Andromache was preparing to resume her descent when she saw a movement above her. It was Kassandra, strolling down the very edge of the path. Andromache's breath caught in her throat. Kassandra spotted her and waved.

'It is a beautiful night,' she cried. 'So exciting!'

Andromache reached out and drew the girl to her. 'What are you doing here? It is dangerous.'

'I needed to see you before you left. Did you speak with Kalliope?'

Andromache sighed. She had buried the bones beneath a tree, and wept at memories of their love. 'Yes,' she said, her voice breaking, 'I told her I missed her, and that I would remember her always. Do you think she heard me?'

'I don't know. I wasn't there,' replied Kassandra brightly. 'I tried to speak to Xidoros, but he is not here. Do you think it is because men are not allowed on the isle?'

Andromache hugged the girl and kissed her. 'Are you going to be happy here?' she asked. Kassandra squirmed away.

'You need to tell Helikaon something,' she said urgently. 'He must go to the pirate islands. Odysseus will be there. And Achilles.'

'We are not here to fight battles, Kassandra.'

'But Ithaka has been invaded and Penelope is held prisoner. She has been beaten and tormented. Odysseus will go there and die if Helikaon does not help him.'

The wind faltered and a cold silence fell on the cliff side. Andromache could almost hear her own heart beating. Odysseus was Helikaon's oldest friend, but he was now an enemy. If he and Achilles were to die it would weaken the Mykene forces, perhaps fatally, and maybe save Troy. The silence grew, and she saw Kassandra watching her. Guilt touched her.

'I need to think on this,' she said, unable to meet her sister's pale gaze.

'What is there to think on?' asked the girl. 'Penelope is a wonderful woman, and she is carrying the son of Odysseus.'

'It is not just about Penelope. There are other factors. The survival of Troy, for one.'

'Other factors,' said Kassandra softly. 'How strange people are.'

Andromache flushed. 'There is nothing strange about desiring to protect those we love.'

'That is my point. Helikaon loves Odysseus, and Penelope. You know that if you tell him he will rush to their aid. Just as he risked his life to come for you, when the Mykene attacked Troy. He is a hero, and he will always desire to protect those he loves.'

Andromache bit back an angry response. Taking a deep breath she said, 'Tell me that the deaths of Odysseus and Achilles will not save Troy.'

Kassandra shook her head. 'No, I will not tell you that. All I know is that Odysseus is rushing to his doom. Which is what the pirates want. Their leader has a blood feud with Odysseus. There are almost two hundred warriors on Ithaka now. Odysseus has thirty men.'

'The Ugly King is no fool,' said Andromache, 'and only a fool would attack two hundred with thirty.'

Kassandra shook her head. 'He loves Penelope more than he loves life. They have cut off her hair, Andromache, and every night the pirate chief has her dragged from a dungeon, dressed in rags, and chained to her throne. The whores of the pirates throw food at her, and screech insults.' She paused. 'The decision is yours to make. I must go now.' Turning, she started swiftly up the mountain path.

Andromache cursed and ran after her, slipping on the wet ground. 'Kassandra, we cannot part like this. Will I see you again?'

Kassandra smiled. 'We will meet again before the end.' She lightly touched her sister's cheek, then walked away.

Andromache watched her go, then turned and continued down the path. As she came closer to the beach she saw a group of men in flowing robes talking with Helikaon. Most of the crew were gathered around. Almost unnoticed, Andromache moved through the crowd. As she came closer she saw that one of the men in robes was Gershom.

'What is happening here?' she asked, stepping forward to stand alongside Helikaon.

'Gershom is leaving us,' he said. He smiled at the sight of her, but quickly the smile faded and there was suppressed anger in his voice. 'He is sailing today with these people of the desert.' Andromache looked at the four cold-eyed bearded men with Gershom.

'Why would you want to leave us?' she asked him.

'I do not want to. I gave a promise some years ago. Now I have been asked to honour it. I have many faults, Andromache, but I keep my promises.'

Turning to Helikaon he offered his hand. For a moment Andromache thought Helikaon would refuse it. Then the

155

Dardanian king shook his head, and stepped in and embraced him.

'I will miss you, my friend,' he said, drawing back. 'My men and I all have reason to be grateful to you.'

There were murmurs of agreement from the crew gathered around, and Oniacus clapped Gershom on the back. Gershom grinned and nodded.

'We hope to hear tales of great adventures,' said Helikaon, forcing a smile.

'More likely you will hear of my untimely death,' replied Gershom. 'But word is unlikely to reach you for I will be travelling under a new name, one chosen for me.'

He turned to the gathered crew. 'My friends,' he said, 'you plucked me from the sea and befriended me. I will hold you all in my heart, as I hold Zidantas, and others no longer with us. May the Source of All Creation protect you, and keep you from harm.'

Finally he looked at Helikaon and Andromache. 'May you both find great happiness,' he said.

Without another word he walked away. In his long robes, with the men of the desert following behind him, Andromache thought he looked like the prince he was, stern and full of authority. She wondered what would become of him, but she knew she would never find out.

They watched in silence as Gershom climbed on to the Egypteian ship, and then Andromache looked into the face of her lover and saw the sorrow there. Placing her hand on his arm, she leaned close to him. 'I am sorry to see you so sad.'

'He is my friend, one of the best I have ever had, and my heart tells me we will not meet again.'

'You have other friends who love you.'

'Yes,' he agreed. 'I value them all.'

'Is Odysseus one of them still?'

He smiled. 'Odysseus first and foremost. He is the greatest man I have ever met.'

Andromache sighed. 'Then there is something we must speak of.'

XII

The beggar and the bow

IN THE DRAUGHTY *MEGARON* ON WIND-TOSSED ITHAKA THE PIRATES were enjoying their nightly revels. Many stood out in the courtyard, seeking the warmth where Odysseus' sheep roasted on spits, but most of them were in the hall, laughing, quarrelling, eating and drinking. A few had already slumped asleep on the cold stone floor. Occasionally a skirmish would break out, but no one had died yet this night, Penelope thought regretfully. And the numbers who were killed each day in these sudden knife-fights were more than made up for by newcomers. More than a hundred of these scum of the seas had arrived in the last few days, drawn across the winter seas by tales of the hospitality on Ithaka. Added to their number were some Siculi tribesmen from the Fire Isle in the west, harsh, savage men, with tattooed faces and weapons of curved bronze.

The queen sat chained to the carved wooden throne and tried, as she did each night, to distance herself from events around her. Though exhausted, she raised her shaven head high and held her gaze on the opposite wall where the huge painted shield of Odysseus' father hung unregarded. She tried to force her thoughts away from the pain of her broken fingers, the throbbing in her bound wrists, and the incessant itching of the lice-ridden rags she had been forced to wear.

She concentrated her attention on the happy days when she and Odysseus were both young, and called to mind the face of her son Laertes. In the first years after he died she could only see him as he had been in the immobility of death, but now she found she could remember the precise hue of his eyes, feel the soft down of his cheek against her lips, and recall the exact expression on his face when his father came into the room. No day passed when she did not remember the boy, but thoughts of him now were calming and sweet, rescuing her, for a few precious moments, from this endless torment.

As always, her mind kept betraying her, raising fruitless hopes that Odysseus would come striding through the *megaron* doors, swinging his sword and carving a path to her, releasing her from her bonds and taking her into the safety of his huge arms. The idea was like one of his stories told in this very hall at night when the fire was banked high and she was surrounded by those she loved. But then cold intelligence would flow across such dreams. Odysseus was older now, almost fifty. The days of great strength and inexhaustible stamina were behind him. His joints ached in the winter, and after a day of labour he would sink down into a comfortable chair with the heavy, grateful sigh of the ancient.

Time, that thief, was slowly stealing the vitality from the man she loved, and she knew that if he came his ageing body would betray him against these vile young men, glorying in the power of their youth.

Then despair would strike, and she would plead: *Don't come, Ugly One! For once in your life do something sensible and stay away. Wait until the spring and bring an army to avenge me. Please don't come to me now.*

But he would come. She knew this with certainty. For all that he was wily, brilliant, and cunning, Odysseus would be blinded to reason by his love for her.

Her thoughts turned bleakly to suicide. If he knew she were dead, Odysseus would still come, but with a clearer mind bent only on vengeance. He would wait until he had raised a fleet and could kill every pirate on Ithaka ten times over. If she could get hold of a knife, or a sharp stick, she could pierce her breast in an instant. Even as the thought came she felt the babe move within her, and her eyes misted with tears. *I could kill myself, but I cannot kill you, little one.*

'Well, your highness, will you do us the honour of eating and drinking with us tonight?' asked the hated voice.

Penelope's gaze reluctantly focused on the gaunt, cruel features of Antinous, her captor and tormentor, as he bowed elaborately before her. He was young, having hardly more than twenty summers, but he was clever and ruthless. The hint of insanity in his green eyes could be feigned, she thought, but it made the older pirates step around him with care. His hair was dark and long, and a single, thin braid, decorated with gold wire, hung from his right temple.

In the nineteen endless days since the attack – days the queen had marked as carefully as she marked the kicking of the child inside her – Penelope had learned a lot about these pirates and their ways. Most were spiteful, stupid men who believed cruelty and murder made them strong. They were undisciplined and prone to sudden outbursts of rage and violence. Of the five pirate leaders who had banded together under Antinous' leadership to attack Ithaka, three were now dead at Antinous' hand. Another had been killed in a fight over a captured woman.

'Well, my lady? Shall I untie your hands and have food brought?' Antinous' grinning face was inches from hers. She smelled meat on his breath but not wine, for he never drank.

Penelope ignored him. His hand snaked out, slapping her face hard, and jarring her teeth. She could taste blood upon her tongue. 'Or shall I give you to my men tonight?' Antinous asked her softly, gesturing to the drunken rabble. 'They will make you squeal.'

The queen focused her gaze on his too-calm eyes, eyes she would see in her dreams as long as she lived.

'Do as you will, pirate,' she said coldly. 'I am Penelope, queen of Ithaka. My husband is the great Odysseus, and he is coming here to kill you. Hear the words of your death, Antinous.'

Antinous laughed lightly and stood back. 'We are impatient for your husband's arrival. I hear that he and a few old men like him are coming to rescue you. All across the Great Green I expect they are speaking of it.' He gestured again around the hall. 'My fighters are young, and strong, and fearless. They will relish cutting out the heart of fat Odysseus.' Then he moved alongside her and whispered in her ear, 'But first I will make him watch you die. He will see you raped by my men, then watch as I put out your eyes and cut his foul get from your belly.'

Despite the terror in her heart, Penelope forced a smile. 'Your words mean nothing, blowhard. You are already dead. This I promise.'

There was movement in the doorway far down the hall and she saw a new group enter. Eagerly she scanned their faces. There was a muscled giant she first thought was Leukon, but as he turned to her she saw the violence in his eyes and realized he was just a killer.

Then she saw a face she knew. Sekundos! An old rogue Odysseus had had dealings with in happier days, but pirate scum none the less. No hope for her there. Others of his crew followed him in, ragged men in threadbare tunics. They looked more like beggars than pirates.

'Looking for rescue, Penelope?' Antinous asked her. 'Old Sekundos is not a saviour. Soft as puppy shit, and close to senile, but he tells me he knows the island well. All the hidden places where your peasants and their women are cowering in fear.'

Penelope closed her eyes, seeking a few heartbeats of release from his presence. But she could not force his face from her mind, and saw again the dreadful day he had come to Ithaka.

His eight galleys had sailed through the morning mist, and two hundred warriors had stormed ashore. The small garrison of thirty fighting men had battled valiantly all day, but by twilight all of her soldiers, most of them boys and ancients, lay dead. The bodies of those brave men had been impaled on spikes upon the beach for Odysseus to see when he arrived. The stench of rotting flesh upon the breeze was appalling.

The pirate chief spoke again. Penelope opened her eyes. 'And Sekundos will show us where the black savage is hiding,' he said.

'I will have him brought here, and slowly dismembered. You can watch him suffer and hear his screams.'

One-armed Bias had defended her through the long day of the attack, killing and wounding more than a dozen invaders, until, as hope faded, he had reluctantly retreated on her stern orders, disappearing into the night like a phantom. Each day she heard whispers among the pirates of the dark demon who picked off sentries and lone stragglers. Antinous had scoured the island for him, but had not found him.

Penelope had been dragged into her own palace and hurled to the floor before the young pirate chief. He had kicked her in the face, and hauled her up by her hair. When she tried to strike him he had grasped her fingers, twisting them until two snapped. Then he had punched her to the ground. Half dazed with pain she had heard his cold voice.

'I am Antinous, son of a father murdered by Odysseus. I am here for vengeance.'

'Odysseus is no murderer,' she replied, spitting blood from her mouth.

'A foul lie. He was on a ship with Nestor and Idomeneos. In a sea battle against my father.'

'Three kings in a sea battle? Ah yes,' she said, staring up at his long, angular face. 'Odysseus spoke of it often, and now I see the resemblance. Your father was the man known as Donkey Face.'

He had punched her again, breaking her nose, then grabbed her hair, slapping her again and again. Finally she had sunk unconscious to the floor, and had awoken in a tiny cell.

Now she watched Sekundos the Kretan walk up to her, an old shield hanging loosely from his shoulder. He looked frightened, and there was sweat glistening on his bald head.

Glancing nervously first at Antinous, he said, 'Greetings, lady. I am sorry to see you brought so low.' She saw his gaze taking in her crippled fingers, the crusted blood round her eyes and mouth.

She smiled gently. 'Greetings, Sekundos. The company you keep brings you only shame.'

'There is so much shame in my life, lady, that a little more would not weigh heavily on me.'

Antinous laughed and pushed the old pirate away. Then he turned towards Penelope. 'You speak of shame in my presence, when I have treated you so well? I fear I must teach you manners!' He raised his left hand to strike her. At that moment there came a hissing sound, and a black feathered arrow hurtling towards his head plunged instead through his forearm. Antinous cried out in pain, and staggered back.

Penelope looked down the length of the hall.

In the far doorway, dressed like a beggar, stood Odysseus, the great bow Akilina in his hand. 'And now, you cowsons,' he bellowed, 'it is time to die!'

Shocked silence fell. No one moved. In that moment Odysseus calmly notched another arrow and let fly. The shaft plunged through the throat of a yellow-haired tribesman, who fell back dead.

Now pandemonium broke out. Some pirates tried to run for cover, others grabbed their weapons and charged at the Ithakan king, but a huge dark-haired warrior carrying two swords stepped into their path. He slashed one blade through the throat of the first assailant before ramming his second deep into the chest of the pirate alongside.

Others of Odysseus' disguised crew drew weapons and attacked. Odysseus ran towards the long feasting table in the centre of the hall. A man reared up before him. Odysseus shoulder-charged him to the floor, then leapt on to the table.

'I am Odysseus!' he shouted. 'You are all dead men now!' His voice boomed like thunder, the words echoing from the rafters.

Achilles and the crew of the *Bloodhawk* were fighting furiously before the doors, forcing the enemy back towards the centre of the hall. Odysseus sent a shaft through the skull of a tall pirate. Two more warriors scrambled on to the table and rushed at him. Odysseus swung Akilina like a club, cracking the bow against the face of the first. The man was hurled from the table. Odysseus twisted to one side and kicked the second man in the knee. The pirate screamed and fell.

A spear flew past Odysseus' head. He shot an arrow into the chest of the man who threw it.

Standing by the throne, Antinous snapped off the arrow in his forearm and, with a cry of pain, dragged the shaft clear. His left hand was useless, the thumb paralysed. Drawing a short stabbing sword he shouted, 'Odysseus! Watch your wife die!' Penelope shrank away as the sword blade lanced towards her throat – to be blocked by the shield of Sekundos. The old man's sword slashed out, but he was too slow and Antinous swayed away from the blade.

'You treacherous cur!' hissed Antinous. 'You brought them here! Now you can die with them.'

Antinous attacked. Sekundos blocked a thrust with his shield, but Antinous dropped to one knee, his sword slicing beneath the shield and cutting deeply into the old man's thigh. Sekundos cried out, and fell back. Antinous glanced down the long *megaron*. Odysseus had jumped off the table and thrown aside his bow. He was now fighting with a sword, slashing ferociously left and right trying to force his way through to his wife.

The balance of the battle was shifting now, Antinous realized. The advantage of surprise had been with Odysseus and his men, but that had passed, and weight of numbers was beginning to tell. There had been almost one hundred and fifty pirates in the *megaron*. The fighting men with Odysseus numbered only forty. They were being forced back slowly towards the great doors. They would have been overrun swiftly were it not for the giant, black-haired warrior with the two blades. His strength was terrifying. Again and again his swords cut through defences, bodies piling up around him.

Antinous turned his attention back to Sekundos, for the old man was advancing on him, shield held high, stabbing sword at the ready.

Antinous laughed. 'Old fool, you should have quit the sea years ago. Your muscles are wasted, your speed gone, your bones brittle.'

Antinous darted in, making a feint towards the groin. Sekundos dropped his shield to block the blow. Antinous plunged his short sword over the shield and into the old man's chest. Sekundos groaned and fell back, his shield clattering to the floor.

In the centre of the hall Odysseus was surrounded by pirates, but he surged into them, shouting curses. 'Take him alive!' shouted Antinous. 'I want him alive!'

Suddenly the great doors were thrust open. More warriors came pouring in, screaming a battle cry.

'Penelope! PENELOPE!'

Antinous stood aghast as more and more fighting men swarmed into the palace. At their centre was a warrior in a full-faced helm and breastplate of glittering bronze. He tore into the pirates, cutting down one man after another.

In panic the pirates fell back once more. Some fled through the side doors to the servants' quarters. Others retreated towards the throne. The bronze warrior followed hard on their heels, his sword cutting and killing, blood spraying from the blade.

The black-haired giant was beside him now. Antinous had never seen such a deadly display of fighting skills, had not believed it was even possible. The bronze warrior was fast, swaying away from plunging blades, his sword lancing out with impossible precision. The giant radiated invincibility, smashing his way into the ranks of the pirates, spilling men from their feet.

Antinous backed away, seeking an escape route.

Then he saw Odysseus advancing towards him, blood pouring from many cuts to his arms and shoulders. The stocky king hurled himself forward, scattering the pirates before him, and charged at Antinous.

The pirate chief shouted a curse and leapt to meet him. Their swords clanged together. Odysseus' left hand snaked out, grabbing the front of Antinous' tunic, and dragging him in to a head-butt that smashed his nose. Half blinded, Antinous struggled to free himself from the older man's grip. But he could not. Pain, hideous and burning, tore into his belly, and up through his lungs. All strength fled from him. The sounds of battle receded in his ears. He found himself staring into the eyes of Odysseus, and saw no pity there.

The sword in his belly was half withdrawn – then twisted savagely.

Agony ripped through the pirate chief. The blade was torn clear of him, his entrails flopping out after it. Hurled aside like a blood-stained rag, Antinous was dead before his body struck the floor.

Old Sekundos, his face ashen with pain, dragged himself along-side Penelope. His strength failing, he sagged against the throne before slipping to the floor.

Outside the palace fleeing pirates were met with a hail of arrows, then a charge led by Oniacus and a score of fighting men from the *Xanthos*. Three survivors broke clear – only to be met by a huge, one-armed black man. Leaping forward, Bias stabbed the first in the neck, then plunged his blade into the chest of the second. The third man raced clear. A black-shafted arrow slammed into his back. He staggered forward for several paces, then pitched face first to the ground.

A group of pirates escaped through the side doors and dashed down to the beach. On the great galley *Xanthos* all was dark, and the survivors raced towards it, hoping to capture the ship. As they started to climb the trailing ropes dark shapes appeared above them, and a hail of arrows ripped into them from the high deck. On the stern of the ship Andromache stood calmly shooting shafts with more of the ship's archers, her arrows slamming into the pirates with cold precision.

Inside the palace the battle was over. Some of the pirates cried out for mercy. None was given.

Odysseus dropped his sword and ran to his wife, kneeling along-side her. Swiftly he untied her hands, then, cradling her shaved head in his hands, he kissed her brow. There were tears in his eyes. 'I am so sorry,' he said. 'This is my fault.'

Penelope clung to him with her good hand and for a moment they were silent, close in each other's arms, scarcely believing they were together again, and safe.

'I knew you would come, Ugly One. It was most foolish of you,' she murmured at last. Lifting her broken hand, she gently stroked his face. 'And look at you, all cuts and bruises.'

The bronze warrior approached them, and lifted clear his helm. Penelope looked up into his sky-blue eyes.

'I had thought there was little left in this world to surprise me,' she said. 'But you prove me wrong. Welcome to my house, Helikaon.' She looked beyond him to the blood-spattered giant.

'I am Achilles,' he told her.

'You could be no other,' she replied.

For the next three days the men of the *Xanthos* helped Odysseus' crew clear away the bodies of the pirates, and prepare the funeral pyres. Refugees moved back from their hiding places in the hills, returning to their looted homes. Andromache joined the women of Ithaka as they moved through the *megaron* and surrounding rooms, scrubbing away the blood, and clearing the filth the pirates and their whores had left in their wake.

Little was seen of Penelope during this time, and Odysseus appeared only rarely.

By the evening of the third day the palace was once more habitable. The cleansing of homes brought a sense of normality, but many had lost loved ones, and there was an air of despondency throughout the settlement. The only surgeon on Ithaka had been killed by the attackers, and the wounded were tended by Bias, Oniacus and Andromache. All three had some experience of herbs and medicinal plants.

Just before sunset on the fourth day Penelope emerged from her rooms, and walked among the wounded, a bright scarf of gold wrapped round her shaven head. She could not assist with the work, for her fingers had been splinted. But she sat with the sufferers, talking to them, praising their courage.

Old Sekundos was dying. Penelope went to where he lay on a pallet bed in the sunshine. He had asked to be carried out so he could see the Great Green one last time.

When Penelope arrived he smiled. 'Too old . . . and slow,' he said. 'Was a time . . .'

'Yes,' Penelope replied, her voice tender, 'you were too old to win. But not too old to save my life, and that of my child.'

A faint smile touched the old man's lips. 'Always . . . wanted to be . . . in one of Odysseus' tales.' He looked up at the clear blue sky. 'Beautiful day to be . . . sailing,' he whispered.

Penelope's vision blurred. 'You are a hero, Sekundos. And I am sorry I spoke of shame when we met.'

The old man rallied at the compliment. 'You . . . remembered my name. That is . . . a great honour for me,' he told the queen. Then, his strength fading, he looked up at her. 'You must leave me now. I have . . . a wish . . . to die alone. Just me . . . and the Great Green.'

Penelope leaned down and kissed his brow. 'May your journey be swift, and the Fields of Elysium welcoming.'

Just then Andromache emerged from the palace. 'Walk with me,' said the queen, then moved away up a gently sloping hill. Andromache saw she was trembling, and her footsteps were unsteady. She took Penelope's arm, and together they made their way towards the crest of the hill.

'You are still weak,' said Andromache. 'You should be resting.'

Penelope took a deep breath. 'Odysseus does not ask, but I feel the questioning eyes of others upon me. They all wonder what violation I suffered, and whether my pride has been shattered.'

'There is not a man alive who could take away your pride, let alone shatter it,' said Andromache.

'Fine words from someone who does not know me.' The rebuke was gently spoken.

'I do know you,' Andromache told her. 'From all that Odysseus has told me of you, and from all that I have seen and heard since I have been here. All speak of their love for you, their respect for you, and their pride in you.'

Penelope did not reply, but led the way to a stone bench overlooking the bay. The pirate ships were still drawn up below, as was the mighty *Xanthos*. The two women sat in silence for a while, then Andromache spoke. 'Odysseus is a good man. I like him greatly.'

Penelope sighed. 'He has not asked me what I suffered. I wonder at that.'

'Do not wonder too deeply,' Andromache advised her. 'I saw Odysseus when the *Xanthos* arrived at the pirate isle. I have never seen a man so tormented, so frightened. He feared losing you. Now he is saddened by your pain, but he cannot hide the joy in his eyes that you are alive. He does not ask because all that matters to him is that you are safe, and he is with you.'

'He is a sentimental old fool,' said Penelope fondly.

Below them Odysseus and Helikaon walked from the palace. Odysseus glanced up and waved. Penelope lifted a hand in response. Together the two men continued down to the shoreline. Penelope looked at the young woman beside her, seeing her face soften as she gazed down at the two men.

'So,' asked the queen, 'why is the wife of Hektor travelling the Great Green?'

Andromache told her of the purpose of their journey, and the visit to Thera with Kassandra, but as she spoke her eyes followed Helikaon. A great sadness touched Penelope then, for she saw the love in Andromache's eyes.

'I am tired,' she said. 'I think I will return to my rooms.'

Andromache helped her back to the palace, and once there Penelope kissed the younger woman on the cheek.

'Despite all that has happened,' she said, 'I will treasure these last few days. It has been good to see Helikaon and the Ugly One together again as friends. And I am glad we met, Andromache.'

'As am I. I see now why Odysseus has such love for you.'

Penelope sighed. 'We have been lucky. An arranged marriage that led to joys I could not have dreamed of. Others are not so lucky. But love is to be cherished wherever it is found. Sometimes, though, love can lead to great heartache, and pain beyond imagining. You understand what I am saying?'

Andromache flushed. 'I think I do.'

'When you reach Troy again bring my greetings to Hektor, a man I have always admired. A good man, a man of no malice or deceit. Tell him Penelope wishes him well.'

'I will tell him,' Andromache answered coolly, but there was anger in her eyes.

'Do not misunderstand me, my dear,' Penelope went on. 'I do not judge you, but we have spoken now and I know you better. You are not sly, or capricious, and the path you are walking will eat away at your spirit. Odysseus told me of Helikaon's love for you. He tells me everything.'

Andromache's anger faded. 'I don't know what to do,' she whispered.

'Come inside. We will sit and talk,' Penelope told her.

In the queen's apartments a fire had been lit, and they sat together on a couch. Andromache talked of her first meeting with Helikaon, and of the battle in Priam's palace. She spoke of Halysia and Dex. She told Penelope of Helikaon's sickness, and the wound that would not heal.

'Then, one night, his fever broke,' she said.

'And you were with him?'

'Yes.' Andromache looked away.

'And no one else?'

Andromache nodded, and a silence grew between them. Penelope did not break it, but sat quietly, waiting. Andromache took a deep breath, and let it out slowly. 'Hektor is a good man, and my friend,' she said. 'He loves my son.'

The shock of the words struck Penelope, though she did not show it. *He loves my son.*

'Does Helikaon know?'

'Know what?'

'That he is the father of your child?'

Andromache's eyes widened as she realized what she had given away. 'No – and he must not! He cannot! All his life he has been racked by guilt, first about his mother, who killed herself in front of him, then because he could not save little Dio, then Halysia. This news would only cause him more torment.'

'Be calm, Andromache. We are friends, you and I. No word will come from me. Not even to Odysseus. I promise you. Does Hektor know?'

'Yes, I told him at the very first,' replied Andromache, the words barely audible. 'But only he and I know, and now you. But it is vital it does not get back to Priam. He would kill Astyanax, and me, and hunt down Helikaon too if he could. It is better this way. It is the only way. But it is so hard,' she whispered.

'Oh, my dear, I am sorry for your heartache. But you must make a decision, and there is only one to make. You know what it is.'

Andromache nodded, and tears began to fall. Penelope leaned in and put her arm round the younger woman's shoulder. There was nothing more to say.

On the beach below Helikaon's crew were loading supplies.

'You are heading for the Seven Hills?' asked Odysseus. Helikaon looked at him, but did not answer. Odysseus understood his friend's reluctance to speak of his plans. Despite the rescue of Penelope they were still on opposing sides.

'I'll not betray you, lad,' said the older man. 'Surely you know that?'

Helikaon nodded. 'I know. The madness of war affects us all. Yes, I am going there. What will I find? Are my men still alive, Odysseus?'

'Of course they are. It hurts me you need to ask. When this war began I gathered all the people together and told them I would suffer no enmities, no feuds. There are brigands and nomadic bands of tribesmen moving through the land. There are raiders of the sea. They have enough enemies to fight without warring amongst themselves. All is well there, Helikaon, and you will be welcomed as a friend by everyone. I take it you seek tin?'

'Yes. We will need all we can find.'

'There are stores there. Take whatever you can carry.'

As they spoke Bias came up to them. Helikaon looked up as he approached, recalling the hatred in the man's voice the last time they met.

I hope you burn, and your death ship with you.

He did not look at Helikaon, but spoke to Odysseus. 'We have loaded most of the supplies you ordered,' he reported, 'but the pirates have left us with scant reserves.'

'Tomorrow you can sail for Pylos,' said Odysseus, 'and trade for more with Nestor's people.'

Bias nodded, but did not leave. The silence grew, then he took a deep breath and addressed Helikaon. 'I do not take back what I said, Helikaon. But I thank you for coming to our aid.' Without waiting for a reply he walked away.

'A good man, but unforgiving,' Odysseus said.

Helikaon shrugged. 'Forgiveness should never be given lightly. How is Penelope?'

'She is strong – far stronger than I. But I do not want to speak of what she must have suffered before we arrived. To think of it fills me with a rage I can hardly control. You spoke of the madness of war, and this attack on Ithaka is an example of it. The son of Donkey Face wanted revenge, but even without that the pirates and raiders are growing in strength. As we gather to destroy Troy our own kingdoms are neglected. When we conquer – and we will conquer, Helikaon – what will we come back to? I fear this conflict will consume us all. There will be no victors then, and even the treasury of Troy will not contain enough gold to rebuild what we have lost.'

Helikaon looked at his old friend. There was more silver than red now in his hair and beard, and his face was lined and anxious.

'All that you say is true, Odysseus – save for the treasury of Troy. I have not seen Priam's hoard of gold, but it would have to be mountainous to maintain the expense of this war. Gold passes from the city every day, to hire mercenaries, to bribe allies. And there is little coming in now the traders are leaving. If the fighting goes on much longer, and you do take the city, you may find nothing of real worth.'

'The thought had occurred to me,' Odysseus told him, nodding. 'If that proves true then we are all doomed to poverty and ruin.' He sighed again, and looked into Helikaon's blue eyes. 'I hope I do not find you in Troy when we take the city.'

'Where else would I be, Odysseus? The woman I love will be there, and I will protect her with my life.'

'I fear for you, lad.' Odysseus looked suddenly weary. 'You and Hektor are the two greatest fighting men of Troy,' he said, his voice low. 'What will happen, do you think, when he discovers his wife is your lover?'

Helikaon pulled angrily away. Then his shoulders sagged. 'Is it so obvious?'

'Aye, it is, when you never stand close to her in a room or look at her when you are in company, when you stare at the floor whenever she speaks, but leave for your rooms within heartbeats of each other. Before long – if not already – there will not be a man among your crew who does not suspect.'

Odysseus laid his hand on Helikaon's shoulder. 'Take her back to Troy, then leave the city. Defend the north, hold open the trade routes, fight battles at sea. But stay away from her, lad, or I fear for the future of you both.'

Book Two
THE BATTLE FOR TROY

XIII

The peasant and the princes

THE WINTER WAS THE HARSHEST THAT ANYONE LIVING IN TROY COULD recall. Storms blown down from the north brought icy sleet and then, remarkably, snow. Icicles formed on windows and walls, and out on the pastures north of the city sheep, trapped in snowdrifts, froze to death. Blizzards raged for twenty days, and even when they passed the routes remained blocked.

In the lower town there were deaths among the populace of the poorer quarters. The price of food rose alarmingly as bad weather and rumours of war caused the numbers of trade caravans from the east to dwindle. Priam ordered all grain stores to ration supplies, and the city seethed with discontent.

Even in the worst of the winter refugees still fled the city, for the news from the south was unremittingly bad. Hektor had won three battles, but overwhelming numbers of the enemy had forced him back to Thebe Under Plakos, and now that city too was under siege.

In the north a Mykene attack on Dardanos had been crushed by the general Banokles and his Thrakians, aided by a regiment of mercenaries led by Tudhaliyas, the banished son of the Hittite emperor. The battle had been close. It would have been lost had the invasion fleet not been caught in a storm. Only a third of the ships

175

had made it across the straits. The enemy force had been reduced to four thousand men, and not the twelve thousand who could have stormed ashore.

On midwinter's day the king's son Antiphones left his house in the lower town and trudged up the icy, near-deserted streets towards the city. An icy wind was blowing, and even the sheepskin cloak he wore could not keep the cold from his bones.

Passing through the Scaean Gate he made his way up the stone stairway to the south battlements. As he climbed he remembered the long days of illness following the palace siege four years before. Knifed nearly to death, he had fought to recover, and to lose some of his prodigious weight, by climbing the battlement steps over and over again. The first time he had tackled the west battlements, where the great wall was lowest. He had thought then he would pass out through pain and exhaustion. But over the months his strength had grown, and now – though he still weighed as much as two men – he was as strong as any warrior in Troy.

He had no idea why his brother Polites had asked to meet him on the Great Tower of Ilion. Antiphones had not been up there since he was a child. Priam forbade it. 'The roof would collapse under you, boy,' he had said, 'and it would be an engineering nightmare to rebuild.'

On the south wall, above the Scaean Gate, he paused for a moment, then opened the oak door in the side of the Great Tower and entered its blackness. Here he waited until his eyes were accustomed to the gloom. The steps crafted on the inner wall of the tower rose up to his left.

When he finally emerged high on the wooden roof the wind hit him like an axe. The four guards manning the corners of the tower stood braced, enduring. Polites, his skinny frame enveloped in a heavy cloak, his thinning hair covered by a sheepskin cap, came hurrying over to him, pushed by the wind from the north.

'Thank you for meeting me here, brother,' he said, half his words snatched away as they left his mouth. 'Are you well?'

'Let us leave mutual enquiries about our health to a more appropriate time,' Antiphones yelled. 'What are we doing here?'

'As usual, I am seeking your advice, brother.' Placing his hand on Antiphones' shoulder Polites urged him over to the side of the tower overlooking the lower town and the bay. The wide battlemented wall offered shelter for the lower part of his body, but still Antiphones could scarcely suck in his breath in the wind. He cupped his hand over his mouth so he could breathe.

'Our father has chosen to make a fool of me again,' Polites said, close to Antiphones' ear. 'He summoned me yesterday and told me he was making me his *strategos*, and that I must plan the defence of Troy. I have spent a sleepless night, brother.'

Antiphones nodded. 'And why are we on the Great Tower?' he gasped.

'From here we can see all of Troy and its surroundings. We can see where the invaders will come, and we can plan our defence.'

Antiphones grunted. He grabbed hold of his brother's skinny arm and dragged him back to the top of the tower staircase.

'Come with me, Polites!'

Without bothering to see if his brother was following him, he descended into the dark, mercifully windless, tower, and made his way back down to the wall. Emerging into the light, he descended the battlement steps.

Reaching the bottom, he summoned a gate guard. 'Fetch me a chariot!' he ordered. The man nodded and raced off up towards the palace.

Antiphones walked out through the open Scaean Gate. Only then, looking over the lower town once more, did he turn to his brother.

'In order to defend the city we must think like the invader,' he told him. 'We cannot think like Agamemnon standing on the Great Tower. We must go where *he* would go, see what *he* would see.'

Polites nodded, his face downcast. 'You are right. I am no good at this. That is why father chose me. To make a fool of me. As he did at Hektor's Wedding Games.'

Antiphones shook his head. 'Brother, you are not thinking this through. True, Priam has made fools of us in the past. He made me his Captain of Horse when I was so colossally fat I would have broken the back of one of Poseidon's immortal steeds. But in this he knows what he is doing. When the Mykene come he has to be ready. They could be here on our shores by spring. We might have just days before we see their ships. He has not chosen you to make a fool of you. He has chosen you because he thinks you are the right man for this task. You have to understand that.'

'In spite of the Games?'

'*Because* of the Games, brother. The Games were important to him. He wanted Agamemnon and his crew of rabble kings to see how the Trojans could organize themselves. He believed you could do it. And you did him proud. You got thousands of men to the correct events, on the right days at the right times. They were all fed and housed. It was a great success. You were too anxious at the time to see it.'

'There were a few fights,' Polites said, reassured a little by the praise.

'There were more than a *few* fights.' Antiphones laughed. 'I witnessed a score myself. Yet the Games were not disrupted, and everyone went home satisfied. Except King Eioneus,' he shrugged, 'and the two men killed in the chariot races. And that Kretan fist-fighter Achilles killed with one blow.' He laughed and clapped his brother on the back.

'I don't see it,' said Polites miserably. 'Yesterday I met the generals, Lucan and Thyrsites. They were speaking in a language I could not understand.'

Antiphones chuckled. 'Soldiers like to speak their own private language.'

A chariot came into sight, clattering through the gateway. Antiphones dismissed the charioteer and took up the reins. 'Come, Polites,' he said. 'Let us take a ride together.'

Polites climbed aboard. Antiphones flicked the reins and the chariot set off through the lower town past the rabbit warren of streets and alleyways under the great walls. Once across the fortification ditch Antiphones drove the chariot down the gently sloping road and across the snow-carpeted plain of the Scamander until they reached the river. It was in full winter spate, and its flood waters lapped around the chariot wheels before they reached the wide wooden bridge. Antiphones drew the horses to a halt and climbed down. Standing at the centre of the bridge they looked back the way they had come.

'Now, what do you see?' asked the big man.

Polites sighed. 'I see a great city on a plateau surrounded by walls which are impregnable.' He glanced at Antiphones, who nodded encouragingly. 'I see the lower town which lies on sloping ground, mostly to the south of the city. This can be defended, but if the numbers of defenders are too few, or the invaders too many, then it can be taken, street by street, building by building. Taking it will be very costly to both sides, but it can be done. Father is thinking of widening the fortification ditch round the town, which will mean pulling down many buildings. But he fears it will send the wrong message. If the people believe Agamemnon is definitely coming, they will flee the city in even greater numbers and the treasury will suffer.'

Antiphones shrugged. 'Agamemnon will come anyway. What else do you see?'

'All around us, to east, west and south, I see a wide plain, ideal for cavalry warfare. The Trojan Horse would destroy any troops exposed on this plain. None could stand against them.' As Polites gazed upon the city Antiphones saw his expression change.

'What is it?' asked the big man.

'The Trojan Horse,' answered Polites. 'Thousands of horses. We could not stable them in the Upper City. There would not be enough feed. Nor could we leave them in the lower town, and the barracks there. What if the town fell?'

'Now you are thinking,' Antiphones told him, though the problem had not occurred to him before. The Trojan Horse was a mobile army, best suited to fast movement, surprising enemy forces. It would be useless in a siege. Fear touched his heart then.

Polites was staring intently at the land around the city, and down to the Bay of Troy. 'We will need more horsemen,' he said, 'out-riders and scouts. Hektor and his men will have to remain outside the city, constantly moving, then hitting the enemy where least expected.' Polites' brow furrowed. 'How then can we supply them with food, and fresh weapons, arrows and spears?'

'You are going too fast for me,' Antiphones told him. 'How can we survive with our army outside the city?'

'Not all of the army. Only the Trojan Horse. We can still man the walls with infantry and archers, and sally out with our regiments when the occasion permits. We must have hidden supplies out in the far hills and the woods where the enemy will not venture,' he continued, warming to his theme. 'And we will need a way to communicate with Hektor, so that we can link strategically.'

'You are a wonder, little brother,' said Antiphones admiringly. Polites blushed at the compliment. 'But,' Antiphones went on, sobering a little, 'we cannot rely solely on the Trojan Horse. It is our spear and our shield, but even the strongest shield can be shattered.'

'Do you believe Agamemnon will bring his own cavalry? Surely not!'

'No, the strength of the Mykene is in their infantry. The Mykene phalanx is the best in the world, experienced and disciplined. We will not want to be drawn into any pitched battles with them.'

'But, brother,' argued Polites, 'we have the finest infantry. Surely the Scamandrian and Heraklion regiments, and your own Ileans, are a match for any army? They are all doughty warriors.'

Antiphones shook his head. 'With the exception of the Eagles, we have no foot soldiers to compare with the Mykene,' he admitted. 'And our infantry are buttressed by Hittite and Phrygian mercenaries, with their flimsy armour. The Mykene would cut through them like a scythe through long grass. Only Hektor and the Horse can defeat the elite warriors of Agamemnon. The Mykene are the finest fighters but, heavily armoured, they are slow to react. Only a cavalry charge will break their formation and scatter them.'

Polites nodded. 'But surely Father's Eagles would be a match for them?'

'Yes, but there are only three hundred Eagles. The Mykene infantry will number in the thousands, and most of them will be veterans of a score of wars. They are deadly, Polites, and they know how to win. They get a lot of practice.'

Antiphones gazed up at the city, his mood bleak. Since his brush with death he had thanked the gods daily for his continued life, and attacked each day with vigour, determined to wring the last dregs of enjoyment from it. But now, for the first time in years, blackness threatened to engulf him. What had started as a mild intellectual exercise, discussing the defences of Troy with his brother, had blossomed into a black dread for the future. He could see in his mind's eye enemy camps on the plain of the Scamander, the river running with blood, the lower town empty and burned, Mykene troops clamouring at the walls of Troy.

Polites said encouragingly, 'We also know how to win, brother. And the great walls are impregnable. The city cannot be taken.'

Antiphones turned to him. 'If the Mykene reach the walls, Polites, then Troy cannot stand. There are only two wells in the city. Most of our water comes from the Scamander and the Simoeis. And how long can we feed all our people? We could not last the summer. And eventually there would be a traitor. There always is. Dardanos was not taken by siege, remember. It needed just one traitor and the enemy troops merely walked in the gates.'

He fell silent. *I* was the traitor, he thought, the last time Agamemnon tried to take Troy. Through my arrogance I almost caused the death of the king, and the fall of Troy to a foreign power. Only the courage of the hero Argurios prevented that. Two Trojans plotted the fall of Troy and a Mykene saved the city. How the gods enjoy such elegant irony.

Antiphones smiled grimly, trying to rouse himself from gloom, cursing his self-pity. 'If only I had remained fat I could have sat behind the Scaean Gate and all the troops in Mykene could never have opened it.'

Polites laughed. 'Then we should head for home and a mountain of honey cakes.'

The big woman trudged through the streets of the lower town, a basket of honey cakes on her arm. As she walked many of the older

181

traders called out greetings. She knew them all. Tobios the jeweller, with his henna-dyed hair, Palicos the cloth merchant, Rasha the spindly meat seller, and more. To them she was still Big Red, the servant of Aphrodite.

But those days were gone now. She was married to Banokles, a soldier of the Trojan Horse. She smiled. A general now, no less. Thoughts of her husband warmed her as she walked through the morning cold.

When young and beautiful she had dreamed of marrying a rich man, tall and handsome, and of living in a palace with servants to tend her needs. There would be perfumed baths, and jewelled robes. Her husband's adoration would shine brighter than the summer sun, and she would walk through Troy like a queen of legend. Such were the dreams of the young. The woman of those times had believed she would never grow old. There would never be a day when men did not desire her, when one glance from those violet eyes did not capture their hearts.

Yet that day had come, creeping unnoticed through the shadows of her life. The rich clients had fallen away, and Red had found herself plying her trade among foreign sailors, or common soldiers, or the poorer merchants and travellers.

Until the night Banokles had come into her life.

Red cut through the alleys towards her small neat house in the Street of Potters, coming on the way to the square where she had first seen the blond-bearded Mykene soldier. He had been roaring drunk, and in the company of thieves and cut-throats. He had called out, then staggered towards her. 'By the gods,' he had said, 'I think you are the most beautiful woman I ever saw.' Fumbling in the pouch by his side he had pulled out a silver ring, which he thrust into her hand. She told him she was finished with work for the night, but it had not concerned him. 'That is for your beauty alone,' he told her.

Despite her years of dealing with men and their hungers she had been touched by the gesture. And she had felt sorry for the drunken fool. She knew the men with him. They were robbers, and before the night was over they would kill or cripple him for the rings he carried.

But she had left him there and walked – just as she had this morning – to the house of the baker, Krenio.

Later, retracing her steps, she had braced herself for the sight of the soldier dead on the stones. When finally she reached the square she saw him sitting quietly drinking, the thieves sprawled out around him.

In the days that followed she had watched him take part, as a fistfighter, in Hektor's Wedding Games, had walked with him along the beach, had slept beside him, listening to his breathing. And somewhere in that time she had realized, with great surprise, that she was fond of him. Why remained a mystery. He was not intelligent, nor intuitive. In many ways he was like an overgrown child, quick to anger, swift to forgive. Even now her love for him surprised her.

Banokles the general. The thought amused her.

Reaching her house she put the basket of honey cakes on the table and poured herself a cup of wine. The fire had died down and she added fuel, then sat before the flames. Banokles was still in Dardania. Word had reached the city that he had won a battle. His name was on everyone's lips.

Red sipped her wine, then reached for a honey cake. Just the once, she promised herself. The taste was divine. Krenio's talent as a baker was second to none.

The old man had wept again when she visited him that morning, telling her over and over how much he loved her. 'I am going to leave the city,' he said once more.

'You have been saying that for a year,' she replied. 'But you haven't done it yet.'

'I am waiting for you to see sense, my dear, and come with me.'

'Do not start that again, old man. I am married now.'

'But still you can't stay away from me, can you? We are destined to be together. I know this with all my heart. Come east with me, Red.'

She could not tell him she pleasured him, as she always had, for his honey cakes. Red bit into a second one. It was so good.

Her mind drifted back to Banokles. 'I miss you,' she whispered.

*

Banokles was bored. Outside the fortress of Dardanos soldiers were still celebrating their latest victory over the Mykene. Banokles could hear laughter and singing, the sounds of joy from men who had survived a battle. He could smell roasting meats, and he yearned to be out among the warriors, drinking and dancing without a care. Instead he was stuck in this chilly chamber while Kalliades and the Hittite with the curly beard and the name that tangled in his tongue spoke endlessly about beaches and bays, landing places and possible battle sites. They had talked about food supplies, scouts, and promotions to replace officers who had fallen in battle. The words washed over him and he found himself growing steadily more irritable.

Truth was he was missing Big Red. Her absence was like a rock on his heart. He pictured her sitting in her small courtyard, her back propped up by cushions, feet resting on a padded stool. The image calmed him a little.

Their parting had not been a happy one. Her violet eyes had glared at him. 'You big oaf,' she had told him. 'This is a war that cannot be won. Troy cannot stand against the western kings and their armies. All the intelligent merchants are leaving the city. We should do the same. Head east. You have gold now, and a reputation. You could find work among the Hittites. We could be happy.'

'I *am* happy,' Banokles had replied, trying to take her into his arms. She had shrugged him off, then sighed.

'So am I,' she had admitted reluctantly. 'And it frightens me. I never expected it. Look at me, Banokles. I am a fat, ageing whore. I thought all my dreams had died a long time ago. I was content in my little house. Then you came along.'

Banokles had stepped in then, putting his arms round her. She didn't struggle, but laid her head on his shoulder. 'You are the joy of my life,' he told her.

'Then you are an idiot, and your life must have been wretched before me.'

'It was, but I didn't know it. Don't worry. I'll be home in the spring. You just rest and enjoy yourself. Get more of those cakes from the old baker.'

'You truly are a numbskull,' she said, but her voice had softened. Then a soldier had called out for Banokles. Red gave her husband his helm and he had leaned in to kiss her.

'Make sure you listen well to Kalliades,' she warned him. 'And don't go getting yourself killed.'

'No danger of that. We've already crushed their army. They won't come again before spring, and by then I'll be home.'

But the Mykene *had* come again, and the battle had been fierce, with slashing blades, and plunging spears. If not for the storm that had scattered their fleet the enemy numbers would have been overwhelming.

Banokles stared with dislike at the Hittite prince. The man was young, but his beard was long and artificially curled. His clothes were of shiny cloth the colour of sky, and they gleamed in the torchlight. He dresses like a woman, thought Banokles contemptuously, seeing the glint of gems sewn into the sleeves. Even his boots, embossed with silver, glittered. There were precious stones set into his sword hilt. The man was a walking treasury.

Banokles drained his wine cup and belched. The belch was a good one, rich and throaty. It caused a break in the conversation. His friend Kalliades looked up and grinned.

'I fear we are losing the attention of our comrade,' he told the Hittite prince.

Tudhaliyas shook his head. 'At the risk of being called a pedant, I should point out that one cannot lose something one never had.' Rising smoothly, the Hittite walked across the room and out on to the balcony.

'The man does not like me,' observed Banokles, scratching his close-trimmed blond beard. 'And I don't like him.'

Heaving himself to his feet he gazed around the room, his eyes focusing on a platter of sliced meat and cheese. 'All the cakes have gone,' he complained. Moving to the door he hauled it open, and shouted for more cakes. Then he slumped down again.

'It is not dislike,' continued Tudhaliyas, strolling back into the room. 'I was raised by philosophers and teachers of rare skill, historians and thinkers. I have studied the strategies of ancient wars, and the words of great generals and poets and lawmakers. Now I am banished from my father's realm, and in the company of a soldier whose chief joy is to piss up a tree. Dislike does not begin to describe my feelings.'

Banokles glared at him, then glanced at Kalliades. 'I think that was an insult, but I stopped listening when he got to philosophers. Never liked the cowsons. Don't understand a word they say.'

'I accept they don't say much that would interest you, my friend,' Kalliades told him. 'But if we can drag ourselves back to the matters at hand I would appreciate it.'

'What is there to talk about? The enemy came, we destroyed them. They are dead. We are not.' He saw the Hittite staring at him balefully.

'We are trying to anticipate where the next invasion might take place, and how to prepare for it. It is what intelligent officers do,' Tudhaliyas sneered.

'Intelligence, eh?' snapped Banokles. 'If you are so clever how come you were banished? How come you ended up here with us peasants?'

'I was banished *because* I am clever, you dolt. My father is sick and senile. He thought I was planning to overthrow him.'

'Then why didn't he kill you?'

'Because he is sick and senile.' Tudhaliyas swung to Kalliades. 'Can we not discuss the essentials of the campaign alone?'

'We could,' agreed Kalliades, 'but that would be disrespectful to the great general here. And perhaps we should remember that it was *his* cavalry charge that ruptured the enemy line, allowing your regiment to scatter the foe.'

'I had not forgotten that, Kalliades,' said the prince. 'Nor do I make light of his courage, or his fighting ability. It is the laziness of his stupid mind that offends me.'

Banokles surged to his feet, drawing his sword. 'I am tired of your insults, turd face, and your stupid beard. Let me cut it off for you – at the throat!'

Tudhaliyas' sabre hissed from its scabbard. Kalliades leapt between the two men.

'Now this is a scene to inspire our enemies,' he cried. 'Two victorious generals cutting each other to pieces. Put away your swords! Perhaps we should meet later, when tempers have cooled.'

For a moment neither of the swordsmen moved, then Tudhaliyas slammed his sabre back in its scabbard and strode away.

As the door closed Banokles sighed. 'What is wrong with you?' Kalliades asked.

'I miss Red. Haven't seen her for months.'

'Red will be waiting for you. But that's not what is troubling you. We have been friends for a long time. Not once in that time have I seen you draw a sword on a brother soldier. You would have killed a good man, a brave warrior. This is not like you, Banokles.'

Banokles swore softly. 'I hate being a general. I miss the old life, Kalliades. Fight, kill the enemy, get drunk and pay for some whores. That's a proper soldier's life. I am just a pretend general. You do all the thinking and planning. The Hittite knows it. By the gods, *everyone* knows it. I used to be *someone*. I was a great fighter, and men looked up to me.'

'You still are and they still do.'

'That's not the point. I knew what I was doing, and I did it as well as any other man. Now I don't, and I have foreigners insulting me to my face. I tell you, one more insult and I'll take his curling tongs and ram them so far up his arse he'll be able to curl the damned thing from the inside.'

Kalliades chuckled. 'I don't know why the beard annoys you. Many of the Hittite warriors sport them and, as we have seen, they are ferocious fighters. Why don't you go out and join in the revels? Get drunk?'

Banokles shook his head. 'Can't do that any more, Kalliades. Men stop talking when I walk up. They go quiet, as if they expect me to piss on their joy fires.'

'You are their commander. They revere you.'

187

'I don't want to be revered,' shouted Banokles. 'I want to be *me*! Why can't you be the general? You are the one who makes all the plans.'

Kalliades looked at him. 'There is more to war than planning, my friend,' he said quietly. 'All the strategy comes to nothing if the men are not willing. When you led that charge the men followed you, their hearts full of fire and belief. That is something gold cannot buy. *You* are their inspiration. They believe in *you*. They would ride into Hades if you asked them to. You need to understand this. You make Tudhaliyas angry not because you are stupid, but because he cannot *learn* to be like you. He can understand the logistics of war, he can master all the skills and the strategies, but he cannot *inspire*. Truth is, neither can I. It is a rare gift, Banokles. You have it.'

'I don't want it!' protested the big man. 'I want everything the way it was.'

'You want us dead back in Thraki?'

'What? I mean I want . . . I don't know what I want. But it isn't this! A pox on Hektor for leaving me in command!'

'Hektor couldn't take the Thrakians back to Troy with him. You know what happened the last time there were Thrakians there.'

'What?'

'Oh, for pity's sake!' snapped Kalliades. 'You and I were there, in the invading army! Troy's Thrakian regiment rebelled and joined us and we almost took the city.'

Banokles sagged back into his chair and sighed. 'I told Red there wouldn't be any more battles here in Dardanos in the winter. Just how many poxy armies does Agamemnon have waiting across the straits?'

'Obviously more than we thought,' responded Kalliades. 'But why come in winter? Food supplies are short, the land inhospitable. Snow and heavy rains make much of Thraki impassable. It makes no sense.'

'If that's true why are you worried?'

'Because Agamemnon is no fool. He has conquered cities in the past, and led successful invasions all across the west. You and I fought in many of them. Common sense tells me that an attack on Troy would need to be coordinated with an invasion of Dardania in the north, and a major push through the Ida mountains in the south. Only then could he bring an invasion fleet to the Bay of Troy. But to attack here in winter, his army isolated? Even if they made a successful landing and pushed on south, reinforcements from Troy could be brought up to destroy them. What is he thinking?'

'Maybe he's lost his mind,' observed Banokles.

Kalliades shook his head. 'It would be good to think so. But I fear he has a plan, and we can't see it.'

XIV

Omens in the stars

LATE IN THE NIGHT KALLIADES WENT IN SEARCH OF TUDHALIYAS. A sentry directed him to the battlements above the Seagate, and he found the Hittite prince staring north out over the moonlit Hellespont.

Five galleys were beached on the bay below, the crews asleep on the sand. In better days they would have come up to the town that clutched the skirts of the fortress, there to drink and purchase the company of whores. But the town was deserted now, the populace fled to the interior, away from the threat of war. The vessels had come in for supplies before maintaining their patrol of the straits.

Tudhaliyas glanced round at Kalliades, but made no greeting.

'You are still angry?' Kalliades asked.

'I have been angry for most of the winter,' replied Tudhaliyas. 'There is no sign of it passing yet. But do not concern yourself, Kalliades. It is not the oaf that fires my rage.'

'What then?'

Tudhaliyas gave a cold smile. 'It would take too long to explain. So, why have you sought me out?'

Kalliades did not reply at once. Tudhaliyas was a prince, raised among foreign noblemen. Kalliades had no experience in dealing with such people. Their ways and customs were alien to him. What he did know was that the Hittite was a proud man, and he would need to choose his words with care.

'Tempers were raised tonight,' he said at last. 'I thought it best not to leave them festering for the night.'

'You are bringing his apology?'

Kalliades shook his head, and spoke softly. 'There is no need for him to apologize. You offered the first insult.'

An angry light appeared in the Hittite's eyes. 'You expect *me* to apologize?'

'No. Banokles will have forgotten the incident by morning. That is his way. He is not a complicated man, nor does he hold grudges. Everything you said was true enough. I know it. Even Banokles knows it. What is important is that we put it behind us.'

'If he were a Hittite general,' commented Tudhaliyas, 'and one of his officers had spoken as I did, an assassin would have been called for, and the officer swiftly dispatched.'

'Happily Banokles is not a Hittite general. And if there was a battle tomorrow, and you were in dire need, Banokles would ride through fire and peril to rescue you. That is the nature of the man.'

'He already did that,' conceded Tudhaliyas, and Kalliades saw his anger fade. The Hittite prince stared out once more over the sea. 'I have never been enamoured of the Great Green,' he offered. 'I do not understand why men yearn to sail it in flimsy vessels of wood. You Sea People are a mystery to me.'

'I have never loved the sea either,' Kalliades told him, 'but then my life has been one of soldiering.'

'Mine too. I was fifteen and beardless when Father sent me to fight at Kadesh. I have fought ever since against the Egypteians, and now against Idonoi tribesmen and Thessalians who came with the Mykene. Men always talk of final victory. I have never seen one.'

'Nor I,' agreed Kalliades.

'And we will not see one here,' said Tudhaliyas softly. 'The enemy will come again. I have less than three hundred men now, and thirty or more of those are carrying wounds. Banokles' Thrakians number a few hundred, with a further two hundred

Dardanians, many of them new recruits. Add to this the fifty Trojan Horse Hektor left us, and you have less than a thousand men to hold Dardania.'

'I have sent to Priam for reinforcements,' Kalliades told him, 'but I doubt we'll get more than a few infantry, with Hektor and the Trojan Horse away fighting in the south.'

'You could hold the fortress for a few months,' said Tudhaliyas, 'but in the end you would be starved out. If the enemy come in great numbers it would be best, I think, to leave the Dardanians here, then stage a fighting retreat south towards Troy. That way you can still be reinforced and counter-attack.'

'The danger of that,' Kalliades pointed out, 'is that we could be outflanked, then caught out in the open. If the enemy are lightly armed tribesmen we could fight our way clear. But if Agamemnon sends heavily armoured Mykene regiments we would be cut to pieces.'

'They are that good?'

'Believe me, Tudhaliyas, there is no better infantry under the sun. Every one of them is a veteran, and they fight in close order, four or six ranks deep, with locked shields. Your Hittites are brave men, but wicker shields will not block heavy spears. Nor will slender sabres pierce bronze disc armour.'

A sudden bright light to the east caught their attention. Kalliades glanced up, to see a falling star streak across the night sky. Within moments several more flashed across the horizon.

'It is an omen,' said Tudhaliyas, gazing at them. 'But is it for good or ill?'

'There were such lights in the sky the night before we sacked Sparta,' Kalliades told him. 'For us it was a good omen. We won.'

'In those days you were a Mykene warrior,' observed the Hittite. 'Perhaps then it is a good omen for the Mykene.'

Kalliades forced a smile. 'Or perhaps they are just lights in the sky.'

'Perhaps,' said Tudhaliyas doubtfully. 'It is said Agamemnon is a wily foe. Is this true?'

'I served him for most of my time as a soldier. He is a fine strategist. He seeks out the enemy's weakness, then strikes for the heart. No mercy. No pity.'

'Then why is a fine strategist wasting the lives of his men in winter here?'

'I have been asking myself the same question,' admitted Kalliades, shaking his head. 'I have no answer.'

The Hittite looked at him. 'Perhaps you are asking the wrong question.'

'And what would the right question be?'

'Is he a risk-taker, or does he choose the cautious route?'

Both men fell silent. Then the Hittite asked, 'The Dardanian fleet is massed now in the Hellespont watching for enemy fleets, yes?'

'Yes.'

'And Agamemnon would expect us to do exactly that?'

'I suppose so.'

'Perhaps that is what he wants. For if the fleet is protecting the Hellespont, then it is not guarding Troy.'

'He cannot attack Troy in winter,' said Kalliades. 'The fear of storms, or bad winds. The lack of supplies for his troops. The invasion – even if successful – would not be coordinated. No reinforcements from the south, or the north.'

But even as he spoke Kalliades felt a sudden cold on his skin.

'Hektor and the Trojan Horse are away in the south, defending Thebe,' Tudhaliyas pointed out. 'The Trojan fleet is small, for Troy relies on Helikaon's Dardanian ships for protection. Those galleys are here guarding against an attack from the north. If Agamemnon invades Troy now, in dead of winter, with all his men and all his western allies, he will catch the city unawares. And, as you say, strike for the heart. No mercy. No pity.'

Old Timeon the fisherman refused to curse his luck. When calamities befell other men they would rail at the gods, or grumble about the unfairness of life. Not Timeon. Luck was luck. It was either good or bad, but it seemed to him that the odds were the same. And mostly – if a man was patient – luck would balance out in the end.

This season had tested his philosophy to the limit. The old fishing boat had sprung a leak back when the shoals of slickfish were moving down from the distant Sombre Sea, swimming down the coast towards the warmer seas of the south. Timeon had missed the best days, for the timbers of his vessel had proved rotten, and repairs had been slow and costly.

Once the boat was seaworthy he was already deeply in debt. Then two of his three sons had announced they were travelling to the city to join the Trojan forces. This left only young Mikos, a good boy, but clumsy. While filleting a catch of big silvers eight days ago he had slashed his palm, and the wound had turned bad.

Now Timeon was forced to fish alone. It was not easy. His old muscles were stretched to their limits hauling in a full net.

With the other fishermen sleeping he had pushed out his boat in the darkness and sailed from the Bay of Herakles, encouraged by the sight of a school of dolphins. They would be hunting the slickfish, which meant a shoal was close by.

A mist lay upon the dark sea, but the sky above was clear, stars shining brightly. The breeze was cold, but Timeon believed he could feel the first breath of spring within it. Twice he cast his nets. Twice he drew them in empty.

A dolphin glided past the small vessel, its dark eye observing the old fisherman.

'You look plump and well fed,' Timeon told it. 'How about sharing your supper?' The dolphin rolled on to its back, its tail sending a spray of water into the air. Then it dived once more, vanishing into the deep. Timeon prepared his net. His eyes were gritty and tired, his muscles weary.

A light blazed across the sky. He looked up. Stars were falling in the east, white streaks on the sable. His breath caught in his throat at the beauty of the display. The sadness of a happy memory touched him. There had been flying stars on the night he wed Mina, so long ago. 'The gods have blessed us,' she had said, as they lay together on the beach, staring up at the sky.

Three sons they had raised, and five daughters. Blessing enough for any man, he told himself. He shivered. How swiftly the seasons fly. They seemed faster now than when he was young. As a child the days had been endless. He remembered how he had longed to be old enough to sail in his father's boat, to bring home the slick-fish, to be hailed as a great fisherman. The wait had been eternal.

Now the days were languorous no longer. They fled by, too fast to hold. Mina had been dead for five years. It seemed mere days since he had sat by her bedside, begging her not to leave him.

Timeon cast his net a third time, then slowly drew in the trailing rope. Almost instantly he knew he had a catch. Moving as swiftly as he could he gathered it in, dragging the haul back towards the low sides of the fishing boat. Scores of big silvers were thrashing in the net. Using every ounce of his once prodigious strength the old man heaved on the ropes. The fish spilled out, flopping round his feet.

Twenty copper rings' worth in one net!

His luck had changed at last. Timeon's heart was beating erratically now, and he sank back to his seat, sweat upon his face. Then he saw a ship gliding through the mist. It was strange to see a galley abroad at night. Probably a Dardanian vessel, he thought, patrolling the bay.

There was a man on the prow with a weighted line. Timeon watched the ship approach. No one called out a greeting, and the galley moved silently past him. Timeon rolled his net, and decided to head for home.

Then another ship appeared. And another.

Dawn light glowed red in the sky as more and more vessels broke clear of the mist.

Twenty.

Thirty.

Timeon sat quietly watching them. He saw armoured men on their decks. They gazed at him silently. The wind picked up, the mist dispersing. Timeon saw then that the sea was full of ships and barges. Too many to count.

And in that moment he knew who they were. The Mykene had come, and the world had changed.

Timeon's heart was beating like a drum now. Fear flowed

through him. How long, he wondered, before these dread warriors decided to kill him?

A galley came abreast of his little boat. He glanced up and saw a stocky man with a red and silver beard. Alongside him were bowmen, arrows notched.

'A good catch, fisherman,' yelled the man. 'You have been lucky tonight.'

Timeon's mouth was dry. 'I don't feel lucky,' he replied, determined that these killers would not see his terror.

The man smiled. 'I understand that. Bring your catch ashore, and I will see you paid for it. When you reach the shore tell them Odysseus sent you. No harm will befall you. You have my word on it.'

Odysseus signalled to the steersman, then the galley's oars dipped into the water and the ship moved on.

With a sinking heart Timeon hoisted his tattered sail, and set off after it.

XV

A legend is born

A STURDY WOODEN STOCKADE HAD BEEN BUILT ACROSS THE MOUTH OF
the narrow pass leading from the beach at the Bay of Herakles to
the plain of the Scamander. King Priam had ordered it built
to protect the pass. Fifty soldiers of the Heraklion regiment
guarded it. In the case of invasion their role was twofold: to hold
for as long as possible, while sending word to the city, and to
protect and guide to safety those of the king's family resident at the
cliff-top palace of King's Joy.

During the day the gates of the stockade were open, allowing
merchants to bring their carts down to the beach to collect the
catches of fish netted by the small fleet. At night the gates were
closed, and sentries patrolled the ramparts.

On this night two fresh sentries replaced their tired comrades at
the appointed time. The first was Cephas, by his own account a
clever man, his many talents overlooked by officers jealous of his
superiority. The second was a young recruit whom Cephas had
taken under his wing. The boy admired him, and Cephas missed no
opportunity to feed that admiration.

Tonight Cephas was tired. He had spent the day in Troy, taking
the youngster to a whorehouse used by soldiers. There they had
drunk wine and spent all the rings the boy possessed. Upon their

return to the stockade Cephas had promised the lad he would win it all back in a game of knucklebones. So instead of resting he had gambled until midnight. At first his luck was sour, but then it had changed, and he had emerged triumphant, a bulging pouch of rings at his belt.

The boy had watched the game. 'You were amazing,' he told Cephas. Then he had yawned. 'I am so tired.'

'Don't worry, lad, I've arranged for us to take the pre-dawn shift. We'll catch some sleep then.'

'We can't sleep on sentry duty,' said the boy nervously.

Cephas shook his head at the boy's naivety. 'You've a lot to learn about being a soldier. Don't worry. Stick by me and I'll teach you.'

Now on the ramparts Cephas waited, watching the door to the officer's hut. 'I'll wager you a copper ring he comes out before you can count to twenty,' he offered.

'I don't have any rings left.'

'Too late to bet anyway,' said Cephas with a smile. Down below the door had opened, and the officer came striding out, placing his bronze helm on his head. He walked across the open ground and climbed the narrow wooden steps.

'Cold night,' he said.

'Yes sir.'

The officer glanced out to sea. 'A lot of mist tonight.' He sucked in a deep breath. 'Keep a good watch, Cephas.'

'Yes sir,' answered Cephas. A good watch! All that ever moved in the darkness were rodents. This entire exercise was a waste of time. If the Mykene did come they would sail into the Bay of Troy and besiege the city. Anyone with a strategic brain understood that.

'Good man,' said the officer, turning and descending the steps. Cephas watched until the door of the hut closed behind him.

'Well, that's him taken to his bed,' he told the youngster. 'So let's stretch out and get some rest.'

'Are you sure?'

'He won't come out again. He never does. He'll have turned in by now.'

'Well, I am tired.'

'Hunker down, lad. We'll have a snooze and wake long before anyone else is up and around. Don't you worry. I sleep lightly. At the first sound of movement I'll be awake and alert. Twenty years of soldiering will do that.'

The boy stretched out on the wooden floor. Cephas took one last look out at the empty beach, then sat down with his back against the stockade wall.

He closed his eyes.

Achilles stood on the prow of the lead ship as the invasion force glided towards the Bay of Herakles under the starlight. Dressed in a dark tunic, two swords belted at his hip, he leaned on the rail staring through the mist, watching for any enemy galleys that might be patrolling.

He saw only a small fishing boat, and an old man casting his net. The fisherman looked up as the galley sailed past, then returned to his task. The old man seemed weary. Several of Achilles' warriors picked up bows. 'Leave him,' he told them. 'He is no threat.'

The galley sailed on. His shield-bearer Patroklos moved alongside him.

'No sign of Dardanian ships,' said the blond warrior. 'The falling stars showed the gods are with us, I think.'

'Perhaps,' replied Achilles, 'but I would sooner rely on our own strength of arms.'

Another warrior moved to the prow, the stocky, shaven-headed Thibo. As always before a battle he had braided his long red beard.

'You should not be risking yourself, my king,' he said. 'Not for the taking of a little fort.'

'You think I should hide on the ship?'

'It is not about hiding, Achilles,' argued Thibo. 'One well-aimed arrow and we'll have no king.'

'That argument could be used for any battle,' Achilles told him. 'Agamemnon wants the fort taken first, and the summer palace secured. He has given me and my Myrmidons that task. It is an honour. What king would allow his men to take risks he was not prepared to suffer?'

Thibo chuckled. 'I don't see Agamemnon here with us. Or Idomeneos. Not even Odysseus.'

'They are all on their way,' said Achilles. 'And none of them lacks courage. Most especially Odysseus.' He smiled. 'I saw him back on Ithaka, rescuing his lady. A sight I will not soon forget.'

Patroklos leaned in. 'Another battle you should not have taken part in. By the gods, Achilles, that was madness.'

'Aye, it was, but madness of the noblest kind. Is everyone prepared?'

'We all know what is expected of us,' said Thibo. 'We'll not let you down.'

'I know that, Redbeard.'

As the galley's hull scraped the sand Achilles leapt lightly down to the ground. He loped across the beach to the entrance of the pass. Keeping close to the cliff wall on the left he gazed at the stockade, some sixty paces distant. There was no sign of movement on the wall, which surprised him. According to the most recent reports there should be fifty men guarding this fort, and two sentries on the wall at all times. Moving back from the entrance he raised his arm. More dark-garbed warriors leapt down from the galley, making their way swiftly to where Achilles waited. Four were archers, and Achilles called the lead bowman to him. 'There are no sentries visible,' he whispered.

The man looked relieved. The plan had been for the archers to silently kill the Trojan sentries – no easy task when shooting arrows at night towards men in armour on a high wall.

'Stay back here with your men until the wall is taken,' Achilles told him.

The sky was starting to lighten now, the dawn not far off. Achilles swept his gaze over the waiting warriors. He had hand-picked them with care. They were fearless and able.

Gesturing for them to follow him, Achilles ran down towards the stockade. The tall lean figure of Patroklos came loping alongside on his right. To his left was Thibo.

As he ran Achilles continued to scan the stockade wall. Could this be a trap? Might they have a hundred archers lying in wait?

His mouth was dry. If so they would show themselves when Achilles and his men were about thirty paces from the wall. At that point the attackers would be at optimum killing range.

Achilles ran on. Fifty paces to go. Forty.

Thibo cut across him from the left. Patroklos moved in from the right. They too had estimated the killing range and were forming a shield in front of him.

For the next few paces Achilles' heart was pounding, his eyes raking the ramparts, expecting at any moment to see archers rearing up, bows bent, bronze-headed shafts notched to the string.

But there was no movement, and the Thessalian force reached the foot of the stockade. Achilles swung towards Patroklos, who was standing with his back to the wall. The slim warrior nodded, cupped his hands and steadied himself. Achilles lifted a foot into the linked hands, then levered himself up. Using the wooden wall for balance he stepped up again, this time to Patroklos' shoulder.

He was just below the parapet now. Straightening his legs he glanced over the battlements. Two sentries were asleep a little way to his right. Climbing smoothly to the ramparts he drew both swords and moved quietly towards the sleeping men. In the last of the moonlight he could see that one of them was little more than a boy.

Which was all he would ever be.

Achilles plunged his sword into the lad's neck. The dying boy gave a low, gurgling groan. The second sentry opened his eyes. He saw Achilles and tried to cry out. Achilles slammed his second blade into the man's throat with such force that it cut through the spine and buried itself in the wooden wall beyond.

Dragging the sword clear, Achilles ran down the rampart steps to the gate. It was held closed by a thick bar of timber. Putting his shoulder to it, Achilles lifted it aside and opened the gates.

Silently the warriors entered the barracks building, creeping forward to stand alongside each bed. Achilles waited at the door until all the men were in place. Lifting his hand he gave the signal to ready themselves. Swords glinted in the gloom, blades poised over fifty doomed men.

Achilles' hand slashed downwards. Fifty swords plunged home. Some of the victims died without ever waking, others cried out and struggled briefly. None survived.

Walking from the barracks Achilles made his way to the gates. He could see sailors from his galley bringing armour, helms and shields for his warriors. Beyond them more soldiers were gathering on the beach. Two sailors approached him, bearing his armour and shield. Achilles strapped on his black breastplate, and settled the shield in place on his left arm.

He glanced up. High on the cliffs above was King's Joy.

According to the spies it was still the residence of Paris and Helen. Agamemnon had ordered that Helen be captured, Paris and the children put to death. Achilles understood the need for the children to be slain. If allowed to live they would – when grown – seek blood vengeance against the men who killed their father. Killing the children of enemies was regrettable but necessary.

Achilles fervently hoped Helen and her children were absent tonight.

High in the palace of King's Joy Helen lay awake in her bed listening to her husband pace the floor. These nights Paris scarcely slept, and she listened to the soft, relentless sound of his bare feet padding back and forth on the rugs of the antechamber.

Helen sighed. She loved her husband dearly, but missed the quiet scholarly young man she had married, long before this dreadful winter with its constant rumours of war and invasion, long before the death of Dios, which had changed Paris beyond all recognition.

When they met four years ago, Helen was a refugee from Sparta. Timid and quiet, she had been terrified in this strange foreign city, with its haughty jewelled women who looked with disdain at her plain clothes and plump little body.

Brought up in the harsh life of the Spartan court, raised among boys and men whose only thoughts were of war and conquest, Helen had found Paris delightfully different. His shyness hid a wry sense of humour, and his curiosity about the world was entirely at odds with the young men she was used to. He taught her to read and write, for he was gathering a scriptorium of documents from all the lands of the Great Green. He pointed out to her the different-coloured birds which flew over Troy, and explained how they travelled from land to land with the seasons. He had a water tank made of marble and silver and brought her sea horses to keep in it, so together they could watch the births and deaths and daily lives of these small creatures. When they had married, quietly, she was full of joy and felt the rest of her days would be blessed by the gods.

The blackness of night outside was turning to dark grey and Helen listened for movement in the next bedroom, where her two children were sleeping. Three-year-old Alypius rarely slept past dawn and, once awake, he always roused his little sister Philea. But the silence now was total, apart from the soft pad of bare feet.

Throwing back the covers she pulled a warm shawl round her shoulders, then stepped out into the antechamber.

Paris was still dressed in the heavy brown robe he had been wearing the previous day. His head was down and he failed to notice her.

'You should rest, my love,' she said, and he looked round. For a heartbeat his face looked gaunt and grey and exhausted. Then he saw her and his features lit up.

'I couldn't sleep,' he said, coming over to her and taking her in his arms. 'I keep dreaming of Dios.'

'I know,' she said. 'But the dawn is coming and you must have some rest. I will sit with you and hold your hand.'

He slumped down on a chair and she saw, with despair, his face fall into its familiar lines of grief and guilt.

'I should have done something,' he said for the thousandth time.

Over the winter she had found only three ways to reply. 'You are not a soldier.' 'It all happened so quickly.' And 'There was nothing you could have done.' But this time she said nothing, merely held his hand.

She glanced out of the balcony doors, where the darkness was fading towards dawn, and a movement caught her eye. She frowned. 'Look, my love, what's that?'

Paris followed her gaze, then they both stood and walked, entranced, on to the balcony. The dark sky to the east was alive with hundreds of bright lights dropping towards the land. Each appeared then disappeared in a flash.

'They are moon fragments,' he told her, his voice full of wonder.

'Are they dangerous?' Helen shot a nervous glance back towards the room where her children slept.

He smiled, for the first time in days. 'Most people believe the moon is Artemis' chariot, but I think it is a hot metal disc which throws off these splinters. Sometimes they stay in the sky and we call them stars, but some fall to earth, as these have. It is a lucky omen, my love.' He put his arms round her and she could feel the tension easing from him. 'They are far away, and will not harm us.' He yawned. 'Perhaps I will sleep now for a while.'

She sat on their bed and held his hand, daydreaming, as the sky grew brighter and the palace started to wake. In the courtyard far below someone dropped a piece of heavy pottery, which smashed amid loud curses, and within moments Helen could hear her son scrambling out of bed next door. There was silence for a long while, and she wondered what he was up to. Then she heard cries of alarm from a distance, and Alypius came running into the room, dressed in only his nightshift, his dark hair flying, a look of excitement on his face.

'Papa, Papa, there are ships! Lots of ships!'

'Sshh! Papa's sleeping.' Helen dropped Paris' hand and put her arms round the boy.

He squirmed away. 'Come, you must see! Lots of ships!'

Then fair-haired Philea came toddling into the room clutching a ragged doll made of blue cloth. 'Thipth!' she lisped.

Paris awoke and sat up groggily. 'What is it?'

'It is nothing, husband. They have seen some winter ships. It is nothing.' But in the distance she could hear shouts and the cold clash of metal and her heart was suddenly clutched by dread.

Paris rose and walked out to the balcony. As he looked to his left he gasped, and Helen saw him start to tremble. She ran to his side. Far below lay the Bay of Herakles, normally brilliant blue in the dawn light. Now the bay and the wide sea beyond were filled with ships as far as the eye could see. Scores were already drawn up on the sandy beach, and hundreds more were heading east towards them out of the light sea mist.

The sandy beach was full of armed men, and a solid line of them was making its way up towards the palace. Dawn light sparkled off their helms and spear-tips. Helen could see they had already over-run the defensive stockade of the beach garrison.

She leaned over the balcony wall. Directly below them was the main palace courtyard. Soldiers and servants were running to defend the gates. Even as she watched she heard the solid boom of a battering ram against timber.

'There are thousands of them,' she whispered in horror. 'The children . . .'

She looked at Paris and saw despair in his face, a hint of mad-ness in his eyes. 'I must go,' he cried. He stumbled into the anteroom and took two swords from the wall.

Helen caught hold of him. 'You are not a warrior,' she implored. 'They will kill you.'

'They will kill me whether I am a warrior or not,' he said.

'We can escape together,' she begged him, her hands to his face. 'If we can get to the north terrace, quickly, we can climb down from there and make for the Scamander before they surround the palace.'

'Escape?' he said. 'Yes, you must escape!' Pushing her aside he darted from the room and she heard him running down the stairs.

Helen paused for a heartbeat, her mind dazed and slow, unable to take in the sudden awful fate that had overcome them. Then she took Philea in her arms, grabbed Alypius by the hand and started downstairs after her husband. The north terrace was her only hope. It was far from the main gates where the enemy was break-ing in. The terrace looked towards Troy, and beyond it the land shelved steeply down, covered with scrub and undergrowth, towards the plain of the Scamander. She could get the children down there and hide them, or even reach the safety of the city.

On the next level down she heard the smashing and rending of timbers and she paused to look out of a window into the courtyard one floor below. The invaders were now pouring through a wide breach in the gates. Palace soldiers who ran to meet them fought desperately, but there were too few of them and they fell under the weight of numbers.

Then she saw Paris running out across the courtyard, waving his two swords. He was ignored at first, then a huge black-haired warrior turned and saw him. He stepped in front of Paris, who attacked him like a madman. His attack lasted mere heartbeats, and then the black-haired warrior thrust a sword through Paris' throat. Paris fell, his lifeblood gouting out from his neck. He trembled for moments, then lay still, his bare feet sticking pathetically out of his brown robe.

An old servant, Pamones, who had served the royal family since the days of Priam's father, tried to defend the prince's body with a spear, but he was casually disarmed by the warrior. The man grabbed the old servant by his neck. In a lull in the fighting the warrior's voice drifted up to Helen's ears.

'Where is the princess Helen, old man?'

'In Troy, lord,' the man cried, pointing in the direction of the city. 'The lord Paris sent them there for safety.'

The soldier flung Pamones aside, then gazed up at the palace. Helen ducked back out of sight.

'What's happening, Mama?' asked Alypius, who could see nothing of the carnage below.

Hearing pounding feet on the floor below, she picked both children up in her arms, and fled up the stairs. The highest level of the palace was the square tower Paris had chosen for his scriptorium. There were shelves and drawers and boxes full of papyrus and hide scrolls. He and Helen had spent many happy days there organizing documents in Paris' own arcane method. In despair Helen looked around the tower room. There was nowhere to hide. In a daze she took the children out on to the shallow balcony, high above the jagged rocks at the base of the cliff.

'What's happening, Mama?' Alypius asked again, his small face creased with anxiety and fear. Philea was grizzling quietly, her blue doll held to her mouth.

Helen heard loud feet on the stairs and the door burst open. A Mykene warrior walked in. His head was shaved, his red beard braided. He brought the smell of the slaughterhouse into the room. Other warriors jostled in the doorway.

Helen clutched the children tightly and backed away. Four warriors approached her slowly, swords in hand.

She retreated across the balcony, her gaze fixed to the four men, until she felt her calves strike the low balcony wall. Carefully she climbed up on to it. The children stopped struggling in her arms. Alypius glanced over her shoulder to the deadly rocks far below. 'I am scared, Mama!'

'Hush now,' she whispered.

The powerful dark-haired warrior she had seen in the courtyard stepped out before her. He was helmless, and blood flecked his hair and armour.

'Princess Helen,' he said gravely. 'I am Achilles.'

Hope stirred in her labouring heart. Achilles was a man of honour, it was said. He would not kill women and children.

'Lady,' he said gently, sheathing his swords and holding out a hand to her. 'Come with me. You are safe. King Menelaus wishes you to return to Sparta. He will make you his wife.'

'And my children?' she asked, knowing the answer. 'The children of Paris?'

An emotion crossed his face, which could have been shame, and he lowered his eyes for a heartbeat. Then he looked up at her. 'You are young,' he said. 'There will be other children.'

Helen glanced down and behind her. Far below the sharp rocks looked like bronze spear-points in the dawn light.

She relaxed then, and felt all tension flowing away. Closing her eyes for a moment she felt the warmth of the rising sun on her back. Then she opened them again and gazed at the warriors.

No longer afraid, she looked each one in the eye, a calm lingering look, as a mother might look on wayward children. She saw their expressions change. They knew what she was about to do. Each one lost his look of hungry ferocity.

'Do not do this!' Achilles implored her. 'Remember who you are. You do not belong among these foreigners. You are Helen of Sparta.'

'No, Achilles, I am Helen of Troy,' she said. Hugging the children to her she kissed them both. 'Close your eyes, dear ones,' she whispered. 'Squeeze them shut. And when you open them again Papa will be here.'

Achilles darted forward, but too late.

Helen closed her eyes, and fell backwards into the void.

XVI

Battle for the Scamander

KALLIADES LEANED AGAINST A DRIPPING TREE TRUNK AND PEERED INTO the darkness in the direction of Troy. The rainy night was thick as a blindfold over his eyes. He turned back to where he could just see the hundred warriors sitting gloomily round sputtering campfires. Riding from Dardanos with all speed, they were merely half a day from the golden city, but had been forced to halt by the moonless night. They were all frustrated and angry, and only consoled by the fact that there would be no fighting at Troy until the dawn.

Kalliades had been a soldier since he was fifteen. He had been in hundreds of battles, had suffered the dry mouth and full bladder before a fight, had seen friends suffer the slow agonized death from a belly thrust or the poison of gangrene. It was the same for every man waiting in this woody glade. Yet they were all, to a man, desperate for the first glimmer of dawn so they could mount up, ride to Troy and take on the Mykene army. Many of them would die.

Perhaps they all would.

The messenger from Priam to the Dardanos garrison had arrived tired and travel-stained at Parnio's Folly. Banokles and Kalliades rode down to speak to him where he stood on the other side of the chasm. Banokles had ordered him to cross, and the man looked doubtfully at the single narrow span Khalkeus' workers had so far erected. But he was a royal Eagle and his head was high and his stride confident as he crossed the narrow bridge. Only as he stepped on to safe ground could they see the fear in his eyes and the sweat upon his brow.

'General,' he said to Banokles, who scowled, 'Troy is under attack! Agamemnon has landed hundreds of ships at the Bay of Herakles. King's Joy is taken and Prince Paris is dead. Our infantry are trying to stop them at the river Scamander. King Priam commands you to ride to the city's aid.'

Kalliades glanced at his friend and saw the excitement on his face.

'We'll ride immediately,' replied Banokles, not trying to conceal his delight. 'We'll leave a small force here and take my Thrakians.'

'Not the Thrakians,' said the messenger, lowering his voice as both Trojan and Thrakian soldiers started to gather. 'The king wants only loyal Trojan soldiers to come to the defence of the city. He said the Thrakians were to guard the fortress of Dardanos.'

Kalliades snorted. Had everyone in Troy forgotten he and Banokles had been Mykene soldiers only a few years previously? He gave orders that the messenger be given food and water, then said to Banokles, 'It is all very well to say "ride immediately", but how? A man can walk across this bridge, but we cannot take horses across. And it is an extra day's ride to go round.'

The stocky figure of Khalkeus, who had been hovering within earshot, pushed forward and said impatiently, 'It is a simple problem, easily solved. My workmen will fix a line of sturdy planks crosswise along the length of the bridge, widening it to the pace of a tall man. Then the horses can be blindfolded and led across in single file. It is quite simple,' he repeated.

'Will it take their weight?' asked Banokles doubtfully.

'Of course,' the engineer said irritably. 'It will take whatever weight I choose it should take.'

Kalliades glanced at the sky. 'How long will it take?'

'The sooner I stop answering stupid questions.' The red-headed engineer turned on his heel and started hurling orders at his workmen. Within moments men were sawing planks and others were running to fetch more timber.

Kalliades and Banokles had walked back to where Tudhaliyas waited quietly with his men, already dressed to ride.

'Will you join us in the defence of Troy?' Kalliades asked, though he guessed the Hittite's answer.

Tudhaliyas shook his head ruefully. 'No, my friend. And you would not want me to. If my men and I were to fight for Troy, then my father could never agree to come to the city's aid. As it is, I shall return and spread word of your plight, and maybe the emperor will send an army.'

'Priam might well prefer the aid of your three hundred men now, to a Hittite army camped at his gates some day in the future,' said Kalliades. 'That might seem more like a threat than the helping hand of an ally.'

Tudhaliyas smiled. 'Perhaps you are right. War makes friends of enemies and enemies of friends, does it not, Mykene?'

With that he turned and mounted his horse, and the Hittite warriors set off towards the north.

Banokles hawked and spat on the ground. 'Good riddance,' he said. 'Never liked the cowsons.'

Kalliades sighed. 'Those three hundred cowsons would have been very useful,' he said. 'As it is, it's just you and me and our fifty of the Horse.'

'I will ride with you, general, with my fifty,' said a voice.

The Thrakian leader Hillas, Lord of the Western Mountain, strode down the defile towards them. His hair and beard were braided, and his face was adorned with blue streaks in the Kikones fashion.

'Priam says the Thrakian warriors should stay here and defend Dardanos,' said Banokles reluctantly. 'I don't know why. Any one of you Kikones boys is worth two of his poxy Eagles.'

Hillas chuckled. 'We all know that if Troy falls, Dardanos is lost. Then the Kikones will never regain their homeland. I have pledged my allegiance to King Periklos and I will fight for him in Troy. My men will ride with you, whether we're wanted or not. Priam will not reject our aid when we stand before him with Mykene heads on our lances.'

Now, in the rain-dark wood Kalliades gave up wishing the dawn to come, and returned to the campfire where Banokles was lying on his back in his armour.

'We'll be in Troy tomorrow,' Banokles said happily. 'We'll have a good fight, kill a hundred of the bastard enemy, then I'll go home and see Red and have a few jugs of wine.'

'The perfect day,' Kalliades remarked.

Banokles lifted his head and turned to him, firelight glinting on his blond hair and beard. 'What's wrong with you?' he asked.

Kalliades lay down beside him on the wet grass. 'Nothing,' he said, and he realized it was true. He was cold and rain-soaked and hungry, facing a battle the next day against overwhelming odds, yet he felt a rare sense of contentment.

He smiled. 'I think we've spent too long together, Banokles,' he said. 'I'm getting more like you every day.'

He saw his friend frown in the firelight, and open his mouth to reply, but suddenly there was a commotion of stamping and neighing among the tethered horses. Some of the men climbed wearily to their feet to calm them down.

Banokles said, 'It's that big bastard black horse again, causing trouble. I don't know why we brought it with us.'

'Yes, you do,' Kalliades told him patiently. 'You were there when Hektor said the horse should be treated with honour as a hero of Troy. We couldn't leave a Trojan hero with Vollin and his Thrakians.'

As well as their own mounts, the small force from Dardanos was leading the last twelve of Helikaon's golden horses, three of them pregnant mares, and the great stallion which had jumped the chasm with Queen Halysia and her son on his back.

'We ought to call it something,' said Banokles thoughtfully. 'We can't just keep calling it "that big bastard horse". It ought to have a name.'

'What do you suggest?'

'Arse Face.'

There were quiet chuckles from the listening men round the campfire. 'You call all your horses Arse Face, Banokles,' said the rider sitting next to him.

'Only the good ones,' said Banokles indignantly.

'We should call it Hero,' suggested Kalliades.

'That's it, Hero,' said Banokles. 'Good name. Perhaps he'll be less trouble now he's got a name.' He shifted uncomfortably where he lay and with a grunt of satisfaction pulled a small branch out from under him. 'By Ares, that was a leap though, wasn't it? Would you have made it, do you think?'

Kalliades shook his head. 'I wouldn't have even tried.'

'I wish I'd seen it,' Banokles mused. 'It must have been a sight. With the queen and the boy on his back.' He was silent for a moment. 'Shame she died. The queen, I mean. After a jump like that.'

Kalliades thought how Banokles had changed over the years. In the days when they had first fought together he had talked only of drinking, rutting, and battles he had fought. His proudest boast was that he could piss up a tree higher than any man.

But the last few years had mellowed him. Kalliades knew his marriage to Red was responsible. He adored his wife and made no secret of it. His ambition now, he often told Kalliades, was to win the war and retire with honour from the Trojan Horse and start a small farm with Red. Kalliades could not see him as a farmer, but he never told him so.

When the priestess Piria died Banokles had been genuinely saddened. He rarely mentioned her, though once, when Kalliades did, Banokles said shortly, 'She died in battle saving her friend's life, didn't she? What any warrior worth the name would do.' Then he would say no more.

And here he was, Banokles One-ear, speaking with respect of a dead woman he had never met.

'General!' Kalliades was pulled from his reverie by a soldier's shout. 'Dawn's coming! We can ride!'

Echios the Rhodian hated blood. Mixed with mud on the flat plain of the Scamander it was slippery and treacherous. Yet drying on the hilt of a sword it stuck like horse glue and made the weapon hard to handle.

A fifteen-year veteran of Troy's Scamandrian regiment, Echios had fought in the distant south in Lykia, as far east as Zeleia, and in the snowy northern mountains of Thraki, but he'd never thought he'd be facing an enemy army in front of the golden city.

A sword flashed for his face. Swaying to his right, Echios swept up a vicious two-handed cut that glanced off the edge of the enemy's shield and smashed into his cheek. The soldier was punched from his feet. Echios stepped over him.

At first light the Scamandrians had engaged the Mykene phalanx south of the river. The Mykene veterans were heavily armoured and in tight formation. There was no give in them, and step by step through the long morning they had pushed the Trojan forces back towards the river bank. The Scamandrians were fighting on the right, the Heraklion regiment to the left. The bastard Heraklions were the first ones to give, Echios thought, and the day would have been lost except for a near-suicidal cavalry charge. A hundred Trojan Horse, the last in the city, smashed into the flank of the Mykene phalanx, a huge man on a great charger at their head. Echios and the beleaguered defenders cheered as they saw it was Antiphones, the king's fat son. That side of the phalanx crumpled and the Trojan infantry rushed in, hacking and cutting. Since then it had been steady hand-to-hand slaughter. The Trojans were gaining back ground, step by bloody step.

A Mykene warrior slashed wildly at him, off balance in the mud and blood, and Echios dodged the cut, deflecting it off his shield. Mykene armour rose high round the throat, so the Trojan dropped to one knee under his shield and speared his sword up into the man's groin. As he fell his helm came off. Echios, leaping up, chopped him across the brow, scattering his brains. Echios stepped over him.

He risked a glimpse to his right, where his little brother Boros was fighting. He could not see him, but it was hard to tell one blood-covered warrior from another. Echios worried about his brother. He had suffered a sword cut to the head in a skirmish in

Thraki and could not see well out of his left eye. Boros had told no one, fearing losing his place. So Echios had found him a tower shield. It was an old-fashioned piece of equipment, and the other men laughed at him, but it protected his left side better than any round buckler. He wondered if the boy was still alive.

A blood-drenched figure stepped in front of him, a Thessalian by his fancy armour. Echios deflected the sword thrust on his shield, then drove his blade into the Thessalian's neck. Fancy armour but no neck protection, he thought, as the man fell in front of him, his lifeblood pumping from his throat.

An enemy stumbled to the mud in front of him with a great wound in his thigh. Echios plunged his sword into the man's face. He shuddered and lay still.

A huge Mykene ran at him. He was fast and powerful and the speed of his attack surprised Echios. Their blades met time and again, and Echios was forced back. The Mykene grinned at him arrogantly. Again he attacked and Echios sent back a savage riposte that opened a wound in the man's cheek. Now it was Echios pushing forward, but the Mykene parried each stroke. Suddenly the Mykene stepped in, their blades clashed and the Mykene sent a right hook at Echios' face. Echios grunted and fell back, stumbling in the mud. The Mykene swept his sword at Echios' head. Echios dodged down and lanced his sword up into the Mykene's belly. As the enemy soldier fell, Echios paused for a breath then stepped over his body.

He realized his sword was getting blunt. He always carried a spare on his back, but he'd used that already. He'd have to watch out for a sharper one. After all, there was a chance he'd meet Achilles the Slayer. Everyone knew he was out there somewhere. Look for the thick of the fight, they said; that's where he'll be. Just like Hektor, thought Echios. And we could do with *him* right now. He'll be here in five days, General Thyrsites said. With the Trojan Horse. Then these pigging Mykene won't know what hit them.

In front of him a Trojan rider he knew called Olganos had been unhorsed. He was bleeding from several wounds and seemed dazed. Two enemy soldiers ran at him. Echios hurdled the horse's dead body and lunged at one of the soldiers. His sword skewered into the man's armpit, and broke. He dived forward and swept up the man's fallen sword, rolling to his feet. The second man lanced his blade into Olganos' chest before Echios could hammer the sword into his skull. Olganos fell face down in the mud and lay still. Echios stepped over the bodies.

Above the clash of battle and the screams of the dying Echios heard the sound of hoofbeats. There was no enemy soldier facing him, so he risked turning to look back towards the river.

Galloping across the plain and thundering across one of the temporary bridges towards them came a troop of riders, led by a big warrior with golden hair and beard. He was waving two swords and his mouth was open in a battle cry as he rode. Behind him Echios could see Trojan Horse and painted tribesmen.

Reinforcements, Echios thought. About pigging time!

He turned back to the battle just in time to glimpse the killing blow that took out his throat.

Later that afternoon Banokles sat on the south bank of the Scamander washing blood and mud out of his hair and beard. The water trickled under his armour and its chill felt good against his hot skin. He had no wounds except for a nick on the arm from a deflected arrow. He was tired and hungry.

The river was red with gore, and men and horses floated there, moving swiftly down towards the bay. On the other bank he could see Kalliades walking among the wounded, dispatching enemy soldiers with his sword, calling stretcher-bearers to Trojans and their allies. Youngsters were running among the wounded and dead, collecting arrows and abandoned swords and shields. Overhead carrion birds gathered.

Nearby six men were trying to drag a dead horse out of the water. Banokles stood up angrily. 'Our men first, you morons!' he shouted, 'not the poxy horses!' The soldiers hurried to obey, and he slumped down again. His back ached and his stub of an ear itched intolerably. I'm getting too old for this, he thought.

A vast shadow fell across him and he looked up.

'Well done, Banokles,' said the king's son, Antiphones. Despite his bulky frame he also seemed to be carrying no wounds. 'Your ride was well timed, thank the war god Ares. We had the enemy on their back foot already. Your charge was the straw that broke the donkey's back.'

'Some donkey,' grunted Banokles. 'Best soldiers in the world, Mykene infantry.'

'Nevertheless, General, we were the better men today.'

'Not a general any more,' said Banokles happily. 'I was ordered to leave my Thrakians in Dardanos.'

'Yet some came with you regardless,' the prince said, amusement in his voice.

Banokles shrugged. 'So I'm no good as a general, then. Dismiss me.'

Antiphones laughed then, and his bass bellow rang out rich and clear over the battlefield.

'To me you are a hero, Banokles,' he said. 'I would grant you any wish that was in my power. But I fear the king may see things differently.'

'The king?'

'We are commanded to attend King Priam at his palace immediately, you and I. So find a horse and come with me.' He turned away.

'Not me,' said Banokles stubbornly, staying where he was. 'I'm going to see my wife first.'

Antiphones turned back. 'Ah, yes, I remember. You are married to Big Red, the . . . former whore.'

'That's right,' Banokles told him proudly. 'She's a good wife. She'll be missing me, and wondering where I am, with all this fighting going on down here.'

'Kings take precedence over wives,' said the fat man impatiently. 'Come with me.'

'What about Kalliades?'

'By Hades, man,' Antiphones exploded in exasperation. 'Who is Kalliades?'

'He's my fr— my aide. Over there.' He pointed in the direction of the battlefield.

'You can send for your aide when you have spoken to Priam. Now, come with me before I have you arrested and brought to the king in chains.'

During the slow ride up to the city Banokles looked longingly down the Street of Potters where his small white house was located. He wondered if Red was there now, waiting.

At Priam's palace he and Antiphones dismounted and entered the *megaron*. Banokles looked around with interest. It was the first time he had been there since the palace siege when he and Kalliades had been among the besiegers. He remembered with nostalgia the battle on the stairs, the great Argurios, unconquerable, turning back the Mykene invaders with relentless strength and skill. Banokles rubbed the scar on his arm where Argurios' sword had punched through it. He remembered the arrival of Hektor, godlike in his power, and the shield wall where the invaders planned to make their last stand. Then their mysterious retreat to the ships, and the screams of Kolanos.

Banokles smiled grimly. That was a day to remember all right.

When the king came down the stairs Banokles' eyes narrowed. He had last seen Priam in a parade at summer's end. Then he had looked strong and powerful, waving to the troops from his golden chariot. The change in him now was shocking. Priam was a frail old man, leaning on his aide's arm on one side, and a wooden staff on the other. His face was white as papyrus and his steps uncertain. His aide, Polydorus, helped him to his throne and the king sat down wearily, staring at the stone-flagged floor. Behind him stood a scrawny man Banokles knew was the chancellor Polites. Six Royal Eagles flanked the throne.

Finally Priam looked up. When he spoke his voice was cracked and feeble.

'So this is the great Banokles, the hero who never loses, who turns the battle with every charge. Do you not kneel before your king, General Banokles?'

Banokles stepped forward. 'I was taught soldiering as a Mykene, Priam King. In Mykene lands we do not kneel before our kings. We show our loyalty in our every action.'

The king smiled thinly. 'It might not be wise to remind me you once fought in this *megaron* with every intention of killing me. But for the hero Argurios you would have been slaughtered where you stood, along with your fellows.'

'Well,' said Banokles, 'you see, Argurios was Mykene, as you know . . .'

'Enough!' The king's voice thundered out, suddenly full of power. 'You are not here to debate me, soldier! Now,' Priam leaned forward in his throne, 'my son Hektor gave you leadership of the Thrakians because you gathered a loyal army in your retreat across Thraki. It seemed to me then a mistake to put a fool in charge. But now it appears Hektor was right and you are a lucky fool.'

Banokles opened his mouth to speak, but Priam silenced him. 'Be quiet and listen, soldier! My general Thyrsites, the idiot, got himself killed in the battle today. So I need a new general for the Scamandrian regiment. I'll take a lucky fool before an unlucky genius any day. So you are a general again, Banokles, general of the finest infantry force in the world.'

'Yes, but I think . . .' Banokles started.

The king stood up angrily. His rage had rejuvenated him and Banokles could now see the powerful man he had once been. 'If you argue with me again, General Banokles, I will have my Eagles kill you where you stand!'

There was an angry silence, then Banokles said mildly, 'What about Kalliades?'

The king frowned. 'Kalliades? I know that name. Ah yes, the tall soldier who took command of the Mykene invaders after the arrest of Kolanos. What of him?'

'He's my friend.'

Antiphones stepped in hastily. 'He is the general's aide, Father.'

'Then he will continue to be his aide. Now,' he turned to his son, 'Antiphones, report.'

'The enemy have been forced back again to the earthwork they erected at the foot of the pass, Father. We calculate they lost at least a thousand over the two days of battle on the plain.'

'And our own dead?'

'Slightly less. Maybe seven hundred dead, and two hundred so grievously wounded they will not fight again soon, if ever. A hospital has been set up on the edge of the lower town, in the Ilean barracks. Many of our physicians and healers have moved there from the House of Serpents.'

'And the Ilos regiment?'

Antiphones shrugged. 'They are soldiers. They will rest wherever they can.'

Priam looked around him. 'And where is General Lucan? The Heraklions are not represented here.'

'The Heraklion regiment is still on the field. I thought it best to leave one general at the Scamander in case of further attack tonight.'

'Do you expect such an attack?'

'No.'

Priam nodded. 'My Hektor will be here in three or four days. We have only to hold until then. When the main force of the Trojan Horse arrives these western jackals will be driven back to the sea, their tails between their legs.'

Banokles saw Antiphones and Polites exchange a glance. Priam saw it too. He leaned forward in his throne. 'I know you think me an old fool, my sons. But my confidence in Hektor has never been misplaced. The Trojan Horse always prevails. It won at Kadesh, and it will win here. Agamemnon and his lackeys will be driven back to the pass. We will retake the pass, and King's Joy, then the enemy will find themselves trapped in the Bay of Herakles, with Hektor on one side and our ships on the other. We will pick them off like fleas off a dog.'

'At present, however, our fleet is trapped in the Bay of Troy, with Agamemnon's ships holding the Hellespont,' pointed out Antiphones. 'The Dardanian fleet was crippled in the sea battle off Carpea. And we don't know where Helikaon is.'

Priam dismissed the comment impatiently. 'When the *Xanthos* returns Aeneas will deal with the enemy ships. All fear his Fire Hurlers. He will destroy the fleet as he destroyed the one at Imbros, then he will break the blockade of the Hellespont.'

Antiphones shook his head. 'We cannot be sure the golden ship even survived the winter,' he argued. 'We have heard nothing since the turn of the year. We cannot rely on Helikaon.' He paused. 'You expect a lot from two men, even heroes like Hektor and Helikaon.'

The king rounded on him. 'Two men like them are worth a thousand of the likes of you! I despise you, all you nay-sayers and doom-mongers. My Hekabe warned me against you. Remember the prophecy, she said. Troy will prevail and be eternal.'

He sat back exhausted and for a while seemed deep in thought. The silence stretched, and Banokles shifted on his feet, anxious to be off.

When Priam spoke at last, his voice had become sharp and querulous. 'Where is Andromache? Bring her to me. I have not seen her today.'

Polites spoke for the first time. He placed his hand on his father's shoulder and said in a voice of great gentleness, 'She is not here, Father. She is aboard the *Xanthos* with Aeneas.' He glared at Antiphones, then said, 'Come, Father, you need your rest.'

'I need some wine,' retorted the old man, but he stood up uncertainly and allowed himself to be led back to the stone staircase.

Antiphones turned to Banokles with a sigh. 'By the war god Ares, I hope Hektor gets here soon,' he said.

Free at last, Banokles hurried from the *megaron*, climbed on his waiting horse and galloped back down through the city. The Scaean Gate, now closed all day as well as at nights, was opened for him, and he sped towards the Street of Potters, his heart full. His mind had already shrugged off the problems of the day, the burdens of leadership, and the battles that awaited tomorrow, in his eagerness to see Red.

He threw himself off his horse as he reached his home, and only then realized that a crowd had gathered at the small white house.

A neighbour, a potter called Alastor, ran up to him, his face pale. 'Banokles, my friend . . .'

Banokles grabbed him by the front of his tunic and looked round at the men's anxious faces, the women's red eyes and tear-stained cheeks.

'What's happening!' he thundered. He shook Alastor. 'What in Hades is going on!'

'It's your wife,' the man stuttered.

Banokles threw him to one side and rushed into the house. Lying on a sheet of white linen in the centre of the main room was Red. Her body had been washed and clothed in a white gown, but no one could hide the blue sheen to her face or the dark bruises round her neck.

Banokles fell to the floor beside her, his mind in shock, his thoughts in turmoil.

'Red.' He took her shoulders and shook her gently. 'Red!' But her body was stiff and cold under his trembling hands.

He stood, his face white with fury, and the people crowding round him moved back nervously.

'What happened? You, potter! What happened?' He advanced menacingly towards the frightened man.

'It was the old baker, my friend,' Alastor told him. 'The one who made the honey cakes she loved. He strangled her, Banokles, then opened his own throat with a knife. He is out there.' He gestured to the courtyard. 'He told his daughter he loved Red and couldn't live without her. He was leaving the city and wanted her to go with him, but she refused him. He asked her over and over, but she laughed at him . . .'

But Banokles wasn't listening. With an anguished roar he threw himself into the paved courtyard where he found the small form of Krenio lying on the ground, one of Red's gowns tightly gripped in one hand, a knife in the other. His blood had soaked the ground about his head.

Banokles tore the dress from the man's hand and flung it furiously to one side. Then he drew his dagger and drove it into the baker's chest. Shouting incoherently, tears running down his face, he plunged the knife over and over again into the dead man's body.

XVII

Hektor's ride

SKORPIOS WAS TIRED. NOT JUST FROM THE LONG DAY OF RIDING. HIS weariness was bone-deep. He was tired of battle, and tired of the war. He longed to see his father's farm again, and to sit at table with his family, listening to their mundane stories of lost sheep, or weevils on the vines.

He glanced down into the grassy hollow where his comrade Justinos, broad-shouldered and shaven-headed, was striking flint, sending glittering sparks into the dry tinder. A small flame flickered, and Justinos bent forward to blow gently. The fire caught and he carefully added a few more twigs.

The two riders were making late camp just beneath the top of a hill. Scouts for Hektor's Trojan Horse, they were ahead of the main army as it made speed to get back to Troy, crossing the Ida range on the well-worn route from Thebe Under Plakos to the golden city. They were expecting the rest of the force to catch up with them by nightfall.

Skorpios sat staring out across the darkening country to the northwest. The air was fragrant with the scent of evening flowers. Finally he sighed, and moved back down to the camp. Justinos glanced up at him but said nothing. He handed Skorpios a hunk of corn bread, and the two men ate in silence.

'You think Olganos will still be in Troy?' asked Skorpios, as Justinos spread his blanket on the ground, ready for sleep. The big man shrugged.

'There are only a hundred of the Horse in the city. They'll be in the thick of it every day until we get there. They may all be dead already.'

'He is tough, though,' persisted Skorpios.

'We are all tough, boy,' muttered Justinos, stretching out and closing his eyes.

'I want to go home, Justinos. I'm sick of all this.'

Justinos sighed, then sat up, adding more sticks to the blaze. 'We are going home,' he said.

'I mean *my* home. Far away from war.'

Justinos smiled grimly. 'Far away from war? There is nowhere on the Great Green that is far away from war.'

Skorpios stared at his friend. 'It must end one day, surely?'

'This war? Of course. Then there'll be another, and another. Best not to dwell on it. The land is quiet here, and we are safe for at least this night. That is good enough for me.'

'Not for me. I dread tomorrow.'

'Why? Nothing will happen tomorrow. We just carry on riding north, watching for ambush. Hektor will stop beneath Gargaron, as he always does, to sacrifice to Father Zeus. What's special about tomorrow?'

'Nothing. I don't know.'

'Then what is there to dread? Listen to me, boy, *now* is all there is. Yesterday is gone. Nothing we can do about it. Tomorrow is a mystery. Nothing we can do about that either, until we get there. Let Hektor and the generals worry about tomorrow. That's their job.'

'And Banokles,' Skorpios pointed out.

Justinos chuckled. 'Yes, and Banokles, I suppose. I'd feel sorry for the man, but anyone with the balls to marry Big Red should be able to cope with being a general.'

'Why would anyone marry a whore?' Skorpios asked.

'Now that is just plain stupid,' snapped Justinos. 'What has being a whore got to do with anything?'

'Would you marry a whore?'

'Why not? If I loved her and if she could give me sons.'

Skorpios looked at him in disbelief. 'But they are ungodly and impure.'

Justinos' eyes narrowed, and his face darkened. 'Ungodly? By the balls of Ares, I am glad I wasn't raised in your little village. You listen to me, Skorpios. My mother was a whore, my father unknown. I was raised among whores. A few were nasty, some evil, some grasping. But most were ordinary, like you and me. Many were loving, honest and compassionate. Just people doing whatever they had to in order to survive. Ungodly and impure? If you weren't my friend I'd ram your head against that tree trunk there. Now shut up and let me sleep.' He lay down once more, turning his back on his friend, and tugging his blanket over his shoulder.

Skorpios sat with his back against an oak tree, and dozed for a while. The moon was high in a clear sky when he heard the thunder of hoofbeats, hundreds of them, that told him Hektor's Trojan Horse had caught up with them. He kicked Justinos awake, and they both quickly lit prepared torches and stood holding them high. Within heartbeats they were surrounded by riders on horseback, dust kicking up around them, their armour shining in the moonlight.

Out of the darkness rode a huge warrior on a bay stallion. He leaned down towards them and his golden hair seemed to flicker in the torchlight.

'Justinos. Skorpios. Anything to report?' asked Hektor.

Justinos stepped forward. 'Nothing, lord. All we've seen all day are birds and rabbits, and some bear. It's as if the countryside is deserted.'

'It is deserted,' agreed the prince. 'I expected Agamemnon to mount an ambush on our route. He knew we would be coming. But it seems I'm wrong. Perhaps he has thrown everything he has at Troy.'

He sat back on his mount and looked up for a moment at the full moon. Then, raising his voice above the snorting of horses and quiet conversation of the riders, he shouted, 'No stopping now, lads! We ride through the night!'

Justinos and Skorpios quickly began to pack their equipment as cavalry surged around them.

'It seems, boy,' Justinos said quietly, 'tomorrow has arrived earlier than we expected.'

The time passed with excruciating slowness as the bloody slaughter on the plain went on. For Kalliades days were starting to blur together. When it was light he fought alongside the men of the Scamandrian regiment, the Sword of Argurios hacking and slashing at the enemy. There was no place here for swordfighting skills, just bloody butchery. At night he rested where he could, sheer exhaustion tumbling him into sleep despite the moans and cries of the dying and the thick stench of hundreds of burning corpses in his nostrils.

On the fifth morning he awoke to find dawn had long passed and the sun was high in the sky, yet the enemy had still not attacked.

Weary beyond words, he sat his horse alongside Banokles, Antiphones and General Lucan of the Heraklion regiment, a small wiry man with bandy legs, his hair grizzled and his face deeply lined, who had served his king and Troy for time out of mind.

Kalliades looked at Banokles, who sat staring at Agamemnon's armies, his face expressionless, his blue eyes as cold as winter rain. When Kalliades heard of Red's death he had rushed to his friend's house and found him slumped in the corner of the courtyard, his eyes fixed on the mutilated corpse of the old baker. Banokles had not spoken, but had stood and left his home without looking again at his wife's body. He had returned to the battlefield and sat all night by the river waiting for the enemy's attack. Since then he had fought like a man possessed, his two swords dealing death wherever he went. The Scamandrians worshipped him as Herakles reborn and they fought like demons beside him, awed by his untiring and relentless attacks on the enemy.

'Here we go,' Banokles said, his voice flat, and Kalliades turned back to the field of battle, where the enemy armies were forming up. In the centre was the Mykene phalanx, but narrower than they had seen it before, and flanked on each side by another infantry phalanx, then cavalry at the wings.

'Thessalian infantry and cavalry on our left. Achilles will be there with his Myrmidons,' said old Lucan, squinting. 'I can't make out who they've got on the right today.'

'Kretans,' said Banokles. 'Kretan horsemen, anyway. Gutsy bunch, they are. I'm surprised they haven't thrown them in before.'

'They may have just arrived,' rumbled Antiphones. 'Ships are sailing into the Bay of Herakles every day, and not just with food and weapons. Mercenaries are coming from all over the Great Green in the hope of winning some of Priam's treasure. That's probably a mercenary regiment on the right.'

'They'll be fresh,' said Kalliades. 'Fresh horses too.'

'Fresh or not, they'll be dead come nightfall,' said Banokles, stepping down from his horse. Kalliades followed him.

Antiphones leaned down from his mount. 'A general should start a battle at the rear of his army,' he said tiredly, as he had said each day. 'He cannot judge the disposal of his forces from the front.'

Banokles ignored him as usual and walked along the ranks to his left to stand at the head of his Scamandrians. The foot soldiers cheered, and Kalliades saw some of the weariness fall away from them as the chant rippled down the infantry front line: 'Banokles! Banokles! Banokles! BANOKLES!'

Kalliades looked up at Antiphones and shrugged, then went to take his place beside his friend, drawing the Sword of Argurios. Antiphones and Lucan turned their horses and guided them back through the ranks.

Antiphones had ordered the Scamandrians to take the left of the field, the Heraklions the right. At the centre were the elite infantry, Priam's Eagles, and behind them a force of three hundred Phrygian archers, flanked on each side by the Ilos regiment and mercenaries from Maeonia. The tiny force of surviving Trojan Horse was left in reserve on the far side of the river. Most carried wounds, as did their mounts.

Kalliades saw sunlight glittering off armour as the Mykene army began to move towards them. He settled his helm into place, and checked the straps of his breastplate.

'What are we waiting for, lads?' shouted Banokles and, drawing both his swords, he started to run towards the enemy.

At the rear Antiphones waited until he could see the faces of the advancing Mykene; then he gave an order and the Phrygian archers bent their bows to rain arrows over the heads of their own troops and into the front lines of the oncoming soldiers. Just three times they shot then, as ordered, they retreated across the wooden bridges to the north bank, ready to halt the enemy if they reached the river.

Kalliades, running side by side with Banokles towards the phalanx, saw the arrows soar over their heads and glance off Mykene shields and helms. But some cut through, gouging into faces, arms and legs and causing the advancing line to falter as men stumbled and fell.

As he ran Kalliades found new strength. He focused on a gap in the phalanx where one soldier had been brought down by an arrow, leaving the comrade on his left unprotected. Kalliades screamed wordlessly as he ran at the man, hacking at his sword arm. The blow half severed the arm above the elbow, and Kalliades ripped his sword up again, catching the Mykene in the face as he fell forward.

A Mykene warrior swung his sword at Kalliades' head. It glanced off the edge of his shield. Kalliades lanced the Sword of Argurios at the man's throat, but the blade was deflected off his heavy armour. Kneeling, he parried a blow from the man's sword, then hacked at his thigh. A bright fountain of blood gouted out. Falling to his knees the Mykene desperately swung at Kalliades again. Kalliades stepped lightly back, leaving the man to die.

For a moment he was clear of the action. He saw Banokles had fought his way into the thick of the battle. The blond warrior was surrounded on three sides by the enemy, both Mykene and Thessalians.

Kalliades started in that direction, but from the corner of his eye he saw movement to his right. He blocked a savage thrust, slashing his sword across the man's neck in a deadly riposte. Glancing left, he raised his shield just in time to block a blow from an axe. He lost his footing in the mud and the axeman swung at him again. He rolled away desperately.

Then a Trojan soldier leapt at the axeman, slashing at his arm, catching him a glancing blow on his mailed shoulder. The axeman turned to the young soldier and swung the axe at his head. The Trojan carried an old tower shield, and the axe was deflected off its edge. As the axeman raised his weapon again Kalliades leapt up and thrust his sword between the man's back ribs. He wrenched it out as the man fell heavily.

Kalliades nodded his thanks to the youngster with the tower shield and turned back to see where Banokles was. He could not see him, and glanced around. Even in the midst of a battle Kalliades could feel the way it was going, and he knew the Trojans were making ground.

He swept aside a sword thrust to his belly from the right, and killed the man with a lightning riposte to the throat.

A gap had opened up in front of him and again he spotted Banokles, fighting with controlled intensity, his two swords flashing and darting, keeping the surrounding enemy at bay. Kalliades ran towards him, hurdled a body and slashed his sword across the raised arm of a Thessalian soldier. The man stood for a moment, staring at his ruined arm. Kalliades lanced his sword into the Thessalian's throat.

He saw Banokles had lost one of his swords, so he picked up the Thessalian's blade and yelled, 'Banokles!' But in his full-faced helm Banokles did not hear him.

Kalliades saw a Mykene kill his Trojan opponent, then turn to see Banokles' exposed back. Grinning, he raised his sword for a killing blow. Kalliades ran forward. But before the blow could fall, Banokles reversed his remaining sword and thrust it, without looking, into the man's belly.

Kalliades hacked his blade into the neck of one of Banokles' opponents. He saw Banokles notice him and threw him the new sword, then looked around for his next target.

Banokles shouted, 'Don't worry, there are enough for both of us!'

Then the two friends were fighting back to back, the pile of enemy corpses around them growing.

And the long morning wore on.

Kalliades knew the Scamandrians, fighting furiously, were slowly battling their way into the enemy ranks. But there lay the problem. The enemy cavalry on the wings, Thessalians and Kretans, would be trying to get round the sides of the Trojans and their allies, hoping to encircle them. Antiphones had only the small force of Trojan Horse and Zeleian cavalry to stop that happening.

In a lull in the fighting Kalliades paused for a breath. His sword arm was tired and his legs felt as if they could not carry him another step. He and Banokles and a dozen or so Scamandrians were deep in the enemy ranks now. Around them were scores of dead and dying, some Trojans, but mostly Mykene and warriors of Thessaly.

Banokles dispatched a heavily armoured Mykene with a deft thrust to the side, then paused too and glanced around to re-orientate himself. To their left they could see Trojan troops falling back in disarray. A giant warrior in black armour was cleaving into them, his swords flashing like lightning, his body moving with awesome power and grace compared with the tired soldiers around him.

'Achilles!' Banokles shouted to Kalliades, pointing his sword in that direction. 'That's Achilles!'

Through the eye-slits of his helm, Kalliades could see Banokles' face alight with anticipation. He nodded to him, and the two set out to fight their way towards the Thessalian king.

Then there was a deep rumbling sound, and the blood-sodden earth beneath them started to vibrate.

'Earthquake!' Kalliades heard someone yell, and the cry was taken up all around them. The fighting started to falter as soldiers on both sides felt the ground tremble under their feet.

Kalliades found two Mykene corpses fallen one on top of the other and, steadying himself with a hand on Banokles' shoulder, he climbed up on to them for a better view.

In the distance to the south, along the line of the Scamander, he could see a great dust cloud rising. As it came closer to the embattled armies, the rumbling in the ground increased. Hoofbeats!

'It's not an earthquake,' Kalliades shouted joyfully to his exhausted men. 'It's the Trojan Horse!'

Skorpios bent low over his gelding's neck and felt the fear in his gut melting away as the Trojan Horse thundered across the plain towards the flank of the enemy.

Only moments before, the riders had trotted their horses out of the treeline on the north bank of the Scamander where the oak-covered foothills ended and the river flowed fast towards the Bay of Troy. There they had stopped, aghast at the sight of the battle being played out before them. Skorpios had only heartbeats to take it in, the plain south of the Scamander filled with battling warriors, indistinguishable in their blood- and mud-covered armour. Then Hektor had plunged his great warhorse Ares into the foaming river and the stallion had breasted his way across, followed quickly by the rest of the Trojan Horse. Once on the southern bank, Hektor had not even turned to see if his men were getting safely across the fast-flowing river before drawing his sword and kicking his mount into a gallop towards the battle.

Skorpios, with Justinos beside him, was in the fourth rank of riders, bearing down on the enemy's flank, his sword in his hand. Rubbing the swirling dust from his eyes, he could see the enemy's cavalry frantically trying to turn their mounts to face the new threat, but they were hampered by the bodies of horses and men littering the ground about them.

Hektor was already far ahead of the rest. His shield-bearers Mestares and Areoan were trying their best to catch up with him, but few horses could keep pace with Ares at full gallop.

The gallant warhorse hit the panicking line of the enemy with the force of a battering ram. One horse fell screaming as Ares broke both its front legs with the power of his attack. Hektor killed the injured beast's rider with a blow to the head, and others fell

231

back in disarray. Then the shield-bearers punched into the enemy ranks too, followed by the rest of the Trojan Horse.

Skorpios slowed his mount to wait his turn as the riders in front of him plunged into the action. Then a Thessalian rider, breaking through the Trojan line, swept towards him with lance levelled. Skorpios swayed to the left, and the lance-point slashed to his right, plunging into his gelding's flank. The animal reared in panic, giving Skorpios the height to plunge his spear down deep into the Thessalian's throat. Maddened with pain, the gelding reared again, then fell.

Skorpios jumped clear and, rolling, rose to his feet, drawing his sword. He ran at the first rider he saw, a heavily armoured Mykene. The man's lance thrust towards him, but glanced from his breastplate. Skorpios grabbed the lance and pulled and, caught by surprise, the Mykene slid off his mount. Skorpios killed him with a lightning sword cut to the throat. Then, sheathing his sword, he grabbed the man's horse by the mane and vaulted on to its back, lance in hand.

He looked round for someone else to kill. He saw the enemy cavalry had buckled under the attack and some wounded riders were trying to make their way back, away from the field. Snarling, he sighted and threw the Thessalian lance at a fleeing rider. It hit the man in the centre of his back, and he slumped from his mount. Skorpios punched the air in triumph.

'Skorpios!' He turned to see Justinos, his face and sword covered with blood. He was grinning. 'Still want to be back on your father's farm herding sheep?'

XVIII

A lucky fool

IN TROY, HIGH ON THE GREAT TOWER OF ILION, POLYDORUS WATCHED the battle unfold with a mixture of pride and deep aching jealousy. His hand itched to hold a sword, to wield it in defence of his king and his city. He watched his fellow soldiers far below chasing the enemy, and he longed to be among them.

After his heroic part in the palace siege four years before, in which he had aided Argurios, Helikaon and Dios in the defence of the stairs, the young Eagle had been quickly promoted, first to Priam's bodyguard and then, to his initial dismay, to the position of personal aide to the king.

'I do not want this!' he had stormed to his wife Casilla. 'It is not fitting for a soldier!'

'Hush,' she had said, 'you will wake the babies. It is a great honour, my husband. King Priam has chosen you himself. That means he trusts you. Perhaps he likes you. You are very likeable, Polydorus,' and she had smiled and tried to put her arms round his neck. But he had pulled away, not to be placated.

'I will be no more than a body servant, bringing him cups of wine, helping him get dressed.' He hushed his voice. 'I am a warrior, Casilla. I have fought for Troy since I was fifteen. This is . . . this is . . .' He lowered his voice again. 'This is an insult,' he whispered, as if someone might be listening in their small house hard by the western wall.

But as time passed Polydorus had become used to his role. True, he had to help the old king with his food, and aid him, soused in wine, to his bedchamber each night. But the young soldier was often privy to the secrets of the city as he sat in on discussions between Priam and his generals and counsellors, and the king had on many occasions sought his quiet, thoughtful views on dealings with foreign kings and the progress of the war.

And in the two years he had grown to care for the old man.

Now he turned to look at him. The king, dressed in thick woollen robes and a sheepskin cloak against the biting wind on the tower, was clutching the battlement wall with his bony hands and gazing avidly at the mêlée far below. His watery eyes were failing him, and he often barked a question to Polydorus about how the fighting was going. The young man saw the pride on his face and the tears in his eyes as Hektor and the Trojan Horse galloped into sight upon the plain.

'Hektor, my son,' he whispered, 'Agamemnon and his lickspittle kings will flee like the rats they are now you're back. They will be fighting each other to get back to their ships now, my boy.'

Polydorus had fought in Thraki years ago, but his experience on the battlefield was limited. Yet he knew Agamemnon could field many times the number of warriors Priam could. Hektor's surprise attack had won the day, he thought, as he watched the enemy soldiers streaming back towards the pass. But what of tomorrow?

He glanced past the king to Prince Polites, who was also swathed in sheepskin, his red-rimmed eyes watching the retreat anxiously. As if he felt the Eagle's gaze, Polites turned to him and gave a rueful smile. Polydorus knew Polites shared his opinion – the war is not over yet, not by a long way.

To his father, Polites said nervously, 'The battle was already going our way when the Trojan Horse arrived. Antiphones would have won the day eventually, Father, although with far more casualties.'

Priam spat on the floor at his feet. 'Pah! Antiphones is a fat fool.

And you are an idiot. You know nothing of war. You should be down there fighting, not up here watching from a safe distance.'

Polites flushed. 'I am not a warrior, Father. You chose me as your chancellor, to look after your treasury. I serve the city in my own way.'

Priam turned on him venomously. 'And how is the treasury, Polites? How well are you looking after it for me? Is it overflowing?'

Stung by the words, Polites said heatedly, 'You know very well, Father, we have to pay for this war. Your mercenaries down there have to be bought, and if they think we are losing they will demand even more of our wealth. We need metal to make bronze armour and weapons, but we have to go further and further afield, and our desperation puts the prices up. Now we badly need tin, and the *Xanthos* is our only hope.'

Strangely, this seemed to cheer the king up. 'The *Xanthos*, yes,' he said with pleasure. 'I trust Aeneas will be here soon, or he'll miss the fighting altogether. I was looking forward to seeing Agamemnon's ships in flame.'

Polydorus turned to look down at the battlefield again. The enemy were retreating to the earthwork they had built to protect the pass. Some seemed to be fleeing blindly, others retreating in good order. Mykene, he thought, or Achilles and his Myrmidons, his elite guard. They would not show their backs to their foes. He suddenly felt a moment of kinship with the disciplined soldiers, enemy or not. He remembered the Mykene hero Argurios holding the stairs, mighty in his courage, and dying with his love Laodike after saving Troy for her sake. Polydorus cherished that day as the best of his young life.

'My lord, perhaps we should return to the palace,' he suggested. 'It will be getting dark soon and the fighting will be over. Even my young eyes cannot see what is happening so far away and in failing light.'

The king sniffed. 'Then I must find myself an aide with better eyesight,' he said, but he allowed himself to be helped back to the stairwell.

As they cautiously descended the gloomy tower steps, Polydorus heard the old king repeating to himself, 'My Hektor is back, and the rats will flee to their holes.'

For two days there was little movement from the armies of Agamemnon. Driven back behind the reinforced earthwork that protected the landward side of the pass, the western forces showed no heart for a renewed attack.

The Trojans, who had put every soldier who could stand up into battle for days on end, took the precious time to honour their dead, to treat the wounded, and to sleep. Hektor was tireless, laying defence plans with his generals, touring the House of Serpents and the barracks hospital to encourage his wounded and dying men, and walking the field of battle where the Trojan army lay in wait for Agamemnon's next attack. Kalliades could see the grey sheen of exhaustion on his features when they met on the plain of the Scamander on the third day.

'You need rest, Hektor,' the old general Lucan told him, as if he heard Kalliades' thoughts. 'Troy needs all your strength for the coming battles.'

Hektor said nothing, and Lucan went on, 'And we are too close to the enemy lines. A well-placed arrow could find you and end all our hopes.'

Hektor and Lucan, with Banokles and Kalliades, stood a mere hundred paces from the enemy earthwork, now bristling with sharpened stakes to deter an attack by riders. The massive bulwark formed a semicircle protecting the mouth of the narrow pass. On the cliffs above the pass and on the white walls of King's Joy the Trojans could see the glint of armour as enemy warriors watched and waited.

'What are you, his mother?' asked Banokles irritably. He made no secret of the fact that he disliked the old general, and Kalliades thought the feeling was mutual.

Lucan smiled thinly, and his eyes were cold. 'If you had ever met Hekabe the queen, Mykene, you would not ask such a foolish question.'

Hektor was staring up at the cliffs, and he appeared not to hear.

Then he said, his voice distant, 'I will not die from an arrow wound, General.'

'Did his soothsayer tell King Priam the manner of your death?' asked Lucan, his tone sceptical.

Hektor visibly shook off his reverie, and clapped the general on the shoulder. 'No, old friend, but Agamemnon would ensure an archer who killed me would suffer a cruel and lingering death. He has other plans for me. He would see me shamed and laid low in public, by Achilles or another champion.'

'Ajax Skull-Splitter is here. I saw him in the thick of it,' said Banokles helpfully.

Kalliades nodded. 'I saw him too. Killed two of our men with one sweep of that great broadsword.'

'Still carrying that old tower shield too.' Banokles' face, normally grim these days, lightened at the memory. 'Big heavy thing. No one else was strong enough to carry it all day. Like an ox, he was. Still is, I suppose.'

Hektor suddenly threw his head back and laughed, and many of the soldiers resting nearby smiled, the sound was so infectious. 'I am sure Agamemnon has many champions anxious to take me on, Banokles. I have heard of Ajax. He is a mighty warrior.'

Thinking of Ajax brought to Kalliades' mind the young soldier who had saved his life. He asked, 'Does anyone know the name of a young Trojan who also carries a tower shield?'

Hektor said without hesitation, 'Boros. He and his brother are from Rhodos, although their mother was Trojan. The brother, Echios, is dead, I'm told. Both Scamandrians.'

There was no reproach in his tone, but Kalliades felt foolish. He was aide to the general of the Scamandrians, yet he knew few of his soldiers. Hektor could greet every man fighting for Troy by name, and he knew the names of their fathers. Only the mercenaries from Phrygia, Zeleia and the Hittite lands were unknown to him.

Lucan pointed up towards the pass and asked impatiently, 'When will we strike them, Hektor?'

Kalliades and Banokles glanced at one another. They had all been present that morning in the Amber Room when Priam had demanded an immediate attack on the pass and King's Joy.

Hektor, sitting at ease in a great carved chair, a goblet of water to his hand, had said patiently, 'Attacking the pass would be suicidal, Father. We could take the earthwork, though it would be costly in casualties, fighting uphill and unable to use the Trojan Horse. Then we could fight our way to the pass. But at the narrowest part of the pass there is only room for swordsmen to fight two abreast. Pitting our best warriors against theirs would win a stalemate. Except,' he went on, his words soft but emphatic, 'they hold the cliffs above. They would be raining arrows and spears down on our fighters. It would be suicidal,' he repeated.

The king strode up and down the great room, his robes swirling round bare feet.

'Then we must attack from the sea,' he said after a while. 'The *Xanthos* will use its Fire Hurlers to destroy Agamemnon's ships.'

'That would indeed be a gift from Poseidon,' responded Hektor patiently. 'If we could coordinate an attack from the sea at night, we could send climbers to take the cliffs, then King's Joy. But this is daydreaming, Father. Our ships are blockaded by Menados' fleets. They are useless to us in the Bay of Troy. And we do not know where the *Xanthos* is.'

'Wrecked by Poseidon on some foreign shore, perhaps,' added Antiphones. He had suffered a wound to his thigh, and was sitting on a couch with one leg raised on cushions. His face was pale and he was clearly in pain, his normally jovial manner subdued.

Priam stopped walking, and he stood as if deep in thought, his mouth working. Then he said craftily, a gleam in his eye, 'We will attack from the sea! The *Xanthos* will use its Fire Hurlers. We'll see how Agamemnon likes that!'

Losing patience at last, Hektor raised his voice. 'We do not know where the *Xanthos* is, Father! And my wife is on board. Would you send the ship into battle with Andromache at risk?'

Priam was startled by his son's unaccustomed tone, and his voice became querulous. 'Where is Andromache? Where is she? Is she here?' He gazed about him anxiously as the other men looked away, embarrassed.

Kalliades dragged his mind back to the present. Hektor was saying, 'We can keep the enemy bottled up in the bay indefinitely. They cannot fight their way out of the pass any more than we can fight our way in. Agamemnon may call himself the Battle King, but the other kings accept his command only as long as there are battles to fight. As time passes they will quickly tire of each other's company, and quarrels will start. They will all be heading home soon if there is no sign of the treasure of Priam they've been promised. Achilles loathes Agamemnon, I'm told, and is only here to avenge his dead father. Old Nestor is here because he fears Agamemnon's power. Only Sharptooth and his Kretans can be relied upon.'

'And Odysseus?' asked Kalliades. 'What of the Ugly King? He is a man of honour.'

'He is indeed,' responded Hektor heavily. 'He has thrown in his lot with Mykene, and will not be moved.'

Banokles had been watching the enemy forces. 'Look!' he said suddenly. 'What are they doing?'

Fifty or so soldiers had moved some distance forward from the narrowest part of the pass and were digging feverishly.

'Shall I tell our archers to shoot them?' suggested Lucan.

Hektor shook his head. 'They are too far away for accuracy, and it would merely be a waste of arrows. We cannot afford to lose more weapons.' His face became grave, and Kalliades guessed he was thinking about the perilous state of Troy's armoury. Khalkeus of Miletos had been recalled from bridge-building at Dardanos to take charge of the smiths labouring night and day to renew bronze swords and spears. Hektor had ordered that every man fighting for Troy should have a bronze breastplate and helm, even though it meant the elite troops had to go without bronze greaves and their shoulder- and arm-guards.

But the shortage of tin meant most of the forges were dark, and the bronzesmiths were being pressed into duty as stretcher-bearers and gate guards. Kalliades knew of a young bronze worker, a master of his craft, who was slaughtering injured horses and butchering them for meat. The whole city awaited the return of the *Xanthos* and its hoped-for cargo of tin.

'They're digging a second earthwork,' said Kalliades, shading his eyes.

'Let them,' replied Hektor, turning away. 'They are wasting their time and energy building more defences. I'm not going to attack them. And it will only hamper any attack they make.'

'But the king,' said Lucan angrily. 'He ordered you to attack, lord.'

Hektor looked the old man in the eye until the general dropped his gaze, then the king's son walked away.

Kalliades mounted his horse and rode slowly round the battlefield. The Ilos regiment was in the front line, drawn up in defensive squares, although the soldiers were relaxing, lying asleep or eating, staring into the flames of their campfires.

Behind them were the Scamandrians. He rode along their lines, looking for the telltale tower shield, but he could not find Boros. He wondered why it bothered him. In each pitched battle of his soldier's life he had been saved hundreds of times by a comrade's well-placed sword or shield, just as he had rescued others. Kalliades gave a mental shrug. Perhaps it was simply that he himself had once carried a tower shield, long lost during the palace siege. Now he favoured a round leather and wood buckler strapped to his arm which gave him more flexibility in battle. The front lines of the Mykene phalanx were armed with waisted tower shields of horn and hide, which worked well for them while they attacked like a giant tortoise, but gave them less manoeuvrability when fighting in a mêlée.

Having toured the entire army, noting Hektor's deployment of the regiments, the Eagles and the Trojan Horse, Kalliades returned to the front line of the Scamandrians to find Banokles. His comrade had stripped off his old battered breastplate and was lying on his back in his undershirt, gazing at the darkening sky.

Kalliades stepped down and handed his mount to a horse boy, then sat beside the warrior. Another youngster brought two cups of watered wine, and a plate of meat and corn bread. Kalliades thanked him.

240

He nudged Banokles and indicated the wine. Banokles sat up and took the offered cup. He sipped absently, and after a while he asked, 'Do you think they'll attack again?'

Kalliades glanced around him, but there was no one within earshot. 'Agamemnon's ambition and Achilles' need for vengeance will feed their determination,' he responded, 'at least for a time. Yes, I think they will attack again. But they must come through the pass, so they cannot use the phalanx. It will be a death or glory charge.'

'I always liked that one,' said Banokles. 'It worked for us. It might work for them. No soft-bellied pukers up there.' He gestured with his head in the direction of the pass.

Kalliades knew he was right. They had served with the Mykene army themselves for many years, and they were both aware the reputation of those grim warriors was well deserved.

The silence lingered awhile. It was a still night, and Kalliades listened to its sounds: the laughter of the men, the crackling of the nearby campfire, the sounds of horses shifting their feet and snuffling gently. Then he asked, 'What did the king say about generals? He'd rather have a lucky fool than an unlucky genius?'

Banokles frowned and scratched his thick blond beard. 'I think that's what he said. Great Zeus,' he said indignantly, 'only a king could get away with calling me a fool.'

'You're not a fool, Banokles. But you have always been lucky in battle.'

Banokles' face darkened and he said nothing. Kalliades guessed he was thinking about luck and about Red, so he stayed silent. Finally Banokles asked, 'How many battles do you think we've been in, Kalliades?'

Kalliades shrugged. 'I don't know. Hundreds.'

'But here we are, waiting for another one. Fit and strong and ready. We've neither of us been badly wounded. Just my ear, I suppose.' He rubbed the nub of his ear thoughtfully, then the scar on his right bicep where the Sword of Argurios had plunged through it. 'Now, we are great warriors, you and I. But we have been lucky, haven't we?'

He glanced at Kalliades, who nodded his agreement, guessing what he was leading up to.

'So why,' Banokles frowned, 'why in the name of Hades does someone like Red, who never did anyone any harm, die like that, when we're still here? What poxy god decided she had to die such a stupid poxy death?' He looked at Kalliades, who saw grief and anger in his friend's ice-blue eyes.

'Whores get killed sometimes,' Banokles went on. 'It's a perilous business, everybody knows that. But Red had given up her whoring when she got married. She just loved those honey cakes, and he was the only baker in the city who was still making them. That was the reason she asked him to our house.' There was another long silence. 'And he was only a skinny little runt.'

'He was a baker,' Kalliades said gently. 'He had strong arms and shoulders. Red would not have stood a chance.'

Banokles was quiet again, watching as the sky darkened to pitch black. Then he said, 'That priestess . . . Piria, Kalliope, whatever she called herself. That was a good death, saving her friend. And that queen on the black stallion. They both had a chance of a warrior's death. Even though they're women. But Red . . .' His voice tailed off. 'They say heroes who die in battle go to the Elysian Fields and dine in the Hall of Heroes. I've always looked forward to that. But what happens to the women who are heroes? Like Piria and that queen? And what happens to Red? Where does she go now?'

Kalliades knew his comrade was consumed by the grief of loss, and by frustration. Banokles had been used to the simple code of the warrior – if someone kills your friend or brother in arms, you take revenge. Yet how could he avenge himself on a dead baker?

Kalliades sighed. 'I don't know the answer to that, my friend. Maybe one day you'll find out. I hope so.' He added sadly, 'We've seen a lot of death, you and I – more than most. You know as well as I do death doesn't always come to those who deserve it.'

Kalliades' mind went back to the farm outside Troy, and Piria standing on the hillside, her blond hair shining in the light from the blazing barn, her face stern, calmly shooting arrows into the assassins who had come to kill Andromache. He had promised Odysseus he would take Piria to meet Hektor's wife, that he would see her safely to the end of her journey. How foolish of him, how arrogant, to think that he could guarantee her safety; as if love was all that was needed. The hurt in him had lessened over the seasons, but the doubt had grown. Had he really loved Piria? Or had Red been right?

He thought of the big whore's words to him long ago. 'We are so alike, Kalliades. Closed off from life, no friends, no loved ones. That is why we need Banokles. He *is* life, rich and raw, in all its glory. No subtlety, no guile. He is the fire we gather round, and his light pushes back the shadows we fear.'

He looked at Banokles, who had lain back again and closed his eyes, his profile barely visible in the firelight. A sudden trickle of fear ran through Kalliades. His old comrade in arms had altered a lot in the last few years. His wife's death had wrought more changes. Would he continue to be the lucky fool Priam called him?

'Help me. Please help me.' The cry came from a dying man, and the young healer Xander, pulling a cart full of severed limbs past the rows of wounded soldiers at the barracks hospital, hesitated before stopping. He pulled a bloodstained cloth over the cart to hide its grisly load, then went over to the man.

He was a rider. Xander, who had seen more injuries in his young life than most soldiers, could tell at a glance. One leg had been severed raggedly below the knee, perhaps by a blow from an axe. The other had been so badly injured, perhaps by an awkward fall from his mount, that it had been amputated high on the thigh. Both stumps were rotting, and Xander knew the man would die soon, and in agony.

He laid his hand gently on the man's shoulder. 'Are you Trojan Horse?' he asked.

'Yes, sir. Phegeus son of Dares. Am I dying, sir?' Xander saw Phegeus had been blinded by a blow to the head. He believed he was being visited by a commanding officer, not a freckle-faced healer of less than seventeen summers.

243

'Yes, soldier,' the youngster said gently. 'But the king knows you fought bravely for your city. Your name is on his lips.'

Xander had long since learned to lie glibly to dying men.

'Is he coming, sir? The king?' Phegeus reached out anxiously, grasping at the air, and Xander took his flailing hand and held it between his own.

'King Priam will be here soon,' he said quietly. 'He is proud of you.'

'Sir,' the man said confidentially, pulling Xander towards him. 'The pain . . . Sometimes I cannot . . . Sometimes . . . the pain is too bad. Let me know when the king comes. I would not have him hear me cry like a woman.'

Xander reassured Phegeus he would tell him when the king arrived, then left to deposit the contents of his cart outside the barracks. He stood for a moment, gratefully sucking in the fresh night air off the sea before going back into the hot, fetid building.

He found Machaon, the head of the house, washing blood off his hands in a barrel of water in the corner of the barracks. Machaon was still a relatively young man but now he looked like an ancient. His face was grey, the cheekbones jutting from pallid skin. His eyes were hollow and deeply shadowed.

'We need hemlock,' Xander told him urgently. 'We have brave men here whose courage falters when they face the torment of their wounds.'

Machaon turned to him and Xander could see the pain in the healer's eyes. 'There is no hemlock to be found in the city,' he responded. 'My prayers to the Serpent God have gone unanswered.'

Xander realized in a moment of dread that Machaon was not just exhausted, he was gravely ill.

'What's wrong, Machaon?' he cried. 'You are suffering too.'

Machaon stepped closer to the youngster and lowered his voice. 'I have had a vileness growing in my belly since the winter. I have tried herbs and cleansing honey, but it continues to grow.' His face suddenly spasmed and he bent over as if gripped by a clawing pain. When he stood up again his skin was ashen and beaded with sweat, his eyes unfocused.

'I have told no one, Xander,' he said shakily. 'I ask you to keep my secret. But I am too ill to travel down to the battlefield. You must go in my place.'

Despite his concern for his mentor, Xander's heart leapt. A chance to leave this place of death and go out in the fresh air, to deal with the lesser wounds of men who were not dying, not in agony. Hektor had decreed all wounded men who could walk should stay out on the plain in case of a further attack by Agamemnon's armies. Those with serious wounds likely to heal were carried to the House of Serpents in the upper city to recover their strength for future battles. Those likely to die were in this hospital, the former barracks of the Ileans. The barracks were in the lower town, inside the fortification ditch, and just a short distance from the funeral pyres which had been burning day and night.

'I will go, Machaon,' he said, 'but you must rest.' He looked into the tortured eyes and saw no chance of rest there. 'Where do I go?'

'There are injured men everywhere. They will not be hard to find. Do your best.' As Xander turned to go, Machaon's hand shot out and grabbed his arm. The boy could feel only cold in the older man's bony fingers. 'You always do your best, Xander,' he said.

Xander packed a leather bag full of healing potions, bandages, his favoured herbs, needles of different sizes, and threads. Then he snatched up a jug of wine, and three water skins, and set off down towards the battlefield.

The evening was cool and as he walked Xander tried to imagine he was back at home on Kypros, strolling the green hills among his grandfather's herds. The muted cries of injured men became the gentle bleating of the wandering goats. He half closed his eyes as he walked, and he could smell the distant sea, and hear the cry of the gulls. He stumbled on the rough path and nearly fell, and grinned at his foolishness. Yes, he thought, walk about with your eyes closed and break a leg, Xander!

Machaon was right. The injured were not hard to find. Xander walked among them, placing clean bandages on wounds, sewing cuts to faces with fine needles, and larger ones to legs and arms with thicker needles and sturdy thread. He boiled his herbs in water over soldiers' campfires to make healing brews, and splinted broken fingers. He urged some of the more seriously injured men to go up to the houses of healing, but all refused. He could not blame them.

The long night wore on, and Xander carried on working. He had met many of the soldiers before; they had come to him with their wounds, and their unexplained pains and minor illnesses, some of them many times over the years. They greeted him as a comrade, and joked with him in the way of soldiers everywhere. They called him Shortshanks, and Freckles, and he flushed with pleasure at the affection in which he was held.

A heavy mist had come rolling down the Scamander valley, making it hard for him to see. He was so tired by now he could hardly stumble from one small campfire to the next, and his trembling hands could no longer sew wounds. Still he walked on.

'Time to go, Xander,' said a familiar voice in his ear.

'Machaon?' he asked, looking about him, but the fog obscured everything. 'Machaon? Is that you?'

'Quickly, boy,' the voice said with urgency. 'Stop what you are doing now, and hurry back to the city. Quickly now.'

Xander packed his leather bag hurriedly and threw it over one shoulder, then picked up the empty water skins and started to make for the river. He could barely see his hand in front of his face, and he was forced to walk slowly, careful not to stumble over waking men or into the flanks of dozing horses.

Then out of the mist came a loud cry, echoing eerily through the darkness and picked up by rank after rank of warriors' voices, 'Awake! Awake! They are coming!'

XIX

The fog of war

EARLIER THAT NIGHT, AFTER THE SUN FELL BELOW THE HORIZON TO reveal a sky full of stars, Odysseus stood on the walls of King's Joy nursing a pain in his shoulder and a wound to his heart.

Three days previously, his valiant force of Ithakans and Kephallenians had been fighting on the Scamander plain when the Trojan Horse punched into the western armies like a battering ram, turning a knife-edge battle into a near rout.

Two of Hektor's riders had charged as one into Odysseus' infantry, each guarding the other's flank, hacking with their swords, killing and wounding all around them. As one rider raised his sword high to slash at a young crewman from the *Bloodhawk*, Odysseus, running up behind, had lanced a spear deep into the rider's side, straight into the heart. The bronze spearhead lodged under a rib. Odysseus tried to drag it out, but instead pulled the dead rider off his horse. With dying warriors all around him, the Ithakan king was slow to get out of the way, and the body fell on him, dislocating his shoulder. The arm bone had been wrenched back into place by Podaleirios, the Thessalian surgeon, but even now, days later, Odysseus was still in pain. He had thrown away the sling he was given, and hid his discomfort from others. But now as he moved his arm experimentally, as if swinging a sword, he cursed as agony fired through his shoulder.

Twenty years ago, he thought irritably, or even ten, I would have shaken off this injury within a day.

The greater agony, though, was in his heart. He remembered Penelope's words years ago on the beach at Ithaka. 'I fear you will have hard choices to make. Do not make bull-headed decisions you will regret afterwards and cannot change. Do not take these men into a war, Odysseus.'

'I have no wish for war, my love,' he had told her, and he had meant it.

How the gods on Olympos must be revelling in the irony, he thought ruefully. Or perhaps his wife's fear should never have been voiced at all, lest the gods were listening and chose to make it real.

For here he was, within sight of the golden city, his loyal men fighting side by side with the Mykene for Agamemnon, whose obsession was to destroy the city, kill Odysseus' former friends, and take its wealth for himself.

And he remembered Helikaon's words to him on their last meeting. 'I have not seen Priam's hoard of gold, but it would have to be mountainous to maintain the expense of this war. Gold passes from the city every day, to hire mercenaries, to bribe allies. And there is little coming in now. If the fighting goes on much longer, and you do take the city, you may find nothing of real worth.'

Odysseus smiled grimly to himself. Agamemnon and his fellow kings still had faith in the riches of Priam. At least they had a reason to fight. *What is your excuse, Ugly One?* he heard Penelope say. *Because you gave your word? Is your word so powerful, so sacred, that you must fight with your enemies against your friends?*

Three days before, battling on the plain alongside the armies of Mykene, he had seen the Trojan Horse thundering down the valley. And he had felt his heart leap as if Hektor and his riders were coming to his own rescue.

Odysseus sighed. War made strange sword brothers. He despised Agamemnon and his fellow kings. Idomeneos was greedy and mendacious. Menestheos of Athens and Agapenor of Arcadia were no better. The weakling Menelaus did whatever his brother told him. Old Nestor was a kinsman of Penelope, and Odysseus liked the old man, yet he had been beguiled by the promise of Priam's treasure too. Only Achilles was at Troy on a mission of honour, to find the warrior who had ordered his father's death, and avenge him.

He thought back to Hektor's Wedding Games when wily Priam had declared Odysseus an enemy of Troy. A less prideful man would have merely left the city. But Odysseus, slighted and insulted, had allowed his pride to force him into the arms of this rabble of kings. It was true, he was guilty as accused of hiring an assassin to kill Helikaon's father, but only to protect Helikaon, whom the same assassin had been paid to kill.

Now Odysseus, sick to his soul, had left his loathsome allies drinking and quarrelling in the *megaron* of King's Joy, and had walked up to the terrace for some fresher air.

He looked around. Agamemnon's Followers, the king's henchmen, had roasted two pigs here earlier, and the terrace smelled of blood and burned meat. Then they had played a game with one of the pig's heads, kicking it about until it was a shapeless black mass. Odysseus picked it up and gazed at it for a moment before throwing it over the wall. He smiled to himself, thinking of the pig Ganny, first rescued from the sea and then, in his yellow cloak, sitting as if listening to Odysseus' tale of the golden fleece on the pirates' beach.

'By Apollo's balls, Ganny my boy, we had some adventures together!' he said out loud.

Cheered by the memory, he strolled to the western side of the terrace. In the starlight he could see down to the Bay of Herakles, its white sand scarcely visible under the hulls of the hundreds of ships beached there. A sitting target for Helikaon's Fire Hurlers, he thought. Had Agamemnon learned nothing from his disaster at Imbros? Odysseus had heard no news of the *Xanthos* since it left Ithaka but, prudently, he had quietly moved most of his own fleet further down the coast to a small hidden cove.

He turned and looked in the other direction, to the walls of Troy lying moonlit in the distance, like a city of magic from one of his stories, and, before him, the plain of the Scamander where the Trojan army was camped, waiting. The myriad lights of their campfires showed they were formed in defensive squares. Hektor would not be stupid enough to attack, he knew, as the idiot Menelaus claimed. A man with no sense of strategy assumes others are as stupid as he is. Odysseus glanced down to where soldiers had laboured to dig an inner earthwork. A waste of time and energy, he thought. And just another obstacle when we attack. The stupidity angered him.

Looking south, along the valley of the Scamander, he saw that a blanket of thick mist was forming over the river and starting slowly to roll towards the Trojan armies on the plain. They cannot see it coming, he realized. Before long they will not be able to see their swords in front of their noses.

His mind working quickly, he left the terrace and stomped back down the stone stairs to the *megaron*, to be greeted by drunken shouts and laughter. Menelaus was lying on the floor in a pool of wine, apparently unconscious. Agamemnon gazed expressionlessly at the Ithakan king. Agamemnon never drank, and Odysseus was always careful not to drink in his company.

'Well,' said the Mykene king, 'the Tale Spinner has chosen to join us again. We are honoured. Have you a story to entertain us tonight, Prince of Lies?'

Odysseus ignored the insulting tone and said nothing, merely standing in the doorway until he had their attention.

'Sober up quickly, you drunken sots,' he bellowed. 'I have a plan.'

Achilles, unarmoured and wearing a simple black kilt and leather breastplate, his face smeared with soot, crouched in the entrance to the narrow pass and stared into the thick mist. 'This is madness,' he said cheerfully.

Odysseus, resting on one knee beside him, chuckled. 'We have to attack at dawn anyway,' he replied. 'Our allies have pledged to be here soon after sun-up. If we attack now, this fog gives us the extra element of surprise.'

'Well, it surprised *me*,' said a red-bearded warrior gloomily. 'It's the middle of the night and the mist is so thick I can't see the end of my sword. We won't know who we're killing.'

'The ones lying down, Thibo, either sleeping or dead, will be the enemy,' Odysseus told him.

He thought the plan through again. Agamemnon was committed to attack today, which meant funnelling his armies through the pass. The heavy mist gave him the perfect opportunity to get them through under cover. Hektor, of course, would expect that, and by dawn he would have his forces ready. By attacking at dead of night they might catch him unprepared.

Odysseus and Achilles, the fifty Myrmidons, and another hundred hand-picked warriors, were to creep out of the pass under cover of the dark and mist, cross the earthworks and descend on the Trojans as they slept. None was wearing armour lest any clink of metal on metal betray their presence. The Trojans would quickly raise the alarm, but Odysseus calculated that as many as a thousand would die first, slaughtered as they dreamed.

Far behind them through the pass the rest of Agamemnon's armies waited restlessly. Once the silent band of killers had done their grisly work and the alarm was raised, the infantry would come charging through. The cavalry would have to wait on the seaward side of the pass until the dawn came and the mist cleared. But the enemy were in the same position. Even the Trojan Horse could not attack if they could not see.

Odysseus moved his shoulder and grimaced at the pain, then licked dry lips. Just one more battle, he thought to himself. You've done this before, old man. He grasped his sword in one hand and a long dagger in the other. He glanced at Achilles, who had his swords on his back and two daggers drawn, and nodded.

The pair crept forward, silent in the muffling mist, their small army moving noiselessly behind them. Odysseus climbed the new earthwork, cursing it under his breath. By the time he reached the main earthwork he had fallen well behind Achilles, who had disappeared ahead of him like a wraith. Hurrying to keep up, Odysseus clambered over the bank of earth and mud, glimpsing dark-garbed warriors, swords and knives in hand, passing him silently on either side. It was an eerie sight.

Then the killing began. Ahead Odysseus heard the small muffled sounds of cold bronze plunging into flesh, soft gasps quickly cut off. He hurried forward. Soon he was walking in the dim light of campfires that had bodies strewn around them, the dead and the dying, blood still gushing from slashed throats, eyes staring up at him, hands reaching out for aid that would not come.

It was so quiet he could hear his heart beating. Then there was a loud cry. 'Awake! Awake! We are under attack!'

In an instant the air was filled with the clash of blades, the screams of the wounded, the snarls and grunts of fighting men, the snapping of bones and the rending of flesh. Odysseus heard Achilles' booming battle cry from somewhere up ahead and moved towards the sound.

A warrior appeared in the half-light, a Thrakian tribesman with a painted face. The Ithakan king leapt to the attack, but the man moved like quicksilver, blocking his thrust and turning in to him. His shoulder struck Odysseus in the chest, knocking him back. The king fell to the ground and rolled quickly as a sword blade thrust into the earth beside him. Odysseus plunged his dagger into the unprotected thigh of the tribesman. Blood sprayed out and the man fell. Odysseus jumped up, and slashed his sword across the man's head.

He bent to pull out his dagger, but one of Priam's Eagles leapt at him with a snarl, recognizing the Ithakan king. Odysseus parried his sword blow and reversed a cut to the warrior's neck. The blade hammered into the breastplate – and snapped. Dropping the useless hilt, Odysseus grabbed the man by his armour and hauled him forward, butting him savagely, then crashing his fist into the man's belly. The Eagle doubled over, then his head snapped back as Odysseus' knee exploded into his face.

He picked up the Eagle's sword and plunged it into the man's neck. Then, screaming his battle cry, 'Ithaka! Ithaka!' he powered into the Trojan ranks, cutting and cleaving, an awesome fury upon him, his injured shoulder forgotten.

An unarmoured Trojan warrior ran forward, ducking under Odysseus' plunging sword, and stabbing his blade towards the Ugly King's belly. Odysseus leapt backwards, and tripped over a body. He rolled and came up swinging his sword two-handed, half beheading the warrior.

He glimpsed a movement to his right and blocked a lightning attack from a sword. Twisting his wrists and returning the blow, he clove the attacker from neck to belly.

There were Trojans all around him now. His sword rose and fell in the mêlée, cutting through leather and flesh and bone. He twisted and swung, then, too late, saw a sword slashing towards his neck. Another sword flashed up to block it, parrying the death blow. Odysseus recognized the braided red beard, and he grinned at Achilles' shield-bearer.

'Be careful, old man,' Thibo shouted. 'I can't watch out for both of us.'

Odysseus ducked under a two-handed cut from his right and drove his sword home in the man's chest. Beside him Thibo leapt and twisted, cleaving and killing. Odysseus saw dawn light gleam off his bloody blade, and realized the night mist was starting to clear.

Two Trojan soldiers ran at Thibo. He blocked a blow from the first, gutting the man with a reverse stroke. His sword stuck in the man's belly. The second warrior's sword arced towards his head. Odysseus parried the blow, chopping his sword through the man's neck.

'Where is Achilles?' he asked, panting. 'You're supposed to be watching out for *him*.'

Thibo shrugged. 'Achilles can take care of himself.'

Daylight was clearing the mist quickly, and Odysseus could see warriors struggling and dying all around him. Three Trojans came at him at once and he cursed aloud as he clove through one neck and ducked under a slashing blade. Then, dropping to his haunches, he charged into the two other soldiers like a bull. He caught one in the belly with his injured shoulder and grunted in agony. The other fell back, stumbling over a body, and was disembowelled by a slashing sword.

Odysseus saw Achilles standing over him, his two blades dripping blood.

'Go back, Ithaka,' the Thessalian king shouted above the noise of battle, 'or that wound will kill you. Only the dagger is saving you.'

Odysseus looked down and saw a knife hilt sticking out of his thigh. Blood had drenched his leg. In the fury of battle he had not noticed it.

'And get yourself armoured,' Achilles ordered. Swaying to one side as a sword scythed past his chest, he chopped his attacker down with a blow to the neck.

Odysseus shouted back, 'You have no armour, Achilles!'

Achilles just grinned at him, and charged back into the fray.

Odysseus realized he was dizzy from blood loss, and he cursed. As he stepped forward he felt his knees give way. Hands grabbed him and pulled him upright, then a powerful shoulder lifted him up under the arm. The sounds of fighting receded as, still cursing, he was dragged from the battlefield.

He was on the Penelope *again, the wind in his hair, the fresh sea air filling his chest. A huge flock of gulls was flying over the ship, darkening the sky with their wings. The clamour of their cries was deafening. Stupid birds, gulls, he said to himself. Then he saw the birds had the faces of women, contorted with hatred and spite. Harpies, he thought, coming to rend his flesh.*

The sharp pain of teeth tearing his leg brought him round and he found himself lying on muddy ground clear of the battlefield. One of his crewmen, the powerful fighter Leukon, was stitching the wound in his thigh, his thick fingers clumsy on the bloodsoaked thread. Leukon's leg had been broken three days before and he could not fight. Now he sat awkwardly, and was clearly in agony from the splinted limb.

Odysseus sat up. 'Give me wine, someone,' he demanded, and he was handed a goblet. He drank it down, asked for another, and watched impatiently as Leukon tied off the stitches. The blood had stopped flowing, and he felt the wine reviving him.

'Back to the battle, Leukon,' he said.

'Aye, my king,' said the huge warrior, and he struggled to stand up.

'Not you, you fool. Me!'

Odysseus made to rise, but a hand on his shoulder held him down and a cold voice said, 'The battle is over for you today, Odysseus.'

He looked up to see Agamemnon. With a massive effort he levered himself to his feet, trying to ignore the torment in his shoulder and the pain of the stitches pulling in his leg. The Mykene king was right. He felt as weak as a pup, and it took all his willpower to stay upright.

They were looking over the battlefield from a vantage point in front of the main earthwork. The early sun had burned off the mist and he could see clearly the battle on the plain before them. It was a mêlée, foot soldiers on both sides fighting desperately, neither side giving any quarter. Agamemnon's cavalry had all deployed to the left, hitting the right flank of the enemy, forcing Hektor to bring the bulk of his Trojan Horse to that side in a ferocious counter-attack. Odysseus could see the Trojans had the upper hand, forcing Agamemnon's riders back from the river. Enjoy your success while you can, Hektor my friend, he thought.

Amid the sea of fighting and struggling men, he could see a group of black-clad warriors forging an arrowhead into the Trojan infantry.

'Achilles and his Myrmidons are fighting without armour,' he said angrily. During their long night of planning, the western kings had agreed that once the alarm was raised the elite killing force would fade back and armour themselves. Achilles, with the battle fury upon him, had ignored that agreement and fought on. 'He can never survive. And his men will not leave him. He is condemning them all to death.'

'That would be a shame,' said Agamemnon flatly.

Odysseus looked at him, fury rising in his chest. 'Have you no loyalty to anyone, Mykene?' he asked angrily. 'Achilles is fighting your war.'

Agamemnon turned and gazed at him, his dark eyes cold and

empty as a winter sky. 'Achilles fights for the glory of Achilles,' he said, and Odysseus knew it was true.

The battle raged on as the sun climbed in the sky. Odysseus could see the western armies were slowly being pushed back, and Achilles and his band were in danger of being surrounded. He glanced at the sun, standing proud of the horizon now, and started watching anxiously southwards, along the river valley. Finally he saw a distant speck, a horseman riding with all speed towards them. The scout edged his way round the rear of the fighting, galloped up and threw himself off his horse before Agamemnon.

'They are coming, lord!' he gasped.

'About time,' said the Battle King with satisfaction.

Sunlight glinted off the spear-points of hundreds of marching men, flanked by cavalry, as a new army marched towards Troy. Odysseus looked back to the battle before him. The Trojans, lower down, had not seen the threat yet.

The approaching army's cavalry broke into a gallop, riding straight for the unprotected flank of the Trojan infantry, lances down. Now aware of the threat, the battle-weary Trojans desperately tried to re-form to face the attack, but the shock as the armoured riders hit them was devastating. Scores of men fell under the trampling hooves of the horses.

Hektor reacted quickly. His Phrygian archers, at the rear of the battlefield, started loosing volley after volley into the coming infantry. Arrows were deflected off shields and conical helms, but some men crashed to the ground, tripping others as they came.

The Trojan Horse were isolated on the wrong side of the field, but at an order from Hektor half of them peeled away and galloped to counter the new threat. Hektor himself dug his heels into his great warhorse and charged at the enemy cavalry. As he reached them several horsemen rode against him. His blade lanced out, spilling the first rider from his mount; the second fell as Hektor's sword, wielded with awesome anger, crushed his skull. Then a lance drove into the chest of the stallion Ares and he fell, throwing Hektor to the ground.

Odysseus could see him no more. Frustrated, he turned his gaze on the leader of the newly arrived army who, surrounded by his bodyguard, rode up the slope towards him.

'Well, Kygones,' he commented as the Lykian king drew his horse to a halt, 'you are not joining the battle today?'

The Fat King pulled off his helm and smiled coolly.

'You should have more gratitude, Ithaka,' he said. 'When last we met you professed great moral outrage at the death of one man, a simple sailor. Now you and your fellow kings ask me to help you kill thousands. Where are your thanks?'

He dismounted and handed his horse to one of his men.

'All our actions have consequences, Odysseus. By barring your ships from my beaches, over the death of that one sailor, you and Helikaon dealt a body blow to Lykia, crippling trade and draining its lifeblood. My people have suffered, and for the first time in a generation children have starved in wintertime. When Agamemnon sought me as an ally, are you surprised that I felt no loyalty to Helikaon and his kinsman Priam?'

Odysseus had no answer for him. He turned back to the battle-field, then heard Hektor's horn blowing – the two short blasts repeated over and over, signalling retreat. Good, he thought. You cannot win the day, Hektor. The Scamander plain belongs to us. Retreat in good order while you can.

But the Trojans were fighting every step of the way, protecting their wounded as they backed slowly towards the river and its four bridges to an ephemeral safety.

No more than a hundred soldiers had retreated across one of the wooden bridges when a bright flame like a huge torch erupted amongst them. Suddenly the entire bridge was ablaze, setting fire to the men upon it. They screamed and thrashed about in agony. Many jumped into the Scamander, but their flesh kept burning and their cries were awful to hear. Then a second bridge caught alight. Within moments all four bridges, the Trojans' only way of retreat, were burning ferociously.

Stunned by the sight, Odysseus turned to Agamemnon. 'Is this your work?' he asked, but the Mykene king just shook his head, as surprised as he was.

They watched as desperate Trojans, trapped between the advancing enemy armies and the river, started throwing themselves into the fast-flowing water, some helping the wounded to cross, others just swimming for their lives. Injured men were being pulled under and swept down towards the bay, too weak to struggle against the strength of the powerful current.

Then Agamemnon gasped and pointed as Hektor, mounted again on gallant Ares, walked the stallion into the Scamander high above the blazing bridges. He reined in the warhorse in the centre of the river, and stood there as the waters crashed around them. Others of the Trojan Horse joined them, guiding their horses to stand by Ares, reducing the force of the current. Soon thirty warhorses stood in the river, enduring as the waters struck them. The riders had only shields to protect themselves and their mounts from the arrows and lances of the enemy, and three fell in the Scamander and were swept away, but most of them stood firm, allowing the Trojan injured to make their way across to safety. The Phrygian archers ran along the river bank to help protect the horses with a rain of arrows at the advancing enemy.

Odysseus wanted to cheer, and he smiled to himself to see the anger on Agamemnon's face.

'Hektor lives,' the Mykene king hissed. 'Can nothing kill him?'

'He charged an army and yet he survives,' said Odysseus happily. 'That is why Hektor is Hektor and we kings are just standing here watching.'

Sick of Agamemnon's company, he set off down towards the battlefield, limping heavily on his injured leg. Stretcher-bearers were on the field now, bringing wounded men away. He saw healers and surgeons helping injured warriors of the western armies, and soldiers dispatching wounded Trojans. The ground was heavy with churned-up mud and blood, and Odysseus felt himself tiring quickly.

Then he saw a figure he recognized, a fat warrior in outsize armour lying in the mud, his back resting against the flank of a dead horse. Odysseus stomped over to him.

The prince was bleeding from a score of cuts. 'Well, well, Odysseus,' he said, his voice a weak rasp. 'Have you come to finish me off?'

'No, Antiphones,' the Ithakan king said, sitting down beside him, suddenly weary. 'I just wanted to talk to an old friend.'

'Are we friends, you and I?' the prince asked.

Odysseus shrugged. 'At this moment, we are. Tomorrow is another day.'

'Tomorrow I shall be dead, Odysseus. This will be the death of me.' He gestured to a deep wound in his side, from which dark blood was pumping out on to the ground. 'A thinner man would be dead already.'

The Ithakan king nodded. 'What happened at the bridges?' he asked.

Antiphones scowled, and his ashen face darkened a little. 'My fool of a father. Priam had secretly instructed his Eagles to torch the bridges using *nephthar* if our forces started retreating. Trojans do not retreat, he says.'

Odysseus felt a wave of revulsion. 'Is he quite insane now?' he asked, shocked by the ruthless cruelty of the Trojan king to his own troops. 'It is sometimes hard to tell the difference between insanity and cold-blooded brutality.'

Antiphones tried to lift himself up into a sitting position, but he was too weak and he sank down again. Odysseus saw the flow from his wound had lessened. He knew the prince had not much longer to live.

'He is the cruel and selfish king he always was.' Antiphones sighed. 'He has times of confusion. We thought it was the wine, for he hardly eats. Then he has insane ideas, like this one. Hektor just ignores them. But this . . .' He gestured towards the river. 'He is cunning still, you see. He told no one except his Eagles. And they would all kill themselves for him on his command.'

A Mykene soldier walked over to them, his sword red with blood, looking for enemy wounded. Odysseus waved him away.

259

Antiphones was silent for a while, and Odysseus thought he had died. Then the big man said, despair in his voice, 'Troy will fall. She cannot be saved.'

Odysseus nodded sadly. 'Agamemnon will win and the city will fall. Once we reach the great walls and the city is under siege it is only a matter of time. There will be a traitor. There always is.'

Antiphones said weakly, 'I thought she would last a thousand years. There is a prophecy . . .'

Odysseus said irritably, 'There is always a prophecy. I do not believe in prophecies, Antiphones. In a thousand years the golden city will be dust, its walls ruined, flowers growing wild where Priam's palace once stood.'

Antiphones smiled weakly. 'That sounds like a prophecy, Odysseus.'

The king leaned towards him. 'But she will not die, Antiphones. I promise you that. Her story will not be forgotten.' Already in his mind a tale was forming of a warrior's wrath and the death of a hero.

The prince's eyes had closed. He whispered, 'I was the traitor . . .' Then he died.

Wearily, Odysseus stood. He saw the soldier he had sent away find another Trojan soldier, gravely wounded and unable to save himself. The Mykene warrior thrust him cleanly through the heart, then moved on. His eye was caught by the body of a young man lying in the mud, and he walked towards him. Odysseus saw the youngster had red hair and was without armour. One arm moved feebly as if he were trying to turn himself over. As the Mykene soldier raised his sword, Odysseus said, 'Hold!'

The man paused and looked at him doubtfully.

'He is one of mine, soldier. Do you know me?'

'You are Odysseus, king of Ithaka. Everyone knows you.' The man lowered his sword and moved away.

The boy was plastered with mud and blood, and seemed dazed by a blow to the head. Odysseus knelt beside him and helped him turn over.

'Xander! I never thought to see you here,' he said. 'Being a hero again, lad?'

*

Xander awoke with a start to find it was evening, and he was on a sandy beach. He could hear the sound of waves crashing against rocks, the distant sound of lyres and pipes, and low voices murmuring close by.

'Lie still, you fool,' said a deep voice, 'and give that wound a chance to heal. It may have pierced your vitals.'

'Then I am a dead man,' said another irritably. 'If I must walk the Dark Road I do not plan to do it sober. Give me that jug.'

Xander's head hurt abominably and as he tried to sit up the world lurched around him and he lay down again with a groan.

'How are you feeling, Xander?' asked a voice.

He opened his eyes a crack and was surprised to see Machaon looking down at him, his face in shadow as the sun fell at his back.

'Where are we, Machaon?' he asked. 'Why are we on a beach?' He tried to sit up again, and this time succeeded. He found his leather satchel was lying by his side.

'Drink this,' the healer said and, kneeling alongside him, brought to Xander's lips a cup of delicious-smelling liquid. The boy sipped it, then drank it down greedily. It was warm and tasted, he thought, of summer flowers. He had never tasted anything so good. He found his head clearing a little and he looked round.

From where he sat all he could see was soldiers, some wounded and lying down, others sitting round campfires laughing and joking. The black hulls of ships pulled up on the sand hid his view of the sea, though he could smell the salt of it. With a sinking feeling in the pit of his stomach he realized where he was.

'We are on the beach you call the Bay of Herakles, and I am not Machaon,' said the healer. Sitting down he poured thick liquid from a clay pot into a cup of water warming over a fire. He looked up. Xander could see now it was not the face of his mentor, though the two men were very alike. This man was older, and nearly bald, and one of his eyes was strange, the eyeball pale and pearly.

'My name is Podaleirios, and Machaon is my brother,' the healer said. 'You clearly know him, Xander. Is he well?'

'No,' admitted the boy regretfully. 'When last I saw him he was very sick, sir. I wish I could help him. He has always been kind to me. Why am I here with the enemy?'

There was a burst of laughter at his words, and someone said, 'You are in the Thessalian camp, boy. You should be proud to be with Achilles and his Myrmidons, the finest warriors in the world.'

The speaker was a slender young man with fair hair braided and pulled back to his neck. He was cleaning blood off his arms, but Xander guessed it was someone else's, for he looked uninjured. Beside him was a huge dark-haired warrior dressed in black, and lying between them a bald-headed man with a braided red beard. His chest was heavily bandaged and Xander could see blood leaking and staining the white material. His healer's eye noted the grey sheen on the man's face and the feverish look in his eye.

'Podaleirios,' Xander asked the healer, 'I don't know how I got here, but can I return to Troy now?'

The men laughed again, and Podaleirios said, 'Call me White-eye, Xander. Everybody else does. You were brought here by Odysseus of Ithaka. He found you unconscious on the field of battle and carried you to safety. And you cannot return to Troy. You are now healer and surgeon to the warriors of Thessaly. This is Achilles, king of Thessaly,' the healer gestured to the black-clad giant, 'and you are now his servant.'

Xander stared in wonder at the legendary warrior. 'Lord,' he said humbly, 'I am not a priest of Asklepios, pledged to help the sick or injured wherever I find them. I am just a helper to Machaon. I belong in Troy.'

Achilles frowned. 'Odysseus tells me you trained with Machaon in the House of Serpents. If such a famous healer sent you on to the battlefield to help the Trojan wounded then he must have faith in your skills. Are you saying you will not help my stricken warriors? Think carefully on your answer, boy.'

Shamefaced, Xander said, 'I'm sorry, lord. I will do what I can to help.'

To White-eye, Achilles said, 'At dawn, when the boy has rested, take him up to King's Joy. He will be valuable there.'

The healer nodded and moved away. A servant came to the

campfire offering platters of meat and corn bread to the warriors. One was placed at the wounded man's side, but he did not touch it, merely swigged on his jug of wine. Achilles pointed at Xander and nodded, and the servant gave the boy some food. It was roasted pig, warm with greasy juices, its crackling salt and tasty. Xander felt his stomach grumble in reaction to the wonderful smell. He realized he had not eaten all day, or the day before. He wondered when he had last tasted any food, then forgot about it as he sank his teeth into the succulent meat.

There was silence for a while as the warriors ate. Then Achilles said to the wounded man, 'I will have you carried to King's Joy, Thibo. It will be cold on the beach tonight. At least there you will be under shelter.'

Thibo shook his head. 'I'll be all right here by the fire. I don't want to be up there with the dead and dying.'

'I am your king and could command you,' Achilles said mildly.

Thibo grunted. 'Would you want to be up there, in that place of torment?'

Achilles shook his head and said no more.

The fair-haired warrior nudged him with his elbow. 'We went there once when we were children. Do you remember, we visited King's Joy with your father? I don't know why.'

Achilles nodded, chewing his meat and swallowing. 'I remember, Patroklos.'

Patroklos went on, 'It was a place of beauty then, the white walls painted with bright pictures of the gods. There were soft rugs on the marble floors – I had never seen such rugs before – and the gleam of gold and gems everywhere. It was wonderful to behold.'

Achilles agreed. 'And now Agamemnon's Followers have made a pigsty of it,' he said. Then he smiled. 'I remember we were told off for playing on the high balcony where Helen fell.'

Patroklos shook his head in wonder. 'I'll not forget that day on this side of the Dark Road. The princess throwing herself to her death with her children.'

Thibo grunted. 'They were dead anyway, the children. Agamemnon would have seen to that.'

Patroklos argued, 'But Helen need not have died. It seems wrong, such beauty smashed to ruins on the rocks below.'

Xander listened with surprise. He had only met the princess Helen once, in Helikaon's chamber when the Golden One was gravely ill. He had seen a plump, plain woman with a sweet smile. Perhaps they were talking about a different Helen, he thought.

'She was not a beauty,' said Thibo thoughtfully.

'Yes, but you don't like them buxom, Thibo,' replied Patroklos, grinning. 'You like your women skinny, like boys.' He winked at his friend.

'It's true,' Thibo agreed amiably. 'But I meant she was not beautiful like an expensive whore . . .'

Patroklos started laughing at this, but Achilles broke in, 'I know what you mean, Thibo. She did not have the beauty of golden-haired Aphrodite. She was more like stern and terrible Hera, before whom even the gods quail.'

Thibo agreed. 'She made me feel like a small boy. She was like the mother you love, but whose anger you fear. The other men on the balcony said the same. They've all been talking about her.'

Speaking so much made Thibo cough. The spasm seemed agonizing, and he held on to his chest with both hands. His face lost all colour and he groaned. Xander could see the blood patch on the bandage spreading.

Taking up his leather satchel, he stood and said to the wounded warrior, 'Sir, perhaps I can help you, if you will let me.'

XX

Andromache's choice

ANDROMACHE STOOD AT THE PROW OF THE *XANTHOS* AND BREATHED in the fresh salt air as the great ship glided through a light swell. She had always loved the days of spring, when the snows melted on great Ida and the rivers and streams around little Thebe filled and sparkled with clear icy water, its wooded hills and valleys clothed in pale green rain-washed leaves.

When she had been sent by her father as priestess to Thera she had thought of Thebe Under Plakos as her home. But by the time she was dispatched unhappily to Troy to marry Hektor, Thera had become home to her. Now here she was, on the *Xanthos* and less than a day's sail from the golden city, and where is your home now, Andromache, she thought? Is it Troy where you yearn to hold your son in your arms again? Or is it on this ship where you have lived, and loved, for long endless winter days of fear, and longing, and bliss?

Once the crew had got used to a woman aboard their ship, had stopped calling her princess or priestess, and had ceased glancing covertly at her legs and breasts at all opportunities, she had found a home on the big ship. She joined the men round their campfires at night, shared their meals, distributed water skins when the ship was under oars, helped sluice down the decks, and was even asked to sew up a ragged rip in the sail after a rough day in stormy seas.

'I am the daughter of a king, and wife to Hektor,' she had laughed, 'and you are sailors. You know more about sewing than I do!' Yet she had done her best with the sharp needle and sturdy thread they gave her, and pretended not to notice when her poor stitches were remade for her by a grizzled crewman whose fingers were more nimble than hers.

One calm day Oniacus had offered to teach her to row, and she had grasped the great oar and learned to pull with the motion of the sea, but within a short time her palms were covered with bleeding blisters, and Helikaon had told her angrily to stop.

Helikaon! She did not turn round, for she knew he would be standing at the stern of the ship, one arm on the great steering oar, watching her. Closing her eyes she could recall every detail of his face, the fine dark hairs of his eyebrows, the exact set of the corners of his mouth, the shape of his ears. In her mind's eye she could see his bronzed arm, with its soft sun-bleached hairs, draped across the steering oar, as she had seen it a hundred times. She knew every scar on his body, by touch and taste. He was wearing a long winter robe of blue wool, the same colour as his eyes when he was angry, and his feet were in old sandals stained by salt and time.

They had tried to follow the counsel of Odysseus at first, and stayed away from each other, not touching, not brushing past each other on the narrow aisle of the ship, barely speaking unless there were crewmen present. Their determination had lasted until they reached the Seven Hills.

Andromache had been astonished by the small thriving city built by Helikaon and Odysseus so far from their homes. The stockaded fort was on a hill overlooking the great river Thybris, and a busy community had developed around it, flourishing in the soft, verdant land so different from Ithaka and Dardanos. The people had started building a stone wall round the fort, for they had to fend off attacks from local tribes who resented the presence of these foreigners from far across the seas. But the king of one of the tribes, Latinus, had welcomed them and joined his forces to theirs.

So the community of the Seven Hills grew. They had purchased tin from pale-skinned traders travelling from far to the north, in the Land of Mists, and Helikaon was able to fill the *Xanthos*' cargo hold with the precious metal.

One night a feast was held in honour of one of the country's tribal gods, and the crewmen of the *Xanthos* joined in with relish. In the firelight Andromache, a little drunk, caught Helikaon's eye and smiled. No further message was needed. Unseen they crept away and found a soft mossy hollow far from the revels, where they made love for most of the night, first with frantic, animal passion, then, later, gently and tenderly until the first glimmer of dawn. Little was said; they had no need of words.

Back on board ship, returning to Troy with all haste, the lovers had stayed away from each other again. Helikaon had steered the *Xanthos* up the coast of Mykene, which was barren of ships, then crossed the Great Green high to the north. They had spent the last night before their return to Troy in a deep cove on the isle of Samothraki. Andromache had remained on board ship, in her small tent pitched on the foredeck, and Helikaon had come to her in the darkness.

The night was pitch black, but she heard the small soft sound of the tent flaps being parted, smelled the musky smell of him as he lay down beside her. He said nothing, but pulled down the sheepskin covering her body and kissed her shoulder. She turned to him. He kissed her mouth deeply, and the swell of suppressed longing in her rose so sharply it was painful. She moaned. He put his hand over her mouth. 'No sound,' he whispered in her ear. She nodded her head, then gently bit the palm of his hand, tasting salt. He smiled against her cheek. He slid under the warm sheepskin and moved on top of her, his body cool against her fiery loins. Her legs rose up to meet him and he entered her, warm and wet in the animal-smelling darkness.

He paused for a few unbearable heartbeats, then moved against her slowly. Too slowly. She squirmed under him, seeking a quick release from the painful longing of her body. He stopped, until she lay still, then he moved again, teasing her. When she climaxed the need to cry out became almost unstoppable, and he put his hand over her mouth again, then kissed her hard. He lay still again for mere moments, then started once more.

At last, drained and exhausted, he rolled away from her and they pushed off the damp animal skin and let the sweat dry on their bodies.

She whispered in his ear, 'Tomorrow we will be back in Troy . . .'

'Not now, my love,' he murmured. 'We will have plenty of time to talk about it tomorrow.' They spoke no more that night.

Now, standing on the foredeck of the ship, Andromache closed her eyes again, and let her body move dreamily with the rhythms of the waves, remembering that wondrous night and its own rhythms.

When she opened her eyes, she could see a dark speck on the blue sea to her left.

'Ship to port!' she cried, pointing, and within heartbeats she felt the great ship move beneath her towards the new threat. She narrowed her eyes. She could see it was a galley under sail, no mere fishing boat, but she could not make out its markings.

'It's Dardanian, lord!' shouted Praxos, new to the crew the previous autumn and with the sharp eyes of the young. 'I can see the black horse!'

There was a lusty cheer from the oarsmen, most of whom were Dardanians and looking forward to returning to their families. As Andromache watched, the other ship's sail was furled and her rowers took up the beat. The two ships glided towards one another. As they met rowers on the approaching sides shipped their oars, and ropes were thrown across, lashing the vessels together.

Andromache made her way along the aisle of the *Xanthos* to the stern. Helikaon glanced at her, his face expressionless. 'It is the *Boreas*,' he said.

They waited in silence as the Dardanian ship's young fair-haired captain shinned up a rope, climbed to the deck and fell to his knees before Helikaon. 'Golden One, thank the mercy of Poseidon we met you,' he said breathlessly. 'We were expecting the *Xanthos* to sail up the coast and most of our ships are off Lesbos, waiting for you.'

'Calm down, Asios. Why was the *Boreas* waiting?'

'Troy is under siege, lord,' the young man told him, 'and the Mykene fleet of Menados holds the entrance to the Hellespont. Agamemnon is camped in the Bay of Herakles with a thousand ships. We hoped to warn you before you sailed unknowing into them.'

Andromache closed her eyes. She had left Astyanax thinking he was safe in Troy. The familiar demon, guilt, clawed at her. She had left her son to be with her lover. Whom had she thought of more often on her journey, her only son, or Helikaon?

Helikaon was asking, 'What of Dardanos?'

'The Mykene have ignored the fortress. Our people are safe, for a while. Agamemnon has pulled his troops away from Thebe as well, lady.' He glanced at Andromache and flushed. 'He has thrown all his forces, and those of the western kings, in an attack on the golden city.'

'And Hektor?' Andromache asked.

'Hektor leads the Trojan defence, but they are outnumbered, and the last we heard they had been pushed back to the lower town. King's Joy is taken and the plain of the Scamander.' He hesitated. 'Prince Paris and his wife are dead. And Prince Antiphones.'

Andromache, stunned by the news, saw the colour drain from Helikaon's face. 'All dead?' he said, his deep voice grave.

'There has been great slaughter on both sides, lord. The funeral pyres burn night and day. If the *Xanthos* had arrived after dark you would have seen their light from far across the Great Green.'

'The city is surrounded?'

'No, lord. All their efforts are on the south of the city, at the fortification ditch. People can still flee through the Scaean Gate or the Dardanian Gate. Everyone is leaving. But that was six days ago. The situation changes daily. The *Boreas* has had no word since then.'

Oniacus stepped forward. 'Agamemnon has left his ships vulnerable at the Bay of Herakles, Golden One,' he said. 'Our Fire Hurlers can destroy his ships in one night, as we did at Imbros.'

Helikaon frowned. 'Perhaps later. But at the moment, sadly, I do not have that choice. The city is awaiting our cargo of tin, is it not, Asios?'

The young man nodded. 'The city's forges are dark,' he said. 'Troy desperately needs weapons and armour.'

Suddenly he glanced towards the coast, startled, and they all turned. In the distance at the tip of Trojan lands, the Cape of Tides, a light had appeared. It was a beacon, blazing brightly.

Helikaon gazed on it and frowned. 'A beacon, but telling what to whom? Asios, is the Cape of Tides in Trojan or Mykene hands?'

'I know not, lord. Trojan, when I last heard.' He shrugged.

'It tells us nothing, then,' said Helikaon briskly, his decision made. 'Oniacus, we will sail on to the Hellespont and the Bay of Troy, then make our way up the Simoeis. We will berth there and, if Athene favours us, smuggle our tin into the city from the north.'

'But Menados' fleet holds the Hellespont,' repeated the young captain. 'Even the *Xanthos* cannot defeat his fifty ships!'

'But,' said Helikaon thoughtfully, 'maybe together the *Xanthos* and the *Boreas* can.'

The Mykene admiral Menados looked up from the high deck of his patrol ship and saw a beacon blazing on the topmost cliff of the Cape of Tides.

'What does it mean, admiral?' asked his aide, his sister's son, a bright enough boy but with no initiative.

'I do not know,' the admiral told him. 'The Trojans are signalling someone, but we cannot tell who, or what the signal means. Much good may it do them,' he grunted. 'They are all dead men anyway.'

Like his crews Menados was bored and frustrated after long days of sailing the Hellespont. Of his fleet of fifty-seven, he had ordered thirty ships to patrol the length of the Trojan coast from the tip of the Thrakian shore to the Bay of Herakles. Seven ships, including his own, the new bireme *Alektruon*, held station against the current in the Hellespont. The remaining twenty ships were beached on the coast of Thraki, their men relieved to sleep and eat. The ships' duties were rotated regularly, but it was no work for fighting men, he thought, travelling back and forth, first under oars, then under sail, over and over again, wearing out the oarsmen and blunting the skills of their captains. Menados privately thought the duty was Agamemnon's punishment on him for the mercy Helikaon had shown him at Dardanos.

Word of the blockade had travelled swiftly through the lands bordering the Hellespont, and no ship had so far tried to break it and sail out of the straits. They had sunk one Dardanian ship trying to break in under cover of darkness, and two Hittite merchants had also tried to run the blockade and get home, angry at Agamemnon's high-handed action in closing the straits to the ships of all lands.

As the doomed Hittite seamen had struggled in the cold, treacherous waters, Menados was asked if the Mykene ships should pick them up. Let them die, had been his order. Personally it would have been his choice to rescue them; he had respect for seamen of all lands, and it would have been easy enough to drop them on the Thrakian coast to make their way home on foot. But word could not get back to the Hittite emperor that his ships were being sunk by the Mykene. The few strong swimmers who seemed likely to make it to the shore were stalked by the ships, then picked off by archers when they failed to drown.

'Ship to the north!'

The admiral turned and shaded his eyes. Members of the *Alektruon*'s crew jumped up to look, eager for action. The distant ship was under sail, pushed towards them at speed by the stiff northerly. Menados could not see its markings in the failing light, but hoped it was Dardanian or Trojan.

Most of the Trojan fleet was bottled up in the Bay of Troy. It could not get out, but equally the Mykene fleet could not get in. Priam had never acquired the strength of shipping justified by such a great city, relying instead on the huge Dardanian fleet built up by his kinsmen Anchises and Helikaon for his trading and defence. There were a mere eighteen Trojan ships trapped in the bay, but many were now said to be equipped with Fire Hurlers, which balanced Menados' numerical advantage. It was stalemate. With more ships at his disposal Menados knew he could easily take the bay, but Agamemnon needed every available foot soldier to capture the city, for they were dying in their thousands.

Menados sighed. The crewmen confined to his ships should be content to stay aboard. Daily they saw in the sky above Troy the evidence of the funeral pyres, pillars of smoke by day and the fiery glow by night.

'It's a Dardanian ship, lord!' cried his aide. 'Your orders?'

Now Menados could see for himself the black horse sail. Not the *Xanthos*, though, he thought. Too small. A pity.

'Five ships,' he ordered. 'Board her. They may have useful information for Agamemnon. The other ships close on her but stand off. There might be Fire Hurlers.'

His orders were given by the display of brightly coloured banners fashioned from linen, a system Menados had himself invented for conveying information at sea. Five ships, four Mykene and one Athenian, set off towards the oncoming vessel, intending to slow her by destroying her sail, then ram and board her. The other Mykene ships all turned to the north too. The Dardanian ship came on, not changing her course, apparently determined to break through the vessels approaching her.

As they closed, flaming arrows shot from the Athenian ship, targeted on the black horse. Two fell in the sea, but five hit their mark and the sail began to burn. As it disintegrated in flame the ship lost way, but she still came on. Flaming debris fell to the deck, there was a mighty whoosh and instantly the whole ship was alight.

At the last moment Menados saw three figures hurl themselves from the deck of the ship into the water.

'Fire ship!' he shouted. 'Come about! Keep clear!'

But the blazing ship came on, and the Athenian vessel could not get clear in time. The fire ship rammed into her hull as she was still turning, and slid along the wooden planking. The force of the collision caused the Dardanian's mast to collapse, and it fell flaming on to the deck of the Athenian ship. Pieces of burning sail, hurled by the high wind, struck the sail of one of the Mykene vessels and it too started to blaze.

'Fools!' shouted Menados, watching two of his ships blazing, their crews throwing themselves into the water. The other galleys were moving clear. And fools aboard the fire ship, he thought. Why sacrifice a ship in such a way?

He spun round. Behind them, powering at full speed through the gathering darkness, he could see the *Xanthos* making its way through the gap between the Mykene galleys and the Cape of Tides. It was a rough and windy night, and the bireme's rowers were hard pressed by the wind from the north and the strong current at the cape.

'The *Xanthos*!' Menados shouted. 'Come about, you idiots! Quickly!'

His steersman leaned on the steering oar with all his strength, and Menados added his own weight. But by the time they turned the ship to chase the great vessel, it was fully dark, and the *Xanthos* had sped away from the light of the three blazing ships and disappeared into the darkness of the Hellespont.

The *Xanthos* moved ahead slowly through the night, making her way east along the Simoeis. The sky was clear and starlit overhead, but a light mist lay over the river. The only sounds were the soft plashing of oars and the harsh braying of donkeys in the distance. It was so quiet Andromache could hear scuffling noises in the reeds as small creatures fled the passing of the great ship.

The *Xanthos* had entered the straits at a dangerous speed in the darkness, overloaded as she was with the crew of the *Boreas*. Only a seaman as experienced as Helikaon would have risked it, for he knew the strong currents and perilous rocks of the Cape of Tides better than any man. But once within the Bay of Troy, the rowers had slowed. Then more vessels had loomed around them in the dark: the Trojan ships trapped in the bay. Andromache would have expected cheering as the golden ship glided past, but there was an eerie silence as sailors lined the decks to watch the *Xanthos* as it headed through the bay towards Troy's northern river.

'Why so quiet?' she had asked Oniacus, who was standing on the

273

foredeck with a sounding pole, peering into the mist ahead. 'We are still far from Troy and the enemy camps.'

Keeping his gaze fixed on the river, the sailor replied, 'At night sound travels over very great distances. We cannot be too careful.'

'They all look so grim.'

He nodded. 'Aye. It seems much has changed here since we left.'

The Simoeis was shallow and marshy, even in spring, and Helikaon steered the *Xanthos* into the centre of the river. Andromache could see little in the misty night and time crawled by slowly. Finally she felt the ship slow to a complete stop. The silence around them was heavy and oppressive.

'This is about as far as we can go,' Oniacus said quietly. 'We will moor here and unload the tin. We can only hope our enemies are not expecting us.'

Andromache felt a shiver of fear run through her. Trapped in this shallow, narrow river, the *Xanthos* would be vulnerable if the forces of Mykene were to find her. Had the admiral Menados been able to send word to Agamemnon of the ship's arrival? Had he had the time?

The rowers shipped their oars, and the sluggish pull of the river floated the vessel gently into the side. Andromache strained her eyes to see into the mist on the bank.

Suddenly a torch flared. A voice called softly, 'Ho, *Xanthos*!' A dark figure, hooded and cloaked, appeared out of the gloom. In the light of the single torch he looked massive.

Helikaon left the steering oar and strode down the aisle to the centre deck. With a long dagger in one hand he vaulted over the side of the ship and landed lightly on the soft ground beneath.

Andromache heard a familiar voice say, 'There is no need for daggers between us, Golden One.' Then Hektor pushed his hood back, stepped forward and threw his arms round Helikaon in a bear hug. She heard him ask, 'Is Andromache safe?' and she stepped to the side of the ship where she could be seen. Hektor looked up and in the torchlight she could see his face was tired and strained. But he smiled when he saw her.

A crewman dropped a ladder from the deck to the river bank

and she climbed swiftly down. She hesitated before her husband, her emotions in turmoil, then stepped into his embrace. She looked up at him. 'Astyanax?' she asked.

He nodded reassuringly. 'He is well,' he said.

They stood back, and the three of them gazed at each other. Andromache had not foreseen this moment. She had expected to return to Troy accompanied by Helikaon, with Hektor away at war, and she had spent sleepless nights aboard ship worrying about keeping their illicit love secret in a city of gossips and spies. Now her future was changed in a blink of an eye. Seeing Hektor again, his face speaking of burdens he could barely shoulder, she felt ashamed of herself and her selfish plotting.

Helikaon seemed genuinely pleased to see his old friend again. 'You are a welcome sight, cousin,' he said. 'How did you know we'd be here?'

'The beacon on the Cape of Tides. I gave orders for it to be lit when the *Xanthos* was spotted. We have looked long for your return, Golden One. We knew you would beat Menados' blockade.'

'Three brave men gave their lives to deliver us safely,' said Helikaon. 'Asios and two crewmen from the *Boreas*.'

'Their names were Lykaon and Periphas,' Andromache told him.

Helikaon looked at her and nodded. 'You are right, Andromache. Their names should not be forgotten. Asios, Lykaon and Periphas.'

'Those three could be the saving of Troy, if you come bearing tin,' said Hektor.

'We have a hold full of it, cousin.'

Hektor sighed with relief. 'Your mad bronzesmith Khalkeus tells me he can cast strong swords from the metal of Ares, but he has yet to show me one. Meanwhile our forges are dark. We could not contine the fight without your cargo. Let them unload with all speed, and we will speak.'

He gestured and from the darkness emerged men leading donkey-carts. Some of the newcomers swarmed up ropes on to the deck of the *Xanthos*. There were quiet words of greeting as old friends met again, then the hold doors were opened, and they started unloading the precious metal. Hektor led Helikaon and Andromache a short way across the flat marsh to where a small hillock hid a glowing campfire. The three sat down. Hektor undid his cloak and Andromache could see he was garbed in full armour.

'The news we hear from Troy is grave,' said Helikaon. 'Antiphones and Paris both dead. And poor Helen.'

'What of her children?' asked Andromache.

Hektor shook his head, and his silence told them everything. In the light from the fire, Andromache could see he had aged ten years since she last saw him. His eyes sat in dark hollows, and sorrow and grief seemed permanently etched on his features. He rubbed his hands over the fire. He seemed lost in thought, then he shivered as if bitter memories were returning to plague him.

He shook his head and said, 'Never in my worst nightmares did I believe Agamemnon could field so many warriors.' For a while he paused, his face haunted. 'Have you heard how we lost the battle for the Scamander? The treachery of the Fat King and his Lykians won the day for the western kings. After that the enemy took the fortification ditch quickly, within a day. They swarmed over it. They had the scent of victory in their nostrils, and we were hampered by trying to save our wounded. We have defended the lower town now for ten days, forcing Agamemnon's armies to battle for every wall, the smallest flagstone, every bloodstained pace. There has been carnage on both sides. But all the while they were fighting to win the town they could not surround the great walls, and we could get women and children out, and your cargo in. This was our hope. Now you are here, and with the protection of Athene we will smuggle the tin into the city tonight. The forges will all be at work before dawn. Then,' Hektor said, looking at them, 'tomorrow night, under cover of darkness, we will pull our troops back, retreat behind the walls, leave the enemy the lower town, and seal the gates.'

There was shocked silence, then Andromache said, 'But you have always believed Troy under siege would be doomed.'

Hektor nodded and stared at his hands, then started rubbing

them together again, as if he could not get warm. 'But I was a younger man then,' he said ruefully, 'who had not seen the horrors I have seen. I always feared treachery. Our history and yours, Helikaon, tells us there is always a traitor. But now we are sealing the great gates. The west and east gates have been bricked up. Only the Scaean Gate will be left open, and the Dardanian Gate. And those can only be opened on my personal command, or Polites'.'

'Polites?' Helikaon asked, frowning.

Hektor sighed. 'With Dios dead and Antiphones too, Father . . . Father can no longer be trusted to make decisions about the war. You have missed a great deal in the season you have been away. From today Polites is in charge of the defence of Troy. I will not go back there tonight. And at dawn tomorrow the Trojan Horse will ride from the golden city, never to return until Agamemnon destroys her or gives up the fight.'

Helikaon nodded his understanding, but Andromache said, 'The Trojan Horse abandon Troy? Why?'

Hektor explained gently, 'We cannot be trapped in the city, Andromache. Cavalry is useless there, and we will not be able to feed the horses if the siege goes on through the summer. Water will also be in short supply. The Trojan Horse must be free to attack the enemy where they least expect it, destroy Agamemnon's supply lines, seek out his weakest links and slice through them.'

Helikaon said, 'I see that they must leave the city. But must you go with them, cousin? If you stay in Troy you will give the people heart. Polites is a good man, but he cannot inspire with his leadership as you can. You are the heart and soul of Troy. You are needed there. Put Kalliades in charge of the Horse. He has a fine strategic mind.'

'I have thought long and hard about it,' admitted Hektor. 'But there will be nothing for me to do in a siege. I need to do the one thing I am good at . . .' He paused and sighed. 'I can fight and I can kill. I cannot do that behind high walls.' Helikaon opened his mouth to speak again, but Hektor held up his hand. 'My choice is made, Helikaon. The walls are impregnable. Polites will have to decide on rationing, the care of the wounded, and the safety of the gates. He will be better at all that than I.'

He looked at them, from one to the other. 'But you must leave as soon as possible, both of you, once the ship is unloaded. Helikaon, the *Xanthos* is like the Trojan Horse. She can do little stuck in the bay. But she is priceless to our cause on the open seas, attacking Agamemnon's supply routes, sinking his ships. The name of the *Xanthos* spreads terror among all seafaring men. You must make Agamemnon fear what is happening behind him, and force the kings to quarrel as they lose ships and their supplies run out. The longer this goes on the more each king will worry about what is going on at home, which leader is rising to take his place and assassinate his family.'

Helikaon drew a deep breath, but he nodded agreement. 'Menados will not expect me to sail again so quickly.' He glanced at the sky, where there was a glimmer of light in the east. 'We might get out again before dawn.'

Hektor said, 'The Trojan fleet has orders to go with you. It is under your command. Sink as many of Menados' ships as you can. But they fear your Fire Hurlers and will probably run.'

'We are low on *nephthar*,' Helikaon said.

'We have brought you two wagons full.' Hektor smiled a little. 'With great care.' He stood up, and said, 'May Poseidon look kindly upon you both.'

'He always has,' said Helikaon.

Andromache looked to both of them, anger rising in her breast. 'You speak as if all decisions have been made. But I decide my own future! I am not going with you,' she said to Helikaon. 'I will return to the city, as planned, and to my son.'

Hektor leaned down towards her and took her hand, pulling her to her feet.

'Escape while you can, Andromache,' he said. 'I beg you! Go with the *Xanthos*. There is a good chance that all these men,' he gestured to the river bank and the men hard at work unloading the tin, 'will be dead by the morning. We have pushed our luck to breaking point getting out of the city tonight. If we smuggle this tin into the city, to the forges where it is needed, it will mean Athene is truly smiling on us.' The shadows round his eyes deepened. 'And her face has been turned away from Troy in recent times.'

'And where would I go, Hektor?'

'To Thera, or to your father in Thebe. It is no longer under attack.'

She shook her head. 'No, I cannot. Agamemnon wants me dead. We have more than enough evidence of that. I bring danger with me wherever I go. If Troy falls Agamemnon will feel free to do anything he wants, even attack Thera and its sisterhood. If there is any safety for me, however ephemeral, it is in Troy. And Astyanax is there.'

Helikaon added, 'And my son Dex is there. Why could you not get them out of the city, Hektor? You said women and children were being smuggled out.'

Hektor sighed. 'Priam would not let the boys leave. They are together in the palace now. Father says as heirs to Troy and Dardanos they will be safest in Troy. Or rather, they would be more unsafe anywhere else. This is your argument, my love.' He looked at Andromache, one eyebrow raised. 'And it is a good one.'

'It is true,' she admitted. 'Agamemnon will hunt them both down. He is right, Helikaon. Dex will stay with Astyanax and me. I will take care of him.'

The three stood, and as they walked slowly back to the river bank, Helikaon told Hektor, 'Menados has a new ship, a great bireme almost as big as the *Xanthos*.'

'I know of it,' said Hektor. 'It is called the *Alektruon*. A cursed name. It has not the heart of the *Xanthos*. It is just a hollow copy.'

'And it was not built by the Madman from Miletos,' Helikaon replied grimly. 'It will break apart when Poseidon swims.'

On the *Xanthos* unloading was complete. Hektor turned to his companions and said, 'I fear we three will not meet again this side of the Dark Road. This is a story with no good endings.'

Andromache took his hand. 'We will meet again, Hektor. I know it.'

He smiled. 'Is this a prophecy, Andromache?'

'You know I am not given to prophecies, visions or prescient dreams. I am not Kassandra. I just know in my bones that this is not the end.' She kissed his hand gently. 'Until we meet again, my husband.'

She caught the expression on Helikaon's face, and she felt as if her heart was being wrenched in two. She was standing with the two men she loved, yet was to lose them both within moments. And she could not say a proper goodbye to either of them. Looking into Hektor's shadowed eyes she felt the familiar stab of guilt that she could never love him as he deserved. And under Helikaon's intense blue gaze she hated herself for hurting him by choosing to stay with her son.

Her heart in pain, she turned her eyes towards the distant city, hidden by the night. One thing was certain. There would be more grief for them all before the end.

XXI

Men of courage

WHEN DAWN ARRIVED IT FOUND THE *XANTHOS* STILL MAKING HER WAY back along the narrow Simoeis. Helikaon stood at the steering oar and watched for signs from Oniacus at the prow. The growing light behind them put the river ahead of the ship in deep shadow, and Oniacus was using a long notched pole to test the depth of the water. Progress was slow, and Helikaon had long since surrendered his first idea of attacking the Mykene fleet before sunrise.

He tried to keep his mind on plans for the battle ahead, but his thoughts kept straying back to Andromache. The moment he had first glimpsed her so long ago on that ill-starred night at Bad Luck Bay his heart had been ensnared. Until then he had always told friends he would marry for love alone. Until then, though, he had no idea what love was. And, arrogantly, he had believed the choice of marriage would always be his. He never dreamed he would fall helplessly in love with someone who was unavailable, already betrothed to his closest friend. The gods watch for such arrogance with glee, he thought.

In many ways these last hundred days had been the happiest of his life. The *Xanthos* was his true home, the one place where he could find total contentment. To share it with the woman he loved had been a pearl beyond price. There were times that winter, as they sailed from island to island, in fair weather or foul, as he watched Andromache sitting at the prow gazing at the sea, or walking like a flame-haired goddess among the oarsmen handing out water skins, or crouched by the mast holding on tightly as the ship ploughed through rough seas, when he thought he could never be happier. She was his north star, the fixed point round which his world turned. For as long as his heart beat, or hers, he believed they would always share a destiny.

He had not expected to lose her so suddenly that night, to watch her walk away beside one of the donkey-carts into the darkness on a perilous journey to the beleaguered city. She had made her choice, and chosen to stay with Hektor's son. She had not looked back. He had not expected her to.

As the sun rose a beam of light speared through the mist, and lit up the ships of the Trojan fleet waiting where the river Simoeis opened out into the bay. They lay as if becalmed in the pale morning, sails furled, the rowers resting on their oars, waiting for action. We are fighting the greatest war the world has ever seen, thought Helikaon, and our likely future is death and ruin, and you are thinking about the woman you love, instead of making battle plans. If this is what love can do to a man, perhaps you were better off without it.

He smiled to himself. I do not believe that, he thought.

He handed the steering oar to the helmsman, and strode to join Oniacus on the central deck. 'Gather the captains of the Trojan ships,' he told him. 'We have much to discuss.'

'I will ask them to join us, Golden One,' replied Oniacus. He turned away, then came back hesitantly. 'It is rumoured,' he said, 'that some of the Mykene ships now have their own Fire Hurlers.'

Helikaon laughed. 'Good news at last!' he said. Oniacus looked mystified. 'They will have no battle experience and little practice, Oniacus,' Helikaon explained. 'We know how dangerous the *nephthar* balls are and we treat them with great respect. In the heat of battle the Mykene will likely do more damage to themselves than to our vessels. This is welcome tidings. Just wait and see, my friend.'

It took a while for the captains of the eighteen Trojan ships to gather. The smaller ships eased in towards the *Xanthos*, until their masters could climb on board, sometimes crossing over several adjacent ships to get there. When he saw the mass of vessels lying together and bumping gently against each other, a new plan formed in Helikaon's mind.

Finally all the ships' masters were mustered on the central deck of the *Xanthos*. Helikaon knew them all, and he felt a thrill of pride. They were all men of courage, and skilled seamen. They had been frustrated by confinement in the bay for many days. Each was eager for action, but the most impatient was Chromis the Carian, master of the *Artemisia*, one of the fastest ships in the Trojan fleet, though the smallest. Chromis, a red-faced, burly man, stood at the front of the group, hands on hips.

'We are nineteen,' said Helikaon, looking round. 'Do we have an accurate report on the number of Menados' ships?'

'More than fifty,' said Chromis. 'Until today half of those were patrolling the coast down to the Bay of Herakles. The arrival of the *Xanthos* has caused Menados to order them all to the Hellespont. We are heavily outnumbered. But he will expect you to make a run for it soon, lord.'

'What Menados expects is a vital part of my plan,' said Helikaon thoughtfully. 'Which of your ships have Fire Hurlers?'

'The *Naiad* and the *Shield of Ilos*,' replied a young dark-eyed man with a heavy limp.

'And what experience have you of using them, Akamas?'

'None in battle, lord. But my men on the *Shield* and the crew of the *Naiad* have spent many long days throwing empty clay balls at targets. There was little else to do in the bay,' Akamas said ruefully. 'Our crews became quite expert at hurling them at the other ships.' Most of the masters smiled and there was some laughter.

'Have any of you seen a ship aflame with *nephthar*?' Helikaon asked, his face hardening, his voice cold.

They all shook their heads. Helikaon nodded. 'I thought not. You must understand, and all your crews must understand, that once a *nephthar* ball hits a ship and breaks, that ship is doomed, as if it already sat at the bottom of the Great Green. Do not wait for the fire arrows. All the crew must abandon ship without hesitation. Is that clear?' He looked round at them all, his violent blue eyes studying them one by one, until they had all nodded.

'Very good. And although I respect what you say, Akamas, I will put some of my own crewmen, with battle experience, on board the *Naiad* and the *Shield of Ilos* to advise and help with the *nephthar*. Do not feel slighted. Be in no doubt we have a mighty confrontation ahead. We need to allocate our skills where they are most needed. And we have extra crewmen, from the *Boreas*, to fill the gaps in any of your vessels' rowing benches.'

'The *Artemisia* may have no Fire Hurlers, Golden One,' said Chromis impatiently, 'but she has greater speed than some of these bigger ships. We can lead the Mykene a merry dance, if you so order.'

'Speed can be vital,' Helikaon replied, 'but usually running away from a battle, not towards it.'

The other captains laughed and Chromis flushed, fearing he was being made a fool of.

'I am not mocking you, Chromis,' said Helikaon. 'I have a part for the *Artemisia* to play, and it is an essential one. You will need all your ship's speed and agility.'

Chromis grinned and looked about him, proud to be chosen. 'So when do we attack them, Golden One?' he asked. 'The sooner our ships can slip out into the Great Green the sooner we can start to fight back, hit the enemy at the Bay of Herakles.'

'We will not attack,' Helikaon told him. 'We will wait for the Mykene to attack us.'

Chromis snorted. 'But how can we be sure of that? They've been content to keep us trapped in the bay like . . . like crabs in a net.'

'You yourself pointed out that much changed when the *Xanthos* arrived,' said Helikaon. He looked around the Trojan captains. 'We must have patience,' he said. 'Something the Mykene do not have. They are an impetuous and aggressive people. We must use that against them. And my plan is not just to slip past Menados, then make a run for it. I plan to destroy his entire fleet.'

*

The day passed with bone-aching slowness on the waters of the Hellespont, and when the sun slid down the sky there was still no sign that the *Xanthos* and the Trojan ships were planning to break out of the bay. Menados forced himself to stop pacing the deck of the *Alektruon*. He sat in his captain's chair, the picture of calm assurance. Inside his head, though, he was seething – with anger at the cunning Helikaon, and with his need to sail into the bay and smash the *Xanthos* into small shards. His captains had wanted to follow the hated galley in, but Menados had refused to chase after it in the dark.

All his fifty-five remaining ships were now at sea, either gathered off the entrance to the Hellespont, or patrolling the strait. The oarsmen were tired, and he ordered that they work in shifts, half the men rowing at a time. It had always been difficult to find rowers. Any man who could afford a soldier's armour and weapons would rather fight in the field than endure the hot fetid conditions on the rowing benches. Some of the ships' masters used slave labour. But chained slaves were unlikely to work as hard as free men, and the *Alektruon* was rowed entirely by Mykene warriors, proud to be on the finest ship of all the Mykene fleets.

As the light started to fail on the second day there was a shout from one of the vessels closest to the Cape of Tides. A craft had been spotted trying to break the blockade. Menados, excitement rising in his chest, ordered the *Alektruon* and the four nearest ships to intercept her. Block her course, he ordered, but do not engage yet.

Peering into the gloom he could soon see her for himself. It was not the *Xanthos*, but a smaller ship, with a dark sail sporting a white full moon. She sped along the line of the coast, perilously close to the rocks of the cape, risking the use of her sail to gain more speed.

'Not the *Xanthos*,' said his sister's son, disappointment in his voice. 'But maybe they are using a small ship to sneak the royal family out of Troy?'

'That would require a very small vessel indeed,' Menados said drily. And, he thought, Priam would never leave the city, or his treasury.

The small ship skipped across the waves, closer to the approaching Mykene galleys, then suddenly her sail was furled, the rowers took over and within heartbeats they had turned the vessel fully round and she was powering back towards the bay.

'Do not follow!' the admiral ordered, and the signal was quickly passed from ship to ship. The Mykene vessels pulled slowly away, reluctantly, Menados thought.

What is Helikaon up to, he wondered? Was it what it seemed? One ship making a run for it? Or another fire ship? No, Helikaon would not use that trick twice. He paced up and down the deck again, his officers watching him anxiously.

Finally he came to a conclusion. If Helikaon were to sneak past him again, two nights in a row, he and his officers would face a slow and agonizing death at Agamemnon's hands. He could not afford to let even one vessel out of the bay. It was another moonlit night, so he had to assume they would try again.

'There will be no rest for our crews!' he told his officers. 'Tonight all our ships will patrol!'

Helikaon was awake before dawn, when the light was just a pink glow in the east. He had slept deeply. The previous night he had put two ships out at the mouth of the bay to act as nightwatchmen. The rest of the crews got a good night's sleep and were fresh for the coming day.

He saw a Trojan galley gliding towards them from the cape, where its captain had picked up reports on the Mykene fleet from the watchers stationed there.

'They patrolled all night!' its master shouted up to Helikaon gleefully. 'Their rowers will all be as tired as dogs!'

Oniacus grinned at his lord. 'Tired crews and tired commanders,' he said.

Helikaon nodded. 'And tired men make poor decisions,' he answered. 'It is time for the *Artemisia* to lure them in.'

For a second time he watched Chromis' vessel head off gamely towards the Mykene fleet. He was impressed by the skills of the captain and his men. Chromis might be a blowhard, he thought, but he is right to be proud of his ship and its crew. May Poseidon keep her safe.

The crew of the *Xanthos* were busy preparing for battle. The clay balls full of *nephthar*, each as big as a man's head, were being carefully transferred from the hold to straw-lined baskets beside the Fire Hurlers. The hurlers themselves were being checked and greased. The specially prepared arrows and braziers were kept at the central deck, far away from the *nephthar*. Each crewman donned a leather breastplate and took up his sword and bow, and a quiver of arrows. Food was passed round to break their night fast, corn bread and cheese.

As the light grew stronger Helikaon ordered his small fleet to form up in two lines abreast facing north, well back from the mouth of the bay. The *Xanthos* was front and centre. The *Sword of Ilos* and the *Naiad*, with their Fire Hurlers, he placed near each end of the front line. The two ships that had watched all night were tucked in at the back in a position of comparative safety.

Helikaon strapped on his bronze breastplate, and sheathed the two leaf-bladed swords in scabbards on his back. He placed his full-face helm within reach. To his second-in-command he said, 'You are steersman today, Oniacus. Are you clear on our strategy?'

'Yes, Golden One,' Oniacus replied. He hesitated. 'We have never lost a sea battle yet,' he added, concern in his eyes. 'And I will follow your strategy without question, as always. Yet we are already trapped in this bay, like a mouse in a jug, and it seems your plan now is to lure a cat into the jug.'

Helikaon laughed, and his merriment rippled out across the water, making other men smile, easing tension.

'It is true we are trapped here,' he answered, 'but the mouse is safe only in his jug. We are seriously outnumbered, Oniacus. We cannot afford to engage the Mykene in the open sea. We would be sunk, or burned, or captured, every last ship. So we must lure the Mykene into the bay, where we have all the advantages. They have been at sea for weeks. They are bored and frustrated, and now they are tired too. Each Mykene captain wants the honour of sinking, or capturing, the *Xanthos*. Especially Menados. I let him live, remember. He is unlikely to forgive me for that.'

Oniacus scratched his curly head. 'Then let's hope they take the bait of the *Artemisia*.'

Helikaon shrugged. 'They will or they won't. If they don't, they will attack before this day is much older. They are Mykene. They won't be able to resist it.'

It seemed a long wait, but eventually the gallant *Artemisia* appeared in the distance rounding the cape, propelled by the northerly breeze. Helikaon watched Chromis' ship glide down the centre of the bay towards them. It was clear she had been attacked. There were arrows stuck in her planks. The ship drew up beside the *Xanthos*, and Helikaon looked down. There were injured men, but none appeared badly hurt.

'We had a close call, Golden One,' the burly Chromis called up to him, 'but I fear they have not taken the bait.'

'Take your place, Chromis,' said Helikaon. He gazed north, in the direction of the Hellespont. 'It appears you are wrong.'

Round the headland appeared the Mykene fleet, dozens of ships rowing in regimented order. As the crews in the Bay of Troy watched, the enemy vessels formed up into an attack formation. Helikaon smiled as he saw the front line was twelve ships wide. The vessels were well spaced out with plenty of room for the oars.

'Twelve abreast,' said Oniacus, grinning. 'Just as you predicted.'

'Menados is not a seaman,' explained Helikaon. 'He is one of Agamemnon's Followers. He was promoted to command a fleet after his successes in the field. So he does not know the Bay of Troy. Neither, it seems, do his captains.'

The rivers Simoeis and Scamander entered the Bay of Troy at east and south bringing a cargo of silt from higher lands. As the years passed the waters were getting shallower, and hidden mud banks had formed on all sides of the bay. Captains who knew these waters took a careful course down the centre of the bay to avoid the hazards on either side.

The mouth of the bay was wide, but it quickly narrowed. No more than eight ships could travel the bay abreast. Menados' twelve would be funnelled into the central channel where, Helikaon hoped, they would foul their oars and lose their attack formation. If the attacking ships started to swing and show their beams, the *Xanthos* could use her ram.

Ramming was a difficult manoeuvre to pull off effectively. Only a highly skilled crew and a captain of brilliant judgement and timing could count on success. At the moment of impact the ramming ship had to be travelling at just the right speed – too slow, and the enemy could back water out of range, too fast and the ram could get embedded so deeply into the target's hull that it would be stuck there, leaving the attacker vulnerable to attacks from other ships.

Khalkeus had equipped the *Xanthos* with a blunt-ended ram shod with bronze which drove through the sea just below the waterline. The purpose of this was not to penetrate the opponent's hull, but to deliver such a blow that it loosened all the planks around where it landed.

'What are we waiting for?' one of the oarsmen asked Oniacus in a loud whisper. The morning was wearing on and the sun climbing high, yet neither fleet had made a move.

Helikaon heard him and replied, 'We are waiting for the Scythe.' To Oniacus he added, 'Today the north wind is our friend. Perhaps Menados thinks it is his, but he is wrong.'

The stiff northerly which whistled through the city of Troy most days of the year was as predictable as sunrise. A light wind in the morning would build up as the sun reached its height. After noon the Scythe could cut through to the bone, then it would die away again as night fell.

Helikaon looked up at the city of Troy standing high above him off the starboard beam. The golden walls shone serenely in the sunlight, and from the bay it was impossible to tell that a war was going on beneath them. He could see movement in the lower town, dust rising, and he could hear distant shouts, but they sounded like the placid mewing of seabirds from this distance. The only indication of the war was the smoke from two funeral pyres, one to the west of the city, and one to the south, on the plain of the Scamander.

He turned his gaze back to the enemy fleet, and at last felt the wind cutting hard against his face. Helikaon raised his sword, the steersmen ran to their stations, and he shouted, 'Oars at four!'

The rowers pulled in to their oars with a will and the *Xanthos* leapt forward, the Trojan ships keeping pace. Out in the mouth of the bay the Mykene ships saw the challenge, and attacked!

Once the enemy oarsmen had built up momentum and the two fleets were racing towards each other, Helikaon raised both arms in the air and brought them down sharply. 'Reverse oars,' he cried. The powerful rowers leaned on their oars to back water. The Trojan fleet slowed sharply, as if their commander was afraid of contact. Seeing this, the Mykene ships powered on, tempted further into the bay. For a while they maintained a perfect attack formation.

Then, as Helikaon watched with narrowed eyes, the ships at each end of the front line hit shallow water and lost their rhythm, veering into the vessels beside them, their tired rowers fouling their oars. Ignorant of this, the centre of the front line kept pressing forward into the narrowing channel. Helikaon gave the order to attack again and once more the Trojan fleet sped forward. At last the officers on the *Alektruon* realized the ships at each end of their line were floundering helplessly, oars locked, in shallow water. The order was given to slow, but by then the second and third lines of ships, rowing hard to get in on the action and pushed by the Scythe, were unable to stop. The fast-moving galleys started ramming the back of their own attack line.

Helikaon saw a ship in the second line collide with the stern of the *Alektruon*, making her start to turn. The *Xanthos* had the Mykene flagship's beam in her sights. 'Ramming speed!' he shouted.

The *Alektruon* was still moving forward, her prow drifting helplessly to starboard, when the golden ship hit her. Only heartbeats before the impact Helikaon yelled, 'Reverse oars!' Again the disciplined rowers started to back water.

The two ships came together with a sound like a thunderbolt from Zeus. The *Xanthos* hit her target just behind the prow, shuddered from stem to stern, then pulled away. On both ships warriors were waiting on the foredeck with ropes and grappling hooks, swords and shields at the ready. But many were thrown from their feet by the impact, and as the *Xanthos* backed away there was clear water between the ships before men from either side could jump across. Helikaon felt a cold thrill of triumph. He knew the *Alektruon* was doomed. At the moment of collision he had felt the fatal give in the other ship as planks below the water-line caved in.

Panic erupted aboard the Mykene vessels. Their once-proud flag-ship started listing to port, and ships on both sides of the fleet were floundering in shallow water and thick mud. There were angry shouts and curses as panicking crews blamed each other for their plight. Then, as Helikaon had predicted they would, they let fly with the Fire Hurlers.

He ordered his fleet to back off as fast as possible. Some of the flying clay balls flopped into the water near the Trojan ships, but none of the enemy's hurlers had the height and range of those on the *Xanthos*. Helikaon instructed the crewmen who manned his Fire Hurlers to stand ready.

But they were not needed.

As the Trojan and Dardanian crews watched, two of the *nephthar* balls loosed by Mykene galleys hit other vessels of their fleet. Helikaon quickly ordered his archers to aim their fire arrows on the two ships that had been hit. Both targets went up in a whoosh of flame. The ships' hulls had been caulked with pitch, and the fires spread across the fleet with sickening speed. Crewmen dived and jumped into the waters of the bay, some to flounder waist-deep in sticky mud.

Before long the whole Mykene fleet was in flame, as the fire reached *nephthar* balls on other ships, and the braziers on listing craft turned over. Crewmen stuck in the centre of the mêlée of flaming ships died screaming. More died as they swam into range of the Trojans' arrows. Others swam and waded to the shore of the

Cape of Tides where they were killed by the Trojan soldiers holding the headland. A few made it to the eastern beach of the bay, to their own armies.

From the distance came the faint sound of cheering, and Helikaon looked to the walls of Troy where crowds had gathered to watch the destruction of the enemy fleet. He ordered two of his ships to pick up survivors for questioning, then strode back down the *Xanthos* to the aft deck.

Oniacus shook his head in awe, his face pale. 'They have lost more than fifty ships and hundreds of men, and we have just three crewmen with arrow wounds,' he said, scarcely believing what had happened. He gazed at Helikaon. 'Many Mykene ships are crewed by slaves, chained to their oars. What a hideous death.'

Helikaon knew he was remembering the events at Blue Owl Bay, when Oniacus had argued against such a fate for the Mykene pirates. 'I would not have wished this death on slaves,' he said. 'War makes brutes of us all. This is no victory to be proud of. These Mykene and their slaves were condemned to death by ignorance, arrogance and impatience.'

'*Alektruon* is a cursed name,' said Oniacus.

Helikaon nodded. 'That is true. Agamemnon is unlikely to anger Poseidon by building another one. We have only one problem now.'

'Yes, lord?'

'We must get out of the bay before Agamemnon has time to dispatch another fleet from Imbros or the Bay of Herakles. And our way is blocked.' Helikaon cursed. 'Those ships could go on burning until nightfall.'

'Although *nephthar* burns fiercely it burns quickly, we've found,' Akamas, captain of the *Shield of Ilos*, called up to them. 'Then you will find, Golden One, that the Shield and her sister ships can go where the great *Xanthos* cannot.'

As he waited for the fires to die down Helikaon interrogated some of the Mykene his crews had fished from the bay. Most were simple crewmen, who knew nothing. They were killed and thrown back into the water. One officer was rescued, but he died of his burns before he told them anything of importance.

The sun was sinking in the west by the time the *Artemisia* set out for the last time towards the Mykene fleet. Using oars as boat poles, the crew of the ship created a narrow channel through the smouldering mass of blackened timbers, finding and clearing underwater hazards, and fishing out large pieces of debris. One by one she was followed by the other ships, from smaller to larger, each widening the escape route to the mouth of the bay.

Finally two of them returned, the *Naiad* and the *Dolphin*. The crew of the *Xanthos* threw down ropes, and the two Trojan ships towed the huge bireme slowly through the channel the other vessels had made. The *Xanthos*' crewmen, oars shipped, watched in silence as they passed the hulls of ghostly galleys bearing hundreds of charred corpses. Some of the burned and blackened sailors still stood, fixed in the moment of death. Most had died chained at the rowing benches, their bodies writhing in the heat of the inferno. Many of the *Xanthos*' crewmen turned away, appalled by the horror of the scene. The timbers of the Mykene ships were still smouldering in places and the stench was sickening.

It was a long time before the fleeing ships reached open water and fresher air. Then, as the sun touched the horizon, the *Xanthos* and her small fleet sped into the Hellespont and out into the safety of the Great Green.

Andromache stood, as she had stood for most of the day, on the western wall of Troy, watching the events in the bay below. She had not joined in the cheers around her as the Mykene fleet burned. She had stood stiff and silent, afraid that if she opened her mouth she would break down in tears. In her heart she was saying a final farewell to the man she loved above all others. As the day cooled the crowds around her went back to their homes or barracks, but she stayed on until only she and her bodyguard of four remained.

Her night journey into the city had proved uneventful. The donkey train had made its way across the plain of the Simoeis, then under the northern edge of the plateau on which Troy stood. As they neared the city Andromache could make out lights high above. They were the windows of the queen's apartments, which faced north above the high cliff. There were unlikely to be enemy soldiers stationed beneath the sheer rock face. But as they reached the foot of the northeast bastion scouts were sent ahead to see if the way to the Dardanian Gate was clear. They waited in darkness, knowing they had only a few paces to go, but that those paces were the most perilous. If Agamemnon's troops had reached the Dardanian Gate, then they were lost. It seemed an age before the scouts returned to say the road to the gate was still open. The donkey train slipped inside the city to safety.

Andromache's reunion with Astyanax had been joyous. As she had embraced the boy, warm and sleepy and bewildered from being woken in the middle of the night, she saw another child, fair-haired and white-faced, standing in the corner of the room clad in a nightshift. Still holding her son to her, she knelt down and smiled. 'Dex?' she asked gently, and the little boy nodded dumbly. She saw his face was tear-stained as if he had cried himself to sleep. She put her arm round him and hugged him to her. 'I am Andromache,' she whispered, 'and I will look after you, if you wish. Would you like to stay here with Astyanax and me?' She sat back and looked into his dark eyes. He said something but it was so quiet she could not hear. She put her ear close to his lips and said, 'Say that again, Dex.'

The little boy whispered, 'Where is Sun Woman? I can't find her.'

Now, standing on the western wall, she watched as the pall of smoke hanging over the fleet of dead ships was blown away by the north wind. She realized that the fog that had clouded her thoughts for the past days, a fog born of conflicting emotions, fear and exhaustion, had dispersed. She was glad to be back in Troy, where she belonged, with her son beside her and his little orphan cousin. She was no one's lover, no one's daughter, no one's wife. If they were all to die, as she feared they would, then they would be together. She would protect the children to the last and would die with them.

She waited until the *Xanthos* reached the mouth of the bay, raised her arm in an unseen farewell and, her heart at peace for the first time in days, made her way back to the palace, to her home.

XXII

Traitors at the gate

ON THE WEST WALL KHALKEUS ALSO STOOD WATCHING, BUT AS THE Mykene ships started to burn he turned and walked away, head bowed. He knew the Golden One would escape the inferno and make his way out to sea in the *Xanthos*. Khalkeus had no wish to see any more.

Truly it was called the Death Ship, he thought, the name given to it by the Kypriot carpenters who had built it but refused to sail on it, fearing it was a challenge to Poseidon who would sink it for its arrogance.

But Khalkeus had designed the *Xanthos* to be a trading vessel, to hold more cargo and to be faster than its competitors and, crucially, to be strong enough to brave the heavy seas of spring and autumn and prolong its sailing season well past the days when other ships returned to their safe harbours. And it had exceeded his wildest expectations, sailing the treacherous waters of winter all the way to the far west and back in the search for tin. Khalkeus had looked forward to its return, so he could discuss the ship's travels with the Golden One, hear him praise Khalkeus' skills as a ship-wright, and talk about modifications he could make to the vessel.

Instead, as on that cursed day at the Bay of Blue Owls, he had watched men burn when the Death Ship sailed.

The Mykene were a callous and ruthless race, he told himself. They brought destruction down upon themselves. But the Fire Hurlers were *his* invention; he had built them for Helikaon to fight off pirates and reavers, and now his mind was clouded by sorrow for the men killed so cruelly in their hasty bid to copy the *Xanthos'* fire weapon. The Madman from Miletos, they called him. Perhaps they were right, he thought. Only a madman would create such a weapon of death.

He elbowed through the excited crowd of Trojans all pointing and cheering at the blazing ships, then climbed down the steps from the western wall, and made his way northeast through the maze of streets. He looked about him as he walked, seeing the city with troubled eyes. When he had first arrived Troy had been a remarkable sight, a city unlike any other in the world. The great palaces of the mighty were roofed with bronze and decorated with red and green marble, their walls carved with creatures of legend. Priam's palace boasted a roof of pure gold, which shone in the sunlight, and could be seen from far out at sea. Wide stone avenues were thronged with noble men and women garbed in rich, brightly coloured clothes, glinting with jewellery, eager to see and be seen. The whole world came to Troy to gasp at its beauty, and to profit from its wealth.

Now the world had come to Troy to bring it to its knees and plunder that wealth.

The streets around him were filled with shacks and shanties built by refugees from the lower town, who hoped for safety behind the great walls. Their rough wood and hide shelters, hundreds of them, leaned low against the tall palaces of the rich and powerful. Traders and craftsmen lived in these hovels, some working – if they had the materials – but most living on the hope that one day the war would end and they could return to their trades and prosper again.

There was an atmosphere of fear and anger in the streets, and few ventured out after dark. Food was becoming scarce and the stores of grain were closely guarded, the bakeries too. Water was also a problem. There were two wells within the walls, but most of the city's water had come from the Scamander, now behind enemy lines, and the Simoeis, from which cartloads of water barrels were still brought from time to time. The city wells were also guarded, to ensure fighting did not break out among the waiting crowds of thirsty people, and to secure the meagre water supply from poisoning by agents of the enemy.

Khalkeus wove his way through the confusing pattern of alleys created by the shanties. It seemed to change from day to day. At one point the path he was following came to a dead end, and he cursed in frustration. He thought he was alone in the smelly, shadowy alley, but then a voice said, 'Give you a ride to remember, lord. Only one copper ring.' A skinny whore was sitting in the doorway of a shack, her eyes heavy-lidded with fatigue and disappointment, bright splashes of red paint on her cheeks. She cocked her head and smiled at him, and he saw her teeth were grey and rotten.

He shook his head nervously and hurried back down the alley, finding his way at last to the square before Priam's palace. The great doors were open and the red-pillared portico was flanked, as always, by a line of Royal Eagles in bronze breastplates and high helms with cheekguards inlaid with silver, and white plumes.

Khalkeus looked up at the gleaming gold roof, a symbol of Priam's wealth and power. The bronze had been torn off the roofs of the other palaces, at Hektor's command, to fashion into weapons. Only this remained, a shining beacon drawing Priam's enemies, taunting them to come and take it.

He walked on. At the Dardanian Gate beneath the northeast bastion he was forced to stop and wait for a train of donkey-carts to come in. Two of the carts carried water barrels. The others were loaded with families and their possessions, tearful children and their anxious mothers, their menfolk plodding alongside. One was piled high with wooden crates filled with chickens.

A burly gate guard strolled over to him. 'You again, smith. You like to take your chances, don't you? One of these days Agamemnon will attack this gate, then we have orders to close and seal it. It wouldn't do if you were stuck outside.'

'It is not in Agamemnon's best interests to seal the city, not yet,' replied Khalkeus, reluctant to get into a conversation with this man.

'He's letting families out,' continued the soldier. 'My wife and children left two days ago for the safety of Zeleia.'

'How many have gone out today, and how many have come in?'

The man frowned. 'I've been here since dawn and I've seen more than fifty people come in. Two families have left.'

'So more are coming into the city than going out,' Khalkeus snapped, irritated by the man's lack of understanding. 'Can't you see, you idiot, that's what Agamemnon wants – Troy packed with refugees, eating the stores of grain, drinking the precious water. They are of no use to the city. They do not bring weapons, most of them cannot fight. They are farmers and their families. They bring only fear . . .' he gestured to the women and children, and spluttered, 'and babies!'

The guard looked angry. 'Then why are the enemy letting people out?' he demanded.

Khalkeus held his tongue with difficulty, and moved towards the gate. In his own mind he knew the soldier's family were already dead, had died as soon as they had travelled out of sight of the walls. Agamemnon would not allow children to leave the city, knowing that Hektor's son and the Dardanian heir were inside.

Outside the walls he glanced to the south, where the enemy were camped a mere two hundred paces away, then followed the stone road round the north of the plateau, hunching his shoulders against the wind. Eventually he reached the line of empty forges.

Troy's forges had lit up this area since the birth of the city. The wind scythed in from the north, hitting the high hillside and making the furnaces roar in a way no manmade bellows could. But when the war started Priam had ordered all his forgemasters behind the walls, and these furnaces were now abandoned. Except by Khalkeus.

Since he was very young the bronzesmith realized he thought in a different way from other people. His head constantly brimmed with ideas. He was impatient with those who could not understand the solutions to simple problems which seemed obvious to him. He was curious about the world, and spotted challenges everywhere. When he saw oarsmen rowing a ship he wondered what could be done to make it go faster. He understood instinctively why one house would fall down in a winter gale, while another nearby remained standing. Even as he had shunned the whore's advances that day part of his mind had been wondering what the red paint on her face was made from, and why some people's teeth rotted faster than others.

But his obsession for ten years or more had been his search for the perfect sword.

Everyone knew of the lumps of grey metal that fell from the skies. Most thought them a gift of Ares. They were prized, more valuable than gold. Priam had several in his treasury, and sometimes small objects – brooches, even arrowheads – were hammered out of the cold grey metal.

The Hittites had learned to make swords of this star metal, it was said, but they guarded the secret closely. Khalkeus had never seen such a weapon, but he believed the stories. He had gathered several slivers of the metal over the years and studied them. He had found they could not be scratched by bronze, only by some gemstones. He believed there had to be a way to cast the metal into a sword stronger than the best bronze, a sword that would bend, not break, would remain sharp, and last a warrior a lifetime.

His greatest surprise, studying the shards, was that they went red and rotted when left in water. The red crumbly remains made him think of the red rocks mined all over the country in the search for gold and the elusive tin, rocks considered valueless and thrown away by the miners. He employed workmen to bring cartloads of these red rocks to his forge, and the other smiths had mocked him when he heated them over charcoal in his furnace. Brought to the heat at which copper could be smelted, the new metal refused to become molten and flow, separating itself from the slag and unburned charcoal. What was left was merely a grey spongy mass which, when cooled, shattered at the blow of a hammer.

Frustrated, he pondered over this for a time. Seeing the metal could be weakened by water, he concluded it must be strengthened by fire. He needed more heat. He had persuaded King Priam to fund bigger furnaces, taller than any seen before in Troy, so the grey sponges could be heated fiercely enough to melt fully and release their pure metal. His neighbouring smiths laughed at him at first, then stopped laughing when the first two furnaces burned down, taking nearby forges with them. Then the war came to Troy and the other forgemasters followed the king's orders and moved into the city.

But not Khalkeus. Now, alone on the hillside at last, away from the prying eyes and jeering comments, he looked up at the great chimney he was building. Surrounded by a scaffold of wood, it was already twice the height of a man. Rubbing his palms together, Khalkeus set to work.

Cocooned in a soft pile of sweet-smelling bedlinen and downy cushions, Andromache slept on long past dawn, deeply asleep in the unaccustomed comfort of a real bed. When the sound of muted sobbing woke her, the sun was high.

Luxuriously she stretched, then rolled over and sat up. 'What is it, Axa? What's wrong?'

Her maid, placing a large bowl of scented water on a table, turned a tear-stained face to her. 'I'm sorry, lady. And you so tired. I didn't mean to wake you.'

'I thought you'd be glad to see me back,' Andromache teased her, running her hands through her thick red hair, pushing it away from her face.

Axa smiled wanly. 'Of course I am, lady. But just as you get back safely my Mestares leaves.' Tears welled up in her eyes again and she hung her head. 'I'm sorry, princess, but I am frightened for my babies. The enemy are letting women and children go. I wanted to travel to Phrygia. It is a long way, I know, but I have family there. My babies would be safe. But Mestares would not let me. He forbade me to leave the city. I could not complain, lady, because he was here with me. But now the Trojan Horse have left in the night. And he said nothing to me. Not a word.'

'I know. They rode out at dawn.'

'No, my lady, they left in the middle of the night.'

Andromache nodded thoughtfully. 'Hektor can trust no one. All the while refugees are entering the city Agamemnon will be sending his spies in with them. Mestares could not tell you he was going. Perhaps he did not even know himself. Hektor told me they were leaving at dawn. You see, he could not even tell *me* the truth.'

Axa sniffed and rubbed the tears off her cheeks. 'Everyone says we're safe behind the great walls. You believe that, don't you, my lady? You came back.'

Andromache could not lie to her. 'I don't know, Axa. I came back because my son is here. Where is he this morning?'

'The boys are playing in the gardens. They are firm friends now. It is nice to see them playing so happily together.'

But Andromache felt a stab of fear at her words. Their talk of spies had made her feel vulnerable. 'In the gardens? Are they being watched?'

Axa nodded vehemently. 'They are guarded at all times, my lady. Prince Hektor picked their bodyguards himself. They are safe.'

Andromache saw the maid's plump face cloud over again as she thought of her own three children, and she said hastily, 'I think the scarlet dress today.'

Surprised, Axa said, 'My, your travels have changed you, lady. You don't normally care what you wear. And you seldom wear that scarlet gown. You said it makes you look like . . .' she lowered her voice, 'like one of Aphrodite's maidens.'

Andromache laughed. 'I have spent the entire winter in just three dresses. I am sick and tired of them. Take them out and burn them. I might even do it myself. Now, Axa, you must tell me all the palace gossip I have missed. I hear the princess Kreusa has fled the city.'

A curtain rattled and one of her handmaids, sloe-eyed Penthesileia, came in. 'The king wishes to see you, lady.'

'Thank you, Penthesileia. Axa, our gossip will have to wait. Quickly, help me get ready.'

It was close to noon and the warm air held the promise of summer when Andromache arrived at Priam's *megaron*, yet the atmosphere inside was chill and gloomy. She felt goose bumps rise on her arms as she walked to where Priam sat on his carved and gilded throne, flanked by Polites and Polydorus, with his guard of six Eagles behind him.

Coming up close to the king, Andromache saw he looked shrunken and frail. She remembered the vital powerful man she had first met on the Great Tower. Then she looked into his eyes and shuddered inwardly. The king she once knew, though cruel and capricious, had a sword-sharp mind. Now all she could see in the eyes was cold emptiness. She remembered Kassandra saying of Agamemnon's eyes, 'They are empty. There is no soul behind them.' Do all kings come to this at last, she thought?

'Andromache,' said the familiar voice, though cracked and thin. 'You have been away from us too long. Tell me of your travels.'

Standing in front of him like a dutiful child Andromache started to tell him of their journey: Helikaon's duel with Persion, her talks with Iphigenia, the winter journey to the Seven Hills, and their return, right up to her arrival with the donkey-carts full of tin. She left out only the attack on Ithaka. She gave a detailed account and it took a long time. She was chilled to the bone by the time she finished her tale. All the while she watched him, wondering how much he was taking in. His gaze drifted from time to time, then slowly turned on her again.

Finally she fell silent. There was a long pause, then he said, 'And Ithaka. You missed that out. Surely one of the most interesting events of your journey.'

'Ithaka, my king?'

He leaned forward, and she saw the whites of his eyes were yellow as egg yolks. 'It is the talk of the Great Green that Odysseus stormed his own *megaron* to rescue his wife. Achilles was with him. And the *Xanthos* was seen there at the time. Aeneas helping his old friend, and *our* adversary. I know everything that happens on the Great Green, girl. Do not seek to fool me.'

Andromache remained silent. The king coughed painfully and went on, his voice harsh, 'I declare Aeneas to be an enemy of Troy.

He will be executed when he returns to the city. Do you hear me, Polites?'

'Yes, Father.' Polites caught Andromache's eye and shook his head slightly. 'You are tired now, Father. You must rest.'

Priam ignored him. 'You are not wearing the gown I gave you,' he said to Andromache.

'My lord?' She looked down at the scarlet dress.

'The gold-embroidered gown with the dolphin shawl. You said you would wear it today.' The old man leaned forward again and stared at her, frowning. Then he reached out a claw-like hand and dragged her to him. He was still a powerful man, and Andromache felt his sour breath on her cheek, hot and feverish. His grip on her arm was like a vice.

'Who are you?' he rasped. 'You are not my Hekabe. Are you one of the ghosts? I tell you again, you do not frighten me!'

She said calmly, 'I am Andromache, wife to Hektor.'

'Where is Hekabe?' He released her, pushing her away, and looked around him. 'She said she would wear the golden gown.'

Polydorus stepped forward and offered the old man a drink from a goblet of gold, and Polites moved alongside Andromache. 'You can go now,' he said quietly. 'I know his moods. He is living back in his past and he does not know you.'

'Hektor said the king could no longer be trusted. He did not explain further,' Andromache said as they walked from the *megaron* out into the fresh air. Polites told her of the regiments' retreat from the Scamander and the burning of the bridges, and she listened in horror.

'But if his Eagles still obey him,' she said, 'Helikaon will be killed when he returns to Troy.'

Polites smiled sadly. 'Father no longer has any Eagles at his command.'

'But the Eagles in the *megaron* . . .' Her voice tailed off as realization struck her. 'I see. They are *not* Eagles.'

'No, they are all Hektor's men, hand-picked by him to guard the king. If you had looked closely you would have seen that one of them is Areoan, Hektor's shield-bearer and one of his most loyal friends. They do not do Priam's bidding. Any order he gives they bring to me.'

'Then you are truly king in Troy, Polites.'

He nodded ruefully. 'Yes, I suppose I am.'

'Then Hektor should not have left,' she said sharply. 'I am sorry, brother, but you are not a military man.'

'I told him that myself. Come, let us walk.'

They wandered into the gardens, where Andromache could see the two little boys playing, watched by their bodyguards. She longed to run to Astyanax and take him in her arms. But instead she paced slowly beside Polites as he talked.

'People say Priam had fifty sons, you know,' he told her. 'But much that's said about the king is nonsense. Many think my own sons were sired by him. It is something of a joke in the city. But it is not true. My wife Suso lived away from Troy for most of our marriage because she feared the king's advances. She died in the winter. Did you know that?' Andromache shook her head, struck dumb with compassion for a woman she had never known. 'It was a coughing fever,' Polites explained flatly as if talking about the weather. 'But our two boys are safe. I sent them far from the city over a year ago. No one knows where they are but me. They were the heirs to Troy before your Astyanax was born. But they will never know that. Even the good merchant and his wife who are raising them as their own don't know who they are.' Polites paused. 'But I am straying from my point, sister. You see, Priam had many sons, but he has been profligate with them. I know for certain he had five murdered, probably more. And now he has lost Dios and my good friend Antiphones, and Paris too. And Hektor, the best of us, is not here. So the only son he has left is poor Polites, who is, as you say, not a military man.'

Andromache started to speak, but he held his hand up. 'Hektor believes the walls cannot be taken, and I think he is right. So there is nothing to do for those of us behind them but to guard and ration the food and water, and ensure the Scaean Gate is not opened by treachery.'

'But if somehow they do break in, and you fall, Polites, who will then order the defence of the city?'

'If I fall, Andromache, its generals will defend the city.'

At that moment there was shouting from the portico, and an Eagle came running through the open bronze gates and into the courtyard gardens. 'The Mykene are attacking the walls, lord! They have hundreds of ladders.'

Polites' expression darkened. 'Where?' he demanded.

'The east and west walls, my lord.'

'Who commands the walls today?'

'Banokles' Scamandrians have the west, Lucan the east.'

'Then I will go to the west wall. Soldier, go and fetch my armour.' Polites glanced at Andromache. 'A prince must be seen in his armour,' he explained shyly

He turned to go and almost collided with a red-headed man making his way towards the palace. Andromache recognized Khalkeus the bronzesmith. The old smith was covered with dust, and he looked exhausted, as if he had worked all night.

'I must see the king,' he said curtly.

'You cannot see the king now,' Polites answered.

'Then I wish to see you, Prince Polites,' said Khalkeus, folding his arms and planting himself in the prince's path. 'It is very important. I must have more resources. My work is vital.'

'Another time, Khalkeus. The walls are under attack.'

Khalkeus raised his eyebrows in surprise. 'Under attack? With ladders?' Polites nodded and pushed past him. 'Interesting!' said the smith. 'I will come with you.'

Andromache watched them hurry off – Polites with his long white robes flapping around skinny legs, stocky Khalkeus trotting along behind him. Her heart full of dread, she turned and walked back to the two boys playing in the sunlit gardens.

Khalkeus followed in the footsteps of the king's son as he made his way through the city, flanked by a troop of Eagles. He had completely forgotten his concerns about the forge, his interest piqued by this new turn of events. He had long since dismissed the possibility of the enemy's attacking with ladders. The great walls were high, and the slant of the lowest section meant ladders would have to be unusually long, which would make them heavy to manoeuvre and extremely unstable.

The scene upon the west wall was one of calm control. The battlements were heavily defended by the Scamandrian regiment. At only one point had the enemy managed to climb to the top. Khalkeus watched the obnoxious Mykene renegade Banokles and his men kill them, strip their armour, then throw the bodies back over the wall.

He peered cautiously over the wall at the scene below. More than fifty ladders had been thrown up against the stones. They were all just short of the battlements and, once the enemy troops had started climbing them, their weight made the tops of the ladders hard to dislodge. Nevertheless, the Trojan soldiers were doing an efficient job, leaning over, hooking the ends of ladder poles to the top rungs, then pushing them away and down, sending enemy warriors crashing back among their fellows, breaking arms, legs and heads.

'Slide the ladders!' Polites yelled, seeing what was happening. 'Wait until they have plenty of men on them, then slide them sideways. Then they'll take others down with them.'

Arrows flew over the battlements, targeting the soldiers trying to dislodge the ladders, and Polites hurriedly donned his breastplate and helm when they were brought to him. Khalkeus looked about him, wrenched a helmet from a dead Trojan soldier and hastily put it on. It smelled of blood and sweat.

A troop of Phrygian archers came running up the stone steps, prepared to target the bowmen on the ground. But tall Kalliades, the general's aide, stopped them with a shout. 'Don't shoot! They are too far away for accuracy. Let them keep shooting at us. We may need their arrows later.'

Kalliades glanced at Polites, who nodded his agreement. 'Yes, we need their arrows. And we need other missiles. They are an open target, all those enemy soldiers milling down below us.'

Banokles strolled up to them, wiping blood off one of his swords on a piece of cloth. 'That was fun,' he commented. He leaned over the battlements, then jumped back as an arrow glanced off his helm. 'Boiling oil, that's what we need,' he said, echoing Polites' words. 'Or water. That'll give them something to think about.'

'There is little oil, and no spare water in the city,' answered Polites. 'We cannot use the water we might need to drink come the end of summer.' The men looked at each other, all no doubt thinking the same thing: *Will we still be here come summer's end?*

Khalkeus stepped forward. 'Sand,' he said. The three men looked at him. 'Sand is what we need. Ordinary sand from the beach. Plenty of it. Is there any inside the city?'

Polites frowned. 'Sand is used in the royal gardens. There are piles of it there. It is mixed with soil where drainage is required.' He saw Kalliades' and Banokles' expressions of surprise, and smiled slightly. 'As has been said already today, I am not a military man. But I do know about plants.' He turned to Khalkeus. 'You can have all you want, smith, but what do you want it for?'

At that moment a powerful Mykene warrior levered himself over the wall beside them. As he cleared the battlements, Kalliades leapt towards him and skewered his heart with a sword thrust. The man slumped across the wall, his sword clattering to the stone floor. Kalliades and Banokles grabbed an arm each and threw him back over. Khalkeus peered down and saw the warrior's leg catch on the ladder he had climbed and bring it down, along with four men climbing behind him.

'They're just wasting their men,' Banokles snorted. 'We can go on doing this all day. It makes no sense.'

'You're right,' Polites replied, his face creased with worry. 'It makes no sense. Agamemnon is an intelligent man.' He looked to Kalliades, his face suddenly clearing. 'It is a diversion!'

Kalliades ran for the steps. 'If they attack the east and west walls, they will expect us to pull our troops away from the south!'

'The Scaean Gate!' Polites shouted, following him. To Banokles he yelled, 'Bring some men!'

Instead of pursuing them down the stone steps, Khalkeus trotted hurriedly along the top of the western wall, then along the south wall as far as the Great Tower of Ilion. Below him, inside the Scaean Gate, there was a furious battle going on. The guards, defending the gate desperately against a group of dark-garbed warriors, were being forced back. As he watched, the last of the guards was brought down and the attackers sprang for the great oak locking bar. It took six men to lift the bar, Khalkeus knew, but there were eight men and they had just laid their hands on it when Kalliades and Banokles arrived at a run.

Banokles charged into them with a roar, half beheading one, and slashing a second across the face. The locking bar had cleared its support at one end. There was a tremendous crash from outside and the gate shifted inward slightly under the blow. Kalliades leapt on the end of the bar and threw his weight on it, helped by soldiers who had arrived behind him. The huge oak bar locked back into place just as a second blow hit the gate from the outside.

On the wall above them, Khalkeus hurried to the other side and looked down. Outside the gate the massive trunk of an oak tree was being wielded as a battering ram by fifty or more men. Behind them warriors waited, armed and armoured. The battering ram powered forward once again, but the great gate barely shuddered. It was firmly locked.

As the bronzesmith watched, one of the waiting warriors turned his gaze up towards him, and Khalkeus saw it was the king of Ithaka. Their eyes locked, and Khalkeus slowly shook his head. Odysseus sheathed his sword, then turned and walked away from the gate.

XXIII

Kings at war

ODYSSEUS TORE OFF HIS HELM ANGRILY AS HE STOMPED THROUGH THE
streets of the ruined lower town. Just as he had predicted, the
Trojans had quickly seen through the ploy. Agamemnon's
diversionary tactic had not been a bad idea, he admitted to himself.
Had it worked it might have been worth sacrificing the hundreds
of men injured and killed in the attack on the walls. But it had *not*
worked, and they had wasted brave soldiers and, more important,
lost eight agents inside the city. Those of the eight who survived
would be interrogated, but they knew nothing that would help
the Trojans. The Ithakan king had no idea how many agents
Agamemnon had infiltrated into the city, but he was certain
there would now be no more. Hektor, or whoever commanded in
Troy, would certainly seal the last gates now to stop more refugees
– and Mykene spies – from getting in.

Odysseus had always predicted that, sooner or later, there would
be a bid by his allies to scale the great walls. He thought back to
two nights previously. He and some of his crew from the
Bloodhawk were camped in the courtyard of a palace once owned
by Antiphones, now the home of Achilles' Myrmidons. There had
been no fighting that day, but fresh deliveries of wine had arrived,
and the mood was festive.

DAVID & STELLA GEMMELL

Achilles' shield-bearer Patroklos, standing with a goblet of wine in one hand and a hunk of roasted sheep in the other, had been arguing for an attempt on the walls.

'Look at them,' Patroklos had said, swaying a little as he spoke, waving his goblet towards the south walls. 'A child could climb them. Plenty of handholds between the stones.' He swigged wine and swallowed. 'We wait for a dark night, then the Myrmidons will be over the west wall before the Trojans see us coming. Fight our way to the Scaean Gate, and the city is ours. What do you say, Odysseus?'

'I say my climbing days are over, boy. And the west wall is a poor choice. Because everyone knows it is the lowest, the weak link in the chain of walls, it is more heavily defended than the others.'

'Which would be your choice, Odysseus?' asked Achilles, who was lying on his back staring at the stars.

'I would try the north wall.'

Patroklos snorted with derision. 'A vertical cliff face with sheer walls above? I wager no one could climb that.'

'I wager,' replied Odysseus, 'that *you* couldn't climb the west wall.'

Patroklos could never resist a wager, as the Ugly King knew well. He and Odysseus and Achilles, followed by a happy wine-soaked band of Myrmidons and Ithakans, left the palace and made their way round to the west wall. Framed by the starlit sky, the walls soared high above them.

'What will you wager, old king?' asked Patroklos.

'Five of my ships against Achilles' breastplate.'

Achilles raised his eyebrows. 'Why *my* breastplate?' he queried.

'Because it is well known that Patroklos has not a copper ring to his name, and always reneges on his wagers. You, on the other hand, are a man of honour, and will pay your friend's debts, as you always do.'

Patroklos grinned, uncaring, and Achilles shrugged. 'So be it,' he said. 'What if Patroklos climbs the wall and is killed when he reaches the top?'

'Then the wager stands and you win five Ithakan ships.'

The young warrior tied his braided blond hair back at his neck, kicked off his sandals, and ran at the wall, leaping lightly on to the first high stone. Then, finding easy hand- and footholds, he swiftly climbed to the point where the wall became vertical. There he paused, looking up. He found a handhold to his right and, stretching, just managed to catch the tips of his fingers to it. He moved his feet up carefully, one at a time, then looked for a new handhold to the left. There wasn't one. The top of the huge stone he was clinging to was far above his searching hand.

Seeing his predicament the Ithakans began jeering, but Odysseus hushed them. He glanced at the top of the wall. He could not see sentries in the darkness, but he knew they were there.

Patroklos carefully moved his right foot up to a narrow crack in the stone. He wriggled his bare toes as far as he could into the poor foothold. He glanced up again to check where he was going. Then, taking a deep breath, he leapt for the top of the stone. He just made it, clinging on with his fingertips. His right foot slipped but he managed to get his right hand to the top of the stone as well and held on, scrabbling for a foothold.

But the sound had alerted the sentries. Odysseus saw a soldier peer over the battlements high above and pull back quickly, shouting to his fellows. An archer leaned over with his bow, an arrow to the string. Patroklos was an easy target.

Then from his right Odysseus saw a flash of movement. In a heartbeat Achilles had drawn a dagger and thrown it at the bowman high above them. Odysseus saw it flash through the air, turning over and over in the moonlight, and thunk into the dark shape of the bowman's head. It was an impossible feat: so small a target, at such a height, and in starlight.

Achilles dashed forward. 'Get down, Patroklos, now!'

His shield-bearer quickly climbed down the wall, jumping down the last section, and the two ran back to the Myrmidons who were covering their retreat, shooting arrows up at the gathering Trojan bowmen. Patroklos was laughing when they reached the waiting Odysseus.

'Well, old king,' he said. 'What of our wager now?'

'You did not reach the top of the wall.'

'I was stopped by enemy action.'

'Enemy action was not taken into account. It was a flawed wager.'

Patroklos had shrugged amiably, and they had all returned to the palace. But word had reached Agamemnon of the young warrior's climb, and the next day the Battle King had come up with the doomed plan to scale the walls and take the Scaean Gate.

Reluctantly, Odysseus smiled to himself as he walked back through the sunlit town two days later. He liked Patroklos. Everyone did. He was always cheerful, often playing the fool to amuse his king, and he was brave as a lion. Strange, Odysseus thought, that the fact that Patroklos clearly liked Achilles made the Thessalian king, often brooding and uncommunicative, more popular among his troops.

Patroklos provided some entertainment through the long days, much needed by Odysseus, who spent as little time as possible with Agamemnon and the western kings. Quarrels were always breaking out amongst them. Nestor and Idomeneos seldom spoke, after Sharptooth had suddenly withdrawn his archers from the field one day, leaving Nestor's troops without cover as they attacked one of the lower town's palaces. Sharptooth avoided Odysseus, for the Ithakan king never failed to remind him that he owed Odysseus his gold and silver breastplate, wagered on Banokles' fistfight long ago at Apollo's Bow. And Agamemnon and Achilles now loathed each other, and were constantly at war over something, even falling out over the ownership of a female slave, the daughter of a priest. Odysseus knew it would suit Agamemnon well if Achilles were to die at Troy. When they returned at last to their homelands he would not want such a strong king as a neighbour and potential enemy.

As he walked through the lower town, the Ugly King looked around him with sadness. There were few palaces in this part of Troy. Here had been the homes of craftspeople – dyers, potters, textile workers – and many of the servants to the great houses of the mighty. Before the war there were children running through the streets and alleyways, colourful marketplaces in every square, traders making deals, arguing and laughing, often fighting. Now all was desolation and the stink of death was everywhere. Bodies had been cleared from the streets, but those Trojan families killed in their homes were still there, the corpses corrupting in the warmth of early summer.

In the distance he could hear the words of a funeral chant: *Hear our words, O Hades, Lord of the Deepest Dark*. Dead warriors of the western armies went to the funeral pyre after an honourable ritual. The families killed by them were left to rot.

Deep in thought, Odysseus arrived at the hospital. It had once been the Ilean barracks, then a hospital for the Trojan wounded, all slaughtered when the lower town was captured. Now it held the injured and dying soldiers of Agamemnon's armies. Odysseus hesitated before going in. He planned to visit his wounded men, but he did not relish the duty. Pausing before the doorway, he met the young healer Xander coming out. The boy looked tired beyond words, his tunic covered in blood, both dried and fresh. There were even blood specks among the freckles on his face.

'Odysseus!' the boy cried, his features lighting up. 'Are you here to see your men? You are the only king to visit his wounded troops, apart from Achilles.'

'How is Thibo? Is he dead yet?'

'No, he has left here. He will be back in action in days. He is very tough.'

'You are the toughest among us, lad,' said Odysseus, laying a hand on the boy's shoulder. 'Dealing with the stench and the screams of the dying every day, the horrors of gangrene and amputations. Even the bravest of soldiers avoid this place. I confess I would rather be anywhere else.'

The boy nodded sadly. 'The enemy . . . I mean, your armies brought few surgeons and healers. They rely on whores and camp-followers to help the wounded. The women have stronger stomachs than the soldiers, but they have no skill. White-eye works all day and all night. I fear for him. Did you know Machaon died?'

Xander seemed dazed with exhaustion and his thoughts were wandering. 'I'm told he died at noon on the day your troops took the Scamander. But he spoke to me, I heard him, late that night, in the mist. He tried to get me to leave. But I was too slow. I should have returned to the city while I still could. I let him down.'

He gazed at Odysseus, his eyes brimming with tears. The king pushed him gently down on to a wooden bench outside the makeshift hospital.

'You are tired, lad, tired beyond reason. When did you last sleep?'

The boy shook his head dumbly. He did not know.

'I will see to it that you get more help. Is my man Leukon here?'

Xander nodded, seeming too tired to speak.

'Listen to me, lad,' Odysseus urged. 'When the city falls you must leave here straight away. Leave this place and get down to the Bay of Herakles as quickly as you can. There are always Kypriot ships there, bringing supplies. Board one of them and tell the master I sent you.'

But Xander was shaking his head. 'No, Odysseus, I cannot. If the city falls I must try to help my friends. Zeotos is still at the House of Serpents, and other healers. And there is the lady Andromache and her son. She is my friend. I am a Trojan now, even if I am aiding your warriors.'

Suddenly angry, Odysseus cursed and grabbed the young healer by the front of his tunic. 'Listen to me, lad,' he rasped, 'and listen to me well. I have seen cities fall, too many to count over the years. Soldiers become animals at such times. Every civilian, man, woman or child, will be slaughtered when the gates open. None will escape. If you are there, they will kill you, maybe even someone you helped, whose life you saved. You will be no more to them than a lamb among the wolves.'

Xander shook his head again, and Odysseus could see he was too tired to protest. He let the boy go, and they sat in silence for a while. Odysseus unstrapped his breastplate and removed it with relief.

Then Xander asked quietly, 'When will Troy fall, do you think, Odysseus?'

'Days or years. Tomorrow – or in ten years' time. I don't know, lad. I'm just a foot soldier in this story of heroes.' He sighed and spoke quietly, as if to himself. 'I made a pledge I sorely regret, a pledge to Agamemnon that his enemies would be my enemies, his friends my friends. Well, the man has no friends. But I swore to stand by his side until his enemy is defeated. So I will stay here until the city falls to us, whenever that is. Then I will take my men and return to my ships and sail away. And I will live with it, boy, though it will not be easy. I also have friends in Troy, Xander, friends I have known a lifetime. But I will not be running into the city to help them. They are beyond help. Everyone living behind those walls is dead, lad. They may be walking Troy's streets, breathing her air, eating, sleeping or making love. But they are all dead.'

After dawn the next day the kings of the west gathered in the House of Stone Horses. Odysseus took grim amusement from the fact that Agamemnon had moved into Helikaon's palace. The Golden One had delivered many crippling blows to the Mykene king, sinking his ships, killing his Followers, raiding his coastline. The destruction of Menados' fleet had been a humiliating defeat. Agamemnon's eagerness to capture his palace in Troy, a home Helikaon cared little for and seldom resided in, revealed a lot about the Battle King. All the servants had long since fled, and the rooms were bare. Odysseus chuckled to himself. Never underestimate the pettiness of powerful men, he thought.

In the *megaron* were the kings with some of their aides. Black-bearded Meriones, one of Odysseus' oldest friends, stood beside his king Idomeneos, and Patroklos lounged in a window, idly watching the empty street below. Kygones, the Fat King of Lykia, was accompanied by his nephew Sarpedon, by all accounts a formidable fighter. Some were breaking their fast with meat and corn bread. Odysseus sipped at a goblet of water.

When Agamemnon arrived, his normally calm demeanour seemed disturbed.

'We lost a supply train last night,' he told them, without any form of greeting. 'Sixteen carts of grain, wine, horse feed and dried meats and fish, coming here from the Bay of Herakles. The Trojan Horse struck on the Scamander plain, more than three hundred of them. They killed the guards and drivers, and took the entire train of wagons. A detachment of cavalry was sent from King's Joy, and they killed them too and took their horses.'

There was silence in the *megaron*, then Odysseus said, 'It could have been predicted. Sending supply wagons across the plain with less than a regiment to protect it is more than foolishness. They are rabbits sitting waiting for a pack of hounds.'

'Yet you,' Agamemnon pointed a thin finger at the Ithakan king, 'travel with your men back and forth to King's Joy all the time. You have not been attacked.'

'One fat old king is hardly worth the effort of killing,' Odysseus replied.

'I have lost five more ships to Helikaon the Burner,' Menestheos of Athens told them. 'The *Xanthos* and the Trojan fleet attacked ten of my galleys off Lesbos two days ago.'

'Did he burn them?' asked Idomeneos, his voice like the noise of a galley being dragged across pebbles.

'No, three were rammed and two captured, the crews killed. But I have a fleet of fifty beached at the Bay of Herakles. They must be protected. We must not forget Helikaon destroyed an entire fleet in the Bay of Troy.'

'We are not likely to forget,' spat Agamemnon, in a rare display of anger. 'My fleets patrol the seas off the bay,' he told Menestheos. 'The *Xanthos* will not get through to attack them.'

'Helikaon will not try,' pointed out Odysseus. 'He wants our ships there, so we can all leave. He has nothing to gain by attacking them. But he will take any supply ship he finds.'

'You seem to know well what is in your friend Helikaon's mind,' commented Idomeneos scornfully.

Odysseus sighed. 'I speak only common sense. Troy's best hope is that our supplies fail and we are forced to give up our cause. The *Xanthos* at sea and the Trojan Horse on land could between them leave us all starving by summer. Soldiers need to be fed, and fed often.'

'The riders of the Trojan Horse also need supplies,' retorted Agamemnon. 'As the summer goes on they will not be able to live off the land, and their horses will need feeding. They might be tempted to attack our supply wagons, even if heavily defended. We might use that to our advantage.'

Odysseus asked, 'Was Hektor leading last night's attack?'

'He was. That is one piece of good news. Hektor no longer commands in Troy. He is out leading raiding parties.'

'Then who does command in the city?' asked Sharptooth. 'Priam? The rumour is that he has lost his mind. They are friends of yours, Odysseus,' he sneered. 'Who orders Troy's defences now?'

Odysseus shrugged, refusing to rise to the bait, though anger was bubbling in his chest. 'With Antiphones dead, I don't know. Perhaps one of the generals. Maybe Polites.'

'That is good news,' said the portly Menelaus, repeating his brother Agamemnon's words. 'Knowing Hektor does not lead the defence, I mean. I think we must try another attack on the walls.'

'Are you insane, man?' Odysseus roared, jumping to his feet and tipping back his chair, which crashed to the floor. 'By Apollo's balls, after the carnage yesterday you would send more men to certain death? How many men did we lose, three hundred, four?'

'My brother might have a good idea,' Agamemnon put in smoothly, as Menelaus stumbled back under Odysseus' onslaught.

'Menelaus never had a good idea in his life,' snapped Odysseus. 'He follows you around like a puppy dog, yapping when you tell him to, and sometimes pissing on your feet. This poxy plan is yours, Agamemnon, and I'd like to know why. Because, unlike your pup here, you're not a stupid man.'

Agamemnon had gone pale and his dark eyes were angry.

'I too would like to hear why we should commit more of our forces to certain death,' put in Menestheos of Athens mildly.

Agamemnon took a deep breath. 'Yesterday a group of my warriors managed to take a part of the wall, and hold it for a short while, before being thrown back by the renegade Banokles and his men. If a brave troop of soldiers could take and hold just a section of the wall, then we could send hundreds up a ladder behind them. The Trojans would not be able to stop them. But we need the bravest of fighters, willing to risk their lives for our just cause.' He looked round the room and his eyes rested on Achilles.

'I will have nothing to do with this insanity,' the king of Thessaly said. 'I and my Myrmidons will take part in no more suicidal attacks on the walls.'

'So,' said Agamemnon icily, 'our champion Achilles fears—'

Achilles rose to his feet and in one swift stride was in front of Agamemnon, the tip of his sword resting lightly on the Mykene's throat. It was done so quickly, so gracefully, that no one had time to move. Odysseus saw Patroklos lay his hand on his sword hilt, as did Agamemnon's two Followers. There was a deathly silence in the *megaron*.

Agamemnon, staring unblinking into Achilles' eyes, continued, 'I was going to say that Achilles fears for the lives of his men. That is understandable and is the mark of a true captain. The valiant Myrmidons have been vital to our success so far.'

Achilles waited for a moment, then sheathed his sword. Without taking his eyes off Agamemnon he returned to his seat.

'We are all men of honour,' Agamemnon went on. 'Achilles is our champion, and none doubts his countrymen's bravery. But our attack will go ahead without Thessaly, if it must.'

'And without Ithaka,' put in Odysseus. 'My men will not be climbing walls to certain death. You can have my archers, and my bow Akilina, to defend your warriors from the ground, and that is all.'

'So be it,' said Agamemnon coldly. 'And what is *your* plan for taking the walls, Tale Spinner? Or are you only here to weave children's stories about magic pigs and flying ships?'

Black-bearded Meriones stood up and said angrily, 'The king of Ithaka has proved himself in battle a hundred times. If it were not for him we would still be languishing on the other side of the Scamander.'

'Yes, yes,' put in old Nestor impatiently. 'We are all warriors here. I had fought a hundred battles before young Achilles was a gleam in his father's eye. What I would know, Agamemnon King, is why you need us all here when you plan to send one troop of your men up a ladder.'

'The attack will be the same as yesterday's,' replied the Battle King patiently. 'With all our ladders and as many men as we can muster. The Trojans must not know where our eye is fixed.'

'And where is it fixed?' asked the king of Pylos.

'Our target is the south wall beside the Great Tower of Ilion. If we can take and hold that small part of the wall we will have access to the Great Tower through the battlements door. Then we will have two ways in – down the steps at the south wall, or down through the tower which, as you all know, opens behind the Scaean Gate. We need get only six men to the gate and the city is ours.'

Odysseus waited a safe distance from the south wall, the great bow Akilina on his shoulder, as the western troops mustered for the new assault. This was to be no surprise attack. He could see the sun glinting off the helms of the Trojan forces lined up along the top of the wall.

Despite his losses Agamemnon could still gather more than thirty thousand warriors for the assault. The Ithakan king calculated there could be no more than five thousand soldiers left inside the walls to defend Troy. That should be plenty today, he thought. Agamemnon's latest scheme might work, but it was unlikely. Each passing day, each failed assault, confirmed Odysseus in his belief that the only way to take the city was by trickery.

The ladders lay lined up on the ground ready. They were constructed of oak from the foothills of Mount Ida, and lashed together with strong leather strips. They were heavy, and each required six men to raise it to the walls.

The command was given and the attackers picked up their ladders and ran with them to the base of the wall. Within moments scores of ladders had been raised and armoured warriors were streaming up them. Odysseus stepped back a few paces, notched an arrow to the string, and waited, just as the defenders waited. The Trojans were waiting for each ladder to be charged with warriors before dislodging it from the wall. Odysseus was waiting for the defenders to lean out from the battlements to shift the ladders.

A bearded Trojan soldier holding a ladder pole stretched out from the top of the wall to hook the pole against a ladder and thrust it sideways. Odysseus could see a tiny patch of white between his helm and the armour at his neck. He sighted Akilina and loosed. The arrow punched through the man's throat and he slumped over the wall. Odysseus notched another arrow to the string and waited.

The ladder beside the Great Tower was downed quickly by the defenders, the warriors falling from it as it crashed to the ground. More soldiers raced to raise it again, and to climb it regardless of the danger to themselves. Agamemnon had promised honour and a sheep's weight in gold to the first man to reach the battlements and live. Odysseus picked off two more defenders at the top of the ladder. He saw a soldier on the wall spot him and point him out to the Phrygian archers. Odysseus grinned. He was well out of range of their puny bows.

The attackers were making a fourth attempt to climb the ladder by the tower. There were seven warriors on it when it was pushed sideways, dislodging the men clinging to it, and those on the next two ladders as it crashed into them. There was a thin sound of cheering from the top of the walls. But the attackers did not hesitate. New soldiers leapt forward and raised the ladders again. Such courage wasted on a doomed venture, thought Odysseus.

Glancing at the top of the wall again he suddenly realized that the defenders had fallen back. He frowned. What are they up to now, he wondered?

All along the south wall he saw men come into view bearing huge shallow dishes of shining metal in cloth-covered hands. Boiling oil, wondered Odysseus, or scalding water? The dishes were tipped up as one and their contents showered down on the invaders below.

Instantly there was a scene of horror as climbing men all along the wall started screaming and writhing, trying to pull off their armour, and falling from the ladders. Those who managed to get out of their armour continued shrieking in torment, their cries hideous to hear.

Odysseus shouldered Akilina and ran towards the walls, shouting at his archers to carry on shooting at the defenders. He reached a Mykene warrior who was writhing in agony, trying desperately to rid himself of his breastplate. Odysseus tore it off him but it did not help. The man went on screaming. Odysseus ripped off the man's tunic.

'What is it, Odysseus? What's happening to them?' Meriones cried, kneeling at his side.

The fallen warrior had fainted from the excruciating pain, and Odysseus pointed at the bright red skin of his chest and shoulders. It looked as if it was boiling.

'Sand,' he said, 'mixed with tiny shavings of metal and heated until it's red hot. It sifts under the armour and burns deeply into the skin. It can never be removed and will always be a torment to the victim. I have heard of this weapon used in desert lands. It is a fiendish torture.'

An arrow thunked into the ground beside him, and he and Meriones swiftly raised their shields above their heads. Then each took an arm of the wounded soldier and started to drag him away from the walls. But another arrow thudded into the man's chest and he died instantly. They let go of him and turned back to the walls to try to rescue others.

'By Apollo's balls,' Odysseus muttered, 'he's better off dead.'

Between them he and Meriones carried several soldiers, all tormented by unendurable pain, away from the walls. Never had the king felt so helpless in the face of hideous injury.

They're *all* better off dead, he thought grimly.

XXIV

With shaft and bow

THE WARM SPRING TURNED INTO A HOT, DRY SUMMER. THE BESIEGED city was parched.

As Andromache walked from the House of Serpents back to Hektor's palace she thought longingly of the cool goblet of water which would greet her when she arrived. She slipped through the gates of the palace, shedding her bodyguards with a nod, and stepped into the gardens.

The plants were all dying. The tender ones were long dead, the pots and troughs fashioned from stone and wood filled only with brown twigs. Even the trees were drooping from lack of water. In the early evening light, Andromache's two boys were running around on the dry cracked earth, playing catch, careless of the dead plants, and of the city's desperate plight.

'Mama!' Astyanax shouted joyfully, and ran to her with his arms out. She lifted the boy up on her hip with a groan. 'You're getting too heavy for me!' she protested. Dex ran up to her too, and she ruffled his fair hair, smiling down into his dark eyes.

He was a thoughtful little boy, still shadowed by grief. Sometimes at night, when he was afraid to sleep because of nightmares, he would creep into her bed and whisper to Andromache about his mother, whom he called Sun Woman, and Grey One and

Old Red Man. She had learned that Grey One was his elderly nurse, and Old Red Man the Dardanian general Pausanius, both killed in the Mykene attack on Dardanos. The little boy would chatter about them, mixing them up with the gods and goddesses whose stories he had been told. He recited the same fables over and over, comforting himself with their familiarity. One night recently he had brought 'Mama' into his tales. She recognized herself and her heart lifted. He was starting to add his present life here in Troy to his past life with the dead of Dardanos. He was still heart-scarred, but she believed he would eventually heal.

She put Astyanax down, and taking both boys by the hand led them into the palace. She passed through the anteroom and found her handmaids Penthesileia and Anio talking together in whispered voices. They blushed when she appeared, and made a show of looking busy, polishing the heavy gold jewellery once worn by Laodike, now left unused in a carved ivory box. Andromache smiled at the two girls and walked out to the pleasantly shady terrace.

Axa bustled about, bringing the boys sweet cakes and milk. She handed Andromache a goblet of water, and the princess drank it down gratefully. The taste was sublime. 'I have put a basin of water in your chamber if you want to wash,' the maid said.

Andromache looked at her sternly. 'I've told you, Axa, we cannot waste water on washing. I do not expect you to wash, or the boys, or your babies.' Before the fall of the lower town, Axa's three small children had been moved into the palace.

'But, lady, Prince Polites has asked you to meet him and the generals tonight. You will want to wash before you change your dress,' the maid added pointedly.

Andromache looked down at her saffron gown, stained from her day working with the sick and wounded in the healing house. 'Why would I get changed?' she asked. 'I have nothing clean to wear.'

'I have ordered six white gowns for you,' Axa told her. 'The dye-makers cannot work, but the seamstresses can. And it gives them something to do,' she added defensively.

'But white cloth is needed for bandages.'

Axa shook her head vigorously. 'I asked Zeotos, and he said since there are few injured these days, he has enough bandages stored away to last for ten years.'

Andromache laughed. 'Then you are right, Axa,' she admitted. 'There is no reason why we shouldn't have clean white dresses. Order some for yourself and for Penthesileia and Anio. But you must still pour that water back into the barrel for drinking.'

'But I have already perfumed it, lady,' her maid replied stubbornly. 'No one can drink it now.'

'Then give it to the horses. They won't mind the taste of rose petals.'

'But . . .'

'Now, Axa. The horses will be grateful.'

Axa fetched the basin, grumbling to herself, then left the apartments. Andromache walked across the terrace, which overlooked the stables in the Street of Bright Dancers, and looked down. Eventually she saw the plump figure of her maid walking from the palace, the water basin cradled in her arms. The woman paused and looked up. Andromache waved at her. Axa walked on into the stables.

Smiling, Andromache threw herself down on a couch. Strange days, she thought. There was a listless stillness in the city she had never known before. The heat lay like a wool blanket, stifling movement and keeping everyone indoors in the shade. The streets were empty except in the evenings when weary people queued for bread and water. No one had enough water, or enough to eat.

Although they all lived under the daily threat of death, Andromache felt strangely content. Her husband and her lover were both away at war, and she no longer felt the exhausting conflict of desire and responsibility. Her choice was made. She would stay with her son, and with Dex, until the end came and the blood-hungry soldiers poured in, and then protect the boys with her life.

Each day she worked in the House of Serpents. It was more than fifty days since the last major attack by the armies of Agamemnon, and the only injuries now were arrow wounds, and broken limbs when soldiers who had received their wine ration tumbled off the walls. The work at the healing houses was not hard. Xander had mysteriously disappeared, and Andromache wondered what had become of him, but most of the priests and healers had stayed. The dying were not fed, and were given only enough water to moisten their mouths. Those thought likely to recover were given water until they complained of hunger, when they were fed as well. Andromache hated being in the palace all day, with its air of heavy anxiety, and she preferred to keep herself busy working among the injured and dying, feeding them, talking to them, sometimes holding their hands until they died.

The truth was, she thought, no one had enough to do. The daily routines of the city had broken down due to lack of supplies, and exhaustion brought on by the shortage of food and water, and the energy-sapping heat. Most people, when not standing in lines for food, stayed at home. Inactivity sparked gossip and fuelled people's fears. Her handmaids Penthesileia and Anio had too much time on their hands, she thought, and spent it discussing the plight of the city with other royal servants.

Her mind drifted back to the previous autumn and Kassandra's words to the girls when she was last in these rooms. *You must learn to shoot! The Women of the Horse with shaft and bow! You see? You see, Andromache?*

'Yes, Kassandra,' Andromache said to the empty room. 'I see now.'

Polites was already waiting in the *megaron* with Banokles and Kalliades when Andromache arrived. She smiled at the two warriors, the one blond-bearded and powerful, the other tall and dark. She would always remember them running down the hillside to her rescue on the night Kalliope died. Then they were Mykene rebels fighting assassins who had come to kill her. Now they were the most respected soldiers in the Trojan army. She had heard of the death of Banokles' wife, and she was filled with sympathy, but the only time she had tried to express her regret to him he had ignored her and rudely walked away.

'I assume,' she said to Polites, sitting on a padded chair and folding her hands, 'that we are to discuss rationing and the care of the wounded. You would not have asked me to a meeting of strategy.'

Polites sighed. 'Our only strategy is staying alive. We have not been attacked for fifty-five days. The heat and lack of food and water are our worst enemies now. Our food will only barely last until the autumn. The wells may run dry any day.'

'Is that likely?' asked Kalliades.

'It has happened before.' General Lucan hurried into the *megaron* alongside the king's aide Polydorus, and Ipheus, the young commander of the Eagles. 'Both wells ran dry in the summer heat some forty years ago,' he explained. 'The rivers were down to a trickle too. It was a hard summer. All the livestock died. We had to slaughter most of the horses. I've never seen its like. But the rains came early that year and we survived.'

'The enemy are suffering too,' put in Kalliades. 'They have water aplenty, but their food supplies are not getting through. We have Hektor and Helikaon to thank for that. Agamemnon's armies have ravaged the countryside all round the city. There are no crops left, no livestock. And hungry soldiers are unhappy soldiers. We know one army of mercenaries departed ten days ago, heading south. Others will start defecting if they see no end to the war.'

'It is our best hope,' said Polites.

'No,' put in Banokles, scratching his beard, 'our best hope is that Agamemnon and his bunch of poxy kings lay down their arms and surrender to us. But it's not very likely.'

The men all smiled, but Andromache said impatiently, 'What are we here to discuss, Polites? The situation at the House of Serpents is the same as it was before, when we met three days ago. Many old people and babies are being cared for now, suffering from the heat and drought. Ten more injured bowmen have been brought in. Two died. Three have infected wounds and are likely to die. The others will live, Zeotos says.' Angrily, she added, 'I don't understand why our bowmen are being put in danger when we are not under attack. Taking pot shots at the enemy below the walls achieves little. If each of our archers was to kill one enemy soldier every day, it would still be like a drop of water in the Great Green.'

'We need to remind the enemy, sister,' replied Polites, 'that Troy is stoutly defended. Each attack, even a single arrow shot over the battlements, has to be met with an answer from the city.'

Kalliades added gravely, 'And if the Scaean Gate is opened, lady, and the city falls, then a few bowmen will not make any difference to our fortunes.'

'It only takes a single arrow to kill a king,' she answered him briskly.

They went on to discuss more stringent rationing, for Polites was concerned about the rapidly dwindling stores of grain. Andromache told them she had visited every baker in the city, gathering advice on keeping grain fresh and free of weevils, and ensuring all bakers knew of it.

When the men started to talk about rotating troops at the Scaean Gate, she left the *megaron*. She was feeling restless, and on a whim she gathered her bodyguard, who were playing knucklebones in the portico, and made her way to Priam's palace. With Polydorus busy in the meeting, Andromache had a sudden urge to speak to the king alone. The young soldier was constantly at his side and, although she liked Polydorus, she felt constrained from speaking openly to Priam when he was present.

She was shown up to the queen's apartments, where the king had resided since the death of Hekabe. She had expected to find him resting. But when a soldier showed her into a chamber she was surprised to find the old man out on the wide stone balcony. He was standing staring at the darkening sky, wrapped in a white wool cloak despite the heat. He turned to her and for a moment she was reminded of the man she had first met on the Great Tower of Ilion. He was still powerful and vital then, and she was a girl of twenty who risked death because she refused to kneel to a king. Such arrogance, the older Andromache thought ruefully, such pride.

'I hope I find you well, my king,' she said.

'Andromache of Thebe!' he cried, and in the torchlight his eyes glittered with life, and she realized this was not the confused old man of recent days, but the powerful and capricious king she had once feared, though she did not show it. 'Come, stand with me and gaze upon our city.' He held out his hand and she took it. He drew her out on to the balcony. She gazed sideways at his profile, the beaked nose and firm jaw, and wondered if mischievous gods had transported her back to her first days in Troy.

'Tell me of the Eagle Child,' he demanded, his voice strong. And he quoted the prophecy of Melite, '*Beneath the Shield of Thunder waits the Eagle Child, on shadow wings, to soar above all city gates, till end of days, and fall of kings.* Astyanax, they call him,' he went on. 'Lord of the City. Foolish old women try to touch his tunic as he walks in the streets, I'm told. He is the hope of Troy.' His voice changed and became more urgent. 'He must stay in the city, Andromache.'

She was about to agree with him when he grabbed her by the arms, pushing her against the stone balcony. 'I will not let him leave Troy!' he rasped, his voice angry in her ear. 'I know what you're thinking, girl! You will smuggle him out of the gates, bundled in a basket, just a soldier's whore with a bag of clothes. But you will not. I will have him guarded night and day. My Eagles will see you do him no harm!' With manic strength he lifted her off her feet, attempting to push her over the wide stone wall of the balcony. 'I will stop you now!' he cried. 'You will not take him!'

She tried to fight against him, but her arms were pinned, and she was helpless as he pushed her out over the high drop to the stones below. Forcing herself to stay calm, she made herself go limp in his arms. Recalling her last interview with Queen Hekabe, she whispered seductively to him the words she had heard, though they meant little to her, 'Where do we sail today, my lord? The *Scamandrios* is waiting.'

His body jerked with shock and he released her. Andromache dragged herself back to safety, her heart pounding, and stepped away from him, watching him carefully.

'Hekabe?' he asked her uncertainly, his voice quavering, his eyes pained and confused.

'Go to your rest, my husband,' she said softly. 'I will join you in a heartbeat.'

Priam hesitated then shuffled over to his wide bed and lay down, lifting his feet up with an effort, and stayed there obedient as a child. Andromache gazed at him, emotions warring in her breast. Fear of the powerful king on the balcony quickly gave way to pity for the confused old man. She hurried from the room. Deep in thought, she was walking down a torchlit corridor when a voice behind her said, 'Lady, are you all right?'

Turning swiftly, her nerves in a jangle, she saw it was Kalliades. She realized she must look flushed and dishevelled, and she collected her thoughts.

'I am glad you are here, Kalliades,' she told him. 'I wish to talk to you. I need any bows and arrows you can spare brought to me in the palace gardens tomorrow. I am going to teach the Women of the Horse to shoot.'

'Women of the Horse?' he queried, frowning.

'They are wives and daughters of riders of the Trojan Horse who died in the service of the city. They are given places in the royal household. My two handmaids are the daughters of a rider called Ursos.'

'I knew Ursos,' replied Kalliades. 'A good man. He died in the battle for Dardanos.'

'His daughters are among many young women still in the city. If the walls fall their fate will be appalling. I would like to teach them how to defend themselves.'

The warrior looked gravely at her, as if reluctant to say what he was thinking.

'Speak your mind, Kalliades,' she demanded.

'When the enemy come, lady, they will come in their thousands. A bow and arrow will make little difference to a woman's fate.' He looked down, unwilling to meet her eye.

'You were at the palace siege,' she said to him.

'I was with the Mykene invaders, with Banokles. It is well known, but that part of our lives is past.'

'I did not mention it to embarrass you. Did you see me there?'

He nodded. 'With your bow you killed and injured many of our men.' He paused, then he said, 'You were magnificent, lady.'

She blushed at his unexpected words.

'But,' he went on, 'we Mykene came ready for hand to hand combat. There were few bowmen in our ranks. Had there been, you would have been dead.'

She accepted the truth of his words, but she said, 'Kalliades, if you were being attacked by armed men, would you rather be completely helpless or armed with a bow?'

Kalliades nodded. 'I will see you have the bows and arrows you need. It can do no harm. How many?'

'There are more than thirty Women of the Horse in the city still.'

'I will let you have what we can spare. But we must not leave our bowmen short.'

Deep in thought Kalliades left the palace and strolled back through the quiet city to the east wall. He followed it along to the east tower, where he climbed the steps to the battlements. Men of the Scamandrian regiment were sitting around, talking quietly, eating, playing games of chance. Many were fast sleep on the hard stones, as only veteran soldiers can sleep, in the most uncomfortable of conditions.

Kalliades looked for Banokles, but there was no sign of his friend, so he eased himself down, back against the battlements, legs outstretched. He sighed and closed his eyes gratefully. He thought about Andromache's words about bowmen. It was not true, although there was nothing to be gained by arguing with the woman. If he were unarmed and facing armed men he would rely on his strength and his skills as a fighter rather than on a flimsy bow. His distrust of bowmen was deeply ingrained. The warriors of Mykene despised archers, or slingers, or anyone who fought from a distance. True warriors armed themselves with sword or dagger, spear or lance, facing their enemies eye to eye. He remembered Kolanos killing the great Argurios with a coward's arrow and, even after all this time, the gorge rose in his throat at the thought. He had asked Father Zeus to curse Kolanos for that act. He smiled grimly, recalling Kolanos' agonized death.

It did no harm giving serving women bows to play with, he thought. It would keep them occupied, and take their minds off their fate. And Andromache was right about one thing: it took only a single arrow to kill a king.

Kalliades gradually became conscious that someone was looking at him, and opened his eyes. A young soldier with floppy flaxen hair was standing in front of him.

'Yes, soldier?' he said, closing his eyes again.

'Lord, general . . .' the lad stammered.

'I am not a lord and I am not a general. I am a simple soldier. Speak up.'

'You wanted to see me,' the youngster said. Kalliades opened his eyes. The young soldier was nodding vehemently as if confirming his own words.

'I did? Why, who are you?'

'I am Boros, sir. Boros the Rhodian they call me.'

Daylight dawned. Kalliades grinned. 'You are the soldier with the tower shield!'

'Yes I am, sir. Although I lost it in the retreat from the river.' Boros hung his head. 'My brother gave it to me. I was sorry to lose it. It was a good shield.'

'Sit down, lad. You saved my life. I only wanted to thank you. I would not have recognized you.'

The soldier blushed, but he sat down nervously beside Kalliades. 'I was told you were looking for me. I didn't know why. I thought I had done something wrong.'

Kalliades laughed. 'But that was long ago, in the spring. You managed to avoid me for all this time?'

Boros smiled nervously, then rubbed at his left eye. 'I was injured. I broke a leg and was in the house of healing. It took a long time to knit.' He rubbed at his eye again.

'Is something wrong with your eye, Boros?'

'No, nothing. I had a blow to the head once. It aches sometimes, that's all.'

'I know what you mean. I suffered a sword cut to my face . . . a long time ago. My face still hurts in cold weather, or when I'm tired.'

They sat in companionable silence for a while, then Boros asked, 'I have never been in a siege, sir. Will they slaughter everyone if they break in?'

Kalliades nodded. 'They will, lad. Pent-up frustration and blood-lust make men do truly terrible things. They will kill the soldiers, anyone in armour, cleanly. That is the Mykene way. But the people of the city, the refugees, men, women and children, face a ghastly fate.'

'But the walls cannot be taken,' Boros argued. 'Everyone says so. They have not even tried to attack since we dropped the burning sand on them. Many of our men say we should seal up the last gate, the Scaean Gate, then wait them out.' He added more confidently, 'The Scaean Gate's our weak point, that's for certain.'

Kalliades nodded. 'What you say is true, soldier. But our generals believe the enemy will lose heart as the siege goes on. Already one mercenary army has left, and others will go too. Most of them are not here for honour and glory, but because they smell plunder. And the plunder smells less sweet if you are camped in a ruined town with little food and no women to entertain you. We know the Mykene will stay, come what may, and Sharptooth's Kretans, and the Myrmidons of Achilles. But when they are the only armies remaining outside the walls we will throw open the Scaean Gate and sally forth and take them on. Then, with Ares to guide our swords, the men of Troy will prevail.'

A cheer arose around him, and he realized he had spoken loudly and the Trojan soldiers had been listening. It was a ragged cheer and it faded quickly away, but talk of victory raised the men's spirits. Kalliades sighed. He did not believe his own words, but some soldiers might sleep more soundly that night because of them.

The following morning Kalliades made his way to the royal gardens, where Andromache was attempting to teach a group of nervous women how to shoot.

The serving women were faring badly with their bows. Most of them were too overawed by Andromache's presence to pay attention to what she was telling them. Many of the bows were strung too tightly for women to draw. He could see the princess was quickly becoming exasperated, and he wondered if she was regretting her idea already.

He heard her say to a slender dark-haired girl, 'Listen to what I say, Anio. Breathe out and when all the breath has left your body, sight the arrow, then release.' The black-shafted arrow missed its target, but only by a hand's-breadth, and Anio smiled as Andromache praised her.

The only woman who showed real promise stood on her own at the end of the line. She was tall: no beauty, Kalliades thought, with a firm chin, heavy brows, and long dark hair in a thick plait down her back. She was strong, though, and had mastered the pull of her bow, and she sent arrow after arrow at her target, determined to learn the skill. He wondered who she was, then heard Andromache call her Penthesileia.

Kalliades was there only a short while before he realized he was not helping. The presence of a veteran warrior was making the women even more self-conscious. They kept glancing at him anxiously and murmuring to one another. He left the gardens swiftly, to find Banokles waiting outside, leaning against a wall.

'I couldn't watch,' his friend said, shaking his head. 'They're all useless.'

'Do you remember the first day you picked up a bow?' retorted Kalliades, finding himself defending Andromache's ambitions. 'You were no better then than they are.'

'I'm no better now,' Banokles admitted. 'Neither are you.'

Kalliades set off towards the west of the city, with Banokles following. The big warrior went on, 'The men told me you were talking last night about riding out and taking them all on. Agamemnon's armies, I mean.'

Kalliades shook his head, and said, 'I was saying that if a few more of the armies give up and go home, we might sally out and take the battle to them. But they still have at least five warriors to every one of ours. And they're stronger. They have water to spare.'

'Well, I was going to say it's a stupid plan,' Banokles replied. 'I'd go along with it, though. I'm sick of this waiting around. Where are we going?'

Kalliades was leading the way through the maze of refugee shanties. Women and children sat dull-eyed in the doorways of the shacks watching the two warriors pass. Babies cried pitifully, but otherwise there was silence in the city of refugees.

'To the Thrakian camp,' he replied. 'I wish to speak to Hillas.'

'Good. I wonder if they've still got some of that drink of theirs, that Mountain Fire.'

'The drink you said tasted like old sandals left to stew all winter then set ablaze?'

'Yes, it was good. I wonder if they've got any left.'

Kalliades stopped suddenly and Banokles walked on a few paces before coming back to him. 'What's wrong?' he asked.

'Banokles, have you thought what we should do, you and I, if we survive this?'

His friend shrugged. 'Go somewhere else, I suppose. We can't go back west any more. We'll go north with Hillas and the Thrakians, maybe, help them get their land back. Why?'

Kalliades took a deep breath. 'I believe I will give up the sword,' he said.

'The Sword of Argurios? Can I have it?'

'No, I mean I will give up soldiering.'

'You can't,' said Banokles, frowning. 'We're sword brothers. Doesn't that mean anything to you?'

'Do you remember when we first came here to Troy?'

Banokles grinned. 'That was quite a scrap, wasn't it? One of the best.'

'We nearly died that day,' Kalliades reminded him. 'A lot of our friends did die. Including Eruthros, the man you say you wanted for a sword brother.' Banokles shrugged and Kalliades went on, 'We've been through a lot since then, haven't we?'

His friend nodded.

'Then I thought the world was divided into lions and sheep. We were the lions, and our strength gave us power over the sheep.'

Kalliades shook his head. 'I don't feel like that now. Everything is more complicated. But I have come to the conclusion, my friend, that the evils of the world are caused by men like you and me.'

'We didn't start this war.' Banokles looked baffled.

'I could argue with that. Or I could argue that Alektruon started it. Or Helikaon. But that's not the point. Look at all those armies out there beyond the walls. Some of them have left. Not because they have given up war, but because there are no battles to be had here, no plunder to be won. They have gone elsewhere to kill and maim. Men like you and me, selling their swords for death or glory, or to plunder a kingdom.'

'Then what will you do? Become a priest?' Banokles asked scornfully.

'I don't know,' Kalliades admitted sadly. 'But I know you understand me, Banokles. Not long ago you were talking about leaving the army and becoming a farmer.'

'That was then,' Banokles said shortly, his face darkening. He turned his back and started to walk on. Since their conversation on the Scamander battlefield, Banokles had not spoken of Red and his short marriage. If Kalliades tried to bring the subject up, Banokles simply walked away from him.

They reached the Thrakian camp in silence. The tribesmen were camped under the west wall. In the evening it was one of the coolest places in the city, but in the heat of the day the Thrakians erected brightly coloured canopies to protect themselves from the ferocious sun.

Young Periklos, son of the dead king Rhesos, and rightful heir to the lost land of Thraki, had abandoned the life of the palaces and was living with his people. The boy was fourteen, and old beyond his years. He chose to dress in the traditional costume of the Kikones, and Kalliades had no doubt that when the boy went to battle, for however brief a time that would be, he would paint his face like his men.

There were only ten of the Thrakians still unwounded. Another five were in the healing houses, but only two of those were expected to live. The rest of the fifty riders had died in the retreat from the river and the defence of the lower town. Looking round the small camp, Kalliades wondered how their leader felt about his sudden decision at Dardanos to bring his men to Troy.

'Welcome to our camp, friends,' said Hillas, Lord of the Western Mountain, standing up to greet them. 'We have a little water to offer you, and some bread.'

Kalliades shook his head. Then, as if he had heard his thoughts, Hillas told him, 'I would not have chosen to end my days in a foreign city, but I do not regret a day of it. We have a saying in my country, "Old age is not as honourable as death, but most people seek it." Kikones warriors do not seek old age. All my sons are dead. If we die with honour it does not matter which land we die in.' He spat on the ground.

'I have come to ask a favour of you, Hillas,' Kalliades said.

'Ask it.'

'You have fine bowmen among your countrymen. I would like to borrow one to demonstrate his skills.'

Hillas frowned. 'I thought the Mykene despised archers? Why do you ask this?'

'The lady Andromache is teaching women to shoot.' At this there were shouts and guffaws of disbelieving laughter from the men in the camp. Banokles grinned with them.

Kalliades explained, 'The princess is a fine archer, but she knows it instinctively, and has no experience of teaching others. Also many of the bows need adjusting for the strength of a woman. Perhaps one of your men . . . ?'

Hillas laughed and shook his head, his braids shaking with merriment. 'No, my friend. My men could teach these Trojan women many things, but not to make fools of themselves with bows and arrows.'

'I will help,' said the boy Periklos, walking over to stand along-side Kalliades. 'The city of Troy and its people have given me sanctuary. The lady Andromache has been kind, taking me and my brother into her home when we first arrived. Our nurse Myrine has been given a place in the royal household, though she is old and infirm and needs caring for herself. If I can do anything to repay the people of the city I will do it.' He turned to the Thrakian tribesman. 'Have you any objections, Hillas?'

The man shook his head. 'No, my king. It is an honourable gesture. And you will be a better teacher than any of this rabble.' He grinned and gestured to his men.

At that moment they heard the sound of shouting from nearby. They heard running feet, then more shouts, screams and the clash of metal.

Drawing their swords, Kalliades and Banokles ran as one towards the source of the noise.

A crowd had gathered round one of Troy's two wells. Three men were on the ground, two apparently dead, one nursing a broken arm. The six guards at the well all had swords in their hands and were facing the angry mob. An empty bucket lay on the ground, its precious water soaking into the earth.

'What's going on?' demanded Banokles.

One of the guards told him. 'The well is dry, general. These fools were fighting over the last bucket of water.'

XXV

Ambush!

FAR TO THE SOUTH OF THE CITY SKORPIOS LAY ON HIS BELLY ON ROCKY ground at the crest of a ridge, gazing down on the long train of wagons stretching along the valley of the Scamander.

Skorpios smiled. In his years as a scout for the Trojan Horse he had never seen such a tempting, slow-moving target. He counted forty donkey-wagons, followed by ten ox-carts. From time to time the donkeys were halted so the slower-moving oxen could catch up. There were more than three hundred riders guarding the train, armed with spears and lances. But behind Skorpios, waiting in the woods for his report, were nearly six hundred Trojan Horse.

Skorpios wondered what was in the ox-carts. Heavy armour, perhaps, for the Mykene infantry, or copper ingots from Kypros. Or jugs of wine from Lesbos.

He rolled on his back, and as he did so his stomach gurgled. He was hungry, and it was a long time since he had tasted wine. The last they had captured was after their final attack on the convoys travelling between the Bay of Troy and the armies camped outside the city. Agamemnon had learned caution since then. Every convoy on that busy route was now surrounded by an army of outriders, heavily armoured and bristling with spears and lances.

Hektor had reluctantly called off the attacks. Instead he targeted the troops Agamemnon sent into the forests and valleys of the Ida foothills to hunt down the Trojan Horse. Hektor's horsemen knew the heavily wooded country far better than the invading forces, and they led the enemy on many a hazardous chase, luring them into blind gulleys to be attacked and killed, or fading away through hidden passes when the Trojans seemed to be trapped. These pursuits always ended in death for the enemy. As a result Agamemnon's ally kings had refused to send their forces into the woods of Mount Ida, even to cut down the oak trees which furnished them with timber and firewood.

But the summer was passing and Hektor's own supplies were running low. These were the first wagons they had seen for thirty days, and the first ever this far south.

Skorpios rolled back on his stomach and peered over the ridge again. The train was almost level with him now. Its leader was a tall rider in black helm and breastplate. Skorpios tried to remember what Mestares, Hektor's right-hand man, had told them about enemy armour. Achilles always wore black armour, everyone knew that, but Skorpios doubted Achilles the Slayer was leading a lowly supply convoy. Some of his Myrmidons, his bodyguard, also wore black in tribute to their leader, although most wore the ordinary armour of Thessaly. The only other warrior who always wore black was Meriones, Odysseus' friend and aide to the king of Kretos. Skorpios could see no Kretan armour below him.

He heard a scuffling on the rocks behind him, and Justinos scrambled up alongside. 'Well, lad? Who do you think they are?' the big man asked, looking cautiously over the ridge.

'I can't tell. Fifty wagons, though.'

'Hmm,' said Justinos. 'Maybe some foreign merchant thought he could make a killing sending supplies to Agamemnon's forces. Thought it was worth the risk. They must have beached their ships in a cove somewhere south.'

Skorpios yawned. They had camped far to the south that night and ridden since dawn. Hektor kept them always on the move. Every night a new camp. The days were long and hard, the nights short. And Skorpios had had nothing to eat since dawn on the previous day.

'I'm hungry,' he complained, not for the first time. 'I'm with Banokles on this. You can't do battle on an empty stomach.'

'Then if Banokles still lives, he'll be moaning even more loudly than you, lad. But those wagons could mean a fine feast for us tonight. It would be pleasant to eat something other than horsemeat.'

They crawled away from the ridge and climbed down the rocky slope to where their mounts were tethered. It was a short ride back to the glade where Hektor and the Trojan Horse were waiting. Some of the riders mounted their horses as soon as they spotted the scouts, but Hektor remained seated by a campfire, burnishing the gold and silver of his great breastplate.

'Can you tell what they're carrying?' he asked them as they slid off their mounts.

Justinos shook his head. 'The wagons are all tightly covered with canvas. But there's about fifty of them. And they're heavy.'

'And their guard?'

'A good three hundred. Their leader is all in black.'

Hektor raised his eyebrows. 'Could it be Achilles?'

Justinos shook his head. 'I have never seen him, but they say he is a big man, as big as you, lord.' Hektor nodded. 'Then it is not Achilles,' Justinos told him. 'This warrior is tall but slender.'

Hektor sat for a while, deep in thought, until one of the riders asked him, 'Do you fear a trap, Hektor?'

'Maybe,' he replied. 'If I were to set an ambush it would be with a large slow-moving convoy. But it is tempting. Our scouts have discovered no enemy forces lying in wait. There are no troops south of us, we can be sure of that.'

Justinos added, 'And we have scouted north to within sight of Troy.'

Hektor made his decision. He stood up. 'Then let's kill them all,' he said grimly.

The riders trotted their mounts back up to the ridge. Skorpios felt the familiar hot fear flaring in his belly as he thought of the battle ahead. There were around six hundred horsemen left in this main force, plus the two smaller groups Hektor had deployed to the country north and east of Troy. They easily outnumbered the riders guarding the wagons, yet Skorpios felt sick with apprehension. His body was covered with cold sweat and his head ached. He knew the weakness would pass when the battle was under way. It always did.

Reaching the crest of the ridge he saw Hektor dig his heels into his mount and gallop down the gentle slope towards the river. The supply train was on the other side of the Scamander, but the river was just a trickle now. The six hundred riders galloped across it, a great dust cloud swirling around them.

Skorpios lay low on his mount's neck and peered through the dust ahead of them. He saw the wagons slow to a halt. The riders guarding them were heavily armed with spears and lances as well as swords. They stood their ground, staying by the wagons and turning to face the charge, rather than peeling off to meet the advancing cavalry. He saw Hektor's sword raised high and swirling in a circle above his head. Surround them!

Skorpios, riding side by side with Justinos, deflected a flying spear with his shield and galloped his mount round the rear of the donkey train. He singled out an enemy rider and charged him. The man launched his spear as Skorpios bore down on him, but it was poorly aimed and the Trojan dodged it easily and plunged his sword into the man's throat. He blocked a vicious sword-cut to the head by another enemy rider, and hacked at the man's arm, half severing it. He spun round just in time to see a lance plunging towards him and got his shield in front of it, but the power of the blow unhorsed him and he hit the ground hard.

Many of the donkeys started panicking and trying to get away from the mêlée, pulling the wagons in every direction. Skorpios rolled out of the way as a heavy wagon wheel rumbled past him; then he scrambled up, looking around for his horse.

At that moment everything changed. The canvas on the wagon in front of him was ripped open from the inside by sharp knives, and twenty or more armed warriors came surging out. From wagons all along the line soldiers were leaping armed with swords.

It was a trap.

Two Mykene soldiers in leather breastplates jumped down from the wagon and ran at him with raised swords. Skorpios deflected one sword-cut off the edge of his shield, and parried the other with his own weapon. A rider appeared out of the dust cloud. It was Justinos. He hacked down one of the Mykene with a killing cut to the back of his neck. Skorpios dodged another sword-thrust from the first Mykene. He ducked and plunged his blade into the man's groin.

His eyes stinging from the dust and grit in the air, he looked around again for a horse. An enemy rider backed towards him out of the dust cloud, defending himself against a furious attack from a Trojan horseman. He did not see Skorpios, who grabbed his ankle and dragged him from his mount. Skorpios plunged his sword into the man's face and leapt on the horse. He turned the beast and galloped towards the front of the donkey train, where he could see the tall warrior in black armour.

Hektor got there first. He too had been unhorsed but he made no attempt to find a mount. He ran with a snarl towards the leader in black, ducked to pick up a spear and hurled it at him with ferocious strength. The rider got his shield in the way but the spear shattered it and punched into his armour, throwing him from his horse.

Despite the power of the blow the warrior rolled and stood up, his helm falling to the ground. He was blond and handsome, his hair in long braids.

'Patroklos!' Hektor whispered.

Patroklos smiled, and launched a vicious sword attack. The two were well matched in skill, but Hektor was the bigger man, and the stronger. He knew that, but he also knew Patroklos might have the better of him in speed.

Their blades met time and again, Patroklos being constantly forced back. Again Hektor attacked and Patroklos sent back a lightning riposte that opened a wound in Hektor's cheek. Now it was Patroklos pushing forward, but Hektor parried each stroke. Suddenly Hektor stepped in, their blades clashed and Hektor sent a mighty punch to Patroklos' jaw. Patroklos grunted and went down. Hektor swept his sword at Patroklos' head. Patroklos rolled, then lanced his sword up at Hektor's groin. As Hektor's blade blocked the thrust he twisted his wrist and the sword flashed back at Patroklos' belly. The blade was deflected off the black breastplate, but lanced into the Myrmidon's side. Patroklos scrambled away and got up, then circled to the left, trying to guard the wound.

Hektor surged forward – into a riposte that all but tore the helm from his head. Still, he knew Patroklos was weakening. He saw the blood streaming from the man's side and down his leg, and knew it was only a matter of time. The Myrmidon had only one chance – a lightning attack and a killing blow to the head or neck. Hektor gave him the opening. Patroklos' sword flashed forward. Hektor ducked and rammed his sword up under Patroklos' breastplate, driving into the heart.

Before Patroklos hit the ground Hektor was turning, checking the thrust of the battle. Donkeys were frantically dragging their carts away, throwing up great dust clouds. Many riders were still mounted, but some of the horses had walked clear of the battle and were standing waiting, as they had been trained. Hektor ran to one and leapt on it. All he could see around him was clouds of dust. The battle was a mêlée. It was impossible to see who had the upper hand.

Hektor saw a movement at the corner of his eye and got his shield up just in time to block a sword-cut to the throat. The enemy rider hacked at him again. Hektor dodged the blow, then thrust his blade into the man's side. The weapon got stuck and was ripped from Hektor's grip as the Mykene's horse reared. Weaponless, Hektor saw another horseman bearing down on him, sword raised. He put up his shield, but a Trojan rider appeared beside the enemy and plunged his sword into the man's unprotected armpit.

Justinos dragged his sword out and the Mykene rider slumped from his horse. Justinos grinned at Hektor, who nodded his thanks.

Just then an enemy horseman rode out of the dust cloud, his lance levelled at Justinos' back. Hektor shouted a warning. Justinos half turned, but too late. The lance plunged through his back with such force that it exited in a bloody eruption at his belly. Justinos gave one agonized look at Hektor, then slumped over his horse's neck. His mount trotted away into the dust.

With a roar, Hektor pulled out his dagger and launched himself at the enemy. The man, having lost his lance, scrabbled desperately for his sword. Hektor grabbed him by his breastplate and pulled him in, slicing his throat with the dagger. He took the dead man's sword, then he heeled his horse and galloped round the battlefield, peering through the dust, counting corpses and wounded. An enemy horseman spotted him and came after him, lance levelled. Hektor swayed his body at the last moment and the lance went by him. Hektor beheaded the rider with one sweep of the sword.

Out of the dust came Mestares on his mount Warlord. His shield-bearer was leaning heavily to one side, guarding a wound.

'They have us, Hektor!' he shouted. 'We are outnumbered. We cannot win!'

Cursing, Hektor dragged his battle horn from his back and put his lips to it. He blew the short notes to signal retreat. For a few heartbeats no one seemed to have heard, then Trojan riders started appearing out of the dust, some injured, some helping wounded colleagues. Within moments they were streaming away, heading back towards the river. Hektor gathered the uninjured riders and forged his way into the chasing enemy horsemen, forcing them back, making space for the Trojan Horse to get away.

Finally, Hektor heeled his mount and galloped back towards the wooded hills.

The next morning at dawn Skorpios sat in the treeline at the point where the Scamander broke out of the woods and dipped under a wooden bridge before joining the flat plain.

He was supposed to be scouting, but his eyes kept misting up. He had always feared for his own life before battles, but never for that of Justinos. The big man had seemed indestructible. The two had ridden together for years, at first with Ennion, Kerio, Ursos, and Olganos, now all dead. He was the only one left of the six.

The power of his grief had quite unmanned him. He had not slept for most of the night. As he listened to the other riders snoring around him, he kept going over in his mind how that last battle should have gone. Justinos had always looked out for him, watched his back, yet he had failed to do the same for his old friend. The thought churned round and round until his brain was worn out, and then he fell into a shallow troubled slumber.

He woke before dawn, his body weary, his mood melancholy. Hektor sent him back to the site of the battle to see if the enemy had taken away their dead and wounded. They had. Even the broken wagons had been carried away for firewood.

In the night Skorpios had decided that when the war ended he would return to his father's farm. A veteran soldier now, with years in the Trojan Horse behind him, he would no longer be afraid of the old man. With the gold Hektor would give him for his loyal service he would buy a small house and help his father with the cattle and sheep. The settlement lay far to the east, on the edge of Hittite lands. Now, for the first time, he wondered whether the farm was still there, his father and brothers still waking in the dark each morning to start work, or sleeping out in the fields to guard the livestock from predators, his mother working from dawn to dusk to keep the family fed. His youngest sister would be twelve now, he thought, almost a woman. He shook his head sorrowfully. He knew nothing about them any more. Perhaps his brothers had left to become soldiers. If they had, maybe they were dead too.

Suddenly Skorpios felt very alone. The last image of Justinos kept flashing into his mind. He found he could not visualize his friend's face smiling, or in repose. Just in the agony of death. He closed his eyes in pain.

When he opened them again he saw the small dot of a rider in the distance, coming from the direction of Troy. The horseman stopped and got off his mount. Skorpios thought he could hear the man shouting something, but he was too far away to make out the words.

345

After a while the rider got back on his horse and continued along the bank of the river. As he got closer Skorpios could see he was garbed in black armour. The young Trojan gazed at him in bemusement. A single armoured soldier all the way out here. He must be one of ours, he thought. Surely he could not be an enemy warrior, riding on his own in such hostile land.

The horseman stopped again. This time Skorpios could hear the words he shouted, borne on the northerly breeze. 'Hektor! Hektor! Come down and fight! Come and fight me, you coward!'

Skorpios watched for a long time, as the rider worked his way down the river, stopping every few hundred paces. He wondered what to do: to go back and report to Hektor, or to keep his eye on the warrior. There were other scouts out, so he settled down to watch, his back against a tree, assuming others would be carrying the strange news to Hektor.

He was observing the rider still when he heard a whisper of movement behind him and turned to find a sword at his throat.

'You would be a dead man now,' said Hektor, sheathing the sword and emerging from the undergrowth.

'I'm sorry, lord,' Skorpios replied, his face flushing. 'I let you down.'

The Trojan prince squatted down beside him. 'You look unwell, lad,' he commented. 'You lost a good friend yesterday.'

Skorpios nodded miserably. Hektor put a hand on his shoulder. 'Justinos was a fine warrior. I have seldom seen better. Make sure you get some food today, then you will sleep better tonight. Now.' He turned his gaze on the rider in black. 'What do you think of this?'

'I think he is a madman. He must know there are hundreds of warriors in these woods who could ride down and kill him in a heartbeat.'

'Yet he knows they will not, because he is a man of honour, and such men believe, against all the evidence, that others are the same.' There was a long silence. 'That is Achilles, lad, and yesterday I killed his friend Patroklos.'

'Will you go down and fight him?' Skorpios blurted out the question without thinking.

Hektor thought for a long moment, then he said, 'The time will probably come, Skorpios, when I will. But I will not fight him today, when there is nothing resting on it, except the honour of two men.'

Is that not enough? Skorpios wanted to say, but he remained silent.

The next day the rider was a priest of Ares. Skorpios sat his horse in plain sight high on the ridge with others of the Trojan Horse. They watched as the priest, garbed in black robes with twin red sashes, travelled up the river, stopping from time to time to shout out the challenge from Achilles to Hektor. The Trojans watched him for much of the day until, as the sun fell into the horizon, he returned to the city.

XXVI

The wrath of Achilles

ON THE THIRD DAY THE RIDER WAS THE KING OF ITHAKA.

Mounted on a sturdy bay gelding and wearing a wide straw hat to guard his head from the blazing sun, Odysseus was sorely conscious that he lacked the grace of Achilles, or even of the priest. He recalled that Penelope had once, teasingly, told him he rode like a sack of carrots. He had confessed, 'A sack of carrots would be ashamed to ride this badly, my love.'

He walked the horse slowly to where the Scamander gushed under a wooden bridge short of the foothills, dismounted gratefully, and settled down to wait. He had brought enough food for two, but he was prepared to enjoy the peace and silence of a day alone.

The sun was starting to fall down the sky when he finally saw a horseman coming towards him out of the treeline. He could tell at a glance it was Hektor, by the rider's size and by his riding style. As he came closer, Odysseus could see the Trojan prince had aged a good deal since they last met. Hektor reined in his mount and regarded him silently for a moment, then he got down. 'Well, king,' he said coolly, 'we meet again in strange times. Are you Achilles' mouthpiece today?'

Odysseus chewed on a piece of bread and swallowed. Ignoring

the question, he gestured to the black horse Hektor was riding. 'Where is Ares? He cannot be old yet. I remember him as a foal not six years ago.'

'Great Ares is dead.' Hektor sighed, his stiff demeanour vanishing as he sat down on the river bank. 'He fell at the battle of the Scamander, lanced through the chest.'

'I saw that,' replied Odysseus, frowning, 'but then I saw him rise up and brave the river to save your troops.'

Hektor nodded, his face sorrowful. 'He had a great heart. But it was gravely wounded. He fell and died before we could reach the city.'

'This one has a wild eye,' the king commented, glaring at the black horse, who looked back at him balefully.

Hektor smiled. 'His name is Hero. He has an angry nature. He is the horse which leapt the chasm at Dardanos. You have heard the story?'

'I *invented* the story,' chuckled Odysseus. 'I am surprised to see the creature does not have wings, and fire flaring from his nostrils.'

Hektor's laughter rang out. 'Truly it is good to see you, sea uncle. I have missed your company, and your tales.' Odysseus saw a little of the weight of war and its burdens fall from the young man's shoulders.

'Here, have some bread and cheese. I doubt if you've had either for many days. It will seem like a feast in the Hall of Heroes.'

Hektor tucked into the food with gusto, and Odysseus pulled more salt bread and cheese and some dried fruit from the leather bag at his side. There was a jug of watered wine in there as well. They each drank some, then Odysseus lay back with his hands behind his head. The sky was of a blue so pale it was almost white. He sniffed the evening breeze.

'There is a scent of autumn in the air,' commented Hektor, swallowing the last of the bread. 'There could be rain soon. The city would likely hold out until the winter then.'

'Without food?' Odysseus snorted.

Hektor looked at him. 'Neither you nor I can guess how much food they have still. You may have your spies in Troy, but a

349

hundred spies are worth nothing if they cannot get their information out.'

Odysseus countered, 'And a lakeful of water is worth little if they have no grain and no meat. We both know the situation in Troy must be perilous by now.'

They sat in silence for a while longer, listening to the plashing of the river blending with the liquid sounds of birdsong high above, then Hektor asked, 'You have come to challenge me to fight Achilles?'

The king took a swig from the wine jug and wiped his mouth on the back of his hand. 'Agamemnon makes an interesting offer. I thought you should hear it.' When Hektor said nothing in response, he went on, 'If you will fight Achilles in a death match, regardless of the outcome, Agamemnon will permit the women and children of Troy to leave the city in safety.'

Hektor looked into his eyes. 'Including my wife and son?'

Odysseus sighed and dropped his gaze. 'No, he will not allow that. No members of the royal family may leave Troy. Nor the Dardanian boy, Helikaon's son. Nor the two Thrakian princes.'

'Do you trust Agamemnon?'

Odysseus burst out laughing. 'By the black balls of Hades, no!' He shook his head in amusement.

'Then why should I?'

'Because I will see the terms of the offer are made public to all the kings and their armies. They are a wretched rabble, most of these kings, but they will not allow the slaughter of innocents if their safety has been guaranteed by all. It goes against their concept of honour. And my Ithakans will give the women and children safe conduct to neutral ships at the Bay of Herakles.'

'And why should I trust *you*, Odysseus? An enemy of Troy who paid an assassin to murder our kinsman Anchises?'

Odysseus struggled to hold his tongue. His pride tempted him to tell the prince the true story of Karpophorus and the plot to kill Helikaon, but he did not. It is Helikaon's story, he thought. He will tell Hektor himself one day if he chooses.

So he said, 'It seems to me, lad, that you have no choice. I have delivered to you a way by which you could save the lives of hundreds of Trojan women and their children. If you turn your back and ride away now, you could never live with yourself. You are a man of honour. You could not do otherwise.'

Hektor nodded, but said nothing. They sat for a long while as the darkness started to thicken and the air cooled.

Finally Hektor said, his voice strangely tight as if suppressing deep emotion, 'You say I am a man of honour. Yet to me it seems that every day of my life is a lie, and each word I speak a falsehood.'

'You are the most honest man I know,' Odysseus replied without hesitation.

Hektor gazed at him, and Odysseus could see the anguish in his eyes. 'If you tell the same lie often enough for long enough, then eventually it can become the truth.'

Odysseus shook his head vehemently. 'Truth and falsehood are two different beasts, as different as the lion and the lizard. They are complex animals and they share many of the same features – they both have four legs, two eyes, and a tail. Yet you cannot mistake the one for the other. I know the truth when I see it, and I know the lie.' He thought for a while. 'Did you ever meet Helen, the wife of Paris?'

Hektor nodded. 'Briefly. She was a shy woman, and deeply in love with my brother.'

Odysseus said, 'I met her once. I thought her sweet-natured, but mousy and plain. You know how she died?' Hektor nodded, his brow darkening. Odysseus went on, 'The men who were there when she threw herself and her children from the heights of King's Joy are speaking of her as a great beauty. Throughout our camps there is talk of the beauteous Helen and her gallant death.'

'What is your point, sea uncle?'

'Only that they do not speak falsely. Soldiers cannot speak of women in terms they do not understand; they do not admire kindness, or modesty, or unselfishness. But they admire Helen's self-sacrifice, so they tell us she was beautiful, like a goddess walking among us. And it is the truth. You are suffering under a great burden, Hektor. We have spoken of this before, and you will not reveal it to me. But not revealing something about yourself does not make you a liar. You show your true nature in each action you take.'

Hektor was silent, and Odysseus wondered if the agony he was suffering was because of the love between Helikaon and Andromache. Yet the young man seemed to be suffering an inner torment, blaming himself for something, rather than cursing others. The king shrugged inwardly. If Hektor chose not to share his problems, there was nothing he could do about it.

'You have soundly beaten Achilles once, at your Wedding Games in a fistfight in front of thousands,' he said, returning to his mission. 'This will be a battle with swords, to the death. Achilles is seeking revenge. You killed his shield-bearer Patroklos two days ago.'

Hektor nodded. 'I know. I recognized him. He was a skilled warrior.'

'He was indeed. And I liked him greatly.'

'Whose idea was the ambush?'

'It was Agamemnon's. He calculated you would be short of supplies by now, and be tempted by the supply train. Patroklos volunteered to lead it. He was easily bored, and the long summer without any action was harder on him than most.'

'Achilles agreed to this?'

'No, he refused to allow Patroklos to go. But Patroklos went anyway, against his king's orders. Now he has gone to the pyre, and Achilles is insane with anger. He believes you targeted Patroklos deliberately, with the intent of paying him back for your victory at the Games.'

'That is madness! Why would he think that?'

Odysseus thought for a long while. Then he said, 'I like Achilles greatly. I have fought beside him on many occasions, and lived cheek by jowl with him all summer long. I like him,' he repeated, 'but, like his sister Kalliope, he has inner demons with which he fights every day. His honour is everything to him, yet this honour means he must constantly be in competition, with himself and with others. Honour to him means always winning, and if he does not win, it eats him up inside, like a vileness of the heart. He assumes, of course, that you feel the same, and that you are spoiling to fight him. He cannot understand why you are reluctant. So he calls you a coward, although he does not believe it.'

He went on, 'Agamemnon is more than happy for this fight to take place. If you die, the Trojan cause will suffer a great blow. If Achilles dies, Agamemnon will celebrate privately too.'

'Why would he?'

'Achilles' father King Peleus of Thessaly was a bully and a coward. Agamemnon could manipulate him, and found him an agreeable northern neighbour. But Achilles will be a strong king and, if they each return to their lands, a daunting new power on his border.'

'*If* they return to the west, Odysseus. These kings are foolish if they think they can stay away from their lands for so long, and not face problems back at home. Things will never be the same for them.'

'Indeed,' Odysseus agreed happily. 'Agamemnon's wife Klytemnestra loathes him, it is said. I'm sure she already has a new husband in waiting.'

Hektor's face darkened at that, and Odysseus cursed himself. Hektor fears Andromache is only waiting for him to die so she can marry Helikaon. What fools we humans are, he thought sadly.

'It is growing dark and I am in no mood for riding again tonight,' Odysseus said. 'I will make camp here. I will wait for you until noon tomorrow. If you do not come I will return to the city alone.'

They both stood up, then embraced as old friends again. Odysseus clapped the prince on his shoulder. 'Come back to Troy with me!' he urged him. 'Fight Achilles! It will be the greatest fight we mortals have ever seen, and the name of Hektor will be remembered to the end of eternity!'

The next day the king's aide Polydorus sat in Priam's gold-encrusted chariot as it jolted through the city streets flanked by heavily armed riders. Beside him the king was wrapped in a heavy wool cloak, although Polydorus was sweating freely under his bronze armour in the stifling afternoon heat.

He shot a glance at the old man, who was peering around, his face a mask of confusion and fear. It was the first time Priam had left his palace since the beginning of summer, and much had changed, none of it for the better.

The king had announced his intention that morning of going to the Great Tower of Ilion. Polydorus had found a reason to postpone the visit, hoping Priam would forget about it, as he had always done before. But this time the old man persisted, and eventually the aide had the golden chariot brought to the gates. He was fearful that the people should see their king addled and bemused, and he ordered the charioteer to make all speed to the tower, and to stop for nothing, even if the king ordered it.

'I do not know this city,' Priam muttered anxiously, as the gleaming chariot passed the squalid shacks of the refugees. 'Where are we, boy? Is this Ugarit? We must make haste for home. My sons are conspiring against me. They wish to see me dead. I do not trust Troilus, never did. Hekabe warned me. She will know how to deal with him.'

Polydorus said nothing and the king quietened, gazing round at a city which was foreign to him. There were few people to be seen on the streets, although Polydorus knew the shanty city hid hundreds dying slowly of hunger, thirst and hopelessness. Babies and old people were the first to succumb. When the remaining well ran dry, which he knew could happen any time, everyone in the city would be dead within three or four days.

They reached the steps to the south battlements. Priam was helped out of the chariot and climbed slowly, his bodyguard in full armour clattering up the stairs in front of him and behind. Soldiers guarding the wall watched open-mouthed as their king shuffled past them. A few cheered, but the sound died away quickly to leave an eerie silence.

Plunging into the darkness of the Great Tower, Polydorus looked up the narrow stone stairs with dread lying heavy in his chest. But

Priam had climbed that way a thousand times, and his steps were firm as he set off. Polydorus came behind him, his gaze fixed on the old man's bony ankles and not on the steep drop to their right. He knew that if the king fell, then they both would. Polydorus would try to save him, of course, but it would be impossible. They would both die, smashed on the stones far below. The old man stopped halfway and rested against the dank wall, then took a deep breath and carried on.

When they stepped out into the daylight again Polydorus breathed a sigh of relief. It was a rare day in Troy when the wind did not blow, yet the air was quite still on the top of the tower. The sky above was pale blue and cloudless.

Priam pulled his cloak more closely around him and stepped over to the south wall. He gazed down at the ruined lower town, his face blank. He looked into the distance. Suddenly he pointed and said, 'Hektor is coming.'

Polydorus looked to where he was indicating and saw two horsemen riding at walking pace from the Scamander plain towards the lower town. He could see one of them was a big man, as big as Hektor, riding a black horse, but he could see neither man's face.

'My son. My son is coming,' the old man said happily.

Polydorus' thoughts went to his own son, as they always did when they were allowed. The boy was still at the breast, and the young aide found himself breathless when he thought of the boy, his wispy dark hair, his soft dimpled cheeks and happy smile. Polydorus had made his decision long since. When the city fell he would abandon the old man to his fate and hurry to Casilla and the boy. He would defend them with his life. It was all he could do.

'Who is that with him?' the king asked.

Polydorus peered again at the riders. They were crossing the wide new bridge the enemy had built over the fortification ditch. In the silent afternoon he fancied he could hear hooves clopping on the wooden planks. With a jolt he realized it *was* Hektor, riding casually, one hand on the reins, the other holding his high-crested helm in front of him. Beside him rode the king of Ithaka. What is Hektor doing riding into the enemy camp, he thought?

355

'Odysseus!' cried the old man, waving his fist. 'Treacherous dog! Cleave the head from his shoulders, my son! Kill the cur!'

Now there were cries and shouts from below and men started appearing from the shadows of the ruins. Hundreds of soldiers – Mykene, Thessalians, mercenaries alike – were running to the main street where Hektor rode. They lined up on each side of his path, watching as the Trojan prince passed, Odysseus riding by his side. There were some jeers, but these were quickly smothered, and then there was silence as the two riders made their way up to the Scaean Gate.

Polydorus hurried to the side of the tower which looked down on the gate. There stood a huge dark-haired man in black armour. Polydorus knew immediately who he was. What is happening, he thought?

There was a brief conversation between the three men in front of the gates, then Achilles stepped aside and walked away, apparently satisfied. Hektor looked up and his voice boomed out. 'Open the gate! Hektor, prince of Troy, commands it!'

Polydorus ran to the inward side of the tower and leaned far over the battlements.

'Open the gate!' he shouted down to the guards. 'Hektor has returned! Open the gate now!'

Andromache was resting on a couch on the east terrace when the distant sound of cheering came to her ears. She sat up and glanced at Axa, who gazed at her in puzzlement. They both rose and went to the terrace wall, but could see nothing from the vantage point. The cheering was getting louder all the time.

'I will go and find out what is happening,' Andromache said.

'Perhaps the enemy has left and we are saved,' ventured Axa.

'Maybe,' Andromache replied doubtfully, and she left her apartments and hurried through the palace.

Outside, the royal guard were also uncertain what was happening. They had unsheathed their swords, ready for action. Then Polites appeared with his bodyguard, looking alarmed.

'Why is there cheering, Polites?' Andromache asked, but he shook his head.

Then a rider galloped up the stone streets towards them. He threw himself off his horse and cried, 'Prince Hektor is back, lord! He is here in the city!'

The sound of cheering came closer, and now Andromache could hear the word repeated over and over, 'Hektor! Hektor! HEKTOR!'

Hope blossomed in her heart, immediately followed by a stab of fear. The summer had been tedious but uneventful. Although the enemy were at the gates, it was impossible to stay frightened all the time, and eventually a complacent calm set in as long hot day followed long hot day. Now the wheel of events was starting to turn again, and something inside her told Andromache this was the beginning of the end.

When her husband finally came in sight, walking his horse slowly up towards the king's palace, he was surrounded by a mob of cheering Trojans. Soldiers had formed a circle of protection round him, but people kept trying to break through in a bid to touch his robe or his sandals. The black horse fidgeted nervously, but Hektor kept him walking steadily on a tight rein. As he reached the palace the royal guard pushed the mob back, but they carried on shouting his name and cheering.

Hektor smiled when he saw Andromache, and reined in his horse. He dismounted wearily, then embraced her, holding a hand out to his brother. 'Andromache. Polites. It is good to see you both.'

'We thank the gods you are here, Hektor,' replied Polites. 'But why and how? You come unlooked-for.'

Hektor shook his head. 'I must speak to Father first.'

'But Father is not well . . .' started Polites.

'I know,' said Hektor, sorrow in his voice. 'Nevertheless he is still the king and I must speak to him first.'

He gripped Andromache's hand tightly for a heartbeat, then let her go, and turned and walked towards the king's palace with his brother. Andromache returned to her apartments, her mind in a whirl. Waiting had never come easily to her, and she found herself pacing up and down the terrace, restless with uncertainty and anticipation. The sky darkened and the two boys went to their beds, but still Hektor had not come.

Finally the door opened with a whisper and he was there, dressed in an old grey tunic and threadbare cloak. She ran into his arms. He held her for a while, his face pressed deep into her hair. Then she looked up at him and said, smiling, 'On the bank of the Simoeis I told you we would meet again.'

Gazing into her eyes, his face grave, he told her, 'There is to be a duel, Andromache.'

She took a deep breath and asked, 'It's with Achilles, isn't it?'

He nodded. 'I killed his friend Patroklos, and he wants vengeance.'

She found anger surging up inside her and pulled away from his embrace. 'This is not a game, husband! This *friend* of his came here, like Achilles, to plunder the city, to kill and to maim. Do you owe it to Achilles to fight him because you killed his *friend*? Hektor, you have killed hundreds in battle since this war started. Do you have to fight all *their* friends too?' She heard the heavy sarcasm in her voice, and hated herself for it, but she could not stop herself. 'This is a grand nonsense, husband!' He opened his mouth to speak, and she cried, 'And do not say the word "honour" to me! I am sick and tired of that word. It seems to me that honour means whatever you men want it to mean.'

Hektor watched her until her rage subsided a little. 'If I fight Achilles, they will let our women and children go. Agamemnon has pledged this and Odysseus guaranteed it.'

'And you believe them?' she asked, but her anger had weakened and she could lean on it no more. 'Will Astyanax be taken to safety?'

He shook his head sadly. 'If they had agreed to *that*, I would not have trusted them.'

'This is still a grand nonsense,' she repeated sadly.

'What is wrong, Andromache?' he asked gently.

She shook her head, trying to clear it. What is wrong with me, she thought? My husband returns to me, having secured the lives of Trojan women and children, yet I am shouting at him like a fish-wife. She smiled at him. 'I'm sorry, my love. But what happens if Achilles kills you? Will Agamemnon then keep his word? Why would he?'

He explained, 'The gates will be opened at dawn and the women and children allowed to leave. They will be escorted to the Bay of Herakles where they will take ship for Lesbos. The gates will close again at noon, when the duel will start. So Achilles and I will not meet until after the innocents are freed.'

'Can you win?'

'I have beaten everyone who has ever come against me. And I have beaten Achilles before. You were there.'

'Yes. It was brutal.'

He nodded. 'Fistfights can be like that. This will be a duel to the death with swords.'

Her blood ran cold as she thought of it. 'It must be quick,' she told him, thinking back to Helikaon's duel with Persion.

'Yes.' He nodded. 'The longer it goes on the more likely he is to kill me. He is very skilled, very fast, and he is younger than I am. But he has weaknesses. Pride and vanity are his constant companions. They are unreliable friends and often give bad advice.'

'That is not very reassuring,' she said, smiling slightly.

He shook his head. 'It is all I have to offer, Andromache.'

Hektor called for food, and he ate a meal of salt fish and corn bread and they both sipped wine as they talked deep into the night. She told him of the desperate situation in Troy, the fact that the entire city now relied for water on one unreliable well, and the dire state of the granaries. They discussed the successes of the *Xanthos*, and those of the Trojan Horse. He asked about Astyanax, and she made him laugh by telling him the trivial gossip of the palace.

At last Hektor, weary beyond words, threw himself on the bed and was instantly asleep. Andromache watched him for a while, her heart aching, then walked back out on to the terrace.

The moon was riding high, and she stood looking at it for a

while. Then she did something she had not done since she left the sanctuary of Thera. She prayed to her own special deity, Artemis the moon goddess.

'O Lady of the Wild Things,' she pleaded, 'protector of small children, take pity on your sister, and protect my husband to-morrow. Guard him so that he can return to guard his son.'

Then she lay on the couch listening to the night sounds of the city, and eventually drifted into a troubled sleep.

It was daylight when she was abruptly woken by a shrill cry. She leapt up, startled, and rushed indoors. There she found little Astyanax standing in the doorway to his bedchamber gazing up in fear at Hektor, who had donned his bronze armour, including the high helm with its black and white crest.

Hektor laughed and pulled off the helm again. 'Don't be frightened, boy.' He knelt down in front of the child and picked him up, holding him in front of his face. 'See, you remember me. I am your father.'

Astyanax grinned with delight, and cried, 'Papa! Did you bring my pony?'

'Not yet, boy. When you are a bit older you will have the pony I promised.'

The child reached out and ran his small finger along the lines of the golden horse embossed on Hektor's breastplate. 'Like this, Papa?'

'Yes, just like this one.' Hektor looked at Andromache and there was anguish in his eyes as he held the boy close to him. He shook his head, and Andromache knew what he was thinking.

'Many other men's sons will live because of what you do today, my love,' she reassured him.

He breathed a deep sigh, looking down on the child's flame-coloured hair. 'It is not enough,' he answered. 'I can never do enough.'

XXVII

The bravest of the Trojans

AS DAWN CAST ITS PINK RAYS OVER THE CITY, THE MASSIVE SCAEAN
Gate swung open a crack and a small girl toddled out. She was
scarcely more than a baby, with big blue eyes and golden curls.
When she saw the armed men lined up outside she stopped in
surprise, then sat down suddenly in the dust and started to wail.

A young woman followed her through the gates crying, 'Susa, I
told you to wait for me!' She saw the enemy soldiers and her face
went ashen, but she ran forward and picked up the child. She
carried a shapeless bag of belongings under one arm, and
she tucked the crying girl under the other. Then she looked
around.

Odysseus stepped forward. 'You know where you are going,
woman?'

She nodded, bobbing her head nervously.

'Then go!' he roared, pointing down the road which led through
the lower town and across the Scamander plain to the safety of the
sea.

'Thank you, sir,' she whispered, passing him by, head down.
'Thank you, lord.'

Next through the gates was a skinny old crone with two
children, a boy and a girl, held tightly by their hands. She glared

when she saw the soldiers, and hurried past the watching ranks as quickly as possible.

As more women came out from the gate Odysseus signalled to his Ithakan riders to accompany the exodus towards the Bay of Herakles. One trotted his horse up to the first woman and, leaning from his mount, picked the crying toddler up by one arm and swung her up in front of him. The girl stopped wailing instantly, startled into silence.

Throughout the morning there was a continuous stream of refugees out of the city until, Odysseus guessed, the line of them stretched all the way from the Scaean Gate to the bay. There were a few donkey-carts and a couple of starved-looking horses, but most of the women walked. There were wives with small children, and some young women travelling in groups, but many of the refugees were sturdy older women, soldiers' wives and camp-followers, used to walking long distances behind moving armies. They did not pale when they passed the enemy warriors; they marched with their heads high.

Odysseus glanced at Agamemnon from time to time. Tall and stooped in his black cloak, the Mykene king was standing watching the refugees. Odysseus was reminded of a hungry vulture deprived of its prey. Alongside him was a thin, swarthy man called Dolon. Each time a woman or child with red hair came out of the gates Agamemnon would look at Dolon, who would shake his head. Odysseus knew the man once had a role in the Trojan royal household, and guessed he would be well rewarded for this day's work.

Shortly before noon the trickle of refugees from the gate stopped. There was an expectant silence among the waiting soldiers, then finally Hektor himself walked out. He was in full armour of bronze, his black and white crested helm held under one arm, and four swords in the other hand. He looked twice the size of any of the men around him, and he gazed at them without expression. The Scaean Gate closed behind him and they all heard the locking bar being firmly rammed into place.

Odysseus walked up to the prince, who asked him, 'Will they be safe, sea uncle?'

The king nodded. 'You have my word. The first ones to leave are already on Kypriot ships. The masters have been well paid to take them to Lesbos. And many will have enough rings for passage far away from here.'

Hektor's face was grave and Odysseus could see the tension round his eyes.

'Then let's get on with it,' he said.

Followed by hundreds of warriors, the two walked round the walls to the west of the city. Here the wall was lowest, and the people of Troy could watch the combat from the battlements. A wide area of ground had been levelled off during the night, and a huge circular trench dug, wider than a man could leap. It was filled with glowing coals, and the heat rising from them made the air shimmer. The arena of combat inside the trench was more than fifty paces wide, and Odysseus knew the ground had been scrutinized closely for loose pebbles which could make a fighter lose his footing. Thousands of soldiers were gathering round the circle, six to eight deep, jostling for a vantage point. The ones at the back pushed forward, those at the front tried to stay back from the heat of the coals.

Achilles was already waiting, alongside the priest of Ares. He was garbed in his black armour and helm, and if he noticed the heat he did not show it. There were four swords at his feet, as agreed. Hektor checked the straps on his breastplate, then put on his helm. He placed his own swords on the ground by the priest. Odysseus noticed the hilts of Hektor's swords were incised with the horse insignia of the house of Priam.

The thin dark-clad priest raised his hands and cried out in a reedy voice, 'O Ares, lord of war, man-killer, bringer of glory, hear our words. Look on these two great warriors. Each has served you well, O hater of mankind. Today, if you will it, one will stalk the sunlit fields of Elysium. The name of the other will echo down the halls of history, and all men will honour him for eternity.'

Two scrawny goats were dragged up and the priest cut their throats with a curved knife as they cried out in fear. Their blood splashed on the ground, drying instantly on the hot earth.

A huge plank of wood, a door, Odysseus guessed, doused in water, was thrown over the trench as a bridge. The two champions each picked up a blade, then walked across the bridge, steam from the coals rising around them. The bridge was withdrawn. Odysseus looked up at the western wall. It was packed with silent watchers. There were thousands of spectators at this death match, but they were so quiet all he could hear was the two men's footsteps as they walked to the centre of the arena.

They touched swords in salute. Then they circled. Achilles attacked first with lightning speed, and Hektor blocked and parried, sending back a blistering riposte that made Achilles step back. They circled again, watching each other's eyes.

'Will you wager with me, Odysseus?' asked his kinsman Nestor, king of Pylos, who was standing beside him. 'Our great Achilles against your friend Hektor?'

'I am proud to call Hektor my friend, but I will not wager on him,' replied Odysseus. 'By Hera's tits, even the gods will not gamble on this battle.'

Hektor hacked and thrust, Achilles parried and countered. Suddenly Achilles launched a ferocious attack, his blade moving like quicksilver. Hektor blocked, then spun on his heel and hit Achilles in the face with the back of his fist. Achilles stumbled, righted himself and swiftly brought up his blade to parry a death thrust to the neck. His riposte was so fast Hektor threw himself to the ground, rolled, and was up again in an instant. They circled again.

Odysseus watched spellbound as the duel continued. Both fighters were endowed with natural balance and speed. Both had honed their skills in a thousand battles. Achilles was the younger man, yet he had spent all his short life seeking fights. Hektor battled and killed only when he had to. Both men fought coolly now and with patience. Each knew the slightest misjudgement could end his life. Each probed for weaknesses in the other; each tried to read the other's moves.

The pace quickened and the swords clashed together in a whirl of glittering bronze. Attacking with controlled fury, Achilles forced

Hektor back towards the fiery trench. They had to move carefully there, for the edges of the trench were crumbling in the heat. Hektor's foot slipped. The crowd on the wall gasped. Achilles lunged. Hektor parried, regained his footing and sent a flashing riposte which slid off Achilles' breastplate. Both men stepped back, as if by consent, towards the centre of the circle.

Odysseus knew most duels began with heat and fury, then settled down to a game of endurance and concentration. No two duellists were exactly matched; all knew this. And there would always come a point when the seed of doubt entered the mind of one fighter – is he better than me? In this duel both men wanted to win. But was the difference between them that Achilles feared to lose? Hektor had no such fear. Indeed, Odysseus wondered if it was Hektor's weakness that at his core he did not care if he lived or died.

Achilles attacked again. Hektor ducked beneath a murderous cut, his own blade flashing out and slicing Achilles' cheek. Achilles stepped back a pace, wiping blood from his face, and Hektor allowed himself a heartbeat's pause.

Then he attacked. Achilles blocked the sword, rolled his wrist and lanced his blade into the meat of Hektor's shoulder. Hektor swayed back, preventing the point thrusting deeply, but his sword fell from his numbed hand. The crowd gasped, and several people on the wall cried out. Achilles moved back two paces and gestured to the Trojan warrior to pick the weapon up.

As Hektor's hand touched his sword, Achilles leapt at him, blade flashing for his head. Hektor blocked the blow with incredible speed but was forced back by the ferocious double-handed assault. Time and again Achilles was within a hair's-breadth of delivering the death blow, but each attack was countered with amazing skill.

The long afternoon wore on, but the crowd was totally absorbed, totally silent, motionless in the monstrous heat.

A lightning thrust, partly parried, had opened up another cut on Achilles' cheek. Hektor was suffering from cuts and gashes on both arms. Each had blunted or broken two blades, replaced instantly by the black-robed priest who tossed them with practised accuracy into the fighters' hands.

Odysseus could see that both men's sword arms were tiring. They circled more warily, conserving strength. Hektor leapt forward. Their blades clashed together, and a high sweet note rose unexpectedly from the dull clash of bronze.

Achilles' sword thrust past the Trojan's defences, hammering into the bronze strap holding his breastplate. It sprang off harmlessly but the power of the blow sent Hektor staggering. Unbalanced, he swung at Achilles' legs. His sword rang off a metal greave, but Hektor stumbled. Achilles hit him across the head with the pommel of his sword. Hektor ducked and rolled, more slowly now, then was up to counter a renewed attack.

He stumbled again, his fatigue obvious. Watching him, Odysseus smiled to himself. It was a ploy he had used himself, only available to the older man in a contest. Achilles leapt forward, certain of the death blow. Hektor swayed away from the thrust. The sword passed his side, just under the lip of his breastplate. Achilles was wrong-footed, expecting a solid target. Hektor smashed the hilt of his sword into the back of his head and Achilles went down. He rolled to his back just in time to block a massive sword-blow to his face. The blades clanged together with a sound that echoed off the walls of Troy like the end of the world.

And Hektor's blade snapped.

Achilles was rolling to his feet as the priest of Ares threw Hektor his fourth sword. The new blade flashed forward, but Achilles blocked it with ease and sent a counter that tore through his opponent's leather kilt, narrowly missing Hektor's inner thigh. Hektor returned the attack with a lightning riposte, his sword ripping into Achilles' helm. Achilles fell back, and shook his head as if to clear it.

Hektor attacked. Achilles parried, and Hektor struck out with his left fist. Achilles swayed away from the blow and sent an uppercut to Hektor's jaw. Hektor rolled with the punch, and spun away as Achilles' sword sang through empty air.

Achilles stepped back and took the moment to lift clear his

damaged helm. He walked over to the edge of the circle and threw
it far out over the heads of the watchers. Hektor dropped his sword
and wrenched off his own helm and tossed it into the crowd. Bare-
headed he picked up his sword again. Then with a roar he ran
across the circle.

Achilles raced in, holding his blade double-handed. Hektor
ducked swiftly and the sword hissed over his head. Off balance,
Achilles stumbled to the earth. He rolled twice then smoothly rose
to his feet. Then in a frenzied attack he landed blow after blow on
Hektor's bronze breastplate. A great crack appeared down the
centre of the golden horse. The Trojan ripped at the remaining
bronze strap and threw the breastplate to the ground. Achilles
paused, then did the same with his black cuirass.

The crowd fell silent as the two men fought on bare chested,
sweat pouring off them. Odysseus watched, caught between
admiration and horror. He had seen many fights in his life, most of
them the dull exchange of huge blows, without skill or fore-
thought. This was a titanic struggle of strength and skill such as no
man watching had ever seen before, or would see again.

Neither champion spoke a word, as far as Odysseus could hear.
Taunts and insults were for lesser men. Each warrior was holding
his concentration in a vice-like grip, planning ahead, trying to
predict the other's moves.

Achilles' sword sliced across Hektor's chest, sending a spray of
blood flying through the air. Hektor groaned, and the sound was
echoed by those on top of the wall, and by many of the watchers
outside the circle. Achilles leapt in for the kill. Hektor swayed to
the right and his blade flashed out. Achilles threw himself back, but
not before Hektor's sword had opened a wound in his side.

Blood was streaming from both men now. And Hektor was
really tiring. Odysseus could see it. Achilles could see it too. He
tried a feint, followed by a lunge to the heart. Hektor parried it and
sent a return cut that pierced Achilles beneath the collar bone,
slicing open the skin.

Suddenly Achilles staggered.

He fell to one knee, shaking his head. Hektor rushed in and

Achilles rolled and tried to stand. Hektor paused, sword ready for the killing blow. With a massive effort Achilles got to his knees, then fell again. Hektor stepped back two paces, frowning. Then Achilles sprang to the attack like a man demented. Abandoning any attempt at defence, he launched a savage assault which backed Hektor right across the arena.

Hektor defended grimly, his back ever closer to the perilous trench. Then suddenly Achilles fell again, his legs collapsing under him.

There were sounds of jeering from the top of the wall. At an order from Agamemnon the makeshift bridge was thrown across the trench and the priest of Ares hurried across to the two exhausted fighters. He took Hektor's sword from his unresisting hand and sniffed at the blade. Then he raised the weapon aloft.

'Poison!' he shouted. 'This blade has been smeared with poison! Achilles has been betrayed by the Trojan!'

'Treachery!' Agamemnon cried, and the cry was taken up angrily by the Myrmidons and the soldiers of Mykene. 'Treachery!'

'Lies!' boomed Hektor's voice, and the word was echoed all along the walls.

'Kill the treacherous dog!' Agamemnon yelled, and before Hektor could arm himself three Followers raced across the bridge to attack him. Hektor ducked under the first sword-cut, then smashed the Follower in the face with his huge fist. As the Mykene went down Hektor snatched his sword and lanced it into the neck of the next attacker. The third Follower died from a sword-thrust through the eye socket.

Achilles' Myrmidons were trapped on the far side of the trench, with no way across, surrounded by warriors packed eight deep. Enraged by the betrayal of their king, all they could do, like those on the walls, was watch helplessly. The soldiers round the circle, their blood already high, were shouting and jostling, and fistfights were breaking out at the back.

Odysseus desperately worked his way through the crowd, cursing, pushing, elbowing a path to where the priest of Ares had retreated with Hektor's sword.

With three Followers dead, Agamemnon sent in the rest of his elite guard. Gravely wounded, Hektor saw the nine coming towards him, picked up a second sword, and attacked. But even he could not stand against so many. He slashed one across the throat. Another went down with a sword in his belly. Hektor snatched up another blade, but the warriors surrounded him, and he was getting weaker by the moment.

Then, amazingly, Achilles stirred and moved. He struggled to his knees, then stood. His face was grey with pain and the effects of the poison. The crowd instantly went silent and the skirmishes on the edge of the crowd ceased.

Achilles swayed on his feet. 'Not . . . Hektor,' he gasped.

Then he slowly raised his sword – and slammed it into the throat of one of the Followers. Agamemnon's remaining men sprang to the attack, and Hektor and Achilles stood back to back to take them all on.

The thousands of watchers were awestruck as the two blood-covered warriors, both beyond hope of life, battled against seven of Agamemnon's elite. Hektor was bleeding from a score of cuts, and one arm was so badly injured it was no longer functioning. It was impossible that Achilles was still standing, let alone fighting. The end was inevitable. Yet it seemed neither champion would allow himself to fall while there were still enemies to fight.

Odysseus, panting and cursing, finally reached the priest, who was watching the battle, his eyes alight with pleasure. Odysseus grabbed him by the throat and, with a roar, lifted him from his feet. The priest grappled panic-stricken in the king's powerful grip, his face turning red. Odysseus delved in the pouch at the man's side, and brought forth a small gold phial. He dropped the priest.

'Enough!' he bellowed, his voice like thunder above the noise of battle.

The fighting in the circle ceased, and the three Followers still alive stepped back uncertainly. Odysseus prised open the phial, which was half filled with milky liquid. He sniffed it. 'Here is your treachery!' he shouted, holding it up. 'And here is your poisoner!' He pushed the priest forward.

Agamemnon strode up and snatched the poison phial. 'What is this?' he asked, his voice shaking with genuine anger.

'It is called *atropa*,' replied Odysseus, raising his voice so everyone could hear. 'It is used by the Scythians of the Sombre Sea to dip their arrows in. It causes dizziness, raving, paralysis and death. It is an evil poison. A coward's weapon.'

'You dog!' Agamemnon grabbed the poisoned sword and plunged it into the priest's belly. The force of the blow knocked the man down on to the hot coals. He started to shriek, his robes bursting into flames around him. Within moments his desperate thrashing ceased and his blackening body was still.

In the arena Hektor fell to his knees with a groan that echoed off the walls of Troy, blood streaming from a score of wounds. Achilles, still standing only by a massive feat of will, raised his sword and, with a last cry, plunged it into the chest of a Follower. Then he fell dead to the ground. The remaining two Followers looked to Agamemnon, uncertain what to do.

With a final effort Hektor picked up Achilles' sword with trembling fingers and placed it on the warrior's breast, then closed the dead hands over the hilt. He rested back on his heels and bowed his head. Odysseus heard his final sigh. Then there was silence.

Hektor was dead.

His heart breaking, Odysseus sank to one knee. Across the circle he saw Thibo, Achilles' shield-bearer, do the same, followed by all the Myrmidons. Then one by one every man round the battle ground knelt in tribute to the two great warriors.

Only Agamemnon stood alone. He turned angrily on his heel and stalked away.

Odysseus bowed his head, sick at heart for the part he had played in the deaths of the two heroes. Then in the quiet he heard a hissing sound. In the trench before him the dying coals were giving off small spurts of steam. Odysseus raised his eyes to the sky. Unnoticed by anyone as the titanic battle went on, thunderclouds had gathered overhead. It became darker as he watched, then there was a deafening crack of thunder, and a bolt of lightning flashed through the sky above Troy's walls. The skies opened and the rain poured down.

He had no idea how long he knelt there in the rain and mud. Eventually Odysseus became aware that people were moving about. He opened his eyes wearily. The Myrmidons were gathered around Achilles, preparing to take him away.

Odysseus levered himself to his feet and walked across to the arena. Red-bearded Thibo was standing by Hektor's body.

'You will return Hektor to his city?' Odysseus asked.

'I will, king,' said the warrior. 'Had he lived, great Achilles would have treated his fallen foe with honour. Then I will take my Myrmidons and we will sail home. Our king will go to the pyre, but not in this accursed place.'

Odysseus nodded. He suddenly realized the men around him had fallen silent, and the only sound was the rain drumming on metal armour. He looked up and saw Andromache. She was walking towards them alone through the rain, dressed in a robe of scarlet flame, her face stern, her head high.

She came up to him. She was ashen-faced and her hair was plastered to her head and shoulders, yet he thought her then the most beautiful woman he had ever seen. Helikaon was right, he thought. Truly you are a goddess.

She looked down on Hektor's body, and when she looked up at him again her eyes were brimming with tears. 'Well, Tale Spinner? Are you happy with this day's work?'

'Two of my friends are dead. What would you have me say, lass?'

'That this will all end now, and you will return to your ships and go home.'

'I will return to my ships and go home.'

She arched her eyebrows, unbelieving. 'Truly?'

He told her, 'Ithaka is leaving this place. I do not believe the priest chose to poison the blade which killed Achilles.' He glanced enquiringly at Thibo, who shook his head.

'I suspect Agamemnon's hand behind this,' Thibo agreed. 'It was an evil act.'

Odysseus told Andromache, 'This is Thibo of the Myrmidons. He will see Hektor's body is returned to the city with honour. Then he will take Achilles' army and go home to Thessaly. And I will be back with Penelope and my new son come the feast of Demeter.'

He saw hope in Andromache's grey eyes and was quick to quash it.

'We once made a pact, you and I, to tell each other only the truth,' he said. She nodded, remembering the Bay of Blue Owls where they had first met. 'Agamemnon will not return home with his armies and fleets. Troy will fall, Andromache. The rain will not save you. In truth, it means only that everyone in the city will be slaughtered before they die of thirst.'

She caught her breath at his harsh words.

'Troy cannot be saved.' He glanced at the listening soldiers, and looked into her eyes. 'But if you wish to save your son,' he told her, 'look to the north.'

He turned away, and left her standing grief-stricken in the rain.

Agamemnon was furious. He strode down the road to his palace, flanked by his Mykene guard and the last two Followers. Can no one follow a simple plan, he thought? The priest was supposed to smear poison on the blade, unnoticed as everyone watched the battle, then drop the phial into the hot coals. Instead, greed had made him keep it, and greed had been his undoing. And as for that interfering oaf Odysseus, it was well past time to do something about him. His nuisance value now outweighed his usefulness.

Agamemnon swept into the *megaron*, where the kings were already gathering, quaffing goblets of wine cheerfully. When they saw him their demeanour changed to watchfulness. He knew they found him hard to predict, and this pleased him.

He looked round, then he sighed and shook his head. 'Our great Achilles is dead,' he said sorrowfully. 'Our champion felled by treachery.'

Kygones of Lykia was watching him narrowly. 'Yes, a tragedy for us all,' he commented drily.

'I heard the Myrmidons say they will leave now and take his

body home,' Menelaus slurred. He had been swigging unwatered wine for much of the day.

'We do not need the Myrmidons. All the more plunder for the rest of us,' said Idomeneos with relish.

The doors opened and Odysseus came in, followed by old Nestor. The Ithakan king stomped up to Agamemnon, his face red with anger.

'Convince me, king,' he stormed, 'that you did not command the poxy priest to poison Hektor's sword!'

Agamemnon replied smoothly, 'This is madness, Odysseus. Why would I poison our own champion?'

'Because, by the great god Zeus, one death was never enough for you. You wanted them both dead! And if Achilles' blade were poisoned and he lived to find out, then he would have killed you himself, as I am minded to do myself for today's foul deeds.'

Agamemnon leapt back and drew his sword, and his Followers moved to his side, blades at the ready. The Battle King was well prepared to fight. To see the meddlesome Odysseus lying on the floor with his lifeblood pumping out was something he had long hoped for. Around them the other kings had their hands to their sword hilts, but Agamemnon realized with shock at least two of them, old Nestor and Menestheos of Athens, were glaring at *him*.

He took a deep breath and said placatingly, 'You are misled by your grief, Odysseus. This is a day of tragedy for all of us. Our champion Achilles is walking the Dark Road. We will never see his like again.' The words of the dying priest in the Cave of Wings came back to him. 'The Age of Heroes is passing,' he added.

'By all the bastard gods, I am sick of it all,' Odysseus told him. 'I will take my army and return to the bay tonight. At dawn we sail for Ithaka.'

Agamemnon felt a flood of relief and pleasure. The fat fool is leaving at last, he thought. The gods must truly love Mykene. Aloud he said coldly, 'So your pledge to me is worthless, Ithaka.'

'It was not the pledge that was worthless, but the recipient,' Odysseus replied scornfully.

Nestor stepped in before Agamemnon could react. 'My army

will leave Troy too. I am an old man, and I wish to see no more killing, no more death,' he said. 'I will start for Pylos come daybreak.'

Agamemnon turned on him. 'Your betrayal will not be forgotten, old man,' he spat. 'You only remain king on my sufferance. When the troops of Mykene return home in triumph, be prepared to defend your flax fields and sandy beaches.'

Nestor flushed and countered angrily, 'Do not seek to threaten me, Agamemnon. My sons are dead, because of the dread Helikaon, but I have strong grandsons aplenty. If your troops march on our borders they will be waiting for you there with sharp swords. *If* you ever return to the Lion's Hall,' he added. 'There are myriad leaves on the tree, and myriad ways to die,' he quoted.

'You pious old fool,' Idomeneos snapped. 'Even the gods are tired of your pompous advice and your tedious tales about when you were a young warrior. We will be better off without you.'

There was violence in the air. Odysseus glanced at his old friend Meriones. He was the only man in the *megaron* who had not drawn his sword. The Ithakan king guessed his friend felt the way he did, but Meriones' loyalty to Idomeneos was legendary.

Then Agamemnon sheathed his blade and sat down on a carved chair. He sipped a little water, and smoothly changed the subject.

'The Trojans will be celebrating tonight,' he commented, as if the angry exchanges had not happened. 'They will have water enough now to last into the autumn. We cannot wait while they die of thirst. So it is time to implement Odysseus' plan to take the city.' He gestured to the Ugly King. 'Remain with us, Ithaka, and by tomorrow night our soldiers could be inside the walls of Troy. You have stayed the course this far. Do not go now on the eve of our triumph.' The words were bitter in his mouth, but the tension in the room eased and men sheathed their swords, picking up their wine cups again.

'We will sail at dawn,' said Odysseus tiredly.

'Good riddance. More plunder for the rest of us,' repeated Idomeneos.

Odysseus turned on him. 'That reminds me, Sharptooth. You

still owe me your breastplate, won by the warrior Banokles in a fistfight. I will collect it from you before I leave.'

Idomeneos scowled. Smiling, Odysseus walked from the company of the kings for the last time.

Book Three
END ⊙ OF DAYS

XXVIII

The Trojan Horse

THE HORSE WAS SWIMMING. SKORPIOS KNEW THE BEASTS COULD swim. *Indeed he had seen many swimming for their lives in the Hellespont after the battle of Carpea. But he had never sat astride a swimming horse. It was very peaceful. The sea was blue, although above them the sky was black as pitch, and the moon hung on the horizon like a hole in the heavens. It was bigger than Skorpios had ever seen, and his mount was floating towards it along a path of silver moonlight.*

Looking about curiously he saw there were fishes all round him. They were very big and were flashing past close to his legs. He wondered nervously if fish had teeth. He was answered when one swam up to him and nibbled his knee. It did not hurt, but it tickled. He kicked out and it darted away.

He noticed Mestares was riding alongside him. His handsome face was corpse grey and one arm appeared to be missing.

'The sea is red,' said the warrior.

Skorpios was surprised to see it was red.

'Go back, Skorpios. Go back while you can,' said Mestares, smiling at him kindly.

Skorpios realized his leg was hurting now from the fish bite. And there was a pain in his side. He had been riding for too long. He was very tired. He turned his mount and headed away from the moon, as Mestares had ordered, but it was dark that way and he felt very alone.

When he awoke he did not want to move. He was lying on the ground with his back against something warm. He opened his eyes and saw his comrades sleeping around him. He realized it was full daylight and, with a groan, sat up.

Then he remembered. They had come in the night, an army of Mykene soldiers, hundreds of them. Caught by surprise, the Trojan horsemen had leapt quickly to defend themselves, and the battle had been vicious. But there were too many of the enemy, and the Trojans were unprepared. Skorpios had been gashed in the knee by a lance, but he managed to kill the wielder, slicing his sword into the man's inner thigh. He thought he had killed four or five of the enemy soldiers before he turned to see the pommel of a sword crashing towards his head.

His head still ached because of the noise of horses screaming. There was a pain in his side as well as in his knee, and one eye was gummy with blood. Moaning, he rolled over and got to his knees, then vomited on the ground. He looked about him. It was still and silent in the woodland glade. Everywhere were dead men and horses. He had been lying with his back to a bay stallion. It seemed to be sleeping peacefully. He could not see a wound. He thought it was Mestares' mount Warlord. Then he recalled his dream. He saw Mestares' body lying close by, a broken sword through his belly, his open eyes full of dust.

Skorpios stood, clutching his side. He pulled aside his bloody shirt to look at the wound. A sword had gone cleanly through the flesh, and he could see the neat shape of the blade on his white skin. It was bleeding, but not much. He could not remember being wounded in the side. He checked his leg. It was a nasty gash and had bled heavily. But most of the blood on him seemed to come from his head. He felt a clot of blood above his right ear. He tried to remember what his friend Olganos had once told him about bandaging wounds. Some must be bandaged heavily, some left free to drain. He could not remember which was which.

His throat was parched and he started looking for a water skin. It was only then that he realized all the Trojan bodies, including his own, had been stripped of armour. They thought me dead, he said to himself.

He frowned. Looking round him he started to count the bodies of his comrades. There were not enough. Some got away, he thought, and his heart lifted.

Staggering around among the corpses of friends and foes, at last he found his own belongings, including a half-full water skin. He threw his head back and drank deeply. The taste was like nectar, and he felt strength flooding back into his body. The pain in his head receded a little.

He found bandages and wound one round his leg, sloshing some water on the wound first. He looked at his side again and decided it would be impossible to bandage. He delved into other men's bags until he had gathered some food. He found a full water skin. His best find was an unbroken sword, hidden under the body of a Mykene soldier. He thrust it into the scabbard still hanging from his waist, and instantly felt stronger. He picked up a bronze knife. It was blunt, but he took it anyway.

Then, with a last look at his dead comrades, he set out for the north, limping on his injured knee.

He had been travelling for some time, and his strength was failing, when he saw a stray horse cropping dry grass under a tree. It was trailing its reins, and still had a lionskin shabrack over its back. He whistled to it and, well trained, it trotted over to him. From the decorative plaiting of the reins Skorpios thought it was a Mykene mount.

With an effort he climbed on its back, then turned again in the direction of Troy. He would meet the enemy soon, and when he did he would kill as many of them as he could before he died.

He felt no fear.

'Great Zeus, I'm hungry!' complained Banokles. 'My belly thinks my throat's been sliced.'

'You've said that every day since we got here,' Kalliades pointed out.

'Well, it's been true every day since we got here.'

They stood on the south wall of Troy gazing down on the enemy armies. The ashes from Hektor's funeral pyre were still floating by on the breeze. The massive pyre had burned all night, fuelled by wood brought by Trojans from all parts of the city. Kalliades had seen young men carrying costly furniture to chop up for fire-wood, and old men bearing armfuls of twigs from dead plants. Everyone wanted to play their part, however small, in the death rites for their hero.

Scented branches of cedar and fragrant herbs had been placed on top of the pyre, then Hektor's body, in a richly embroidered robe of gold, his dead hands clasped round his sword hilt, a gold ring in his mouth for the ferryman.

As the huge pyre blazed Kalliades had seen King Priam helped out on to the balcony of the palace to watch. He was too far away to see the old man's face, but Kalliades felt a stab of pity for him. Hektor was the king's favourite son and, Kalliades believed, Priam had loved him as much as he was capable of loving anyone. Now all his sons were dead, except Polites. Priam had the boy Astyanax close by his side on the balcony. The child had cried out in excite-ment and clapped his hands as the crackling flames climbed high into the night sky.

After the funeral rites, back on the walls the familiar lethargy had returned. The duel and the death of Hektor had angered the men, and the coming of rain had refreshed them. For two days they had walked with pride. Like Hektor they were warriors of Troy, and would fight to the last for the city. But quickly the lack of food, and the long uneventful days, had taken their toll and they had lapsed into idleness and boredom again.

Kalliades was watching a dust cloud in the far distance. The dry earth had sucked all the rain into it, and the ground was as dusty now as it had been before the storm.

Boros the Rhodian was standing alongside Kalliades and Banokles. 'Can you see what that is?' Kalliades asked the flaxen-haired lad. 'Your eyes are younger than ours.'

'I'm not sure, sir,' the soldier admitted. 'Is it a cow?'

Banokles looked at him in amazement. 'Is what a cow, you moron?' he asked.

'Over there.' The young soldier was pointing towards the Tomb of Ilos, where a stray bullock, destined for sacrifice, was chewing grass.

'I meant in the distance beyond the Scamander,' said Kalliades. 'There is a cloud of dust, probably riders, maybe a battle.'

The soldier squinted his eyes and confessed, 'I don't know.'

Banokles suggested, 'Perhaps it's a herd of pigs being driven to Troy for roasting.' He frowned. 'They'd have to be invisible pigs to get past the enemy. But,' he argued with himself, 'we cannot open the gates, so how will they get in? Then they must be invisible poxy pigs with poxy wings, ready to fly over the walls straight on to spits.'

Kalliades smiled. Boros, apparently encouraged by his ramblings, asked Banokles, 'General, I have a request.'

'What?' Banokles grunted without interest.

'When we have won this war I would like to return to my family in Rhodos.'

'Why tell me? I don't care what you do.' Banokles scowled at him.

Boros regarded the general uncertainly, as he would an unknown and possibly dangerous dog, then he said, 'But I have no rings, sir. I have been with the Scamandrians more than a year, but I have only been paid once, at the feast of Persephone, when I received three silvers and six coppers. That is all gone now, and my brother's rings were plundered from his body. I cannot return to Rhodos unless we are paid.'

Banokles shook his head. 'I don't know why you're worrying about getting home. We'll probably all die here anyway,' he said. 'Of hunger,' he added gloomily.

Kalliades grinned and clapped his friend on the back. 'What have I told you about motivating the men, *General*?' he asked.

Banokles grunted again. 'Well, there's no point worrying about poxy rings when we've got these goat-shagging lumps of cow turd to deal with first.' He waved at the enemy camps below them.

Banokles was right. Besides, Kalliades knew there was nothing left in Priam's treasury for the regular troops. The mercenaries from Phrygia, Zeleia and the Hittite borders had been paid. Trojan troops, he thought, are expected to die for Troy without pay.

'If we live, I will see you get rings enough,' he promised Boros, knowing his promise was probably meaningless.

'More of the enemy have left,' the lad commented. 'That is a good sign, isn't it?' he asked hopefully.

'It is not a bad sign,' was all Kalliades could say. They had watched as the Myrmidons marched out, and two other armies, but he could not tell whose. He wondered at the political in-fighting between the western kings which had brought it about. Achilles had been poisoned, but by whom? It was certainly not Hektor. Even the enemy did not believe that. His body had been returned to the city with honour by the soldiers of Thessaly. Was Achilles murdered by someone on his own side? It was a mystery Kalliades knew he was unlikely ever to solve.

'What will you do if you return to Rhodos?' he asked Boros.

'I will join my father, who is a goldsmith. He will train me in his craft.'

Kalliades raised his eyebrows. 'Great Zeus, lad, if my father were a goldsmith I would have stayed at home and learned his trade and not sold my skills with a sword.'

'My mother is a Trojan woman and she told me I must fight for the honour of our city. And she wanted me to find out if Echios was still alive. He was her firstborn, you see. She had not seen him for fifteen years.'

Banokles narrowed his eyes against the sunlight and commented, 'Horsemen.'

The far dust cloud had resolved itself into two dust clouds, and both were heading for Troy. They were moving fast, as if one group of horsemen were chasing the other. Kalliades leaned forward on the battlement wall, frustrated by his inability to see more clearly. He glanced at Boros, and saw the young man was peering in the wrong direction.

'Boros,' he said. 'Can you see anything out of your left eye?'

The lad shook his head ruefully. 'No. I used to be able to see light and shadow, but that has gone now,' he admitted. 'Everything is dark. I was injured in Thraki, you see.'

Kalliades knew a one-eyed soldier could not last long in a pitched battle. It was extraordinary that the lad was still alive.

He turned his attention back to the horsemen in the distance. There were two groups of riders. In front were about fifty men, being chased at a furious pace by maybe two hundred. They had crossed the Scamander and were racing across the plain towards the city. The men on the walls shouted to their comrades to come and watch the race, and below them enemy soldiers were being ordered from tents and from the shadows of ruined houses. They were arming themselves quickly, putting on swordbelts and helms, collecting lances and spears, bows and quivers of arrows.

Then someone cried out, 'The Trojan Horse!'

Now Kalliades could see the riders in front bore the black and white crested helms of Hektor's cavalry. They were lying low on their horses' necks, urging their mounts on with whipped reins and shouts. The chasing horsemen were hampered by the dust being thrown up by their quarry, and they had fallen back some way as both groups galloped up the slope from the plain towards the city.

As the front riders thundered across the wooden bridge into the lower town, enemy soldiers started loosing arrows at them, and from all sides lances and spears were thrown. Some appeared to hit their targets, and two horsemen on the edge of the group went down. The soldiers watching from the walls were yelling to urge the riders on.

Kalliades found his heart in his mouth as the leading horsemen galloped up through the ruined town. Come on, he thought. Come on, you can make it! The enemy riders seemed to have slowed further.

'Open the gates!' someone shouted, and the cry was picked up all along the walls. 'Open the gates quickly. Open the gates! Let them in!'

Then realization hit Kalliades like a blow to the face. His blood went cold. 'No!' he shouted. Pushing desperately through the ranks of cheering soldiers, he raced along the wall to the battlements above the Scaean Gate. Below him men were gathering eagerly to lift the massive locking bar and open the gates.

'No!' he bellowed down at them. 'Stop! Don't open the gates!' But his voice could not be heard above the shouts of hundreds of men, and he ran down the stone steps, waving his arms and yelling frantically. 'Don't open the gates! By all the gods, don't open the gates!'

But the massive oak doors were already groaning open and, with split-second timing, the riders thundered through the gap. There were more than fifty of them, garbed in the armour of the Trojan Horse and armed with spears. Their horses' hooves kicked up a storm of whirling dust as they slowed and circled inside the gates. Behind them the guards started to close the gates again. They were heaving the locking bar back into place when one of them fell with a spear in his belly.

Kalliades drew his sword and ran for the nearest rider. He shouted, 'Kill them! They're the enemy!' and lanced his blade into the man's side, behind his breastplate.

He saw a sword sweeping towards his head from another rider, and he ducked under the horse's belly and leapt up to spear the man from the other side. As the rider fell Kalliades grabbed his shield.

He glimpsed Banokles beside him. His friend powered into the enemy horsemen, slashing and killing. Kalliades shouted to him, 'Defend the gates!' But both of them were blocked from reaching the gates by the press of horses and riders.

Kalliades gutted one enemy warrior and parried a blow from a second, back-handing his shield into the man's face. He glanced desperately at the gates again. Enemy warriors in the stolen armour of the Trojan Horse had their hands to the locking bar and were attempting to lift it. Kalliades slashed and cut, pushed and shoved his way towards them. He brained one of the men with his shield and threw his weight on to the locking bar.

He realized young Boros was at his side, and he yelled, 'Help me here, soldier!'

Boros grinned at him, then punched him hard on the jaw.

As Kalliades staggered back Boros kicked him in the face and Kalliades went flying, dazed, barely holding to consciousness. Bright lights were whirling around his head. He lay stunned, watching in horror as more of the enemy horsemen grabbed the great oak locking bar and heaved it off its brackets. The high gates started to open slowly, then more quickly as they were pushed from the outside.

And the enemy poured in.

Kalliades, lying shielded in the space behind one of the open doors, tried to get to his feet, shaking his head to clear it. Then he realized the flaxen-haired soldier was standing looking down at him. As Kalliades tried to rise, the young man placed the point of his sword at Kalliades' throat, pushing him back to the ground.

'Boros!' he whispered.

'Boros died long ago, at the battle for the Scamander,' the soldier replied triumphantly. 'I am Leitos, first son of Alektruon, loyal servant of Agamemnon King, and I am here to avenge my father and bring the proud Trojans to their knees.'

He leaned forward, pressing on the sword at Kalliades' throat. Blood started to flow. Kalliades could not speak or move.

'It was so easy to take that idiot's place when his entire company had been wiped out, and when the general of his regiment couldn't even be bothered to learn his soldiers' names. And it amused me to fool the great Kalliades, the thinker, the planner – the traitor to Mykene. Die, then, traitor!'

His face hardened and he tensed to thrust his sword through Kalliades' neck. At that last moment Kalliades saw Banokles step up behind the boy, sword raised. With one ferocious sweep of his blade he beheaded him. Hitting the gate, the head bounced on to the ground.

Banokles put out his hand and dragged Kalliades to his feet. 'He was talkative,' he observed. 'Always a mistake. Are you all right?' Kalliades nodded, swallowing blood, still unable to speak. 'Come on then,' said Banokles grimly. 'We've got a city to die for.'

XXIX

The last barricade

ENEMY WARRIORS HARD ON THEIR HEELS, KALLIADES AND BANOKLES ran up the stone steps to the west of the Scaean Gate. On the top of the wall Banokles nodded to his comrade, then turned and raced away. He was heading for the next steps down, so he could work his way round behind the new barricade. Kalliades would stay and ensure the wall was secure.

A Mykene warrior, heavily armoured, appeared close behind him at the top of the steps. Two Trojan soldiers were waiting, eager for a chance at the enemy. One hacked at the warrior's sword arm, the other lunged for his throat. He fell, blood gouting from his neck. He clattered down the stairway, knocking down the man behind him.

Kalliades grinned at the two defenders. 'Pace yourselves,' he ordered. 'There will be plenty more.'

Looking down from the wall, he surveyed the killing ground inside the gates.

The Trojan generals had been planning this day for a long time. If Agamemnon's forces won the freedom of Troy's streets, then the only sanctuary for the city's defenders was the king's palace. Because the best hope lay in keeping the enemy confined at the gate for as long as possible, soldiers had laboured throughout the summer to demolish buildings high in the upper city, taking them apart stone by stone. The stones had been used to fill in the roads and alleyways leading from the Scaean Gate, blocking them to twice the height of a man.

Fire gulleys had been dug all round the circle of open ground inside the gate. These had been filled with anything that would burn: brushwood, the branches and twigs of dead plants, and fuel left from Hektor's funeral pyre. Amphorae filled with the last oil in the city stood ready at points around the killing ground.

As the blood-hungry invaders poured in through the gate, they found themselves trapped in a space less than forty paces across, with the high walls of stone buildings all about them. There were just four ways available to them – up the steps to the battlements on either side of the gate, up the steep stairs inside the Great Tower of Ilion, or straight ahead.

Straight ahead was the only road left unblocked, the stone avenue that led to the heights of the city and Priam's palace. Polites had ordered the entrance to the road barricaded on both sides, with only a central gap remaining for daily traffic.

It was here that defenders were now converging from all parts of the city.

Kalliades turned to the battlements door in the wall of the Great Tower. This would be easy to hold. To get to it the enemy had to climb the steep tower steps in darkness. When they reached the door they would be emerging from dark into light, through a narrow doorway above a high drop. One steady warrior could defend the door all day, sending enemy after enemy falling to break his bones on the stone floor far below.

There were a hundred men holding this part of the wall. Kalliades knew not one of them would fall, or step back, without a fight to the last.

After the long summer of waiting it was almost a relief that this day had arrived. Kalliades looked around him and breathed deeply. The air seemed fresher, the colours clearer. This is what you know, he told himself, the only life you have ever known. If you are not a warrior, what are you, Kalliades?

An enemy warrior appeared at the tower door. A Scamandrian soldier leapt forward and lunged at his chest. The Mykene had his shield up, but the force of the blow unbalanced him. He fell back into darkness with a cry. Any invaders braving the tower steps would have to pass a mounting pile of dead and injured men, Kalliades thought with grim satisfaction. In time this would wear on their resolve.

He surveyed the scene below. More and more invaders were pushing in through the Scaean Gate, eager to get in on the action, and the killing ground was packed with armed men. The Trojan defenders had fallen back, as planned, to the narrowest section of the great road. Here just thirty men, Eagles all, were facing the main thrust of the enemy attack. Behind them the gap in the barricade they were defending became narrower as soldiers laboured to close it with stones, timber and rubble.

Kalliades watched with pride as the Eagles battled to hold back the enemy horde. When ordered, one by one the warriors at each end of the line stepped back and slipped through the gap. Finally just three Eagles remained. Kalliades heard the order for them to retreat. Instead, as one, they charged! They were cut down swiftly, but the gap behind them was plugged and the barricade secured.

Then an order was given, the brushwood was doused with oil and flaming torches were thrown from the heights of the surrounding buildings. Within heartbeats the fire had run along the length of the gulleys, the oil-fuelled flames leaping high and setting alight anything close by. The nearest enemy soldiers tried desperately to get back from the flames, but more warriors were still pushing in through the gates behind them. The padded linen kilt of a Kretan soldier caught alight and within moments he was a screaming, writhing human torch, blundering into his comrades and setting them ablaze. Other men near the fire gulleys were set alight as the leaping flames were blown about by gusty winds.

For a moment it looked as though the flames would jump from man to man, dooming them all. But the disciplined Mykene warriors were not to be panicked. Those armed with lances used them ruthlessly to kill the burning men or to hold them at bay until they dropped dying to the ground. Dozens of burned and blackened soldiers lay moaning on the stones – but the fires had been stopped.

On top of the buildings all round the Scaean Gate and on the walls behind the invaders bowmen were gathering. Arrows started to pepper the enemy troops from all sides and Kalliades saw several go down, hit in neck, throat or face.

Satisfied the south battlements were well defended, Kalliades followed Banokles' footsteps and ran round the wall and down the steps to make his way to the rear of the main barricade. Here he found Polites conferring anxiously with General Lucan and Ipheus, the commander of the Eagles.

'Your Eagles are fine warriors,' Kalliades told Ipheus. 'Would that we had a thousand of them.'

'Would that they followed orders,' growled Lucan. 'Those three at the barricade died needlessly. Three warriors might have made a difference come the last days.'

'They were valiant men,' said Ipheus quietly.

'I'm not denying it,' grunted the old general. 'But, just as we have learned to conserve food and water, and weapons, so we must learn to conserve valour. We have deep reserves of it, but it cannot be thrown away on suicidal adventures.'

Polites pointed out grimly, 'We hoped the fires would spread and send the enemy fleeing. What next? How long will this barricade hold?'

Kalliades replied, 'They have hundreds of men ready to attack it, but on a narrow front. There are thousands more outside the gate waiting to come in. If they keep throwing warriors at it, which they will, eventually they will break through. We can probably hold the barricade into the night, possibly through tomorrow. I cannot see it lasting longer.'

He glanced at Lucan, who nodded his agreement. At that moment Banokles arrived at a run. 'We need more archers,' he demanded. 'They're packed like cattle in there. Good bowmen could pick them off like ticks off a dog.'

Kalliades admitted, 'We are short of bowmen.' Then reluctantly he added, 'The lady Andromache has been training the Women of the Horse to shoot. Some remain in the city. They might—'

'No!' Polites cut across him with unaccustomed anger. 'When the enemy breaks through those buildings will be cut off and the bowmen in them doomed. I will not put the women in danger.'

Kalliades thought any women still in the city were doomed anyway, but he responded, 'Then I will call on the Thrakian leader Hillas. His archers are the finest in Troy.'

In front of them a burly warrior in Kretan armour was the first to cross the fire gulley and clamber over the man-high barricade, killing a Trojan soldier with a massive axe-blow to the head. He was cut down immediately, but two more Kretans followed close behind. One slipped and fell on the shifting timber and stone of the new barricade, and was lanced in the side by a Trojan warrior. The other managed a wild sweep with his sword before he was stunned by a blow from a shield, then half beheaded.

Kalliades turned away to seek out the Thrakians, and found the tribesmen waiting mere paces away. They had painted their faces for battle and were armed to the teeth, including the boy king Periklos.

'This will not last long,' tall Hillas commented as he walked up, waving dismissively at the barricade. 'When it falls we will be waiting. A barricade of flesh and bone will be stronger than one of stone and timber.'

'We need more bowmen,' Kalliades told him. 'On the killing ground the enemy are sitting targets for your shafts.'

Young Periklos stepped forward. 'I and my archers will go where we are needed. Where do you want us?'

Kalliades was torn. If he placed the young king and his Thrakians on a building, they would be trapped when the enemy broke through. But if he put them on the wall, along which they could escape if necessary, there would be no cover from enemy arrows.

'Do not fear for my safety, Kalliades,' the young man urged, seeing him hesitate. 'Put us where you need us. I will take the same risks as my men.'

'How many are you?'

'Just eight bowmen, plus Penthesileia.'

Only then did Kalliades realize that one of the archers, standing slightly apart from the men, was the stern-faced woman he had seen at Andromache's first training session. She was wearing a short leather cuirass over her white ankle-length tunic and a Phrygian bow was slung from one shoulder. In one hand she held two quivers.

'Penthesileia is one of Andromache's handmaidens. She has a wondrous natural skill with a bow,' young Periklos explained, flushing slightly. 'She will be a valuable warrior.'

Kalliades wondered what the other Thrakians thought of this newcomer. He asked the woman, 'Why did you not leave the city while you had the chance?'

'My father Ursos gave his life for Troy,' the woman told him. Her voice was husky and he saw she had piercing green eyes under heavy brows. 'I can do no less.'

Kalliades was reminded suddenly of Piria. Yes, he thought, she would have been here with her bow. He told Periklos, 'Go round to the wall to the east of the gate. If you stand well back you will have some protection from enemy arrows.'

The battle for the barricade went on all day and long after sunset. Fortunately for the beleaguered Trojan defenders, the night was moonless and starless. Fighting continued by torchlight for a while, but at last the enemy troops were ordered back to the gate. The Trojans immediately set about rebuilding defences pulled down during the day.

When they stood down for the night Kalliades and Banokles walked to the temple of Athene where food and water were being handed out. They waited in line in the darkness. Around them exhausted men lay sprawled asleep on the ground. Others sat in small groups, too tired for conversation, just staring with deadened eyes.

'Weevil bread and a sip of water,' Banokles snorted, dragging off his helm and scratching his sweat-soaked blond hair. 'A man can't fight all day on that.'

393

'If Agamemnon had held his troops back for another ten days, we wouldn't even have had weevil bread to fight on.'

'That was a good ploy, though, wasn't it? The Trojan Horse. Who wouldn't open the gates for them, riding like that?' Banokles shook his head in admiration.

'I expect Odysseus had a hand in it,' Kalliades replied. 'He has a cunning mind.'

'Do you sometimes forget who you're fighting for?' asked Banokles suddenly.

Kalliades frowned. 'No, but I know what you mean. We see Mykene warriors coming over the barricade to be cut down, and know some of them were our comrades. If our fate had been slightly different we'd be the ones on the other side.'

'That's not what I mean.' Banokles shook his head. 'I mean, *what* are we fighting for? Troy? There's nothing left of it. The lower town is wrecked, and most of the city. Agamemnon King wants Priam's treasury, they say, but Polites tells us there's nothing left in it. So are we fighting to save the king? He doesn't even know who he is any more.' He scratched his head again. 'It doesn't matter, not really. We're warriors, you and I, and we've picked our side, and we go on fighting until we win or we're killed. I just wondered . . .' He tailed off.

Kalliades thought about it, standing there in the queue for food. They had fled Mykene lands to escape Agamemnon's wrath, and since then they had taken the line of least resistance. They had joined Odysseus on his way to Troy because he offered them a way off the pirate island. By the fickle will of the gods they had been there to rescue Andromache when she was attacked by assassins. That had won them a place in Hektor's Trojan Horse. Kalliades smiled to himself. And Banokles' baffling success as a leader of men had rescued them from the jaws of defeat at Carpea, at Dardanos, and outside the walls of Troy.

He shook his head and laughed, the sound echoing across the square and making tired soldiers turn their heads in wonder.

'We are dogged by good luck in battle, you and I,' he answered his friend. 'Only the gods know why.'

Banokles was silent and Kalliades turned to look at him. 'I would give it all to have Red back,' the big warrior said sadly.

There was stalemate throughout the night, the invaders holding the Scaean Gate, the defenders holding the barricade forty paces away. There were jeers and taunts in the darkness from Agamemnon's troops, some of whom had yet to see battle and were raring to go.

With the coming of first light Kalliades and Banokles took their places behind the barricade. Kalliades checked his breastplate straps, settled his helm more securely, hefted the Sword of Argurios, and waited as the blackness gave way to dark grey. Banokles slashed his swords from side to side, stretching his shoulder muscles, and grunted to his neighbours, 'Make room, you sheep-shaggers!'

Then enemy warriors were scrambling over the barricade.

Kalliades batted aside a sword-thrust, then brought his blade down, two-handed, on a man's neck. He dragged the weapon clear, in time to parry a slashing cut. A thrown lance bounced off the edge of his shield, missing his head by a hair's-breadth. His sword lunged forward and twisted, disembowelling an attacker, who fell screaming at his feet. He threw his shield up to block a murderous cut, then his blade slashed high in the air, braining a warrior who had lost his helm. He felt a searing pain in his leg and saw that the injured man at his feet, holding his entrails in with one hand, had thrust his dagger into Kalliades' thigh. He plunged his sword into the man's neck. Beside him Banokles suddenly leapt up on to the barricade and with two dazzling cuts slashed the throats of two attackers climbing for the top. He jumped back down again and grinned at Kalliades.

The morning wore on, and defenders on either side of the two friends fell and were replaced, then replaced again. Through his focus on the fighting, as his sword hacked and slashed, cut and parried, Kalliades slowly registered a change. He was tiring and his concentration was starting to fail. His thigh hurt, though it had stopped bleeding. He had other cuts and scrapes. He stole a glance at Banokles. The big man was battling with grim determination, his two swords moving like lightning, seemingly without effort. But Kalliades, who had fought beside him for many years and many battles, guessed he was tiring too. He was using his swords economically, with not one wasted flourish, conserving his strength.

And the attackers were getting harder to kill. Kalliades realized he was facing Mykene veterans now. Agamemnon must have kept them in reserve, he thought. He felt a lull in the fighting, as if something had shifted, and he knew it was the battle's momentum.

The Trojans were losing.

Over the barricade came a giant of a man, with a full black beard and shaven head. He bore a tower shield of black and white cowhide edged with bronze. He dwarfed the men around him, and he grinned with pleasure when he saw who it was he was facing. Ajax Skull-Splitter leapt down from the barricade with the grace of a much lighter man.

'Banokles! Kalliades! You soft-bellied sons of whores!' he rumbled with relish.

He leapt to the attack, swinging his great broadsword, cleaving a passage towards them. On either side of him other Mykene veterans formed a wedge, driving the Trojan ranks back from the barricade. Banokles attacked, his two swords hacking and plunging. He killed a man at Ajax' side, but the Mykene champion's huge tower shield and the power of his great broadsword made him unstoppable.

Kalliades desperately hurled himself backwards as an arcing blade from the right sliced through his shoulder guard. He rolled, leapt up and skewered the wielder through the armpit. Then he heard the triple blast of the horn ordering retreat to the palace.

Banokles was being forced backwards by the power of Ajax' attack. He had lost one sword and replaced it with a bronze shield. The Mykene champion hammered the other blade aside and stepped in to crash a huge fist into Banokles' jaw. Banokles staggered, but recovered to block the downward sweep of the broadsword on the shield. Kalliades ran in. Ajax raised the broadsword again and brought it arcing towards them both in a massive sweep. Banokles ducked low and Kalliades swayed back-wards. Unbalanced, Ajax tried to recover but Banokles leapt up and brought his shield smashing down on the huge warrior's head. Ajax was dazed but still stood. Banokles hit him on the head again, then again, and he finally went down, crashing face first into the blood and dust.

'Is he dead?' Banokles asked, panting.

Kalliades brought the Sword of Argurios up two-handed, pre-pared to drive it into the Mykene champion's back. For a heartbeat he paused. The Sword of Argurios, he thought. If it were not for Argurios' loyalty and Priam's mercy they would not be there. Loyalty and mercy. He glanced at Banokles, who shrugged. Kalliades lowered his sword. He heard the horn again ordering retreat, and they both turned and raced for the palace.

XXX

The advice of Odysseus

LATE ON THE SECOND DAY A GREAT CHEER ROSE FROM THE SOLDIERS waiting patiently outside the walls for their comrades to break the Trojans' barricade. The young healer Xander shivered in the hot afternoon as he watched the thousands of warriors rush in through the Scaean Gate.

He remembered the first time he had arrived in Troy, in a donkey-cart with Odysseus and Andromache. He was a child of twelve, and had left his grandfather's goat herd on Kypros to go on a great adventure. He had felt that same shiver of fear as the cart trundled through the great gate and he had first glimpsed the city of gold with its bronze-roofed palaces, verdant courtyards and richly dressed people.

He thought of his father, who had died fighting the Mykene pirate Alektruon, and Zidantas, who had been a father to him for a few brief days, and wondered what they would think of him now, giving aid and comfort to the armies of Agamemnon who were pouring into that city to rape, plunder and kill.

He turned and walked slowly back to the barracks hospital. From beside his pallet bed he fetched his old leather satchel and delved in the bottom of it. He pulled out the two pebbles he had carried with him since he left Kypros to remind him of home. He weighed them in his palm for a moment, then walked to the door and threw them out into the street. Then he started packing the satchel with his potions and herbs.

'Remember the advice of Odysseus, young Xander.'

The boy looked up and found the surgeon White-eye standing beside him. He was watching anxiously as Xander carefully wrapped bunches of dried herbs in scraps of cloth and placed them in the satchel.

'Run to the bay, son,' the older man urged him, 'take ship to Kypros and return to your mother and grandfather. These people are past help now.'

'You are still here, White-eye,' Xander answered, not looking up from his task, 'though the Myrmidons have left.'

'Some of our ships are still loading their final cargo, mostly horses. When the last galley sets sail for Thessaly I shall be on it. There is nothing we can do here, lad. Troy will be a charnel house, full of death and horror. Walk through those gates and you will die, that is as certain as sunset follows day.'

Xander carried on packing his bag. 'I must help my friends,' he whispered.

'You make friends wherever you go, boy. It is your nature. I am your friend. Do this for your friend White-eye.'

Xander paused. He turned to the man and said, 'When I first came here, on the *Xanthos*, there was a great storm and I nearly drowned. Two men saved my life – an Egypteian called Gershom and the Mykene hero Argurios. Both held on to me beyond the limits of their strength, at the risk of their own lives. They felt my life was worth saving, I don't know why. I cannot explain it very well, White-eye, but I would be letting them both down if I turned my back on the Trojans and ran home. I know I came here for a reason, even if it is one I don't understand.'

White-eye shook his head sadly. 'I cannot argue with you, lad. The ways of the gods are unknowable. I do not know why the serpent god sent me here. I thought perhaps it was so that I would meet you and take you back to Thessaly. You have it in you to be a great healer, Xander, but your skills will be wasted if you throw away your life now.'

'I am sorry you did not meet your brother again before he died,' Xander said, anxious to change the subject. He feared his resolution would drain away.

'So am I, lad, but the truth is, Machaon and I never got on. Though we look alike, we have very different ideas on the ways of the serpent god. We would probably have come to blows.'

Xander smiled at the idea of the two gentle healers circling each other with their fists cocked. For a few heartbeats he was tempted to go with the older man, to take ship to Thessaly and a new life far across the Great Green. But instead he said, 'Remember me, White-eye.'

White-eye nodded, and Xander thought he saw tears in his eyes before he hurried away. Taking a deep breath, the young healer picked up his heavy satchel. It was just starting to rain as he walked up the hill towards the city.

When news came of the fall of the barricade, Andromache was installed in Priam's palace, the last refuge. With her were the two boys and her handmaid Anio.

On the day of Hektor's death, when women and children were allowed out of the city, Axa had left tearfully with her three babies, bound for Phrygia and the family of Mestares. She had begged the daughters of Ursos to go with her. But the sisters had refused, saying their father had died defending the city and so would they. Andromache had made no effort to make them change their minds. She told them she respected their decision, though privately her heart bled for their fate.

Then Penthesileia had gone to the barricade with the Thrakian archers. The boy king Periklos had come to Andromache himself and asked that Penthesileia be released from her service. Andromache had been surprised, though she did not doubt the girl's skill with the bow, and she was moved by her courage. When Penthesileia left with Periklos, Andromache was sure she would never see her again.

The great palace was empty. Priam was in his apartments, she was told, but she had not seen him. There were few servants, and even Andromache's bodyguard had been ordered to the barricade. The boys were playing noisily, excited to be in this new home. Andromache felt frustrated by her confinement. She left the boys and walked down to the empty *megaron*.

She had seldom lingered in that great room in recent years. It held only memories of death and horror. On a whim she walked over to Priam's carved, gold-encrusted throne and sat down. She looked round at the high stone walls, decorated with the shields of heroes. The Shield of Argurios was there, the Shield of Hektor now beside it. She gazed at the great stairway where Argurios was fatally wounded. The silence in the *megaron* echoed off the high stone walls, and the distant sound of clashing metal and shouting men seemed as thin and fragile as the twittering of birds on a summer afternoon.

She looked up at the Shield of Hektor, and one hand fell to touch the belt round her hips. It was cunningly crafted of bronze discs threaded with gold wire, marking her as a Woman of the Horse.

For the first time in days she was alone, and in that great empty stone chamber she felt her control slipping, and tears started to roll down her cheeks. They called him the Prince of War, but she had never seen Hektor as a warrior, only a kind, compassionate man shouldering burdens that no man should have to endure. She remembered that moment in the palace gardens when she had watched him playing in the dust with Astyanax, an expression of deep tenderness on his face which had wrenched her heart. She felt an agonizing stab of guilt, so physical she doubled over from the pain, that she had never loved Hektor as he deserved; that he had gone to his death knowing she yearned not for him, but for another man.

Then she wondered, as she did each day, where the *Xanthos* was, and whether Helikaon still lived. Her traitor heart, one moment mourning Hektor, now ached for Helikaon. The blissful time she had spent with him, more than a hundred days, on their voyage west now seemed as though it had happened in another lifetime.

Sitting on the high golden throne she wept for both the men she loved.

Suddenly she started, and swiped the tears from her cheeks. A young messenger, hardly more than a boy, raced in through the high doorway. He stopped, gawping to see her on Priam's throne, and she stood up.

'The enemy have broken through, lady. They are coming!'

Andromache stood by the throne, feeling a tension which was almost unbearable. She knew she should be doing something, but she did not know what. Outside she heard the sound of distant thunder rolling over the sea.

After what seemed a lifetime of waiting, two soldiers staggered into the *megaron* supporting a comrade. All three were injured, but the one in the middle was dying, she could see. Blood was pumping out of a deep gash in his leg and she knew a vital blood vessel had been torn.

'Take him to the queen's apartments,' she ordered, pointing up the stone staircase. 'We will care for the wounded there.' She wondered how many healers, if any, were still in the city.

Soon people started pouring in through the doors: wounded soldiers, old men and a few women. There was fear and exhaustion on every face, and they all looked to her to tell them what to do. She sent the wounded to the queen's apartments, and ordered the women to tend to them as best they could. The men she set to work stripping the weaponry off the walls.

At last Polites arrived, looking ten years older than when she had last seen him two days before. His thin body was lost in someone else's cavalry armour, and he pulled the high helm off with evident relief.

'The enemy have won the city,' he told her briefly. 'Our generals believe they will not attack the palace until tomorrow. So we have time to prepare.'

'I have sent the wounded to the queen's apartments,' she said. 'There is some food and plenty of water in the kitchens. We need an armoury.' She pointed to three women coming in with armfuls of spent arrows to be sorted through.

402

'Why are there still women here?' Polites asked with anguish. 'Why did they not leave when they could?'

'For the same reason you did not, Polites,' Andromache replied. 'They are Trojans who are prepared to stay and die for their city, like you. You could have left long ago, as Kreusa did. Or you could have fled in the days after the taking of King's Joy. These women made the same decision you did. Respect them for it.'

'See they stay within the palace,' Polites told her. 'The city will be a place of horror tonight for anyone outside the palace walls. Agamemnon's troops will be working off the frustrations of an idle summer. No one will be left alive.'

Andromache thought of her two boys. They were safe for the moment, but would not be for long. Feeling panic rising in her breast, she ruthlessly pushed it down. 'Where is Polydorus?' she asked briskly. 'He should be here. He has planned the defence of the palace.'

'I saw him at the barricade,' Polites answered. 'He is a soldier. He could not wait here doing nothing while the city was under attack.'

'Sometimes it is hardest just to wait and do nothing.' She felt anger replacing the rising panic. 'Polydorus was charged with command of the palace. He has deserted his post. And his king.'

'You are being too harsh, Andromache,' Polites chided her. 'Polydorus has always been a dutiful son of Troy. He found it frustrating looking after Father. His city is in danger. He is a soldier,' he repeated.

Andromache looked at him with surprise. 'As a soldier,' she said scornfully, 'his duty was to look after the king, not to fight in the streets. Any common soldier can do that. Polydorus was honoured for his valiant part in the palace siege by being made the king's aide, Priam's bodyguard. He has now abandoned his charge. How can you defend him, Polites?'

Frowning, he answered, 'Sometimes there is a higher duty, sister, a duty to one's conscience.'

Andromache took a deep breath and sighed. 'I am sorry, Polites. I should not be arguing with you. It is getting dark and I must say goodnight to my boys. Then, if Polydorus has not returned, we will get together and make our own plans. Perhaps the generals will be here by then.'

She hurried up the stone staircase, feeling her heart beating noisily. Ruefully she admitted to herself that her fear for her boys had expressed itself as anger. In the queen's apartments she made her way to the boys' bedchamber. Anio was not to be seen. Then she remembered she had told the girl to look for cloth to make bandages. She found little Dex on his own, sitting on the floor playing with his favourite toy, a battered wooden horse with blue eyes he had brought from Dardanos.

She looked round, then squatted down with the boy. 'Where is Astyanax?' she asked him, pushing his fair fringe back off his face.

'He went with the man,' the child said, handing her the toy to play with.

She frowned, and a trickle of dread entered her heart. She heard again the distant sound of thunder. 'What man, Dex?'

'The old man took him,' he said.

XXXI

Death of a king

'I WILL FIND YOUR SON,' THE WARRIOR KALLIADES PROMISED Andromache. 'I will not return to you without him.'

They had searched the palace high and low, but there was no sign of Astyanax. Or of Priam. The king's body servant told Polites he had left the old man wrapped in a blanket in a chair on the balcony. He was feeble and lost, the man said defensively, living in his comforting world of the distant past. Since the death of Hektor he had lived there all the time.

Back in the *megaron*, Kalliades swiftly stripped off his armour, until he wore only his bronze-reinforced leather kilt and sandals. 'Find a dark cloak for me to wear,' he told Andromache. She glanced at him, annoyance overtaking the anxiety in her eyes, but she gestured to one of her handmaids.

'Make that two,' said Banokles, loosening his breastplate.

'General,' Kalliades urged his comrade. 'You will be vital here, to rally the troops.'

'They won't attack tonight,' replied the blond warrior confidently.

'No,' agreed Kalliades, 'Agamemnon will give them free rein tonight to plunder as they will. But by first light we must be ready for them. We have barely enough soldiers left to man the palace walls as it is. Our warriors trust you and will fight to the death for you.'

Polites stepped forward nervously. 'I will go with you, Kalliades,' he suggested. 'If you will have me. I know my father and I can guess where he will be going.'

He had expected the tall warrior to refuse his aid, but instead Kalliades said, 'Thank you, lord. He cannot have got far. We can only hope he has not been captured, and the boy with him.'

The handmaid returned with two dark hooded cloaks. Kalliades swiftly donned his swordbelt, then the cloak. Polites watched him, then awkwardly did the same.

Kalliades told the prince, 'The storm will be our ally tonight. We will stay in the shadows until we find two Mykene warriors. Then we will take their armour.'

Polites nodded without speaking, fearing his voice would quaver. He had never been a warrior. He had left that to his brothers Hektor, Agathon and Dios. He had always been in awe of soldiers who spoke as casually of killing as he did of cutting his roses.

Turning to Andromache, Kalliades said, 'Soon we will need your women with their bows. Place them on the front palace balcony to cover any retreat from the palace walls. If the walls and courtyard are taken, pull them back to the gallery of the *megaron*. Finally, if it comes to that, retreat to the queen's apartments.'

She nodded. 'They will do us proud,' she promised him.

As they left the palace Kalliades paused and Polites looked round at him. Torrential rain was driving at them sideways, lashed by a vicious wind. Lightning lit the sky to the north, and beyond the walls to their left a huge brush fire was burning. They could see no enemy troops, although shouts, screams and the clash of metal echoed from lower in the city.

'Which way?' Kalliades asked, his voice whipped away by the gusting wind.

Polites put his mouth close to the warrior's ear. 'The Great Tower,' he shouted.

Kalliades raised an eyebrow, and Polites nodded vigorously. 'I'm sure of it,' he yelled.

They set off, and made swift progress, running through the streets down towards the tower. Whenever Kalliades paused Polites froze, his heart thumping. Then the tall warrior would lope on, staying in narrow alleys and skirting open spaces. There were fires everywhere, despite the driving rain. They saw many bodies, some townsfolk but mostly soldiers, and several wounded men. Kalliades stopped only once, kneeling to speak briefly to a badly wounded Trojan soldier who lay with his entrails strewn around him. Kalliades took out a curved dagger and sliced the man's throat, then moved on, his expression grim.

In one narrow alleyway Kalliades stopped when they heard the sound of marching feet above the racket of the rain. Coming towards them through the darkness were enemy soldiers carrying torches. They were not running, laughing or shouting; they marched in silence, as if on a mission. Kalliades shoved Polites back into the nearest doorway, but it was shallow and they would be seen once the soldiers came close. Kalliades opened the door and stepped through. Polites followed, his heart in his mouth.

They were in a courtyard. More than a dozen Mykene soldiers were in there too, but their attention was on someone unseen on the ground. The pair heard an agonized cry and a woman's voice begging. Polites looked in anguish at Kalliades. The warrior's face darkened, but he shook his head. Polites saw pain in his eyes.

Unnoticed they slipped back into the alley and ran on. Polites saw Kalliades was limping slightly. He wondered at the severity of a wound that would make a warrior like Kalliades limp.

At last they found two Mykene soldiers in armour. One was leaning against a wall, hands on hips as if getting his breath back. The other was berating him about something, leaning in and shouting in his ear. Kalliades gestured to Polites to wait. Then he walked over to them. They both glanced up, unconcerned. Before they could move Kalliades sliced his dagger across the throat of one. The other leapt back, cursing, drawing his sword. He scowled at Kalliades and lunged at the warrior's face. Kalliades swayed and ducked in one graceful movement, then sank his knife into the man's groin. Only then did he unsheathe his sword. The Mykene fought on bravely for a few heartbeats, then collapsed beside his comrade. Polites could see his lifeblood pumping out on to the rain-soaked street. Glancing round, Kalliades swiftly started to remove the dead man's armour, handing it to Polites to put on. By the time it was done the other man was dead too, and Kalliades donned his armour.

They moved on, and the base of the Great Tower was within sight when they encountered another band of Mykene soldiers. The leader beckoned them to him and Kalliades staggered up, emphasizing his limp.

'Your name, soldier?' the leader demanded.

'Kleitos of the Panthers, sir,' Kalliades replied, slurring a little. 'This is Thoas. He's drunk.'

'We are hunting for children,' the leader told him. 'Agamemnon King wants any brats still in the city found and taken to him.'

'We're looking for women, not their brats.' Kalliades laughed.

The leader grinned. 'Of course you are, soldier, but the two often come together. And Agamemnon is offering a silver ring for any child brought to him. A silver ring will buy you as many women as you need when we get home.'

'I'll bear it in mind,' Kalliades said cheerfully. 'But better to ride one woman now, than ten as a promise. And tonight's will cost me nothing!' He turned to Polites. 'Keep up, you drunken sot,' he shouted, and they hurried on.

The area by the Scaean Gate, a killing ground only the day before, was empty of life. A few blackened corpses lay in the wet, but no one living could be seen. The great gate was closed and the heavy locking bar in place, trapping them inside the city as effectively as it had once kept the enemy out. Polites looked up at the tower and for a moment thought he saw movement at the battlements door. He pointed and Kalliades narrowed his eyes.

'Are you sure?' the warrior asked, doubt written across his face. Polites nodded, and they both made for the stone steps. Kalliades ran up lightly, despite the heavy armour and his injured leg. Polites followed more slowly.

Inside the tower it was pitch black, but it was a relief to get out of the wind. The only sound now was the drumming of rain on the wooden roof far above. They no longer had to yell at one another.

'Stay to the left, as close to the wall as you can,' Polites advised. 'The steps are well worn but they should not be slippery.'

The climb in total darkness was terrifying, even for Polites who had been this way by torchlight many times. He was assailed by doubts now. Could Priam have got this far? Could he have taken Astyanax up these steps in total darkness? He told himself they should have checked at the bottom of the tower first, to see if there was a small body there. By the time they reached the top Polites had convinced himself they were chasing chimeras.

At last he felt the clean night air on his face, and the rain, and he saw Kalliades step out on to the roof ahead of him. The sky had lightened, and he realized it was almost dawn. The thunder and lightning went on unabated. A new fear struck him. He had heard of men in armour being struck down by lightning.

He stepped on to the roof. For a heartbeat he could see nothing, his senses blunted by the wind whipping rain across the high tower. Then the thunder rolled overhead and a brilliant flash of lightning forked down through the sky. By its light they could see Priam standing on the parapet on the far side. His long white hair and grey robe were flying behind him in the wind, as if he were falling already. He held the child out in front of him, motionless in his arms.

His heart hammering in his chest, Polites stepped towards his father, fearing he would plunge out of sight at any moment.

Priam turned and saw him.

'What are you doing, Polites, you fool?' The king's voice, loud and rich with contempt, carried towards them on the wind. 'I did not order you here.'

'I came to find the boy, Father. Andromache was concerned. She did not know where he was.' Polites could see the child's face now. His blue eyes were open and he stared at Polites in terror.

'He is with his father,' the king told him. 'Who else can keep him safe, Polites? Not you, you fool. Nor his whore of a mother. I am showing him to great Zeus. He is the Eagle Child and precious to the All-Father.'

His father? Polites wondered what he meant. Beside him Kalliades asked him with wonder, 'How did he manage to get here without being captured?'

Polites replied, 'The king knows his city better than anyone. And when he is lucid he is cunning as three foxes.'

As they spoke Priam looked down at the child, and confusion appeared on his features. They saw his pale face fall into its usual lines of fear and despair.

Polites stepped forward quickly, afraid the old man would drop the boy in his panic. 'Let me take baby Hektor,' he offered. 'The queen is asking for him.'

Priam looked down at the child. 'Hektor,' he crooned. 'My best boy.'

Polites reached out and Priam handed Astyanax over. Only then did the boy begin to cry quietly. Polites thrust him at Kalliades. 'Take him to his mother,' he ordered.

Kalliades looked at him, then at the king, hesitating.

'Go now, Kalliades. He must be saved. He is the Eagle Child.'

Kalliades frowned. The words clearly meant nothing to him. But he nodded. 'Yes, lord,' he said, and in an instant he was gone, disappearing swiftly down the steps, the boy in his arms.

'Come, Father, you must rest,' Polites said gently, taking his father's hand and drawing him down from the parapet.

'Where am I?' cried the old man fearfully. 'I don't know where I am.'

'We are on the Great Tower of Ilion, Father. We are watching for Troy's enemies. When they come we will destroy them.'

The old man nodded and slumped to the floor. Polites could see he was beyond exhaustion. He sat down as well, and started removing some of his armour. He knew they would both die there.

When at last the enemy came, there were just two of them, Mykene soldiers. One was big, with long unkempt red hair and a full beard. The other was thin and small. They climbed up on the roof and both grinned, exchanging feral glances as they saw the sick old man and his son.

Polites stood wearily, dragging out his sword and trying to remember the lessons he had been taught in the long-distant past. Two-handed, he held the blade up before him, and stepped in front of his father.

The red-headed soldier unsheathed his sword and walked towards him. The other stood and watched, smiling in anticipation.

The soldier lunged at his chest, but Polites skipped nervously back and the sword glanced off the bronze discs of his breastplate. The soldier feinted to the left and, as Polites moved slowly to block the move, he stepped in and sank the blade into Polites' side. It felt like the blow of a hammer. His legs crumpled and he went down on the rain-soaked roof, agony coursing through him.

He looked up as the soldier raised his sword for the killing blow, then was suddenly showered with blood as the man's throat was ripped open by an expertly thrown dagger. Priam stepped forward, growling, 'Die, you dogs!' and picked up the dead man's sword.

The other Mykene ran in, fury on his face. 'By Hades, you'll pay for that, you old bastard!' he shouted, and he swung his sword at the king in a ferocious arc. Priam got his sword up and the blades clashed together, sparks flying in the half-light.

The king stumbled back, then his old legs failed him and he went down on one knee.

As the soldier loomed over him, Polites snatched the dagger from the dead man's throat and lunged at the attacker's inner thigh. He missed his target, merely cutting the skin, but as the soldier swung round at him Priam hefted the sword and plunged it into the man's back. The Mykene fell to his knees, his eyes staring, then he toppled forward, dead.

Drowning in a sea of pain, Polites dragged himself over to the king. 'You killed them, Father,' he panted weakly. 'But there will be more.'

Priam bared his teeth in a confident grin. 'My son will save us,' he promised. 'Hektor will arrive in time. Hektor never lets me down.'

Polites nodded, clutching his side and watching the blood

pumping through his fingers. 'He is a good son,' he agreed sadly. Then he closed his eyes and slept.

It was full daylight when he opened his eyes again. More than a dozen Mykene warriors were walking towards them across the roof. Polites sighed and tried to move, but his limbs would not work and he lay there helpless. He was terribly tired, but he felt no fear. He turned his head and saw his father had somehow climbed back on to the parapet. The words of Kassandra came to him. Priam will outlive all his sons, he thought, and he smiled.

'Goodbye, Father,' he whispered as the old man threw himself from the tower. The last thing he saw was a sword swinging at his neck.

The storm had swept in from Thraki, from the cold heights of the Rhodope mountains. Its burden of icy rain did little to slow the north wind, a wind strong enough to flay the roofs from peasants' cottages and fishermen's huts and tear stout branches from trees. Centuries-old oaks, their deep roots loosened in the bone-dry summer, toppled under its might on the slopes of Mount Ida, and wild animals ran for shelter from its howling fury. The gold roof of Priam's palace clattered in the gale as the wind tried to pry its precious covering free. All across the city terracotta roof tiles were flung about the streets like leaves and the walls of ruined palaces collapsed.

On the steep hillside outside Troy, Khalkeus the bronzesmith looked into the teeth of the gale and rejoiced.

'Boreas, the north wind. The Devourer, they call him,' he muttered happily to himself. 'Let the Devourer eat up the star stones and spit them out for me!'

He gazed up proudly at the towering furnace, the biggest he had yet built after many failed attempts. The stone tower was square at the base, just two paces to a side, yet it was as high as the walls of the city. His first attempt had toppled over, confounding his calculations on the necessary thickness of the walls. The second and third had been torn down by enemy soldiers while he hid close by in the woods, seething with fury at their casual destruction of his labour. But he had braved the Mykene camp and spoken to Agamemnon. Since then the soldiers had left him alone. His last two attempts had been successful, in their way. They had built up the necessary heat, but both had burned down, taking the remaining structures on the hillside with them. Khalkeus had simply started again.

'Patience, patience,' he told himself. 'Nothing useful was ever wrought without patience.'

He regretted he had no one to discuss the project with. The Golden One would have been interested, would have understood the construction of the furnace, and praised Khalkeus for the valuable work he was doing. With the metal of Ares Khalkeus would make the perfect sword, one which would not bend or break, and would never dull.

He had been pleasantly surprised by his conversation with Agamemnon. Khalkeus loathed the Mykene as a race. They were plunderers, pirates and murderers. He had always imagined their king would be a brute without intelligence or imagination. But he had asked thoughtful questions about Khalkeus' work and promised to fund his experiments once the war was over. Khalkeus did not entirely trust him, but the bronzesmith could certainly expect no more support from the Trojans.

A tiny flicker of doubt entered his mind. Another weapon, Khalkeus, he asked himself? After seeing so many men die because of your inventions, do you really want to create another weapon to put in the hands of violent men? He shook his head, shaking free the annoying thought.

Khalkeus had forecast the storm as early as the previous day, and to heat up the furnace he had worked all night. Like a madman, he chortled to himself, the madman from Miletos!

The furnace had been filled with dry olive branches and white limestone chips for purity. Then he had piled in the batches of grey sponges which were all he had succeeded in making from smelting the red rocks. At the bottom of the furnace was a square door, and inside the door was a shallow pottery bowl to receive the molten metal. At the base of the bowl a tube ran out of the furnace to the sword-shaped casting mould. The door controlled the updraught. It was now fully open, and the ferocious wind gusting round the plateau had built up the heat far beyond what he had achieved before.

Nervously, Khalkeus stepped back a few more paces from the intense heat. I cannot stop it now, he told himself. It is in the hands of the gods. Rolling thunder overhead could scarcely be heard for the deafening roar of the furnace. The howl was like the voice of Cerberus in the gathering darkness.

Then, just as he had feared and dreaded, the huge furnace trembled and suddenly shattered. A roaring blast of heat ripped across the hillside, knocking Khalkeus over. As the fire leapt out from its confines, rocks and debris rained down, narrowly missing him. Half dazed, he cried out in frustration, and beat feverishly at his singed hair and beard.

Rolling over, he crawled on trembling limbs to the edge of the hill and looked over, shielding his eyes from the blaze. Only paces from where he lay, in the midst of the debris, he saw with amazement that the furnace had fulfilled its task before its destruction. The furious heat had turned the Ares metal to liquid and it had poured, as intended, into the sword mould even as the chimney collapsed.

Hope surged in the old man's breast. There was a sword, but was it the perfect sword he had dreamed of?

As Khalkeus watched, unbelieving, the last section of chimney toppled slowly towards the mould. The smith cried out in an agony of fear as it hit the edge of it, flipping it over, throwing the white-hot sword into the rain. The blade screamed as if alive as it instantly vaporized the water into steam.

Khalkeus scrambled down towards it, struggling to put on the heavy leather gauntlets which hung round his neck. As he touched the glowing sword the glove smouldered and he snatched his hand away. He sat gazing greedily at the weapon, only half aware that the fire had set light to the remaining trees and shrubby under-growth unscathed by previous blazes.

Slowly, very slowly, the light in the sword died as it cooled under the relentless rain. Khalkeus reached forward and cautiously picked it up.

It was just before sunrise and the storm was past when Kalliades returned to the palace with Astyanax. Departing the Great Tower it had dawned on him how Priam had got there – he had walked along the walls. This must be the first time in generations, he thought, when the walls are not manned. Striding swiftly along them, he had met only a couple of soldiers. Both were drunk, and on this night no one questioned a man in Mykene armour carrying a child.

When he came within bowshot of the palace Kalliades started shouting, 'Open the gates! It is Kalliades!' He did not want any over-enthusiastic archer shooting him down. He heard his name yelled on the wall, the high bronze-reinforced gates slowly opened and he slid through the gap. Andromache and Banokles were waiting for him on the other side. He handed the child to the princess, who clutched him close to her. 'Mama,' the little boy said sleepily.

Tears of relief and joy ran down Andromache's face. Gently she kissed her son's cheek. 'I am in your debt, Kalliades. Be certain I shall not forget,' she said gravely. 'But what of Priam and Polites?'

'I left them together.' He was unwilling to give her false hope. 'I do not expect them to live. Even now this child might be king of Troy.'

She nodded sadly, then turned and walked back to the palace, holding her son tightly.

Banokles asked, 'Are you going to keep that on?' pointing at the distinctive Mykene armour. 'You don't want one of our lads killing you by mistake. That would be annoying.'

Kalliades grinned and sent a soldier to fetch his own armour. Then wearily he followed Banokles up the steps to the top of the ramparts. The palace walls were twice the height of a man. The attackers would need ladders, but they had had plenty of time to make them.

'Well, *strategos*,' he commented to Banokles, looking round at the waiting soldiers. 'What is our plan?'

'I spoke to the men,' Banokles replied, 'and told them to kill every bastard who comes at them, and keep on killing until they are all dead.'

'Good plan,' said Kalliades. 'I like it. It has the advantage of simplicity.' He smiled and felt all his tension ease away. Banokles was right. They had reached the end now and there were no more decisions to make. They would fight, and they would live or die.

Banokles grinned back at him and shrugged. 'Everyone likes a plan they can understand.'

'How many are we?'

'Less than three hundred now, mostly with wounds. Fifty or so Eagles still. And some Trojan Horse. We could do with Hektor here now.' He lowered his voice to a loud whisper, 'And there's that woman.' He nodded his head, indicating along the wall, where Penthesileia stood, bow in hand, looking out at the city. She was wearing a high helm now, as well as the breastplate. Gazing at her profile, Kalliades thought she looked like the goddess Athene garbed for war.

'Hillas reckons she's a wonder,' Banokles confided. 'Can shoot the balls off a flea at fifty paces.'

'*Hillas* does? This is the same Hillas who thinks women warriors should be buried alive for their insolence?'

'I know. I wouldn't have believed it either. Perhaps he's in love,' Banokles mused. 'Though she's plain as a rock and thin as a blade. I don't like bony women. I mean, what's the point?'

Only half listening, Kalliades sat down with his back to the wall and yawned. He was tired beyond reason, his wounded leg ached, and he was heavy of heart. He had never wished to be a Trojan. The warriors of the Lion's Hall had always despised the armies of the city of gold. True warriors were lions among the sheep, they believed, taking the battle to the enemy in the name of the war god Ares. The soldiers of Troy hid behind their high walls, resting on the riches of Priam.

Banokles had been right to ask what they were fighting for. There was no treasure, no king, and the high walls had been rendered meaningless.

416

Kalliades thought back to the day when, as a child, he had hidden in the flax field as brutal men raped and killed his sister. On that day he had vowed to avenge her by seeking out such men and killing them. He had joined the forces of Mykene still firm in his intention. Yet somehow over the years his vow had been forgotten, and he found he was fighting side by side with such brutes. Kalliades had never raped a woman or killed a child, but many of his comrades had, men he was proud to call friends. Rescuing Piria from the pirates had changed his life in many ways. It had made him remember his pledge in the flax field. And he knew he could never turn away from it again.

'In answer to your question . . .' he said to Banokles.

'What question?'

'You asked me what we are fighting for. That little boy. Astyanax is king of Troy now. We're fighting for him. But not because he is the king. We fight today for all the women and old men relying on us in the palace. People who cannot fight for themselves. We will use our swords to protect the weak, not to kill them and take what they own. That is for lesser men.'

Banokles shrugged. 'If you say so,' he answered. Then he squinted into the growing light. 'Here they come!' he said.

Kalliades rolled to his feet and risked a glance over the crenellated wall. His heart sank. They were still facing a horde. It seemed the hundreds they had killed at the Scaean Gate had counted for nothing. At least most of the defenders had had a night's rest, while the attackers had been carousing and killing.

He heard the clatter of ladders hitting the other side of the wall.

Suddenly Banokles stood up and roared at the enemy, 'I am Banokles! Come at me and die, you scum!' A volley of arrows soared over the wall. One shaft grazed his ruined ear and he ducked down quickly, grinning.

Looking at each other, they both waited a few heartbeats, then as one they leapt up to face the enemy. A huge Mykene warrior had reached the top of the ladder and the Sword of Argurios ripped into his face. Kalliades sent a reverse cut into the bearded face of another attacker, then glanced along the outside of the wall. Only twenty or so ladders to this section. All we have to do, he thought, is kill twenty warriors, then keep on doing it until the attack fails.

To his right Banokles swept his sword through the throat of an attacker, then brained another. A warrior with a braided beard came over the wall, an axe in one hand. Banokles let him come then, as he cleared the ramparts, ducked and plunged a sword into his belly. As he fell Banokles stabbed him in the back. He grabbed the man's axe and swung it at the next attacker, smashing through his shoulder and breastplate.

Arrows soared over the wall. Most were too high, and flew harmlessly into the courtyard, but two defenders went down, and one shaft stuck high in Banokles' breastplate.

To his left Kalliades saw three Mykene warriors had forced their way to the ramparts, giving the enemy a foothold and allowing more to follow. Kalliades charged the group, cutting one down instantly, and shoulder-charging the second, who crashed down, his head bouncing against the rampart wall. The third man lunged with his sword at Kalliades' belly. A Royal Eagle blocked the blade and slashed his sword through the attacker's neck. The second man tried to rise and Kalliades plunged his blade down through the man's collar bone and into his chest. He glanced at the Eagle who had helped him, and saw it was Polydorus.

'For the king!' shouted the young aide, gutting another attacker and hacking at the neck of another.

And the battle raged on.

XXXII

The Trojan women

ANDROMACHE LAID HER BUNDLE OF ARROWS ON THE BALCONY WALL.
She dragged her unruly hair back with a leather strip, then dried
her damp palms on her tunic. She looked along the palace balcony
at the other women. Some were watching her, nervously following
her example; others stared transfixed at the ferocious battle taking
place across the palace courtyard. It could not last much longer,
they all knew. Their gallant warriors defending the ramparts had
beaten back wave after wave of enemy attacks. Now, in the sultry
afternoon, Andromache knew by the chill in her bones that it was
nearly the end.

She watched stretcher-bearers, most of them old men, struggle
back to the palace with their burdens. Why, she wondered? Our
wounded soldiers are just being saved for a later death, when the
enemy breaks into the palace. We cannot hold the wall. It is not
high enough and we do not have enough men. We cannot hold the
palace. She closed her eyes. Despair threatened to overwhelm her.

'Lady, can you help me?' Her young handmaid Anio was
struggling with the leather breastplate she had been given. Though
intended for a small man, it was too wide, the straps falling off her
thin shoulders.

Patiently Andromache unthreaded the straps then tied them

closer together. 'There,' she said, 'that's better. You look like a tortoise who's been given too big a shell.'

Anio smiled and another girl laughed, and Andromache felt her tension ease. There were ten Women of the Horse left, women and girls as young as fifteen who had not fled the city. Some had stayed because they had no family and nowhere to go, others because their families had remained, convinced the great walls would never fall. As Kalliades had ordered, she had brought them to the high balcony overlooking the courtyard. Only Penthesileia had gone to the ramparts to fight with the Thrakian bowmen.

Andromache frowned, angry at herself for giving in to despair, however fleetingly. You are the daughter of a king, she told herself. You do not whine or complain about your lot. Little Anio can find it in herself to smile, despite the odds. You should feel privileged to stand beside her.

She watched the men on the wall and pride surged in her breast. They are Trojan warriors, she thought. *We* are Trojan warriors. We will fight here, and we may die, but our tale will be told and the name of Troy will not be forgotten.

A familiar voice whispered in her ear. 'Yes, Andromache, yes! Be strong! Look to the north and help *will* come. We will meet again before the end, sister.'

Kassandra! The girl's voice was so clear, so *present*, that Andromache looked round. Inside her head she called her sister's name, but there was no reply. Look to the north, Kassandra had said. Odysseus had told her the same thing.

At that moment, with awful suddenness, the enemy broke through on the wall. Eight Mykene warriors fought their way clear, racing down the rampart steps and across the paved courtyard towards the palace.

'Be ready!' she yelled to her archers, snatching up her bow and notching an arrow to the string. The other women did the same. 'Wait!' She watched coolly as the warriors approached.

Then she shouted, 'Now!' and a volley of arrows tore into the running men. The women had time to loose two or three shafts each, and five of the attackers were hit. Two fell, three stumbled on. When the men reached the closed *megaron* doors there was nowhere to go, and they tried to scale the sheer stone walls. Only one managed to reach the balcony. As his hand gripped the top of the wall Andromache pulled out her bronze dagger. She waited until his face appeared then plunged the blade into the man's eye. He fell without a sound.

She looked again to the struggle on the ramparts. The line of defenders had fractured in several places and more Mykene were breaking through. The Trojans started to fall back in an organized retreat, pace by pace, trying to hold the line while being relentlessly forced towards the palace.

'Wait!' she ordered the women, seeing some of them raise their bows again. 'Lower your bows. Now! Remember our orders.'

Beneath them they heard the groan and rumble of the *megaron* doors opening.

With a loud clatter of hooves on stone, the last horsemen in the city rode out from the palace. In the centre of the battle line defenders broke swiftly to left and right. The riders galloped straight for the exposed centre. With lance and spear they slammed into the enemy. Every horse left in the city was there. Andromache saw the black stallion Hero which had carried Hektor on his final ride. He was rearing, kicking out with flailing hooves at the enemy soldiers. Then all she could see was a mêlée of warriors and horses, all she could hear the shouts of men and the neighing of their mounts, the clash of metal and the rending of flesh.

It was a gallant last strike, but it was not enough. The gates in the palace wall had been opened and hundreds more enemy warriors were joining the rear of the horde. The Trojans were still retreating, battling bravely but losing ground all the time.

'Be ready,' Andromache ordered the Women of the Horse. 'Don't shoot wildly. Take time to aim. We cannot risk shooting our own men. Make each arrow count. Always aim high. If you miss one man's face you might hit the man behind him.' This was the instruction she had drummed into her archers over and over in recent days, until she found herself muttering it in her sleep.

Enemy warriors had fought their way within bowshot now, but

still she waited. Then she saw a bearded bloodstained soldier in a Mykene helm look up at her and grin. 'Now!' she shouted. Sighting high on his face, she loosed her arrow. The shaft plunged into the man's cheek. She had a new arrow to the string in a heartbeat. She shot it at a soldier with his sword raised. It bit deep into his bicep and she saw the sword fall from his hand.

For a moment she paused to glance at the other women shooting at the oncoming horde. Their faces were determined, the movements confident. Arrow after arrow was finding its target. Her heart soared.

'We are Trojan women,' she yelled at the enemy. 'Come against us and we will kill you!'

She could no longer see the Trojan defenders beneath her, hidden by the jutting balcony. She and her archers kept shooting into the mass of enemy faces. She did not hear the *megaron* doors close.

No time seemed to pass as she carried on shooting, yet she realized it was growing dark. Her shoulder hurt.

'Andromache, fall back! Andromache!' She felt a hand on her arm and found herself being dragged from the balcony. Struggling, she looked up.

'Kalliades! We must fight on!' she cried.

'We *are* fighting on, Andromache. But you must rest. You are wounded.'

'Are the doors closed?'

'We have retreated to the *megaron* and the doors are closed. The enemy are bringing ladders to the balcony. The fighting there will be hand to hand. It is the only place they can hope to break in until they can force the *megaron* doors. Your women have been magnificent, and they still have a part to play. We need you and your bows on the gallery. But you must rest first,' he urged. 'There is time. Then you will be ready to fight on.'

She nodded, and looked at the wound on her shoulder. Blood was flowing freely. She guessed an arrow had made the deep groove, though she could not remember it. 'I will have my wound dressed once the other women have been attended to.'

'That has already happened. You were the last to leave the balcony.'

'Are any of them hurt?'

'Yes, but minor wounds only.'

'Then I must see my son.'

He nodded. 'Very well. Go, see your son. I will find someone to tend your wound.'

Andromache walked through the palace, pushing her way through the *megaron* packed with men and horses, hardly seeing the frenzied activity around her, her mind in a whirl. She could still feel the smooth wood of the bow in her palm, the straightness of each arrow in her fingers, the muscles in her arm tensing as she drew back, the smooth release. Over and over again.

The queen's apartments were dusty and dark. Stillness lay on the rooms as heavily as the dust. Wounded men were being cared for in the queen's gathering room, so she skirted past it and made her way to the rear chamber where the boys slept. Astyanax and Dex were fast asleep, tucked up in the same bed.

Andromache watched them breathing, and stroked each small head, one red, one fair. Her mind slowly calmed.

Behind her a voice said hesitantly, 'Andromache?'

She started and turned. 'Xander!' she said in surprise, embracing the freckle-faced healer. Kalliades, who had brought him, raised an eyebrow.

'This lad says he is a healer. Clearly you know him.'

'He is a good friend of mine, and of Odysseus. We voyaged together. I feared you dead, Xander. You have been gone so long.'

As he examined her shoulder and applied ointment and a dressing, she told him of her travels, and of Gershom's sudden departure from the *Xanthos*. Xander explained how he had ended up in the enemy camp, and talked about the time he'd spent with Odysseus and Achilles.

'You should have taken the Ugly One's advice,' she told him, 'and fled the city.'

'You did not,' he countered quietly.

She remembered her last talk with Polites and shook her head, smiling. 'You are right, Xander. It is not my place to judge you.'

Xander examined the deep gash on Kalliades' thigh. 'It is very angry,' he said, frowning, 'and I think corruption is setting in.' From his satchel he brought out some dry brown vegetation. 'This is tree moss,' he explained to them. 'It is old but it still has virtue to purify.' He bound it to the wound with a bandage. 'The wound should have been stitched long since,' he told the warrior. 'I fear it will always pain you.'

Kalliades told him, 'If I live through this day, I will rejoice in the pain.'

After healer and warrior had left, Andromache sat with the sleeping boys. She scanned Astyanax' face, seeking something of his father in the angle of an eyebrow, the curve of an ear. She wondered again where Helikaon and the *Xanthos* were. Then the familiar demon, guilt, rose in her heart and she thought of Hektor. She realized how much she missed him, and found herself wishing he was here beside her. She always felt safe with Hektor. With Helikaon there was always danger.

She wandered to the north window, where light was fading on the plain of the Simoeis. She recalled her trip by donkey-cart into the city with the cargo of tin. That night she had looked up at these high windows and wondered if anyone was up there staring down. Now she looked down into darkness and guessed no one was there. With the city open to him, Agamemnon would not waste men guarding the sheer north walls.

The north walls. Look to the north. Suddenly Andromache realized what the words meant. She leaned over the window ledge and looked far down to the bottom of the cliffs. If she could find rope, could she get two children down the vertical drop? She moved her wounded shoulder. Back and forth did not hurt much, but when she lifted the arm above her head the pain was agonizing. She could never do it.

Yet Odysseus and Kassandra always gave good advice, each in their own way. And they were right. It was the only path left to her now if she hoped to save her son. She leaned over the window ledge again. Darkness was gathering, but as she looked down she could just make out a figure climbing towards her.

Her heart seemed suddenly to slow, and its thudding echoed in her ears. She could not see the climber's face, nor even his age or build, but she knew without a doubt that it was Helikaon.

Earlier that day, while the sun still sat high in the sky, Helikaon stood impatiently on the prow of the *Xanthos* as the great bireme made her last journey up the Simoeis.

His emotions had been in disarray since, off Lesbos two days before, they had encountered a Kypriot vessel loaded with refugees from Troy, and had heard of Hektor's death and the fall of the city. Hektor dead! He had found it impossible to believe. Hektor had been feared dead before. But he heard the refugees' tales, of the duel with Achilles, the poison and betrayal, and of the great funeral pyre, and with a pain in his heart he knew it to be true.

There was no news of Andromache, but he was sure she still lived; he knew every bone in his body would ache if she was no longer in his world.

Now, as the galley slipped up the narrowing river, he looked south towards Troy. The oarsmen too kept glancing at the city, their faces grim, watching the flames leaping from the walls, darkening the pale sky to the colour of bronze.

Suddenly Helikaon could wait no longer. He ordered the starboard rowers to ship their oars, and the oarsmen to port guided the galley into the side. Even as she bumped gently into the reed-covered bank, Helikaon turned and addressed his crew.

'You are all Dardanians here,' he told them, his deep voice sombre. 'My fight is not yours. I am going to the city and I will go alone. If any of you wish to return to Dardanos, leave here and now and may the gods walk with you. For the rest of you the *Xanthos* sails at dawn. If I do not return, Oniacus will be your captain. He will first take the ship to Thera, then follow the Trojan fleet to the Seven Hills.' He glanced at his right-hand man, who nodded. They had discussed this at length, and he knew Oniacus would follow his orders loyally.

But there were cries from the men, 'We will go with you, Golden One!'

Helikaon shook his head. 'I will go alone,' he repeated. 'I do not

425

know if anyone can get into the city now. And if we could, even the eighty of you, brave men and true, would make little difference against the hordes of the enemy. Go to the Seven Hills. Many of you already have families there. It is your home now.'

There were more shouts and entreaties from the crew. But Helikaon ignored them, strapping to his back the scabbard with its twin leaf-bladed swords, then hefting a thick coil of rope on to his shoulder.

The cries died down, then a single voice asked, 'Do you plan to die in Troy, lord?'

He stared coldly at the questioner. 'I plan to live,' he told him.

Then he vaulted smoothly over the side on to the river bank. Without a glance back at the *Xanthos*, he set off at a steady lope towards the golden city.

As he ran his thoughts were of Andromache and the boys. If she still lived then Dex and Astyanax must be alive. She would fight to the death for them, he was certain. Two nights and two days had passed since the enemy entered the city. Could anyone still be alive? How long could they hold Priam's palace? In the previous siege the defenders had numbered a mere handful, yet they had held back the invaders all night. This time the number of the enemy could be a hundred times greater. He shook his head, trying to dislodge the endless speculation. First he had to find his way in.

It was getting dark when he reached the north walls of the city. He made his way to the point directly beneath the queen's apartments. Looking up he could see lights in the high windows. They seemed so close. Yet to get there he had to scale a dry, crumbling vertical cliff face. That was the easy part. Above that was the sheer limestone wall of Troy itself.

When he and Hektor were young men they had once competed to make this climb. Scaling the lower cliff, with its numerous hand- and footholds, and rocky outcrops, they had ascended quickly, shoulder to shoulder. Then they had reached the point where the cliff ended and the wall began. There was a wide ledge there, and they paused. They had both looked up at the golden stones from which the wall was fashioned. They were massive, each more than the height of a man, and so cunningly crafted there was not the narrowest fingerhold between them. The pair had turned to one another and laughed. They agreed it was impossible and had climbed down, their friendly contest over.

Now, a man ten years older, he was planning to try something a youngster at the height of his strength could not do. Only desperation would make him attempt it, but he could see no other choice.

He started to climb. As he remembered, the hand- and footholds were plentiful, although dry and crumbly after the hot summer. The initial ascent was not difficult, and within a short space of time he was on the ledge which marked the top of the cliff and the bottom of the wall. He paused for breath, looking up again. He had come this far. He could not stop now. But in the gathering dark he could see not one single handhold.

He dropped the coil of rope on the ledge beside him. In desperation he looked up again. Miraculously, leaning over the window ledge high above him, her chestnut hair a halo of flame in the light from the window, was Andromache.

Goddess, he whispered to himself. I am truly blessed.

'Andromache!' he called. 'Catch the rope!'

She nodded silently. He picked up the rope again, carefully trapping the loose end under one foot. He steadied himself, then with a mighty effort threw the coil upwards. But his caution made it fall short. Andromache grasped vainly at thin air, and the rope fell back, missing Helikaon and looping far down the cliff. Patiently he wound it up again. Now he had the measure of the throw, and at his second attempt he hurled the coil harder and it landed straight in Andromache's waiting hands.

She disappeared from sight, then was swiftly back, calling down to him, 'It is secure!'

He cautiously leaned his weight on the rope, and it held firm. Within heartbeats he had shinned up it and was over the window ledge.

Andromache fell into his arms. Only then did he allow himself to fully believe she was still alive. He pressed his face into her hair. It smelled of smoke and flowers. 'I love you,' he said simply.

'I can't believe you are here,' she answered him, gazing into his eyes. 'I feared I would never see you again.'

There were tears in her eyes and he pulled her close, feeling her heart beating. For a long moment time slowed. He forgot about the war and surrendered himself to their embrace. The fears that had been plaguing him – that he would find her dead, their sons murdered – evaporated as he held her close and their hearts beat as one.

'Dex?' he whispered. She drew away from him and took his hand. She led him to the little bed in the next room where the two boys lay. He bent down to look into his son's face, and touched his fair hair.

When he turned back to Andromache her face had become grave. They walked back out of the room, then she put her arms round him, and drew a deep breath. She said, 'My love, there is something I must tell you.'

At that moment the door of the chamber opened and two warriors burst in. Kalliades and Banokles stopped in shock. Helikaon did not know which surprised them more, his presence in the room, or the fact that he held Andromache in his arms.

Kalliades recovered first. 'Helikaon! You come unlooked for!' He glanced towards the window, seeing the knotted rope.

Helikaon said quickly, 'Do not expect an army to come swarming up the walls. I come to you alone. But you have my sword, if it will make a difference.'

'You will always make a difference, lord,' said Kalliades. 'Though the situation is grave.'

'Tell me.'

'Agamemnon has thousands waged against us. We number less than a hundred. They have seized the palace wall. It is taking them a while to break through the *megaron* doors, but they cannot last much longer.'

Helikaon remembered that Priam had had the doors renewed after the previous siege. They were fashioned from three layers of oak, cross-grained, reinforced with metal bars which locked into holes in the floor and ceiling. It was unlikely they could be forced, only hacked slowly to pieces.

'The king?' he asked.

'Priam and all his sons are dead. Astyanax is king.'

Andromache cast Helikaon an agonized glance, and looked towards the window. He nodded. 'I have a duty here,' he told her. 'Then we will save the children.'

The warriors walked through the palace to the *megaron*, where Helikaon was proud to see order and calm, though the air was thick with the scent of death. There were the hundred heavily armoured soldiers, most of them wounded and bloodstained, all so exhausted they could barely stand. A few stood ready facing the doors, where even now the wood was starting to splinter under the heavy heads of axes. Most sat or lay, conserving their energy, too tired to speak. But one of them, in the armour of an Eagle, scrambled up as they passed.

'Helikaon!' he cried.

Helikaon turned and smiled. 'Polydorus, it is pleasant to see you alive.'

'Have you brought an army, my friend?'

'No. I bring only my sword.'

'Then you bring us hope. There is little enough here now.'

Helikaon nodded. Looking down he saw horse droppings on the floor. He frowned. 'Horses?' he asked.

Banokles grinned. 'There are a few left. I've had them locked away somewhere safe.'

'Who commands here?' asked Helikaon. 'Lucan?'

Banokles shook his head. 'Lucan fell at the Scaean Gate. Tough old bastard. Thought he'd live for ever. You're the only king on this side of those doors, lord.'

But Helikaon shook his head. 'You have fought for this city all summer, general. You know every man here and what he is capable of. You command here. I am just a foot soldier, Banokles. My sword and my life are yours.'

Banokles sighed and shot a glance at Kalliades, who threw his head back and laughed. The laughter rang round the *megaron* and men turned their heads at the unaccustomed sound. 'Tell us your plan then, General,' Kalliades asked his friend, grinning.

'There are thousands of the bastards, most of them Mykene veterans,' Banokles replied, 'not one soft-bellied puker among them. We're just a hundred. When the thunder rolls they'll have the better of us. But by the bloody spear of Ares we'll make them pay for every step they take!'

The hundred defenders stood in line three-deep facing the doors. In the front two lines were the last of the Eagles. Front and centre was Helikaon, wearing the armour of a Royal Eagle, with Banokles and Kalliades. Behind them stood Polydorus. Out in front, on either side of the doors, were two Thrakian archers.

Andromache was on the gallery watching them, bow in hand. She remembered the last time the four men were together in this *megaron*, when Banokles and Kalliades fought for the Mykene, and Helikaon and Polydorus defended the stairs. And she wondered at the irony of life and the tyrannical whims of the gods that had brought them together again.

She could see Helikaon's profile, and saw him turn his head briefly to glimpse her. She wondered if this would be her last sight of him alive. She knew he had come here with the intention of rescuing her. Yet once here he could not leave friends and comrades to fight on without him. In the heat of the battle he would forget about her and her boys. For a moment only she felt sorry for herself. To be in his arms once again, then to have him snatched away by duty and loyalty seemed so cruel. Then she hardened her heart. Helikaon must follow his duty, and he would live or die. *Her* duty today was to fight until the battle was lost, then escape with her sons, somehow, down the cliff. She thought again of Kassandra's words, 'We will meet again, sister, before the end,' and took courage from their message.

The axe heads tearing relentlessly at the heavy oak doors had finally cut a hole. She could see movement on the other side. Then she saw Banokles step forward from the front line, hefting a lance, and with astonishing accuracy and strength throw it through the gap. There was an explosion of curses on the other side, and the Trojans all cheered. The cry was taken up all round the *megaron*, 'Banokles! Banokles! BANOKLES!'

Then the hole in the door was hacked wider, and warriors started forcing their way through. The two archers loosed arrow after arrow into them. Six Mykene fell before their comrades managed to get as far as the Trojan line. At first they only climbed in one at a time and the men on the front line dispatched them with ease. Then they started pouring in, and succeeded in releasing the metal bars. The ruined doors groaned open.

Andromache watched with pride and fear as the small band of Trojan fighters held back the forces of Agamemnon. Despite the power of the Mykene attack, the slaughter was terrible in their ranks. Helikaon, Kalliades and Banokles fought with cool efficiency, each armed with shield and sword. Every attacker fell swiftly to their blades, and for a moment Andromache gave in to hope. Then she looked through the doors and saw the ranks of the enemy, all armed to the teeth, ready to replace their fallen comrades, and all hope drained away.

She looked around. The narrow Trojan line across the *megaron* was protecting the stone staircase and the gallery. If it were pushed back even a few paces the enemy could reach the side of the gallery, throw ladders up, and get behind the defenders. The Mykene would not make the mistake they made last time, and be drawn by arrogance to attack the stairs while neglecting the gallery. Agamemnon, a cool thinker, would have made sure of that.

The women archers had been ordered to protect the gallery. With them were some civilians, traders and farmers, and a number of old soldiers well past their fighting years, who were charged with pushing away the ladders, and with guarding the women.

The brute strength of the Mykene advance soon started to take its toll on the exhausted defenders, and the line was being forced back at each end. Andromache saw Trojans falling, to be instantly replaced by their comrades behind. Yet slowly the two wings of the line were being bent back. Only the centre held.

'Be ready!' she shouted, and the women raised their bows.

Ladders were passed from hand to hand over the heads of the Mykene, then she heard one bang against the gallery wall. Half a dozen arrows slammed into the first warrior to climb it.

Below them one wing of the defending line had been pushed back further. 'Hold the line!' someone shouted. A group of old soldiers hurried down the stone stairs bellowing their battle cries to lend their support to the collapsing wing.

More and more ladders were raised and soon Mykene warriors were climbing on to the gallery. Andromache saw the civilians attacking them with swords and clubs, fighting without skill but with desperation. Still the women stood their ground, raining their shafts into the enemy.

The defenders below had been forced back to the stone staircase, and Andromache saw a few Trojan soldiers fleeing up the stairs. Then she realized they were racing to defend the gallery.

Kalliades left Helikaon and Banokles fighting side by side on the stairway and sprinted up the steps towards her. As he passed he snarled, 'Retreat now, Andromache!' Armed with two swords now, he slammed into the advancing Mykene.

Andromache shouted to the women to retreat to the queen's apartments. One was already dead, but several wounded archers limped past, including little Anio, blood streaming down one arm. The others fought on, loosing arrow after arrow into the Mykene. Two were cut down. Penthesileia stood her ground alone, then fell with a dagger in her side.

Andromache grabbed her bundle of arrows and turned to flee – and saw two Mykene warriors stalking towards her, cutting off her path of retreat. The first lunged at her with his sword. Instinctively she blocked the blow with her bundle of arrows, then grabbed an arrow in her fist and stepped in. With a cry she plunged it into the eye of the attacker. He fell, clutching the shaft.

The second warrior raised his sword for a killing blow. Then he fell to his knees, hit on the head from behind by a man wielding a club. The Mykene, dazed, twisted round and rammed his sword into the belly of his attacker. Andromache picked up the first Mykene's sword and hacked at the second man's neck until he was still. She stepped over the bodies to reach her rescuer, who was slumped against the wall, thick blood staining the front of his clothing. She knelt down.

'Remember me, lady?' the man whispered, blood trickling from his mouth.

For a heartbeat Andromache did not. Then she saw three fingers had been cut away from his right hand, and the memory came back to her of a moment in a street when a drunken man, a veteran of the Trojan Horse, had called her goddess.

'You are Pardones. I thank you for my life, Pardones.'

The dying man said something, but his voice was so weak she could not hear. She bent down to him. 'Kept it,' he murmured. Then the rasp of his breath abruptly stopped.

She sat back, tears in her eyes, and saw on the floor beside his dead hand the golden brooch she had given him then for his courtesy and loyalty.

Wiping her face on the back of her hand she got up, cast a last glance at the *megaron* where Helikaon fought on, then followed Kalliades' orders and ran back down the stone corridor to the queen's apartments.

The gathering room was a scene of carnage. Dozens of gravely wounded soldiers lay on the floor, dragged there by comrades or civilians. There were a few injured women. Andromache saw Penthesileia had been brought there, still alive but ashen-faced. Lying with her was Anio, her head in her sister's lap. Young Xander was moving from person to person, overwhelmed by the number of injured yet carrying on, staunching wounds, comforting the wounded, holding the hands of the dying. He looked up at her and she saw his face was grey.

Kalliades had followed her in, covered in blood, some of it from a wound high in his chest.

'They have the gallery,' he told her urgently. 'We can hold the stone corridor for a while, but you must get ready to leave with the boys.'

'Helikaon?' she asked, her heart in her mouth.

But at that moment Helikaon and Banokles entered the

433

gathering room, carrying Polydorus, who was badly wounded. They laid the Eagle on the floor, then Helikaon turned to Andromache.

'You must go now,' he told her, and she heard the agony in his voice. *You* must go, she thought, with a stab of fear. Not *we* must go. She knew he would stay and fight to the end. She would not try to change his mind.

They hurried to the room where the little boys slept. She woke them and they rubbed their eyes and looked wonderingly at the blood-covered warriors around their bed.

Helikaon lifted Andromache's hand to his lips, and she winced. 'You are wounded?' he asked anxiously.

'Yesterday,' she admitted, showing him her shoulder. 'It has opened up again. I will need help with the boys.'

'You cannot take two children down the rope on your own anyway,' he said. 'I will carry them down.' Hope flared in her, then died when he dropped his eyes. 'Then I must return,' he told her.

'You take Dex,' Kalliades suggested. 'I will carry Astyanax. He knows me and we have shared adventures before.' He picked up the little boy, who confidently put his arms round the warrior's neck.

'Whatever you're going to do, do it quickly,' urged Banokles, who had been listening to the fighting in the stone corridor.

'Strap the child to me,' Kalliades told his friend, handing him a length of bandage. In a moment Banokles had wound the bandage round him, tying the child tightly to his chest. Kalliades walked to the window. Astyanax grinned over his shoulder at Andromache and waved his hand at her, thrilled by the excitement.

'You had better take this,' Banokles said suddenly. Kalliades looked at the weapon he was holding out.

'The Sword of Argurios! I had lost it!'

'I found it on the stairs. Take it with you.'

'It will hamper me on my climb. Keep it until I get back.'

'You don't know what might happen down there. Take it.'

Kalliades shrugged and sheathed the sword. He climbed out of the window, disappearing into the night.

'You next, my love,' Helikaon said to Andromache. 'Can you climb down with that wound?'

'I can make it,' she reassured him, although privately she had doubts. Her heart was thudding in her chest. She cast a last glance at the blond warrior. 'Thank you, Banokles,' she said. It seemed inadequate after all he had done for her. Before he could step back she darted forward and kissed his cheek. Banokles nodded, his face reddening.

Andromache sat on the window ledge and swung her legs round. Then, grabbing hold of the rope, she started her descent.

XXXIII

The last king of Troy

HIS SMALL SON DEX STRAPPED TO HIS BODY, HELIKAON CLIMBED HAND over hand down the rope after Kalliades and Andromache. He was anxious to return to the palace quickly, and could think only of the coming struggle. He knew Agamemnon would show himself at the last, and Helikaon would be waiting for him. No matter how many elite warriors the Mykene king sent against him, he was determined to survive long enough to confront Agamemnon, and kill him if it was in his power.

His feet reached the ground, and Kalliades deftly pulled away the bandages holding Dex to him. 'It is still dark,' pointed out the tall warrior. 'Andromache will need a torch.' He shouted up to the window, 'Banokles, throw down a torch!'

Within moments a flaming brand flew through the air and fell some paces away. Kalliades ran to get it, stamping out the sparks on the dry vegetation, and returning the torch to Andromache's hand. Standing tall in the torchlight in a flame-red dress, she had never looked more beautiful, Helikaon thought.

He said to her urgently, 'The *Xanthos* will only wait until the sun clears the horizon, so you must make haste. Keep directly north. See, the north star is bright tonight.' Realizing her arms were trembling from the effort of the climb, he pulled her into an embrace. Andromache cast a glance of entreaty at Kalliades, who moved out of earshot.

'Please, my love, come with us,' she pleaded. 'I swore to myself I would not say this to you. But you and Kalliades will both go back to certain death.'

Helikaon shook his head. 'You know I cannot. I have friends in there, comrades I have known most of my life. Some of them defended Dardanos for me. I cannot leave them. It is my duty.'

'We both chose the path of duty before,' she argued. 'It was a hard road, but we walked it knowing each of us was doing the right thing. But Troy is now a city of the dead. The only reason to return would be to die with your friends. How will that benefit them? We must leave the dead behind us and set our faces to the sunrise. Your duty now is to your ship and to your family – to me and your sons.'

But her last words were lost as Kalliades cried out. He had pulled on the rope, ready to climb back up the cliff, but it fell towards him, looping to the earth from the high window. Helikaon stared at the coils of rope, and at the cleanly cut end. His chest tightened with fury at the betrayal.

Kalliades shouted up angrily at the figure they could all see outlined in the window. 'Banokles!'

His voice floated down to them. 'May Ares guide your spear, Kalliades!'

Helikaon saw Kalliades lower his head for a moment, his face becoming grave, then he took a deep breath and called up to his friend, 'He always does, sword brother!'

They saw Banokles raise his hand in farewell. Then the window was empty.

Helikaon felt the fury in his chest. 'What in the name of Hades is that idiot doing?' he stormed.

Kalliades replied quietly, 'He is saving my life.' He rubbed his eyes roughly with the back of his hand, then added, as if to himself, 'It's something he does.'

Helikaon looked up at the sheer walls. 'I will climb alone,' he promised.

Andromache turned to him, her face angry. 'You cannot climb back! There will be no one to throw a rope to you this time – unless it is the enemy. You must leave now, Helikaon. Accept this gift that fate, and Banokles, have presented to you. Return to the *Xanthos* and sail away from the dead past.'

She glanced at Kalliades, but the warrior still stood gazing up at the high window, lost in his own thoughts. She placed her hand on Helikaon's chest and leaned in to him. 'You did not hear what I said, my love. I had hoped for a better time to tell you. But Astyanax is your son. Our son. You must save your son.'

Helikaon stared at her wonderingly. The words made no sense. 'How can that be?'

She smiled a little. 'Trust me, Helikaon. It is true. It was when you were ill, deep in delirium. I will tell you about it when there is time, and we are alone. But both these boys are your sons. You must help me take them to safety. Dawn is coming and I cannot get them to the *Xanthos* in time on my own.'

Helikaon shook his head, bewildered. He felt suddenly like a ship adrift; the certainties which had guided his life were being washed away by the storms of fate.

He looked up at the window, an agony of indecision in his breast. Every instinct in his body told him to climb back up to the palace. Even now he believed he could make a difference and somehow defeat the hordes of the enemy, despite the odds. Then he thought of what he had said to his crew. *I plan to live.*

He nodded his head then, accepting his fate. 'Very well, we will go to the ship. Kalliades?'

The warrior turned towards him, and admitted, 'I cannot climb the cliff without a rope. My leg is not strong enough. I accept the gift my old friend has given me. I will come with you to the *Xanthos*, if we can get there in time.' He looked to the east, where the sky was showing dark red on the horizon. 'But it will be a close-run thing.'

The going was difficult in the torchlight. The land was flat horse meadows divided by small streams, but all was bone dry now, and they had to leap the ditches, or stumble across them. Helikaon, who knew the country well, led the way holding the torch and young Dex. His mind still in confusion, he thought of what Andromache had told him. He recalled erotic dreams he had had about her as he lay in a fever in the palace of Hektor. He had guarded the dreams in his thoughts all these years, until the wondrous reality of her body replaced them in his memory. He wondered that she had kept silent about it throughout their voyage together, then he thought of Hektor's death, and he understood.

He paused and glanced back to where Kalliades was following them with Astyanax in his arms. The warrior's face was pale; his leg clearly troubled him.

'Do not fear for me, Golden One,' he said, seeing Helikaon's look. 'I will keep up.'

'I am sorry about Banokles.'

'Banokles lived each day as if it were his last. I never knew a man take so much from life. We should not grieve for Banokles.'

The light was starting to strengthen when Helikaon stopped, hearing a sound, and out of the darkness loomed a group of men. Helikaon swiftly set the boy down and drew his blades. Kalliades moved alongside him, the Sword of Argurios in hand.

They were a ragged army, twenty or more of them, some in armour, many wounded. All had the ferocious look of men pushed beyond desperation. From among them walked their leader. He wore a black and silver chin beard. He seemed greyer now, and leaner, but Helikaon's blood ran cold when he recognized the Mykene admiral Menados.

'Well, Helikaon, this is a strange meeting on a night's walk,' said the admiral affably. 'The Mykene renegade Kalliades, the Burner – most hated of Mykene's enemies – and a refugee family. Two boys. Let me see? Could it be that one of these boys is the rightful king of Troy?'

Helikaon said nothing, watching the men, calculating their strength, planning in which order to take them. He and Kalliades edged apart, making room to swing their swords.

'Thanks to you, Helikaon, these brave men and I are now

outcasts. Agamemnon was not pleased that you destroyed an entire Mykene fleet. But we might win back the king's favour by delivering to him the last heir to Troy.'

Helikaon spat out, 'Make your play, Menados. We haven't got all night.' From the corner of his eye he saw the sun's first rays lancing over the horizon.

Menados ignored him, addressing Kalliades. 'You are free to join us, Kalliades, as an outcast yourself. We are not going to the golden city, but back to Mykene and the Lion's Hall, there to suffer Agamemnon's judgement – if he ever returns.'

Kalliades answered him coolly. 'The Law of the Road states that Helikaon's battle is mine. I will stand with him.'

Menados nodded, as if he had expected the response. 'Loyalty has been much prized among the Mykene, although that loyalty seemed often misplaced. You are not the first Mykene warrior to stand side by side with the Trojans. The great Argurios was a comrade of mine. We fought together in many battles. I admired him more than any man I have ever known. Now, Helikaon, when last we encountered each other, you chose the path of mercy. You are undoubtedly regretting that now. And you told me that if we were ever to meet again you would cut out my heart and feed it to the crows. Is that still your intention?'

Helikaon snarled. 'Try me, Menados!'

A voice behind Menados yelled, 'Let's take them, admiral! The Burner is accursed and must die!'

Another shouted, 'The gods are with us, lord. They have brought the Burner into our hands!' There was a chorus of agreement and in the pre-dawn gloom Helikaon heard swords rasping from scabbards.

Menados turned to his men, annoyance in his voice. 'I was speaking of loyalty and mercy, two qualities which used to be admired by the Mykene.'

Behind Helikaon one of the boys started to cry, from tiredness or from fear.

Menados sighed and sheathed his sword. 'Go on your way, Helikaon. Matters are now equal between us. I give you and your people your lives, just as you once gave me mine. In the name of the great Argurios.'

There were angry shouts from Menados' men, but no one made a move. Helikaon guessed their loyalty to Menados, or fear of him, was stronger than their need for vengeance.

Swords still at the ready, the two warriors walked watchfully past the Mykene band. Andromache, with Astyanax on one hip, holding Dex by the hand, followed them.

As they raced on Helikaon strained his eyes to find the dark bulk of the *Xanthos* in the distance. The ball of the sun, rising out of the mist to their right, was almost clear of the horizon now, and they still had a way to go.

'We cannot make it,' Kalliades said. Helikaon's heart sank. The man was right. It was impossible to get to the ship before she sailed.

Then, from out of the west, he heard a shout. He paused and turned. A horse was cantering towards them across the rough ground, leaping the ditches, its rider waving to them and shouting. As he came closer Helikaon saw he was wearing the armour of the Trojan Horse.

'Skorpios!' Kalliades cried out in delight. 'How in Hades are you here? We thought you long dead!'

'It does not matter!' Helikaon shouted. 'Get down, lad! I don't know who you are or what you're doing here, but I need that horse!'

The fair-haired rider slid quickly off his mount, and Helikaon vaulted on. He grabbed the reins and kicked the beast into a run, heading north towards the river at full pelt. Behind them he heard the newcomer ask, 'Where's he going with my horse? And where's Banokles?'

Banokles watched Helikaon climb down the rope into the night. Then he heard Kalliades' voice call to him for a torch. He grabbed one off the wall and threw it down to him. He watched it spiral into darkness, then he returned to the crowded gathering room to see who else could be saved. But among the many wounded and dying there was no one who had the strength to lower themselves to safety. Only the healer.

He told the boy curtly, 'On your way, lad. There is a rope from the window of the rear chamber, leading to the ground. Climb down it and save yourself.'

The boy carried on sewing a soldier's scalp wound. There was blood everywhere, and his fingers kept slipping on the bronze needle as he worked. Without looking up, he replied, 'I will stay.'

Banokles grabbed the boy by the front of his clothing and dragged him upright, shaking him like a rat. 'That was not a polite request, boy, but an order. Go when I tell you!'

'With respect, sir,' said the healer, his face reddening, 'I am not a soldier for you to command, and I will not go. I am needed here.'

Frustrated, Banokles flung him down. He could hardly force the boy to go. What could he do – throw him out of the window? He stalked back to the rear chamber and without hesitation cut the rope. He waited, grinning to himself, and shortly he heard Kalliades' voice shouting, 'Banokles!'

He leaned over the window ledge and called down to his old friend. 'May Ares guide your spear, Kalliades!'

There was a moment's pause, then Kalliades shouted back. 'He always does, sword brother.'

Banokles waved farewell. Red had always told him Kalliades would get him killed, and here he was saving his friend from certain death. In a high good humour, he went out to the stone corridor where the last three Eagles were holding back the enemy. There was only room for one man at a time to swing a sword, so each combatant faced a duel to the death. He saw one Eagle cut down, a sword through his belly, and a comrade take his place. Two more to go, he thought, and went back into the gathering room.

He saw the king's aide Polydorus lying propped against a wall, blood drying on his chest and stomach. He had always liked the man. He was a thinker, like Kalliades, and a doughty fighter too. Looking at Polydorus' face with his veteran's eye, he guessed the warrior would probably survive, if given time to heal. Banokles always told Kalliades he knew if a wounded soldier would live or die, and he was very seldom wrong. Well, actually he was often wrong, but he was the only one keeping score.

He squatted down.

'How are we doing?' asked Polydorus with a faint smile.

'There are two Eagles left, holding the corridor, then I'll go in.'

'You'd better go now then, Banokles.'

Banokles shrugged. 'In a moment. You Eagles are a gutsy bunch.' He frowned. 'Can you believe that boy refused to leave?' He nodded towards the healer.

Polydorus smiled. 'You could leave, Banokles. You chose not to. What's the difference?'

For a moment Banokles was astonished. It had never even entered his head that he could have climbed down the rope too.

'I'm a soldier,' he answered lamely.

'Yet you are under no man's orders. Has it occurred to you, Banokles, that now Hektor's son has left the city you, as the senior soldier here, are truly king of Troy?'

Banokles was delighted by the idea, and he laughed. 'The king? I never thought I'd be a king. Shouldn't I have a crown or something?'

Polydorus shook his head weakly. 'I never saw Priam wearing a crown.'

'Then how will people know I'm king?'

'I suspect you will tell them, my friend, if you get the chance.' Then Polydorus' face became grave. 'May the All-Father guard you, Banokles. It is time now.'

Banokles stood up, then turned and walked to the corridor.

The last Eagle was battling courageously. The stone corridor was littered with bodies, and Banokles dragged two corpses back into the gathering room, to give himself some space to fight. One Trojan soldier lay slumped against the corridor wall, clutching a wound in his belly. He raised a warding hand as Banokles approached him. 'I would rather die here than in there,' he said.

Banokles nodded. He closed the oak door to the gathering room behind him and waited. He did not have to wait long. The last

Eagle, weakened by his wounds, fell to one knee and his Mykene opponent swung his sword at the man's neck, half beheading him.

Banokles stepped up. The Mykene warrior looked familiar, but he could not name him. It doesn't matter anyway, Banokles thought. He wrenched one sword from his scabbard, blocked a fierce overhead cut and sent a slashing riposte across the warrior's face. The man stumbled and Banokles plunged the blade into his chest.

He turned briefly to the injured Trojan. 'One,' he said.

Then he unsheathed his other sword. He felt a familiar calm settle on him. The only contentment he had felt since Red's death had been in the heat of battle. His grief for his wife, the burden of his responsibilities, all vanished away, and Banokles rejoiced.

A huge warrior in a lionskin tunic leapt towards him, sword raised. Banokles parried the blow and reversed a cut to the warrior's neck. The blade hammered into armour and broke. Dropping it, Banokles ducked away from a second blow, then twisted his wrist and his other sword hissed through the air into the man's groin. As he stumbled Banokles chopped him on the back of his neck, severing his spine. He picked up the man's sword as he fell to the floor.

'Two,' he heard the injured Trojan say, and he laughed.

The next warrior took longer to kill. He inflicted two minor wounds on Banokles, one on the leg, one on the cheek, before Banokles blocked a lunge, spun his blade and thrust it under the man's helm.

'Three.'

With the fourth warrior it became a duel. Banokles tried a feint, followed by a lunge to the heart. The Mykene parried it and sent a return cut that struck Banokles' neck, slicing open the skin. The pace picked up, with both men hacking and slashing, blocking and moving. Banokles realized he was tiring. He knew he could not afford to get weary. He had to end each contest quickly. He feinted with his left sword and as the Mykene parried it, he swept the right sword up through the man's belly and chest, disembowelling him.

There were a few moments of rest while the Mykene dragged

away their dead and dying, then the next warrior stepped towards him.

As the morning dragged on, Banokles felt his concentration wavering. After one kill he glanced down at himself to see blood still flowing from the gash in his leg. There were other minor wounds, including one on the left shoulder. That arm was reacting too slowly.

'You are dying, Banokles,' someone said. He realized it was the man in front of him, a Mykene in the old armour of Atreus' personal guard. Banokles staggered as the man's blade lanced beneath his ribs, deflected off the bronze discs of his leather breastplate. Then Banokles got his feet under him and surged forward, his right sword swinging in a high, vicious arc. It tore into the man's neck protector, ripping through it and opening a deep wound in the man's throat. He fell back, choking on blood, and Banokles leapt on him, plunging his sword into the enemy's face.

'How many now?' he shouted. There was no reply, and he glanced behind him at the injured Trojan, but the soldier had died.

Seventeen, Banokles decided. Maybe more. He picked up the last opponent's shield to replace his left sword and guard that side.

A huge warrior walked down the corridor towards him. Banokles prepared to meet him, but his sword seemed very heavy and he dragged it up in front of him with a massive effort.

'Banokles,' the warrior's deep voice rumbled, and Banokles saw it was Ajax Skull-Splitter. Banokles was glad the veteran Mykene champion had survived the battle at the Scaean Gate. He knew he would have to bring all his strength and concentration to bear to kill the man. But he felt badly in need of a sleep.

'Kalliades?' Ajax queried.

Banokles managed a grin. 'He's back there, having a rest and something to eat. He's up next. And you know he could teach me a thing or two about swordfighting.'

Ajax laughed, the deep rumble making the stones of the corridor vibrate. 'Then you will walk the Dark Road together,' he promised.

He attacked with a speed which belied his great size. He was fast, but Banokles was already moving. He ducked under the slashing sweep of the broadsword, and kicked out, catching Ajax on the knee. The big man staggered but he was so well balanced that he recovered in a heartbeat and lunged for Banokles' throat. Banokles blocked the blow and leapt back a pace.

Ajax attacked again. Their blades met. Ajax hacked and slashed, but Banokles blocked every blow, moving on instinct, his body awash with pain. Suddenly Ajax spun on his heel and crashed his massive fist in Banokles' face. Banokles fell back.

He blinked. There was sweat in his eyes, or blood, because his vision was fading in and out. Suddenly he found he was down on one knee and could not get up. I'll have that sleep soon, he thought.

He was surprised to see Ajax sheathe his sword, then turn and walk back down the corridor. Banokles knew he should leap up and ram his blade into his old comrade's back. He was planning to do it, but time passed and he found he was still kneeling on the floor. Angry voices echoed down the corridor. There were armed men there, watching him.

'I order you to kill him,' shouted one man furiously. His deep voice was familiar, but Banokles could not remember whose it was.

'I'll not dispatch him for you, Agamemnon King,' rumbled Ajax, anger in his voice. 'You were a warrior once, too.'

Banokles' last sight was of a tall figure walking down the corridor towards him. He realized it was Red, and he grinned up at her as the light faded.

Today was a good day, he thought happily.

XXXIV

The god of mice

AGAMEMNON WRENCHED HIS SWORD OUT OF BANOKLES' CHEST AND handed it to an aide to clean. He was in a good humour. Killing Banokles put an end to an irritating fleabite he had not been able to scratch. He had no doubt that the traitor's accomplice Kalliades lay dead somewhere in the mounds of Trojan corpses he had seen between the Scaean Gate and this last corridor.

He had waited all morning with his brother kings Menelaus and Idomeneos, his anger growing as warrior after warrior sent into the stone corridor failed to kill the renegade. But now he was dead, and nothing stood in the way of Agamemnon's twin ambitions: to kill the boy king, Hektor's get, and finally to win his prize – the treasure of Priam. He knew he must be close to them both, for so many Trojans to have died guarding this way.

At the end of the stone corridor was a simple oak door.

'Open it!' he ordered, and two axemen ran forward. But it was not barred, and opened at a touch. Preceded by the axemen and flanked by his bodyguard Agamemnon strode in.

The room appeared to be a hospital. Dead and dying Trojans, perhaps forty of them, including a few women, lay on the floor of a great square room. The stench was appalling and death hung in

447

the air like woodsmoke. All eyes turned to him. Some were full of fear; most held acceptance of their fate.

Standing in front of the wounded, holding a sword raised in both hands, was a short young man in a blood-drenched robe.

Ignoring him, Agamemnon looked round. There were no children in the chamber. They must have hidden them. He frowned, his good humour evaporating.

The boy with the sword was saying something. Agamemnon listened impatiently. 'Do not kill these people,' the boy said, his voice trembling. 'They can no longer harm you and your armies.'

'Kill him,' Agamemnon ordered.

'Wait!' Meriones, Idomeneos' aide, stepped forward in front of the boy. The axemen paused and looked to Agamemnon uncertainly.

'I know you, lad,' Meriones told the boy. 'I have seen you with Odysseus.'

The young man nodded, and lowered his sword slightly. 'I am Xander. I was privileged to be healer to great Achilles and his Myrmidons. I am a friend of Odysseus.'

'Then what are you doing here, lad, with the Trojans?'

'It is a long story,' Xander confessed.

'It is a story I would like to hear,' Meriones told him, looking at Agamemnon. 'Spare the boy, Agamemnon King. We could do with a tale or two now Odysseus has departed.'

'Good riddance,' barked Idomeneos. 'I want no more tall tales. Kill the boy and let's find the treasury.'

Irritated almost beyond endurance by the Kretan king after the long summer in his company, Agamemnon snapped, 'Very well, Meriones. As usual, *you* give me good advice. Healer, I will spare you and your wounded if you tell me where Hektor's son is.'

The young man replied nervously. 'Astyanax is gone, sir. The Golden One took him away last night.'

Helikaon again! Agamemnon felt his fury rising with the speed of a summer storm. 'Helikaon was here? Only last night? How is that possible? You are lying, boy!'

'No, sir. I am telling you the truth. He climbed the north wall and took the boys away. The lady Andromache went with him, and—'

'The north wall? But that cannot be climbed!'

'It is true, lord. I expect the rope is still there for you to see.'

He pointed towards the rear rooms and Agamemnon gestured for a soldier to go and look. Menelaus followed him.

Always Helikaon, the Battle King thought, spoiling my plans at every turn! Even at my moment of victory.

Idomeneos rasped, 'I have no interest in the killing of Hektor's son. Troy is finished, whether Priam's line survives or not. Do you fear that Helikaon and the boy king will raise an army and try to take the city back? Why would we worry? We will find Priam's treasure and return to our lands.'

Agamemnon nodded. Sharptooth was, as usual, motivated only by his own greed, but in this he was right. The boy could be hunted down at leisure. Nowhere on the Great Green was safe for him. Once Troy was securely in Mykene hands, and in the charge of a commander loyal to Agamemnon, the king could go back to the Lion's Hall and his wife and son, and celebrate his victory over Priam and his golden city. Agamemnon King, Conqueror of the East! His name would go down in legend as the destroyer of Troy.

Good humour restored, he turned to Xander. 'I am a man of my word, boy. Tend to your wounded. No more Trojans will die at the hands of the Battle King.'

'Brother!' Agamemnon turned. Menelaus had returned from the rear rooms pale-faced.

'Well? Was the rope there? Is the healer speaking the truth?'

'Yes, brother, but there is something else you must see.' He gestured urgently for Agamemnon to join him.

The Mykene king sighed. His bodyguard at his side, he followed Menelaus into a small rear room. The window looked out to the north, and to its stone pillar was tied a strong rope. It had been cut near the top.

At Menelaus' urgent bidding Agamemnon walked to the window and looked out.

It was well past noon and the sun shone warmly on the meadows flanking the river Simoeis. Dry throughout the summer, the wide plains had been made verdant by the recent rains. But little greenery was now visible. As far as the eye could see the plain was covered with armed men, cavalry and infantry in disciplined ranks, motionless, waiting for orders.

Menelaus gasped, 'Hittites, brother! The Hittite army is here!'

On a rocky cliff top to the east of the city the old smith Khalkeus lay in an exhausted sleep, his body curled protectively round the perfect sword. His hands had been badly burned trying to handle the weapon. The numbness in his fingers had masked the pain at first. He had also, he thought, not eaten for several days, although he was interested to find he no longer seemed to need food. His dwindling store of water smelled bad, but he sipped it from time to time.

At twilight he decided to return to the city to present the sword to the king. His few belongings, along with the tent that had sheltered him all summer, had been destroyed in the fire. He tucked the half-empty water skin under one arm and, gingerly cradling the sword across both forearms, he set off.

The pain in his hands was torture. He was angry with himself. A smith with his experience should not make the mistakes of an apprentice. The raw red palms would take a long time to heal, and he would be hampered in his work.

He encouraged himself forward by visualizing the expression of awe and delight on the Mykene king's face when he saw the sword, his urgency as he begged Khalkeus to tell him how it was made. The old man felt a moment of regret that it would not be Helikaon who would receive the weapon. He had always done his best work with the encouragement of the Dardanian king, but he had no doubt that by now the Trojans and their allies had been destroyed. As he walked towards the city he could see flames leaping high from within the walls, and hear the sounds of battle. He was curious to know how the western kings had finally taken the city. The idea of a great battering ram suspended on chains on a wheeled platform had been forming in his head. Distracted, he stumbled on the rocky ground and nearly fell. Careful, he thought to himself in a moment of clarity, you cannot afford to fall on your hands. He moved more slowly, picking his way in the darkness.

He paused for breath under the walls of Troy, beneath the northeast bastion, and drank some of his water. He sat down for a moment and fell instantly asleep.

It was well past dawn when he woke again. His hands were on fire and his head ached abominably. He drained the water skin in one long gulp, then vomited most of it on to the ground. He threw away the skin and slowly got to his feet. A long look at the perfect sword invigorated him and he set off round the walls. He passed the Dardanian Gate and the East Gate but found them both closed and sealed, so he headed for the Scaean Gate.

But when he got there that too was closed. He craned his neck to see the top of the wall, but he could not make out any guards. He wandered around the ruined lower town, but it was deserted. His strength exhausted, he sat down in the dust outside the wall. The six stone statues guarding the Scaean Gate watched him balefully.

It was a long time before there was a creak and a groan and the gates opened to allow a troop of soldiers out. He saw they were Mykene by their armour, and he struggled to his feet.

'You, soldiers, take me to Agamemnon!' he cried. Ignoring the waves of agony he took the sword in both hands and waved it at them.

The troop ignored him and marched off down through the town.

'Your king is expecting me!' he shouted despairingly. 'This sword is for him, you idiots!'

A single soldier peeled off from the rear of the troop and walked towards him, sword unsheathed. Khalkeus saw that half the man's face was hideously scarred. Sand, he thought with sudden interest. That must be what red-hot sand does to flesh and skin.

The warrior did not hesitate. 'Idiots, are we?' he asked. He rammed his sword through Khalkeus' chest, dragged it out, then rejoined his comrades.

It was like being hit by a hammer, Khalkeus thought as he fell,

451

the perfect sword cast into the dust beside him. The pain in his hands had disappeared, he realized with relief.

He had a curious dream. He dreamed he was on the *Xanthos* and a stiff breeze was filling the black horse sail. The ship clove through the water, which was deep green and strangely still. The Golden One was striding towards him, the sunlight behind him outlining his form but putting his features in shadow. Khalkeus could not see well and he felt very weak. Then he realized the golden man was bigger than Helikaon. In fact he was a giant, and the light around him was not from the sun, but was emanating from the man himself. Is it Apollo, the sun god, he wondered? Then with a shock of realization he saw the god was limping.

The god leaned down to him and gently took the perfect sword from his hands.

'You have done well, smith,' his deep voice boomed. 'Sleep now, and tomorrow we will set you to work.'

Tudhaliyas IV, emperor of the Hittites, strode into Priam's *megaron* surrounded by his retinue. Xander watched with interest. He had never seen an emperor before. Apart from the Hittite mercenaries he had treated, who seemed the same as any other mercenaries, the only Hittite Xander had met was Zidantas. Zidantas was huge, with shaven head and forked black beard. This emperor was thin and very tall, with a curled beard, and dressed in shiny clothes like a woman. His retinue were even more strangely garbed in brightly coloured kilts and striped shawls. But they were all armed to the teeth, as were their hosts.

Xander had wanted to stay with the wounded, but as Agamemnon left the queen's gathering room he suddenly turned to Meriones. 'Bring the healer,' he had ordered. Xander now stood nervously at Meriones' side, feeling the black-clad Kretan was his only friend in the room.

Emperor and king met in the centre of the *megaron*, which was still heaped with corpses and abandoned weapons. Tudhaliyas looked around silently, his dark eyes revealing nothing.

Agamemnon spoke first. 'My condolences on the death of your

father. Hattusilis was a great man and a wise leader,' he said, and Xander was surprised at the sincerity in his voice. 'Welcome to Troy, a city of the Mykene empire.'

Tudhaliyas regarded him for a moment, then he replied mildly, 'The Hittite emperor is accustomed to see his vassals prostrating themselves before him.'

Agamemnon's eyes hardened, but he replied evenly, 'I am no man's vassal. I fought for this city and you enter it with my permission. I opened the Scaean Gate to you as a gesture of friendship. Everything here belongs to me. And to my brother kings,' he added swiftly, seeing Idomeneos frown.

'You fought to win this charnel house?' Tudhaliyas commented, looking round again at the corpses, the blood and the gore. 'You must be very proud.'

'Let us not misunderstand one another,' Agamemnon replied smoothly. 'The allied kings of the west fought to win this city, and by superior strategy and military strength, and the will of the gods, we succeeded. Your fame as a *strategos* precedes you, emperor. And you know that for a people to dominate the Great Green they must first dominate Troy.'

'You are right, Mykene,' said Tudhaliyas. 'It is important that we do not misunderstand one another. Priam ruled this city on the sufferance of the Hittite emperors. Under his kingship Troy flourished and became rich, and the land was at peace. The city guarded the Hittite trade routes by sea and land, bringing prosperity to our great city Hattusas. Trojan troops fought for the empire in many battles. My friend Hektor,' he paused for the words to sink in, 'was partly responsible for the triumph over the Egypteians at Kadesh.

'Now,' Tudhaliyas went on, his voice hardening, 'Troy is in ruins, its bay unnavigable. All its citizens are dead or fled, and its army is destroyed. The countryside is barren, crops ruined and livestock dying. That is why I have taken the trouble to come here myself, with my thirty thousand warriors.'

He paused, and a thoughtful silence hung in the air.

'The Hittite empire cares little who holds Troy, if the city prospers and showers its wealth around it. But a dead city in a dying land attracts only darkness and chaos. The empire is forced to intervene.'

Xander felt the atmosphere in the *megaron* become icy. There were fewer Hittites in the chamber than there were Mykene warriors, but they were fresher, better armed, and looked as though they were spoiling for a fight.

Agamemnon gazed round him assessingly, perhaps thinking the same thing. 'Troy will prosper again under Mykene rule,' he vowed. 'By next summer the bay will be full of trading ships once more. The city will be rebuilt, and under our strong leadership it will flourish again.'

Tudhaliyas suddenly stepped forward, and Agamemnon instinctively moved back. The emperor, his bodyguard shadowing him, strode over to Priam's gold-encrusted throne, and sat down gracefully. Agamemnon was forced to stand in front of him to speak to him.

'The Bay of Troy has been silting up over the last hundred years, I am told,' Tudhaliyas said. 'Now a Mykene fleet lies wrecked there and already new mudbanks will be building around the hulks. My experts predict that within a generation the bay will have disappeared and the city will be landlocked. Trading ships will pass it by in favour of the young cities flourishing higher up the Hellespont. Troy is finished, Agamemnon, thanks to you.'

'I did not start this war, emperor!' Agamemnon spat it out, his composure lost. 'But I saw, before all others, the danger Troy offered to the nations of the Great Green. Priam's ambition, backed by his son's cavalry and the Dardanian pirate fleet, was to subdue all free peoples to his will. And while others were bribed or seduced by him, Mykene was not fooled.'

Tudhaliyas leaned back in the throne and laughed, his voice echoing richly in the great stone hall. Then he said, 'This nonsense might have fooled your puppet kings as you sat round your campfires at night, telling each other Priam was a monster of ambition determined to conquer the world. Yet this monster brought forty years of peace until you chose to destroy it.'

'I have fought for this city,' Agamemnon roared. 'It is mine by right of arms.'

At that moment a Hittite warrior walked into the *megaron* and nodded to the emperor. Tudhaliyas flicked his eyes to him, then back to the Mykene king.

'So you invoke the right of arms,' he responded, smiling. 'At last, something we can agree on.'

He stood up and looked down at Agamemnon. 'Outside this city are thirty thousand Hittite warriors. They are all well fed and well armed, and they have marched a long way without the chance of a good fight.'

He paused as a Mykene warrior came into the *megaron* and hurried up to Agamemnon. He spoke in the king's ear, and Xander saw Agamemnon blanch.

'I see you have heard, king,' Tudhaliyas said. 'My warriors have taken the Scaean Gate and are already starting to dismantle it. They will unseal all the great gates and take them apart one by one. For a while Troy will be a truly open city.'

Xander held his breath as he waited for the explosion he was sure would come from Agamemnon. But it did not.

'We discussed misunderstanding earlier,' Tudhaliyas went on smoothly. 'I do not want Troy. Before I left our capital Hattusas with my army I consulted our ... soothsayers, I think you call them. One told me a tale of the founding of this city. He said that when the father of Troy, the demi-god Scamander, first voyaged to these lands from the far west he was met on the beach by the sun god. They broke bread together, and the sun god advised Scamander that his people should settle wherever they were attacked by earth-born enemies under the cover of darkness. Scamander wondered at the god's words, but that night when they camped on this very hilltop a horde of famished field mice invaded their tents and nibbled the leather bowstrings and breastplate straps, and all their war gear. Scamander vowed his people would remain here, and he built a temple to the sun god.

'But the gods the Trojans brought from the western lands were not our gods. Your sun god is called Apollo, also the Lord of the

Silver Bow, and the Destroyer. He is a god of might and of battle. *Our* god of the sun is a healer called the mouse-god. When our children are sick they are given a mouse dipped in honey to eat, as a tribute to the healing god. Over the years, as the city grew, the mouse-god's temple became neglected. The Trojans built greater temples, decorated with gold, copper and ivory, to Zeus and Athene and Hermes. When the great walls were built round the city the mouse-god's temple was outside them. When the small shrine collapsed during an earthquake, it was not rebuilt and eventually grass grew over it and, with perfect irony, field mice ran in its halls. Now the last Trojans have left and taken their cruel and capricious gods with them. You, who worship the same gods of the west, will follow them. Perhaps the mouse-god will stand on the beach again and watch you go, wondering why you all came here.'

As the emperor told his tale more heavily armed Hittite soldiers moved quietly into the *megaron*. Agamemnon looked about him, and Xander could see his face was pale, his eyes wild, as he watched his ambition come to nothing as the heartbeats passed.

Tudhaliyas stood up and his voice darkened. 'I proclaim that this city will be destroyed,' he ordered. 'It will be taken apart stone by stone, then the very stones themselves will be smashed. This city of darkness will vanish from the land.'

Idomeneos stepped forward. 'I care not for your stories, nor for Troy and its fate,' he rasped at the emperor. 'I came only for the fabled riches of Priam. That much is due to us. You cannot deprive us of our plunder!'

'And you are?' asked the emperor scornfully.

'Idomeneos, king of Kretos,' said the man, flushing with anger.

The emperor waved his hand dismissively. 'Go, little kings, seek out your plunder. But carry it back to your ships quickly. Any galley still in the Bay of Herakles come the dawn will be taken and its crews dismembered.'

He turned and gave a brief order in his own tongue, then stalked out of the *megaron*. His retinue followed him, but the rest of the Hittite warriors remained.

Agamemnon seemed smaller now, shrunken by the Hittite's

contempt. He glared round the chamber, and his eyes, full of unfocused anger, settled on Xander.

'You!' he cried. 'Healer! Take me to Priam's treasury!'

Xander stood frozen for a moment, then Meriones gave him a gentle push, and he said, 'Yes, king.'

He knew where the treasury was. It was not a secret. He led the kings down a corridor to the rear of the *megaron*, then down a long flight of steps. Along a wide corridor deep below the ground they walked. Above them on either side of the tunnel carved shapes of stone stared down at them, mythical beasts with teeth and claws, their eyes flickering blindly in the torchlight.

At the end the corridor opened out into a round chamber. Xander and Meriones, the three kings and their guards crowded in. There was a strong animal smell, Xander noticed. In front of them was a high door lavishly decorated with bronze, horn and ivory. In the days of Priam the door was guarded by six Eagles. Now there were no guards, and only a simple oak and bronze bar stopped intruders.

Kleitos the king's aide ran forward and raised the locking bar. He pulled open the door and Agamemnon stepped forward. The smell wafting out was pungent, and Xander's nose wrinkled.

The Battle King walked into the darkness of Priam's treasury, followed by Idomeneos and Menelaus, then they all stopped. There was a gasp, then a volley of curses. Xander squeezed round the side of the door to see what was happening.

A dozen horses stood blinking at them in the light of the torches. They shifted about nervously, stepping in the piles of horse manure which covered the floor, and the acrid odour from the chamber grew even stronger.

Agamemnon cursed and grabbed a torch from a soldier. He pushed his way among the animals, looking for treasure. He searched frantically round the low square chamber, followed by Idomeneos and Menelaus. It was empty, except for the horses and their droppings. Only in the far corner did they find two dusty goblets and a large wooden chest, its lid flung open. Agamemnon reached in and drew out three copper rings, then flung them on to the stone floor. Fury in his voice, he turned to the other kings.

'Helikaon!' he raged. 'The Burner has stolen Priam's treasure from under our noses!'

Menelaus frowned. 'But brother, that is impossible!' he offered nervously. 'How could he get it out of the city?'

'He and his crew must have lowered it down the north wall in the night,' Agamemnon guessed. 'That was why the rope was cut! To stop anyone following him and stealing it back! They will be far away on the *Xanthos* by now.'

'It is the fastest ship on the Great Green,' Menelaus added miserably. 'We will never catch it.'

'We will if we know where Helikaon is going!' cried Agamemnon. Turning to Xander he grabbed him by his tunic. 'Tell us, boy,' he snarled into his face. 'The Hittites will not save your wounded friends. They will not care if they live or die! Tell us where Helikaon is going, or I will have them taken apart one by one in front of you!'

Xander looked round anxiously, but he could not see his champion Meriones, only the faces of the three kings staring greedily at him.

Please forgive me, Golden One, he thought.

'They are going to Thera,' he said.

XXXV

The flight from Thera

ANDROMACHE WAS WATCHING CLOUDS OF BIRDS IN THE SKY OVER Thera, wondering what they were. They were small and black and there were thousands of them, swirling, diving, climbing, splitting into two clouds, then three, then four, then coming together again, in smooth graceful flight. All the crew of the *Xanthos* were watching, and the ship was drifting in the warm morning breeze. Suddenly, as if under orders, the birds formed a single flock and headed away from the island. For a heartbeat they were over the ship, myriads of them blocking the light. Crewmen ducked instinctively, then the birds had passed, racing for the north, and soon vanished from sight.

The oarsmen picked up the beat again and the *Xanthos* glided on towards the Blessed Isle. Andromache sat back on the wooden bench at the mast and peered down into the lower deck where the boys were playing happily. She smiled to herself. For the first few days of their voyage she had watched them all the time, frightened one would fall overboard. But she found that on the *Xanthos* the boys had more than sixty fathers watching out for them. The oarsmen, most of whom had children of their own, treated them as they would their own sons, playing games with them and telling them stories of the sea. Sometimes they would sit the two boys on

459

the rowing benches and let them pretend to row the great galley.

Astyanax and Dex had thrived during their time at sea. They were both nut brown from being in the sun all day, and Andromache was sure they had both grown taller in the few days. Dex was still watchful, a little shy, and slower to laugh than his brother. Astyanax was bold, sometimes reckless, and whenever he was on the open upper deck Andromache still watched him with the anxious eyes of mother-love.

Since leaving Troy Helikaon had set a fast pace towards Thera. His intention was to stop briefly at the Blessed Isle to take Kassandra on board, then sail on to Ithaka, where Kalliades and Skorpios would leave the ship. Then the *Xanthos* would make the long voyage, perhaps for the last time, to the Seven Hills in time for winter.

Once at sea and safely out of Trojan waters, they had no reason to race to Thera, yet Andromache felt a feeling of urgency all the time. She could not understand it. They no longer had to fear the Mykene, and the weather was mild and still, but she suffered a constant sense of subdued panic, as though they were late for something. Helikaon felt it too, he admitted, and they believed the rest of the crew did, although it was never discussed.

Andromache stood and walked down to the foredeck where the two warriors were resting. She liked the fair-haired rider Skorpios. He was unlike any soldier she had ever met. She would talk to him in the long idle evenings spent on rocky shores and sandy beaches. The young man knew the names of birds and the small creatures in the rock pools. He had his own names for the star-pictures in the night sky and would tell her tales of them. He had bought a set of pipes from a trader on Lesbos and would sometimes play soft laments as the sun set. He told her stories of his childhood, sad ones about his brutal father and careworn mother, and happier ones about his brothers and sisters and the daily life in their village. He planned to leave the *Xanthos* at Ithaka, but she hoped he would stay on with them to the Seven Hills.

Kalliades looked up as she approached, and she gave him a warm smile. Rested by the voyage, his leg had at last started to heal. Each day she had re-dressed his wound, until today she had thrown away the spent healing plant Xander had placed on it.

A sailor shouted, 'Dolphins!' and she looked to where he pointed. They often saw a dolphin or two on their travels, and she wondered at the excitement in his voice. Then she realized he was pointing to not one dolphin, or two, but hundreds of them, passing the ship to starboard, their sleek grey backs rising and falling as they surged towards the north.

'Doffizz, doffizz!' she heard one of the boys cry, and they ran up on deck and raced to the rail. She saw two crewmen catch them and hold them securely as they craned their necks to watch the creatures pass.

'Unusual,' murmured Kalliades, who had stood up to watch. He sat down again, but Skorpios carried on gazing at the sea until long after the dolphins had disappeared. When he sat down his face was flushed with excitement like the boys'.

'I have never seen dolphins before,' he explained. 'In fact I have never been to sea before, except to cross the Hellespont.'

'Then you have never seen Thera, the Blessed Isle,' she told him. 'It is unique.'

'How so?' he asked, peering at the island looming ahead of them. 'Because no men are allowed there?'

'Partly,' she told him. 'But it is fashioned like no other island. It is in the shape of a ring, with just one gap where the ships sail in. In the centre is a wide round harbour, which is very deep. No ships can anchor there, for the stone anchors will not reach the bottom. In the centre of the harbour is a small black isle, called the Burned Isle.'

Soon they were passing into the harbour, and Kalliades, who was watching ahead, commented, 'Not such a small island!'

Andromache looked round and gasped. The Burned Isle, black and grey like a pile of coals, was twice the size she remembered. It now filled more of the harbour and the *Xanthos* had to skirt round it to reach the Theran beach. From its summit she could see thick black smoke arising and trailing off towards the east. She looked back to the aft deck where Helikaon and Oniacus were talking urgently, pointing and gazing at the growing isle with wonder.

Young Praxos shouted, 'Ship ahead, lord!'

Andromache also could see a galley drawn up on the far beach. She could make out nothing of it at this distance, but within moments sharp-eyed Praxos cried, 'It is the *Bloodhawk*, Golden One!'

Odysseus! What good fortune! Andromache smiled. But at that instant she heard the rumble of an earthquake beneath them, the sea churned, and she saw a landslip on the Burned Isle go crashing into the water. The waves it created lashed the *Xanthos*, and the ship rocked back and forth. Andromache looked to the children, but they were both safely on the lower deck. She gazed up at the isle again and shivered.

Within a short space of time the *Xanthos* had reached the beach and crewmen were shinning down ropes ready to draw the ship up alongside the *Bloodhawk*. Helikaon slid down a rope, and a ladder was thrown over the side for Andromache. When she reached the beach Odysseus was already waiting, one arm round Helikaon's shoulders. They were both grinning at her and she smiled back. With a touch of sadness she saw the Ithakan king's once-red hair was now all silver.

He took her hand and kissed it. 'By Zeus, goddess, it does my old heart good to see you both safe. I heard Troy was taken and overrun, but there was no word of survivors. I'll wager you have a stirring tale to tell me!'

'Indeed we have, Odysseus, but it is a tale of sadness too,' replied Helikaon, gazing fondly at his old friend. 'What are you doing here? We thought you would be safe in the arms of Penelope by now.'

'Would that I were. I have a son I have not yet seen. But I came to rescue Kassandra. With Troy taken, Mykene scum have no reason to respect the sanctity of Thera. But the place seems abandoned.' He looked around. 'We arrived at sunset last night, and we have seen no one. There is always a priestess to greet arriving ships...' He shrugged. 'I was debating defying the demi-god and climbing to the Great Horse myself. Then we saw the *Xanthos*.'

At his words a chill passed through Andromache and the feeling of urgency returned full force. It was as much as she could do not to go running up the steep cliff path. To Helikaon she said swiftly, 'I will go and find Kassandra and bring her to the ship.'

'If she is still here,' her lover replied, gazing up frowning at the top of the island where the horse's head could just be seen.

'I know she is here,' she told him, 'though I do not know why she has not come to greet us.' She saw his expression and guessed what he was thinking. 'You must not anger the Minotaur by climbing to the temple. I will go and find her.'

Helikaon glanced at the sky, then took her hand. 'If you have not returned by noon I will come and get you, and no demi-gods or monsters will prevent me.'

'And I will come with him,' added Odysseus. 'There's something dangerous about this island now, and it's not the danger of violent men.' He shivered in the sunlight and nodded towards the Burned Isle. 'And tell me that island is growing, and it is not just a delusion of old age.'

'They say the Burned One only rose from the sea a hundred years ago,' Andromache replied. 'And yes, you are right, it is growing very fast, and I fear it is a bad omen. I will make haste.'

With a smile for Helikaon she turned and strode across the beach of black sand, then started up the cliff path, her old rope-soled sandals carrying her surely. Halfway up she stopped and looked down on the men and ships below. Her gaze travelled to the Burned Isle, and she was shocked to see it was nearly as high as the cliffs of the circling island. Smoke was rising from the summit and the air was thick with it. On her arms and shoulders was a light sprinkling of grey dust. She hurried on, dread and foreboding pushing her along with whips of fire.

As she reached the top of the cliff she paused again, gazing up at the Great Horse. The colossal white temple seemed to sway above her, and she wondered if it was she who was swaying. Then, with a deep rumble which made her teeth ache, another earthquake rippled across the isle. Andromache threw herself down and clung to the rocky ground, fearing it would tip up and throw her back down the cliffs. She heard a whoosh of wings and a raucous screeching. Looking behind her she saw a huge flock of gulls flying past the edge of the cliffs, heading south.

'All the creatures are leaving the island,' said a voice. 'Even the birds of the air and the fish of the sea.'

Andromache scrambled to her feet. Walking towards her slowly from the Great Horse temple was the First Priestess. Iphigenia saw the surprise on her face and chuckled.

'You thought me long dead, Andromache. Well, I have made old bones, but my time has not yet come.'

'I am glad to see it,' Andromache replied, and it was true. Iphigenia looked older than the world, but the gleam in her eye was as intelligent and calculating as ever. 'Are the women all leaving the island too? It seems deserted.'

Iphigenia frowned. 'When the earthquakes started, at the time of the feast of Artemis, Kassandra convinced all the girls the island would be destroyed. With her dreams and her visions she can be very persuasive, your sister. One by one they left, despite all my efforts to stop them. The last one, little Melissa, departed two days ago.' She gave a barking cough which Andromache recognized as a laugh. 'She even took the donkeys, saying she did not want them to suffer when the end came. A ship full of donkeys.' She shook her head. 'Foolish girl,' she said tenderly.

'How is Kassandra?'

Iphigenia looked at her with compassion, and Andromache wondered why she had ever thought the old woman unfeeling.

'She is dying, Andromache. Her visions . . . they injure her mind and give her hideous fits. Each fit takes something vital from her, and they have been getting more frequent. She is very frail, but the visions go on relentlessly.'

'Where is she? I must help her.'

'She is in the temple. Walk with me, my dear.'

Andromache's sense of panic was almost uncontrollable now.

Nevertheless she took the old priestess's arm and walked with her slowly into the dark building.

Kassandra was lying on a narrow bed in a corner of the high bleak chamber. It was dark and very cold. The only windows were high above, and she was staring at the dusty shafts of light they shed, her mouth moving as if in conversation.

'Kassandra,' Andromache said gently.

After a long delay her sister looked at her. Andromache was shocked to see her condition. She was dirty and her hair was in rats' tails. She was skeletally thin, and looking into her fevered eyes was like staring into a black furnace.

'Is it time?' she asked feebly. 'Can I go now?'

There was a jug of water and a goblet beside her, so Andromache filled the goblet, then gently lifted her sister up and dribbled some water into her mouth. After a few mouthfuls Kassandra drank greedily, holding on to the goblet, water running down her filthy gown on to the floor.

'Andromache,' she said at last, clutching at her with bony fingers. 'I'm so glad you've come. There is much to tell you and little time . . .'

'Listen to me, sister,' Andromache urged her. 'You must come with me. I will take you to the *Xanthos*. It is here, with Helikaon. We will travel together again.'

'She is too ill to be moved,' Iphigenia told her reprovingly.

'I will bring men from the *Xanthos*. Helikaon will come and fetch you, my love.'

'Men will not defile this temple,' the old priestess barked. 'Do not be so arrogant, Andromache, as to bring down the god's wrath on us.'

'Then I will carry her myself,' Andromache told her defiantly.

'Listen, Andromache. You never *listen*,' Kassandra cried, pulling her close. 'I am dying, and I have always known I would die here. You know that. I told you so many times. It is my fate, and I rejoice in it. I will see Mother again. She is waiting for me, just beyond, so close I can almost touch her. She knows I am coming. It is my fate. You must let me be.'

Andromache felt tears running down her face, and Kassandra brushed them gently away. 'Tears for me, sister? You cried for Hektor, too. I saw you. They never should have killed him, you see. Hektor and Achilles were the last great heroes. And after the Age of Heroes comes the Age of Darkness.' Kassandra seemed to gain strength as she spoke. 'Even now they are coming down from the north, the barbarians, sweeping down through the lands of the western kings. Soon they will learn the secret of the star metal, then nothing will stop them. Within a generation they will tear down the stone palaces of the mighty. In the Lion's Hall where the heroes walked there will be only rats and beetles feeding, then green grass will cover the ruins and sheep will graze there.'

'But what of Troy, sister?'

'Troy will be a place of legend. Only the names of its heroes will live on.'

'Did they all die?'

But Kassandra had paused, listening to her voices. 'Astyanax and Dex,' she asked suddenly. 'Are they safe?'

'Yes, they are safe. Was Melite's prophecy true, sister? Is Astyanax the Eagle Child?'

Kassandra smiled then. Her manner became less anxious, and her voice was that of a normal young woman, the passion and urgency gone. 'Prophecies are slippery things,' she told Andromache, patting her hand. 'Like oiled snakes. Priam and Hekabe searched for many years for the meaning of Melite's words. Finally they found a soothsayer who interpreted them to their liking. He told them the prophecy meant that a king's son born to the Shield of Thunder, you, would never be defeated in battle and that his city would be eternal.'

'But you do not believe that?' Andromache asked. 'Is Astyanax not the Eagle Child? Priam believed he would found a dynasty.'

Kassandra laughed, and the sound was bright and merry as it echoed off the roof and walls of the temple. For a moment the dust motes seemed to dance in the shafts of light.

'Like his father Hektor, Astyanax will have no sons,' she said, smiling at the paradox. 'But because of him a dynasty *will* be founded, and it *will* last a thousand years. It is true, Andromache. I have seen it set in the stones of the future.'

'But that is not the prophecy of Melite.'

'No, it is the prophecy of Kassandra.'

A shudder ran through the temple as another small earthquake hit, and a corner of the roof gave way, collapsing to the floor, sending a new cloud of dust boiling around the chamber.

'You must go now,' Kassandra told her. They looked at one another calmly. Andromache felt the turmoil in her heart cease, and acceptance take its place. She nodded, then embraced her sister for the last time. But Kassandra suddenly pulled away from her, her eyes wild again.

'Go now!' she shouted, flailing her arms. 'Agamemnon is coming! You must go now!' She pushed urgently at Andromache until her sister stood up.

'Agamemnon?'

'He is coming to rescue me,' explained Iphigenia. 'Kassandra tells me he will be here before noon, with a fleet. I will return with him to Mykene.'

Andromache hesitated no more, but ran to the door, pausing for a last wave to Kassandra. But the girl had turned away and was speaking to her unseen friends again. Andromache picked up her skirts and raced from the temple towards the cliff path.

On the beach Helikaon watched as Andromache strode away up the path towards the temple. Her back was straight and her hips swayed delightfully under the flame-coloured dress.

Odysseus observed him, grinning. 'You are a fortunate man, Helikaon.'

'I have always been fortunate in my friends, Odysseus. You taught me to face my fears and conquer them. Andromache taught me that life can only be savoured if you look to the future and leave vengeance to the gods.'

'A good woman and a fine philosophy,' Odysseus agreed. 'And if Agamemnon were to walk up this beach now?'

'I would kill him in a heartbeat,' Helikaon admitted with a

grin. 'But I will no longer seek out revenge and let it rule my life.'

'You are sailing to the Seven Hills for the winter?'

Helikaon nodded. 'The Trojan fleet has gone ahead of us. With all the extra men in the settlement there will be a great deal to do.'

'Many men and not enough women,' Odysseus observed. 'There will certainly be work for you to do, arbitrating disputes and settling grievances. Try to do it without severing their heads from their bodies.'

Helikaon laughed, and the feeling of urgency in his chest eased. Then he saw Kalliades and Skorpios walking towards them and his heart sank. He had tried to persuade the two warriors to stay on the ship to the Seven Hills, but he guessed what they had come to ask.

'Kalliades!' Odysseus cried. 'It is good to see you! Where is our friend Banokles?'

'He fell at Troy,' Kalliades told him.

'Then I wager he took a good few of the enemy with him?'

'Banokles never did things by halves. He was a brave man and a fine comrade. He often spoke of the Hall of Heroes. I'm sure he is supping there now with Hektor and Achilles and telling them what a fine warrior he is.'

The other men smiled, then Kalliades went on, 'This is Skorpios, of the Trojan Horse. We both wish to go to Ithaka. Will you grant me passage one last time, Odysseus?'

'Aye, lad, with pleasure. And you can tell me tales of the fall of Troy to pay your way.'

The tall warrior unstrapped his sword belt and held it out to Helikaon. 'I owe you my life, lord, and I owe it to Argurios too. Take the Sword of Argurios with you. It belongs to the people of Troy, not one wandering Mykene.'

Helikaon received it silently. He slid the sword out of the scabbard and gazed on it with awe. 'It is a wondrous gift. But will you not need it, my friend?'

'I do not yet know the shape of my future, Golden One, but I know I will not be carving it out with a sword.'

They sat on the black sand then and Kalliades spoke of the last days of Troy, and Helikaon told Odysseus of the escape from the city. The sun was rising fast towards noon when Helikaon spotted the flame of Andromache's dress on the cliff path once more. She appeared to be hurrying, though she was treading with care on the treacherous slope. There was no sign of Kassandra.

He stood and strode over to meet her. As he did so he saw dozens of rats running from their holes in the base of the cliff and scurrying towards the sea.

'Where is Kassandra?' he asked, taking Andromache's hand.

'She will not come. She is dying.'

As Helikaon frowned and moved towards the path, Andromache stopped him. 'She wants to die here. She says it is her fate. She will not come and it would not be right to make her.'

'Then I will go and say goodbye to her.'

She grabbed his arm. 'She says Agamemnon is coming with a fleet. He will be here by noon. I know you do not believe her predictions. It is her destiny never to be believed. But the First Priestess confirms her brother is coming for her. We must leave, my love, as fast as we can.' There was an edge of panic in her voice.

He looked up the cliff path, but turned back to her, the woman he loved above all others. 'As always, I will take your advice. Come.'

As they walked back to the ship Helikaon shouted to his crew to make ready. He quickly told Odysseus the news, and without a parting word the Ithakan king hurried to the *Bloodhawk*. Helikaon felt something brush against his foot and looked down. There were more rats heading for the ships, dozens of them, running over his feet and climbing the trailing ropes.

He heard cries as the crew spotted them, and he looked back up the beach. The black sand was now swarming with thousands of the creatures. And they were all heading for the shoreline.

There were shouts and curses from the crew of the *Xanthos* as the rodents started scrambling on board. Men were leaping about, skewering rats on their swords, but more and more were appearing all the time.

'Don't try to kill them all!' Helikaon bellowed. 'Get the ship off the beach!'

He handed Andromache quickly up the ladder. He saw her face was pale with anxiety for her boys as she stepped on to the rat-infested ship. Then, trying to ignore the creatures running over his feet and biting his legs, Helikaon put his shoulder to the hull with others from the crew. He saw crewmen running from the *Bloodhawk* to help move the *Xanthos*. Slowly the great bireme began to shift; then, with a rasp of wood on sand, she moved into the sea and floated free, surrounded by swimming rats.

The *Bloodhawk* crewmen ran back to their ship and Helikaon went with them. It was impossible to run through the carpet of rats without treading on them and the men slipped and slid in squashed bodies and rodent blood. They leaned in to the planks and within heartbeats pushed the smaller ship into the water. Helikaon climbed on board. Men were frantically killing the rats, stabbing them with swords and daggers and throwing them overboard. Fewer were getting on to the ship now as she drifted out into clear water. Helikaon glanced at the *Xanthos*. She was also floating clear and the oars were being run out.

He skewered a dozen more rodents and threw their carcasses in the water, then walked over to Odysseus, who was energetically stabbing any rat he could see.

'This will make a fine tale for you, my friend,' Helikaon told him, laughter bubbling up as he watched the fat king dancing about impaling rats on his sword.

Odysseus stopped, panting, and grinned. 'I need no more tales, even rats' tales,' he countered. 'Stories are always buzzing in my head like a hive full of bees!' Then his expression sobered. 'Get back to your ship, Helikaon. We must both make haste. We cannot take on an entire Mykene fleet.'

Helikaon stepped forward and embraced his old mentor for the last time. 'Good sailing, my friend.'

Odysseus nodded. 'Look for me in the spring,' he promised.

With a parting salute to Kalliades and Skorpios, Helikaon ran to the foredeck and dived into the sea. As he swam towards the *Xanthos* he tried to ignore the floating carpet of dead and dying rats, and the scratch of claws as drowning animals tried to scramble on to his back. He grabbed the rope his crew had lowered for him and climbed on deck. Only then did he allow himself to shudder and brush phantom rats from his shoulders.

He looked around. Andromache stood at the mast, gazing up at the Great Horse. Oniacus was ready at the steering oar. The oarsmen watched Helikaon, waiting for his words.

'By the mark of One!' he shouted, and the oar blades sliced into the water. Following the *Bloodhawk*, the *Xanthos* left the island as the sun rose towards noon.

XXXVI

Fire in the sky

AGAMEMNON LIKED TO THINK OF HIMSELF AS A PRAGMATIST. STANDING on the deck of his flagship as it raced towards Thera, he was still angry, but looking back on the last day in Troy, he knew he could have made his vital decisions no differently.

That blowhard Idomeneos had berated him for opening the Scaean Gate to the Hittite horde, but had he any choice? If they had barred the gates to keep the Hittites out, Agamemnon's troops would have been trapped in the city as surely as the Trojans were before them, with little water or food. They would have starved within days, then been forced to sally out weakened and vulnerable to face superior Hittite numbers.

And although it had been humiliating to be ordered from Troy by the upstart emperor, it actually worked in his favour. Agamemnon had no intention of rebuilding the ruined city. His aim had been accomplished. Everyone throughout the Great Green knew he had destroyed Troy, defeated Priam and killed all his sons. He was Agamemnon the Conqueror, and all men quailed before him. His name would echo for ever in hearts and minds, as the priest in the Cave of Wings had predicted.

He smiled to himself. Once he had found Priam's stolen treasure he would return to the Lion's Hall in triumph. The boy king

Astyanax need not concern him. Mykene soldiers, spies and agents would hunt him down relentlessly, and Helikaon the Burner too, and the bitch Andromache – although he still held hopes of finding them on Thera. He would take great pleasure in their deaths, which would be lingering and agonizing.

As the fleet approached its harbour the Mykene king could see a heavy grey pall lying over Thera. The black isle at its centre was much bigger than he remembered, and a column of smoke was rising from the top. He heard the rumble of a small earthquake like a portent of doom. He shivered.

'My king,' said his aide Kleitos, 'the beach is empty. The *Xanthos* is not here.'

'Then the vile Helikaon must have been to the island already and left. He can be no more than half a day ahead. He will not expect to be followed, so he will be taking his time.'

'What do we do, my king?'

Agamemnon thought swiftly. 'Send six of our ships round the black isle, to ensure the *Xanthos* is not hiding on the other side. We will go ashore and find Priam's insane daughter. I will make her tell us where Helikaon is. She claims to be prescient, and now she can prove that claim. If she is no longer here, and we find no treasure, we sail on to Ithaka.'

My visit to Ithaka is long overdue, he thought. I will revel in the deaths of the fat fool Odysseus and his family.

Agamemnon's flagship and the Kretan war galley beached on the black sand and the three kings stepped ashore with their body-guards. There were hundreds of dead rats on the strand and it was difficult to cross the beach without treading on their carcasses. A pungent smell of blood and burning lay over the island.

'Why are all these rats here?' Menelaus questioned nervously. 'And that black isle is growing. There is the stench of witchcraft here. I do not like this place.'

Idomeneos, who as usual was garbed in full armour, growled, 'An island of women is an abomination. We have all heard tales of the unnatural practices they revel in. It will be pleasant to see the witches sold into slavery.'

473

Menelaus was astonished. 'But they are all princesses, some of them daughters of our allies!'

Idomeneos turned on him. 'And will you go running to tell them, you fat lapdog?' he spat.

Irritably, Agamemnon told them, 'We are near the end of our journey. We will not have to suffer each other's company much longer. Now, follow me!'

He set a fast pace up the cliff path, with bodyguards in front and behind. They were near the top when there was the low grumble of another quake. They all froze for a heartbeat, then threw themselves to the ground as the earth shook under them. Two guards ahead of them were dislodged from the path and fell, plummeting to the rocky shore below. Agamemnon closed his eyes and waited grimly for the ground to stop moving. Something deep inside screamed at him to run to his ship and race away from this witches' isle. He ruthlessly suppressed it.

It was a while before the kings cautiously picked themselves up. A thick layer of grey ash lay over them and they brushed it off their clothes. Agamemnon stalked off angrily. 'This island is cursed,' he agreed with his brother. 'We will take what we need and leave quickly!'

Menelaus looked around. 'It is very quiet,' he muttered.

As Agamemnon breasted the top of the cliff he saw the Great Horse temple looming above him. A faint, elusive memory touched the edge of his mind, but he forgot it as he saw one of the priestesses stumbling towards him. She was an old crone and had difficulty walking, but she struggled forward holding her arms out in front of her as if to touch him. Agamemnon drew his sword. He lanced it into the old woman's skinny breast and walked on, leaving her in a pool of blood.

Agamemnon handed the etched and decorated sword to a soldier to clean, then returned it to its scabbard, feeling more elated than he had done for days. He strode between the horse's front hooves and into the temple.

It was cold and very dark in there. All he could see at first were bright shafts of daylight streaming vertically from the roof. He paused to give his bodyguard time to fan out in front of him. There were only women here, but he felt unnerved by the strangeness of the isle.

'My king!' With his sword the Follower indicated a gloomy corner where a dark-haired young woman lay on a pallet bed. She was singing quietly to herself, her eyes closed.

Without opening them, she cried, 'Fire in the sky, and a mountain of water touching the clouds! Beware the Great Horse, Agamemnon King!' The words nudged the elusive memory in Agamemnon's mind.

Then the girl sat up and turned to look at them, sitting on the edge of the bed swinging her legs like a child. She was an ugly creature, he thought, dirty and thin as a blade.

'Words of prophecy, king!' she told him. 'Words of power! But you did not listen then and you will not hear me now.' Agamemnon realized the mad girl had been quoting the words of the priest of the Cave of Wings long ago. How could she know? He was the only one still alive who'd heard the prophecy.

The girl cocked her head and frowned. 'You killed Iphigenia,' she said sadly. 'I did not foresee that. Poor Iphigenia.'

Agamemnon heard a gasp and turned to see Menelaus hurrying from the temple. So that old crone was our sister, he thought. I never could abide her.

'You have defiled the temple with your bright armour and sharp swords,' Kassandra told him. 'You have killed a virgin of the temple.'

Agamemnon snorted. 'Will the demi-god eat me up?' he asked scornfully.

She looked up at him and locked eyes with his. 'Yes,' she told him simply. 'Something is rising.'

He felt a cold trickle down his spine, and realized the ground was trembling continuously now, making an infinitely deep sound that set his teeth on edge. A headache formed screaming behind his eyes.

'Stand her up!' he ordered, unsheathing his sword again.

Two soldiers grabbed an arm each and lifted Kassandra up. She hung like a doll between them, her toes barely touching the ground. The Mykene king placed the tip of his sword against her belly, but the blade seemed to shimmer and buckle in front of his eyes, as if it had been placed in a furnace. He blinked and it was whole again. He rubbed at the ash and grit in his eyes.

'Where is Helikaon?' he demanded, and was relieved to hear his voice was firm.

'I would have offered you a forest of truth, but you wish to speak of a single leaf,' she quoted. 'Helikaon is far away.' Her gaze went inward. She frowned. 'Hurry, Helikaon. You must hurry!'

'Is he going to Ithaka?'

She shook her head. 'Helikaon will never see Ithaka again.'

'And Priam's treasure, girl? Does he have the treasure?'

'There is no treasure, king. It was all spent long ago. On sharp swords and shiny breastplates. Polites told me. I have seen him with his wife. They are very happy. Just three copper rings left,' she told him. 'The price of a whore.'

In frustration Agamemnon made to strike her, but another fierce quake made them all stumble. Kassandra fell from the soldiers' grip and slipped past the armoured men and out of the temple. Agamemnon followed her, cursing.

She had not gone far. She was standing outside staring at the Burned Isle, where dense black smoke was boiling from the summit. A thick layer of ash now lay on the ground. Nearby Menelaus sat weeping beside the body of his sister. Both were covered in ash and looked like stone statues.

Kassandra glanced at Agamemnon. 'You see, there is a great chamber under Thera, full of fire and burning rock. Perhaps it is where the god lives – I don't know. But it has been growing for generations, and now it is about to burst from its restraints. Hot air and dust and rocks will come spewing out. Then, as the fire chamber empties, its roof will collapse and the sea will pour in. Seawater and fire are enemies, you see. They will battle to get away from each other, and the island will soar into the sky like a pebble thrown by a child. We will ride with it. It will be glorious!' She turned towards him with a brilliant smile, inviting him to join her rejoicing.

'The girl is demented,' cried Idomeneos, but his voice sounded thin and frightened.

The sky darkened and Agamemnon looked up to see a huge flock of birds fly overhead towards the west, thousands of them blocking out the grey hazy light, their screaming voices like harpies'. Kassandra waved at them, a childish gesture, her hand waving up and down. 'Bye bye, birds,' she said. 'Bye bye.' The Mykene king shuddered and he felt panic tightening his chest.

'Everyone is waiting for me,' Kassandra told the kings happily as the ground shook violently again. 'Mother is waiting for me. And Hektor and Laodike. They are just beyond.'

Suddenly she stood on her tiptoes and pointed to the Burned Isle. There was a noise like a thousand thunders and a hot black pillar erupted from the top of the volcano and soared into the sky. The monstrous sound it made broke something in his ears and Agamemnon screamed and fell to the ground as blood poured out of them. Hands to his head he looked up to see the tower of black fire roaring higher and higher. The sound was intolerable and the blast of heat from it scorched the skin of his face. Great boulders were flung from the volcano, soaring like pebbles through the sky, to crash into the sea and on to the isle near them, destroying buildings and narrowly missing the temple. The noise was appalling and Agamemnon thought he would go mad from the power of it.

Kassandra was the only one still standing, without fear, as she gazed at the tower of fire. It seemed to go up for ever, then it slowed and the top of it started flowing outward, spreading its canopy of smoke and ash wider and wider, darkening the earth and blotting out the sun.

She looked down at Agamemnon compassionately. She seemed to have grown taller and stronger, and he wondered why he had thought her ugly. Her face was radiant, and she blazed with beauty like a sword in a flame. Then she pointed again and from the top of the volcano a red-brown flow like a glowing avalanche started to belch out and move down the slopes. It slithered swiftly over the black rocks of the Burned Isle and soon reached the sea. Agamemnon got to his feet with difficulty, for they were all knee-deep in warm ash. He saw his ships were under oars, beating their way as fast as they could row towards the harbour entrance. The cowards are leaving me, he screamed inside his head. He saw Idomeneos shouting, but could not hear what he said.

Agamemnon thought the red-hot avalanche would stop when it reached the sea, but instead it carried straight on, rolling across the surface towards the fleet. Long before it reached the first ship the vessel burst into flames, burning hotly before it was engulfed in the hideous flow. One by one the galleys were overtaken and destroyed, their crews blackened and charred in an instant. When it reached the base of the cliffs on which they stood the rolling avalanche of fire started to crawl up towards them, but then it slowed to a halt. Agamemnon breathed out shakily.

His relief lasted only for heartbeats. There was another terrifying sound from deep in the earth beneath them. As he watched he saw the sea in the harbour dent in the middle, and an enormous whirlpool start to form, sluggishly at first, then with greater speed. There was another great noise, an army of thunders, and the sea suddenly fell away from them, swallowed instantly into the earth. The entire fleet of charred ships disappeared in moments, as water rushed into the harbour to pour into the hole in the world.

There was a building roar, and the ground started to shake wildly.

Agamemnon's last sight was of Kassandra, a joyous smile on her face, as she waved him goodbye.

He closed his eyes.

Then the island rose up under them and flung the kings screaming into the sky.

Not far to the west Helikaon stood on the aft deck of the *Xanthos*, his arm draped loosely over the steering oar, looking up at the sail stretched taut against the wind. He was at his happiest when the black horse danced over the waves. Although there were sixty or more men lounging about on the decks, gossiping, eating and drinking, laughing and telling tall tales, he felt alone with his ship when she was under sail. He could feel the shift and groan of the timbers beneath his bare feet, hear the finest vibrations of the huge sail, and sense through the oak of the steering oar the valiant heart of the galley. You are the queen of the seas, he told his ship, as she cut through the waves, rising and falling with grace and power.

His eyes moved, as they always did when given the chance, to Andromache. She was sitting on the forward deck under the yellow canopy. The boys were curled up beside her. They had been running around the ship all morning, delighted to have the oars-men at their beck and call, to play games with them and tell them tales of the sea. Now, tired out, they were both asleep under the awning, protected from the noonday sun.

Andromache was gazing back towards Thera, though the island was now out of sight. Helikaon knew her heart now, and under-stood she did not regret leaving Kassandra, as the girl had asked. Yet it had made Andromache sad to leave her sister to a lonely death, cared for only by the old priestess. Helikaon had spent some time since their departure cursing himself for not climbing the cliffs to fetch the girl, then had ruthlessly put the feelings aside. The decision was made. He would always remember Kassandra with love, but she was now part of the past.

He left the steering oar to Oniacus and walked down the length of the ship, drawn helplessly towards his lover. He made himself pause, as if to inspect the racks of weapons, swords, shields, bows and arrows stored beneath the rails. As usual, thanks to Oniacus' watchful eye, they were all immaculate, cleaned and ready for action if needed.

'Where will we beach tonight, Golden One?' asked grey-bearded Naubolos, a veteran who had sailed on the *Xanthos* since the launch in Kypros, and on the *Ithaka* before that.

'At Pig's Head Cove, or on Kalliste if the east wind is our friend.'

There were shouts and grunts of approval from the men. Even before the war, the whores on Kalliste were more welcoming than any on the Great Green. Now there were fewer ships sailing these waters, and a galley the size of the *Xanthos* would receive an enthusiastic greeting.

Helikaon moved on. He checked the great chests holding the

nephthar balls in their protective cocoons of straw. There were only ten left. He frowned, then dismissed the problem. It could not be helped. There was a good chance they would reach their final destination without seeing another ship, let alone a hostile one.

His feet registered a minute shift in the direction of the ship and he looked back along the deck. Oniacus was steering the galley to catch the wind as it shifted slightly north. Helikaon gazed back the way they had come. There was no longer any sign of the *Bloodhawk*. The *Xanthos*' greater speed had left the smaller ship further and further behind.

'How are you, Agrios?' he asked a leathery old sailor sitting on the deck with his back to a rowing bench. The man had suffered a terrible injury to his arm in a battle off Kios in the summer, when a Mykene warship ploughed along the side of the *Xanthos*, ripping into its oars. Agrios had been hit by an oar as it whipped back at him before he could get out of the way. His arm had been broken in so many places that it could not be set, so it was cut off close to the shoulder. The old man had survived the amputation, and when he was recovered Helikaon allowed him to return to the rowing benches, for Agrios swore he could row as well with one arm as most men could with two.

The man nodded. 'All the better for knowing we'll be on Kalliste tonight.' He grinned, winking.

Helikaon laughed. 'Only if the wind stays fair,' he warned.

He walked to the forward deck, aware that Andromache was watching his every step. She looked wonderful today, he thought, in a saffron robe cut roughly off at the knees. She was wearing the finely carved amber pendant he had given her, and the sparks of warmth in the stone matched the fire of her hair.

Her face was grave, though. 'You are thinking of Kassandra,' he ventured.

'It is true that Kassandra is never far from my thoughts,' she confessed. 'But at that moment I was thinking of you.'

'What were you thinking, goddess?' he asked, taking her hand and covering her palm with kisses.

480

She raised her eyebrows. 'I was wondering how long we were to pretend we are not lovers,' she told him, smiling. 'It seems I have my answer.'

Facing away from the crew, Helikaon felt a hundred eyes on his back, and he heard the lull as the men stopped talking. Then, almost instantly, the normal chatter of sound resumed as if nothing had happened.

'It seems they are not surprised,' he told her.

She shook her head, her face glowing with happiness.

'Golden One!' Helikaon turned to see Praxos running down the deck towards them. The boy was trying to point backwards as he ran. 'There is a storm, I think!'

Helikaon looked quickly in the direction Praxos was pointing, towards Thera. On the clear line of the horizon there was a small dark smudge. Like a storm. But not a storm. As he watched it rose into the shape of a dark tower. A feeling of dread formed in the pit of his stomach. There was a distant roll of thunder, and all the crew turned to watch the black tower rising ominously into the pale sky.

Heartbeats passed as it climbed and climbed, then suddenly it was consumed by a massive eruption of fire and flame, filling the sky to the east. The sound of the eruption hit them, like the noise of thunder increased a hundredfold; like the deep blast of Ares' war horn, or the crack of doom itself.

'It is Thera!' someone cried. 'The god has burst his chains!'

Helikaon glanced at Andromache. Her face was white as clean linen and there was fear in her eyes. She pointed to the horizon and he looked again. The cloud of the explosion, spreading swiftly out and upwards, darkened the eastern sky. But it was mysteriously vanishing from sea level upwards. Baffled, Helikaon gazed at the horizon. It was rising as he watched.

With awful clarity he knew what was happening.

'Take in the sail!' he shouted. 'Get to your oars now!'

He ordered Oniacus to turn the ship round, and as his second-in-command shouted to the rowers he grabbed a length of rope from the deck. With his bronze dagger he sliced it in three pieces. He thrust them at Andromache.

481

'Get the boys on to the lower deck and tie them securely to something solid. Then tie yourself down.'

She stared at him. 'Why?' she asked. 'What is happening?'

'Just do it, woman!' he bellowed at her. Pointing towards the high horizon he addressed the crew. 'That is a wall of water coming towards us, as high as a mountain! It will be upon us in moments. We must all tie ourselves down. Anyone who is not securely tied will die! We will row straight into the wave and the *Xanthos* will climb it! It is our one chance!'

Now they could all see it for what it was, a dark line of horizon much too high in the sky, coming towards the ship with the speed of a swooping eagle. In front of it was a huge flock of gulls, flying frantically away from the great wave. As they passed over the *Xanthos* the sky darkened, their screams beat on the men's ears, and the thrashing of their wings created a wind that rocked the ship.

Rowers were at their benches, rowing for all they were worth to turn the great galley round. The other crewmen were tearing down the lines, cutting lengths for themselves and the oarsmen. All kept glancing up fearfully as the giant wave bore down on them.

Helikaon grabbed some rope and ran to the aft deck, where Oniacus needed all his strength to brace the steering oar to one side. The *Xanthos* was turning in a tight circle. Helikaon lent his strength to the oar, and took another swift look at the wave. It was mountainous, and getting bigger by the moment, filling the whole of his vision. Can the ship climb it, he asked himself? All he was certain of was that it must not hit them beam-on. It would destroy the galley in a moment. Their only hope was to steer straight into it. The oars, and the wooden fins Khalkeus had bolted to the hull, would keep the ship stable.

'We will tie the oar centrally,' he told Oniacus, 'but it will need the strength of both of us as well to keep it steady.'

'If we can do it at all,' his friend replied grimly, his terror palpable.

The ship was heading into the wave now. Helikaon cut the rope in half, then looped half round his waist and tied it to the side rails.

He did the same for Oniacus, who was holding the oar in a death-grip.

'The *nephthar*, Golden One!' he cried suddenly. 'What about the clay balls? If we survive this they will be smashed and broken.'

Helikaon looked up to the wave, which was nearly upon them. 'They will be washed away,' he shouted. 'That is the least of our worries.'

The prow of the ship began to rise as the swell in front of the wave reached them. All along the deck Helikaon saw the wide eyes of terrified men leaning in to the oars, horror at their backs, rowing like men possessed.

'Row, you cowsons! Row for your lives!' he bellowed at them.

The wave hit them and Helikaon felt the whole ship shudder as if she was snapping in two. Then there was a hideous groan and she started to climb. It is not possible, he told himself. The wave is too high. He fought down the panic in his chest. If any ship can do it, the *Xanthos* can, he thought.

Then they were under water. Helikaon could see nothing but swirling sea all around, and he felt the air punched out of his chest as the galley lurched to one side, throwing him against the steering oar. He was tossed about like a rag doll, concentrating only on keeping his hands to the oar, holding it tight, feeling Oniacus' hands there too. It was impossible to steer. All they could do was hold on tight and try not to drown.

For a moment he emerged from the water, and caught a terrifying glimpse of the ship suspended vertically above him, the oarsmen rowing like madmen, though most of the oars were out of the water. Then the sea came over his head again, and all he could glimpse was the blue and green of its depths.

The ship lurched and spun, pitched and heaved. It went on so long Helikaon thought it would never stop. He could no longer tell which way was up, or down, or if he was rising up in the sea or sinking down through the depths. He could not tell if the hideous sounds in his ears were those of the ship groaning, or the men crying, or the screaming of his tortured lungs.

Suddenly there was air to breathe again, and he took a quick breath, ready to plunge down again. But then he realized they were no longer under water. The ship had crested the great wave.

For an instant he feared they were falling, that the ship was plummeting into a deep trough behind the wave. But, looking ahead, he realized there was no hideous drop, only a gentle slope. It was as if the great-hearted *Xanthos* had climbed a giant step in the sea. Helikaon leaned over and vomited up a stomachful of seawater.

He looked along the deck. Nearly half the rowing benches were empty, the oarsmen claimed by Poseidon. Many of the men were hanging, drowned or unconscious, from the ropes tying them to the benches. The mast had been ripped away, as had most of the rails and many of the oars.

Oniacus lay on the deck beside him, half drowned, one arm hideously dislocated from its socket. Helikaon started to untie his ropes, dread in his heart. He had to find Andromache and the boys. If he had nearly drowned on the top deck, how could anyone still be alive lower down in the ship?

He felt a hand on his arm. Grey-faced with pain and shock, Oniacus had pulled himself up, and put out his good hand to stop Helikaon untying himself. He pointed ahead of them, terror in his eyes.

'There's another one coming!' he cried.

XXXVII

Dawn of a new day

THE MAN WHO HAD ONCE BEEN CALLED GERSHOM STOOD IN THE darkness which lay over Egypte and gazed towards the north.

Patience was a skill he had learned only recently. As a young man he had needed only such patience as was required by a royal prince, accustomed to his every whim being instantly obeyed. That is, none at all. Then had come the day when, in a drunken anger, he had killed two royal guardsmen. He had the choice of being blinded and buried alive, or fleeing the country of Egyptc. He fled. As a fugitive, working in the copper mines of Kypros, he had little use for patience either. He worked until exhausted, then slept, then worked again.

Then he had fallen in with the Sea People, roving traders, pirates and raiders from the far northern fastnesses of the Great Green. He seldom thought of those days now, of his time with Helikaon on the great galley *Xanthos*, of his good friend Oniacus, of Xander, and the people of Troy he had known for a few brief years. Word had reached him of the armies besieging the city of Troy, and only in recent days he had heard of the death of Hektor, and grieved for a man he hardly knew. He wondered at the fortunes of Andromache and her son, and hoped she was with Helikaon and that she was happy.

The affliction that had fallen on Egypte two days before had come out of the north: great waves that had devastated the land, and a dark cloud of ash that rolled across the sky, bringing perpetual night. The waves had swept up the river Nile, over-flowing its low banks, destroying crops, demolishing houses, and drowning thousands. Then, from out of the river, polluted by ash-fall, and turned to the colour of blood by the violent churning of the red Nile mud, came millions of frogs and clouds of flying, biting insects. The frogs had invaded the land and crawled and hopped through meagre food supplies. The insects filled the air, so it was hard to breathe without sucking them in. They bit any exposed skin, spreading sickness as they flew.

Standing on a rooftop in the darkness, the prophet heard a sound behind him. He turned to find hawk-faced Yeshua. 'The sun will not rise again today,' his friend said, and there was fear in his voice. 'The people are crying out to you to save them. They believe you have caused this catastrophe.'

'Why would they think that?'

'You asked the pharaoh to free the desert people from their slavery. He refused. Then the sun disappeared and the waves came. The Egypteians believe our god, the One God, is stronger than their own deities, and He is punishing them.'

'But does the pharaoh believe that?'

'He's your brother. What do you think?'

Ahmose had gone to see the pharaoh, his half-brother Rameses, risking bringing on himself the brutal punishment he had long fled, and asked the ruler to allow the desert slaves to leave the land of Egypt. Rameses had refused. Seated on his high, gold-encrusted throne, his beloved son beside him, Rameses had laughed at his brother for his naivety.

'For the sake of our childhood friendship,' he had said, 'I will not have you killed, this time. But do not presume on that friendship further. Did you really expect me to wave my hand and release the slaves, just because you, a known criminal, ask me to?'

As Ahmose walked away, disappointed, the pharaoh's son came running after him. Ahmose stopped and smiled down at him. The boy was about ten, with a mop of black hair, intelligent eyes and an eager smile.

'They say you are my uncle,' he asked. 'Is that true?'

'Perhaps,' Ahmose told him.

'I am sorry we cannot be friends,' the boy said. 'But I will speak to my father about the slaves. My mother says he can refuse me nothing.' He grinned, then turned and ran back to his father's throne.

Standing in the darkness, Ahmose told Yeshua, 'I think Rameses is a stubborn man, and contrary in his nature. I have told him what I want from him, therefore that is the last thing he will give me.'

'Then perhaps you should have asked him to force our people to stay here in Egypt.'

The prophet looked round, startled, and realized cold-eyed Yeshua had made a joke. He laughed and the sound echoed strangely over the land of despair.

'I will go and speak to him again. Perhaps he will relent now.'

As he set off for the palace he thought back to the night long ago on the island of Minoa when he lay by a burning bush, and the dreams and visions he had endured, dosed with opiates by the fey priestess Kassandra. He had seen mighty waves, rivers running red, darkness at noon, desolation and despair. He had seen his half-brother raw-eyed with grief. He wondered what tragedy could make the cold-hearted pharaoh suffer so.

Yeshua hurried after him, grabbing him by the arm.

'You cannot go! He will surely have you killed this time.'

'Have faith, my friend,' Ahmose told him. 'God is great.'

It was the morning of the third day since the destruction of Thera and the coming of the waves. Helikaon and his son walked through the twilight along the grey shore of an unnamed island, splashing their bare feet in the shallows.

Astyanax kept stopping to peer into the shallow water. One of the crewmen had fashioned a shrimping net for him, and he was eager to catch some of the creatures. So far there were just a handful of the tiny transparent shellfish flopping about in the bottom of his net. Helikaon waited patiently each time the boy stopped to add one or two more. After all, there was nothing to hurry for.

Astyanax held up the net again for his father to inspect. 'Good boy,' Helikaon told him. 'Now, let's go back to the camp and eat them.'

The sky was still clouded with ash and there was a constant light ashfall, leaving a grainy greyness on everything. Even the crew's campfires had to be protected from it, otherwise they would quickly go out. As father and son passed the cairn of small rocks raised to mark the bones of their comrades, Helikaon saw that it now appeared as if carved from a single smooth stone.

The *Xanthos* had survived all four of the great waves, each one smaller than the one before. After the brutal punishment of the first, Helikaon had not even tried to steer the ship. He just held on grimly, one arm round the aft rail, one round Oniacus, who was by then unconscious. Yet gallantly the ship had unerringly plunged like a lance into each mountainous wave, as if steering herself. When the fourth wave had passed Helikaon gazed out over the sea. They had been swept into unknown waters. He had no idea where they were. He quickly untied himself and Oniacus, then raced down to the lower deck.

He would never forget the awful sight that struck his eyes. Andromache hung, helpless and still, from the ropes she had tied to a rear rowing bench. Her face was pale and her hair drifted like seaweed in the shallow water on the planks of the deck. She still held the boys in a vice-like grip. Both were alive, but they were sodden and white-faced, silent with shock.

Helikaon untied them, then he picked Andromache up, dread in his heart. Her head lolled loosely and her eyes were half open, unseeing. He threw her down on the waterlogged deck, turning her to her stomach and pressing down on her back to try to expel the water. It seemed to make no difference. Her body was limp, unmoving. Crying out with anguish, he lifted her by the waist, so her head was down, and shook her like a rag doll. At last she gave a faint sigh, then water gushed out of her mouth and she gave a weak cough. He shook her again and more water gouted out, then she started coughing harder and trying to struggle free from his grip. He picked her up and pulled her tightly to him, tears of gratitude and relief falling down his cheeks.

They had lost twenty-nine of the sixty-eight souls on board. Strangely, the one-armed veteran Agrios had survived, but the youngster Praxos had been swept away. Of the survivors, many were injured and two died later that day.

Helikaon had wrenched Oniacus' dislocated shoulder back in place, tied it securely, and given the injured man the steering oar. Then he and Andromache had joined the uninjured crewmen to row the ship slowly through the ash-covered sea. It had been hard to see in the constant greyness, and Helikaon had almost despaired of finding a sanctuary for the night when a darker shape appeared out of the half-light. It was a small low island, much of it scoured clean by the waves. They could not beach the ship, for they had not the manpower to launch it again. So they dropped the stone anchors in the shallows and struggled to the shore as best they could. Exhausted, they all slept where they lay, regardless of the waves lapping at their feet. In the morning Helikaon had sent out men to look for fresh water. They quickly discovered a clear spring nearby and, for the first time since they left Thera, Helikaon knew they were safe for a while.

That night they had known when sunset arrived only by the astonishing display of colours – bronze, red and purple – in the darkened sky. Helikaon now knew which way was west, and he felt encouraged by the knowledge.

The next day they had held funeral rites for their comrades. With no beasts to kill for sacrifice, the men poured libations from their one surviving jug of wine to placate Poseidon, who had brought them to this place, and to Apollo, begging him to bring back the sun. As captain, Helikaon had taken part in the rites, but he had walked away as soon as possible. He found the men's simple devotion unfathomable, and remembered a conversation he had had with Odysseus concerning the men's faithfulness to such unreliable gods.

'All seamen are superstitious, or pious in their devotion,

however you see it,' had said the Ithakan king. 'They are constantly in peril, at the mercy of the wind and the treacherous sea. Giving names to the elements and treating them like living men with human emotions makes them feel they have control over events which would otherwise seem random and meaningless. They are simple men and revere the gods as they revered their own fathers. When angry their fathers could lash out at them and hurt them. When happy they would feed them and keep them safe. So they try to keep the gods content, giving them food and wine, and praising them, worshipping them. Do not sneer at their faith, Helikaon. We all need something to have faith in.'

'You do not believe in the gods, Odysseus.'

'I did not say that,' the older man had replied. 'I do not think the sun god Apollo drives his chariot across the sky each day, like a slave tasked with a very dull chore, but it does not mean I do not believe. I have travelled all round the Great Green and I have met men who worship the weather god of the Hittites, and Osiris, the Gypptos' god of the dead, and the child-devourer Molech, and the grim lonely god of the desert folk, but no nation seems more blessed than any other. Each has its triumphs and tragedies.'

He had thought for a while. 'I believe there is a being beyond comprehension who guides our path and judges us. That is all I know.' He grinned, and added, 'And I fervently hope there is no Hall of Heroes, where we must spend eternity supping with the blood-boltered Herakles and Alektruon.'

On the grey beach in their still, twilight world, Helikaon looked towards the east. He thought he could detect a breath of breeze, and the sky seemed to be lightening in that direction. He wondered if they would ever see a cloudless day or a starry night again. Then he smiled. Ahead of him he could see Andromache and Dex walking towards them along the shore. Even her dress of flame seemed diminished in the grey light.

They met and stood facing each other. He put up his hand and brushed ash from her cheek, looking into her grey-green eyes.

'You are beautiful,' he told her. 'How can you be so beautiful when covered with ash?'

490

She smiled, then asked, 'You walked to the headland again? Do you still hope to see the *Bloodhawk*?'

He answered her ruefully. 'No, I do not. The ship is smaller than the *Xanthos* and was closer to Thera. I do not think it survived. But perhaps its crew did. Or some of them. Odysseus was a strong swimmer, although it was a long time before I found that out.' He smiled at the memory. 'And he claimed he could float on his back all day, a goblet of wine balanced on his belly.'

She laughed, and the air seemed to lighten at the sound. She looked up. 'The sky is getting brighter, I think.'

He nodded. 'If the breeze picks up we might sail today.'

The main mast of the *Xanthos* had been swept away by the sea, and the black horse sail, but there was a spare mast lying the length of the ship and it had been raised in readiness. There were extra oars stored in the bowels of the galley, and a new sail of plain linen. When the men had rolled it out and checked it for weaknesses or tears, Oniacus had asked him, 'Will we paint the Black Horse of Dardanos on this one, Golden One?'

Helikaon had shaken his head. 'I think not.' We need a new symbol for the future, he had told himself.

'But you do not know where we are. How can you know where we are going?' Andromache asked.

'We will sail west. Eventually we will see familiar land.'

'Perhaps we have been swept far beyond the known seas.'

He shook his head. 'In our terror, my love, the great waves seemed to last an eternity. But, in truth, it was not very long. We cannot be far from the lands we know, but they might have been changed by the waves, and be hard to recognize.'

'Then we will still reach the Seven Hills by winter?'

'I am sure we will,' he told her honestly. His heart lifted at the thought of the fledgling city where families from Troy and Dardanos were building their new lives. The land was lush and verdant, the air sweet and the soil rich, the hillsides teeming with animal life. They would start again there as a family, the four of them, and leave their old world behind them. He wondered if he would ever return to Troy, but even as he thought it, he immediately knew he would not. This would be the *Xanthos'* last great journey.

He said, 'Once we reach mainland, or a large island, we should be able to enlist more oarsmen.'

'I can row again, if needed.'

He gently took her hands and turned them over. The palms were raw and blistered from helping row the *Xanthos* to this barren island. He said nothing, but gazed at her quizzically.

'I will bandage them, as the men do, then I can row,' she argued, her face stern. 'I am as strong as a man.'

His heart filled with love for her. 'You are the strongest woman I have ever known,' he whispered. 'I loved you the moment I first saw you. You are my life, and my dreams and my future. I am nothing without you.'

She gazed at him in wonder and tears started to her eyes. He took her in his arms and held her close, feeling the beat of her heart against his chest. Then they turned and walked hand in hand back along the beach, their two sons trailing behind.

The light breeze from the east picked up. The sky started to lighten, and after a while the sun came out.

EPILOGUE

QUEEN ANDROMACHE STOOD ON THE GRASSY HILLTOP, MOTIONLESS, AS she had been since the morning. Now the sun was falling brightly into the west, and still she watched the preparations on the old ship below. She was dressed in a faded brown robe and wrapped in her ancient green shawl. She felt the weight of her years. Her knees ached and her back was on fire, but still she stood.

She saw someone move out of the crowd on the beach below, and sighed. Yet another serving maid with a cup of warm goat's milk and advice to rest for a while? She squinted short-sightedly, then smiled. Ah, she thought, clever.

Her small grandson trotted up the hill and without a word sat down on the grass at her feet. After a moment she knelt beside him, ignoring the pains in her knees.

'Well, Dios,' she asked, 'what did your father tell you to say to me?'

The seven-year-old squinted up at her through his dark fringe and she impatiently brushed his hair from his face. So like his namesake, she thought.

'Papa says it's time now.'

She glanced at the sun. 'Not yet,' she told him.

They sat in companionable silence for a while. She saw his gaze was fixed on the *Xanthos*. 'What are you thinking, boy?' she asked.

'They say Grandpapa will dine tonight with the gods in the Hall of Heroes,' he ventured.

'Maybe.'

He looked up at her, his eyes wide. 'Isn't it true, Grandmama? Grandpapa *will* dine with Argurios, and Hektor and Achilles, and Odysseus?' he persisted anxiously.

'Certainly not Odysseus,' she told him briskly.

'Why not? Because he is the Prince of Lies?'

She smiled. 'Odysseus is the most honest man I've ever known. No, because Odysseus is not dead.'

The people of the Seven Hills had last heard from Ithaka some ten years before. The collapse of the Mykene empire, its leaders dead, its armies in ruins, its treasuries empty, had opened the way for barbarians from the north to sweep down through the mainland, and where once-proud cities had ruled there lay only darkness and fear. But little Ithaka still stood, as Penelope and her growing son Telemachus stood on the cliffs each sunset watching for their king to come home. Andromache remembered Odysseus carving his wife's face in the sand, and wondered if he was doing it still, somewhere.

'How do you know he's not dead?' little Dios asked.

'Because Odysseus is a storyteller, and storytellers never die as long as their stories live on.'

Invigorated by the thought, she stood up, cursed as her knees cracked, then set off down the hill, the boy running after her. Spotting her, two men peeled away from the crowd and raced up the hillside to meet her where a campfire blazed in a small hollow. Andromache's old bow and specially prepared arrows lay beside it.

She took each of her sons by the hand and gazed at them fondly. Astyanax had her flame hair and Helikaon's blue eyes, and his handsome face bore a dreadful sword-wound, a legacy of a battle with the Siculi eight years before when he had nearly died saving his brother's life. Still, when he smiled he looked just like his father. Dex had his mother's fair hair, and the powerful build and dark eyes of his Assyrian sire. He had taken the name Ilos as an act of fealty to his adopted people, but the local folk called him Iulos.

'I am ready,' she told them. 'I have said my goodbyes.'

She had lain all night racked with grief by the king's funeral bier, her heart cracked and drained, her soul bereft, her tears staining his face and hands. Then in the morning she had dried her eyes, kissed his cold lips, and his forehead, and walked away from him for ever.

Now Astyanax turned and signalled, and a score of men leapt to put their shoulders to the *Xanthos*. There was a rumbling of wood against gravel, a groan of protesting timbers, then the old ship was once more afloat. Her mast had been dismantled and the steering oar tied. The galley was heaped with fragrant cedar branches and herbs. At its centre the body of Helikaon lay on a cloth of gold. He was dressed in a simple white robe, and the Sword of Argurios was on his breast. On his right foot only he wore an old sandal.

As the drifting ship reached the centre of the river and was snatched by the current, the sun touched the horizon. Andromache bent to pick up her bow. She put an arrowhead to the fire, where it blazed brightly. She notched the arrow to the string, and closed her eyes briefly to summon all her remembered strength and courage. Then she sighted and loosed the arrow.

It soared into the sky like a rising star, dipped again, and hit the golden ship at the stern. A blaze started instantly. Within heartbeats archers all along the riverbank shot their fire arrows into the ship, there was an explosion of flame, and the *Xanthos* was alight from stem to stern. It was so bright that people in the crowd shaded their eyes, and the roar of burning timbers was the sound of thunder. High above an eagle rose through the blue sky, lifted on the warm air.

Unbidden, faces appeared in Andromache's mind: Hektor, the bravest of the Trojans, his brothers Dios and Antiphones, the talespinner Odysseus, the valiant Mykene warriors Argurios, Kalliades and Banokles. And Helikaon, her lover, her husband, the keeper of her heart.

I have walked with heroes, she thought.

Andromache felt her heart fill again, and she smiled. Then she raised her bow in her fist in a final farewell as the blazing ship sailed into the west.

THE END